Willy Russell was born in Whiston, near Liverpool, and left school at fifteen. He worked as a ladies' hairdresser for six years, stacked stockings at Bear Brand and cleaned girders at Ford, before getting into writing, first as a songwriter then as a playwright. He is the author of, amongst others, the multi-award-winning plays – later made into films – *Educating Rita* and *Shirley Valentine*, and the award-winning West End musical hits *Blood Brothers* and *John, Paul, George, Ringo and Bert*. He and his family live in Liverpool.

Critical acclaim for *The Wrong Boy*:

'Blending comedy, tragedy, pathos and farce into a readable cocktail is a difficult task, even for the most able of literary barkeeps. Few have the talent to serve up genuine belly laughs and follow through with the kind of insightful, dramatic vision that has your top lip quivering and your eyes filling with moisture. Through his plays and films, Willy Russell has proved himself to be a true master of verbal optics, offering the sharpest of one-liners to characters seeking desperately to escape from the mundane reality of everyday life. Now with his début novel, *The Wrong Boy*, 53-year-old Russell has proved himself a novelist as well . . . Unusual, funny, unsettling and rich with sadness, *The Wrong Boy* manages to work on a multitude of levels. It also showcases Russell's gift for sinking deep into the minds and motivations of his characters, offering a voice to the dispossessed. Russell can now add the label of novelist to the tags of playwright, lyricist and composer. Once again he has proved himself to be a multi-facted Renaissance man' *The Times*

'A warm, funny, poignant story' *Sunday Telegraph*

'The dialogue – as you might expect from a dramatist – is cracking stuff: a colloquial poetry reminiscent of Roddy Doyle. Like Doyle, Russell is capable of pushing light fiction into some disturbingly dark corners. Though the laughs never flag for long' *Guardian*

'In his first novel, Willy Russell has created a character to stand alongside his celebrated progeny, Shirley Valentine and Rita, and has eased the transition from stage writing to prose fiction by presenting his story through a series of letters which could cheerfully work as dramatic monologues . . . a deliberately heartwarming tale . . . his real achievement is to present the exaggerated horrors of childhood and adolescence with an unusual wit and sympathy' *Observer*

'His remarkable first novel, and bestseller-in-waiting . . . yo-yos manically between hilarious highs and gut-wrenching lows . . . it's as tightly plotted as anything by Ruth Rendell . . . He wrote the book, he says, with the aim of producing something that sounded spoken rather than written. He's succeeded. And in his new voice as a shy, misunderstood teenager, Willy Russell is every bit as convincing, funny and life-enhancing as he's ever been'
David Robinson, *The Scotsman*

THE WRONG BOY

Willy Russell

BLACK SWAN

THE WRONG BOY
A BLACK SWAN BOOK : 0 552 99645 9

Originally published in Great Britain by Doubleday,
a division of Transworld Publishers

PRINTING HISTORY
Doubleday edition published 2000
Black Swan edition published 2001

7 9 10 8 6

Extracts from lyrics by Morrissey are used by permission of the
artist: 'Half A Person' – Words © Morrissey 1987; 'This Charming
Man' – Words © Morrissey 1983; 'There Is A Light That Never
Goes Out' – Words © Morrissey 1986; 'I Know It's Over' – Words
© Morrissey 1986; 'Vicar In A Tutu' – Words © Morrissey 1986.

Set in 11/12pt Melior by
Falcon Oast Graphic Art.

Black Swan Books are published by Transworld Publishers,
61–63 Uxbridge Road, London W5 5SA,
a division of The Random House Group Ltd,
in Australia by Random House Australia (Pty) Ltd,
20 Alfred Street, Milsons Point, Sydney, NSW 2061, Australia,
in New Zealand by Random House New Zealand Ltd,
18 Poland Road, Glenfield, Auckland 10, New Zealand
and in South Africa by Random House (Pty) Ltd,
Endulini, 5a Jubilee Road, Parktown 2193, South Africa.

Printed and bound in Great Britain by
Clays Ltd, St Ives plc

For Annie

'And if you have five seconds to spare
I'll tell you the story of my life:
Sixteen clumsy and shy
I went to London and I . . .'

Morrissey, 'Half A Person'

16 June 1991
Birch Services,
M62 Motorway

Dear Morrissey,

I'm feeling dead depressed and down. Like a street-lamp without a bulb or a goose at the onset of Christmas time. Anyroad, I thought I'd pen a few lines to someone who'd understand. I know you probably won't answer this; I don't know if it'll even get to you. And, anyhow, even if you wrote back which I know is highly dubious it wouldn't get to me because I'll have gone. The above address is just a service station I'm stopped at. I'll probably not even post it. I'm writing this in the book I use for writing my lyrics and putting my ideas down. It's sort of a journal, I suppose; although that makes it sound more important than it really is. Anyroad, that's what I'm writing in as I sit here amongst the truckers and the tourists and the travellers and the transients. It's just occurred to me that you might have been in this cafeteria yourself, perhaps in the early days, on the way back from a gig and you and the lads pulled in for a cup of tea. It's a sort of comfort, the thought that you could have been here, Morrissey, perhaps even sitting at this very table that I'm sat at now. I wonder what your thoughts were as you sat in this shrine of self-service gratification, with its granary bar and its battered cod and its breadcrumbed haddock beached on a hotplate, far far from the rolling sea. I'm sitting here opposite a dead fat truck driver who's giving me a lift. I wish the bastard hadn't stopped for me. I could have walked here faster. It's taken nearly two hours to get from Manchester to here because he can't drive past a café or a service station without stopping for something to eat.

When I climbed into his cab he said, 'Where y' goin'?'

I said, 'Grimsby.'

He said, 'What for?'

I said, 'To work.'

He nodded over at my guitar. 'What,' he said, laughing at me, 'busking?'

'No,' I said, 'working on a building site!'

He looked a bit dubious.

'Just doing a bit of labouring,' I said, 'and making tea and that.'

He nodded. And then he said, 'How come you're going all the way over there to find work?'

I thought about it. And then I said, 'Because of Morrissey.'

'Morris who?' he said.

'Morris*ey*,' I told him, 'not Morris who. Morrissey, the greatest living lyricist. He used to be with The Smiths.'

'Oh,' he said, 'that boring twat!'

I didn't talk to him any more. He put a Phil Collins cassette on and farted a few times which, in the musical circumstances, I thought was rather apposite.

He's just stuffed another bacon buttie between his teeth and he's laughing again so that you can see all the chewed-up bread and bacon and saliva in his mouth. He thinks it's dead hilarious 'cause I said I was a vegetarian. That's what started him laughing.

'I don't know what you're laughing for,' I said, 'because all sorts of people are vegetarian; like George

12

Bernard Shaw was vegetarian. And Mahatma Gandhi! And the majority of the world happens to be vegetarian,' I said, 'including Morrissey. And me.'

He just laughed even more.

'And that's why I became a vegetarian,' I told him. 'Because of Morrissey.'

But I was wasting my breath so I shut up and let him laugh. What can you say to a Philistine who's into Phil Collins and Dire Straits and other such frivolity? I've got my Walkman on now so at least I can't *hear* him laughing. The only saving grace in having a lift from him is that he's so fat he makes me feel really thin. It's not that I'm obese or anything, not any more, Morrissey. But even though I'm not fat nowadays, I sometimes forget and still think of myself as being corpulent. And I hate having to look at pictures of me when I was fat. Photographs are just like computers – they never tell the truth. It's like that picture of Oscar Wilde, Morrissey, you know the one where he's got those boots on and he's leaning against that wall. And if that was the only surviving picture of Oscar Wilde everybody'd think he was a fat person, wouldn't they? But Oscar Wilde wasn't fat, not on the inside. And I wasn't fat, not on the inside, I wasn't. It was just a phase I was going through. And probably it was just a phase that Oscar Wilde was going through and he couldn't help it just like I couldn't help it. They used to call me Moby Dick! When we moved to Wythenshawe and they put me in that comprehensive school where I didn't know nobody and it was already the middle of term by the time I started, I walked into the classroom and Steven Spanswick looked up and said, 'Fuckin' hell, it's Moby Dick!'

And everybody in the classroom started laughing, even the teacher!

But I don't care about them now. I don't care about Spegga Spanswick and Barry Tucknott and Mustapha Golightly and all that lot. Hilarious bastards! Because I'm grateful really. It was because of people like Steven

Spanswick and Jackson and all those other pathetic persons that I wrote my first ever lyric. It was called 'I Don't Care'.

I don't care
If you pull my hair
I don't care if you laugh at me
I don't care
If you point and stare
I don't care if you throw crap at me
I don't care
If you strip me bare
I don't care if you say I'm fat
I don't care
If you rob my share
I don't care if you call me twat
I don't care
I don't care
I don't care
Because I'm not there.

Looking back on it now it seems deadeningly didactic and somewhat simplistic. In fact it's highly embarrassing, predictable and derivative. But every artist has to start somewhere and the important thing is that despite what my lyrics were like, I had at least started writing them. Oh shit, what's the Greasy-Gobbed Get saying to me now . . . ?

Later,
The Back of a Carpet-
Fitters' Van
Somewhere in the Pennine Chain
(Apparently)

Dear Morrissey,

I'm still dying of embarrassment. I couldn't get out of that service station fast enough. These carpet fitters are headed for Halifax and they said they'd drop me there. I don't even know if Halifax is on the way but I would have accepted a lift to anywhere just to get out of that service station.

I'm glad that at least it happened in such a transient sort of environment and so hopefully I'll never have to see *her* again!

Having my Walkman on and writing to you, I hadn't realised he was talking to me, the Incredible Bulk. By the time I took my earphones off he was *shouting*, 'Hey! Look, look!'

I looked to where he was pointing. And that's when I saw her, stood there by the mix-it-yourself muesli counter. She was smiling at me and she sort of half waved. And though normally I don't have a great facility for a smile, I just couldn't help myself smiling back at her; because although I hadn't ever seen her

15

since that one time at the bus stop by the bottle bank on Failsworth Boulevard, I'd never forgotten her, the girl with the chestnut eyes. I didn't know her, and she didn't know me. We'd just been stood there, with all the other people in the bus queue. She was almost at the front of the queue and I was stood at the back. I was slightly shocked at first, when she'd just nodded at me. I must have looked puzzled though because she smiled again and opened her denim jacket so that I could see her tee shirt. And I understood then. And I smiled back at her. Because she was wearing exactly the same tee shirt as me! The same one that I'm wearing today, the one with the picture of Edith Sitwell on the front and *Morrissey* written on the back of it. And it's always brilliant, that is, when you meet another Morrissey fan. Even though you've never seen them before, you know there's something important that you share with that person. She called back to me, from where she was stood up at the front of the queue, she said, 'Where was it that Morrissey lost his bag?'

I laughed. I said, 'That's easy, Newport Pagnell.'

She laughed then and all the people in the queue were starting to look at us as if we were soft or the sort of decadent drug-crazed delinquents that they read about in the *Failsworth Fanfare*. But I didn't care. We didn't care. We were Morrissey fans!

I said, 'What job did he apply for at the YWCA?'

She laughed again and she said, 'That's easy and all: backscrubber.'

We were having a great time, just stood there at the bus stop, me and the girl with the chestnut eyes.

'What was Morrissey carrying', she asked, 'when he broke into the Palace?'

We both shouted out the answer together, shouted out, 'A sponge! And a rusty spanner!'

And we both laughed then. And that's when I noticed her eyes, noticed that they were as dark and as shiny as chestnuts that have just come out of their skin. I think I must have been staring at her then because she sort of shrugged a bit. And then she asked me, she said, 'Have you got the New York mix of "This Charming Man", the one with the misprinted cover?'

I nodded. And she looked at me like she was really really impressed. The bus turned up then though and someone behind her told her to get a move on and stop holding up the queue. She moved along towards the bus and got onto it. I hoped she didn't think I was being sort of superior or gloating about it when I'd told her I'd got the New York mix of 'This Charming Man' with the misprinted cover. I didn't want her thinking I was bragging about it. As I moved along the queue I decided that if I got to talk to her again when I was on the bus I wouldn't mention that I had the New York misprint cover of 'Hand In Glove' as well! She might very well think it was somewhat ostentatious or even slightly vulgar, a person having not just one but *two* of the most collectible Morrissey collectibles in existence.

As it turned out though, I never did get to talk to her on the bus. I never even got to get onto the bus! Because when I got to it the driver said, 'No more. We're full up!' and I started to protest but he just hit the lever and the doors snapped shut in my face.

And I never saw her again after that, the girl with the chestnut eyes. I never saw her anywhere. I always hoped that I'd bump into her again but I knew it was highly unlikely, especially as I never venture into the outside environment unless it's absolutely necessary. Most of the time I'm quite happy being miserable in my bedroom. And even if I did go out more, like my Mam was always urging me to do, I still don't think I would have bumped into her again, the girl with the chestnut eyes. I knew from her accent that she wasn't even from Failsworth. So that day when I'd met her at the bus stop, it was probably the only time she'd ever been in Failsworth in her entire life. That's why I knew I'd probably never see her again. And sometimes I started to think that I'd never even seen her in the first place and perhaps she'd just been the sort of person I wanted to see, the Girl with the Chestnut Eyes.

But then, today, as I sat there opposite that Incredible Bulk of a truck driver, there she was, in the service-station cafeteria! And she'd recognised me and was smiling at me again and bringing her tray over to the table where I was sat. But she never arrived! She never got to where I was sat. Because as she approached, I suddenly heard him, the Greasy-Gobbed Get of a truck driver, heard him as he said, 'Yeah. You come and sit by me, sweetheart. An' I'll tell y' what: play your cards right and I'll be up you like a rat up a drainpipe.'

Morrissey, it was suddenly like the eerie calm and quiet that descends after a bomb has just exploded. The smile on the face of the Girl with the Chestnut Eyes slowly started to fade. And the worst thing was she was still looking at me, but now there was only hurt and pain in her eyes, like she'd just been mortally wounded. Still looking at me but with disillusionment and disappointment written all over her face now, she suddenly stopped and turned and walked away to a different table where a pair of seasoned citizens welcomed her with their warm, watery-eyed smiles. And then, as I sat there, still almost catatonic with shock at what the Greasy-Gobbed bastard had said to her, I suddenly realised: she must think that I was with him! That I was the sort of person who could be acquainted with the sort of person that the sort of person the Greasy-Gobbed Get of a truck driver was! I scrambled out of my seat then and went across to her to try and explain! But as I did so, *he* started shouting out again, all crude and witless and shag-brained sort of stuff so that she looked up and saw me approaching and immediately went to move off again. That's when I reached out, to try and stop her and tell her and explain and apologise about it all. But as my hand touched her arm she snatched it away and all her mix-it-yourself muesli went showering over the two pensioners who just sat there with rolled oats and cracked wheat and sultanas all over their bacon and egg breakfasts.

'Just leave me alone,' she said, the Girl with the Chestnut Eyes. And she stood there shivering slightly like a bird that's been brought down from the sky with a pellet in its wing.

'Yes, go on! You just leave the poor girl alone!' the female pensioner person said.

'And leave *us* alone an' all!' the man said. 'Look! Look!' he said. 'Look what you've done, you! I can't drink that tea now. It's got bloody seeds and fruit and all sorts of bloody tackle floating on top of it now.'

I said that I'd gladly get him another cup of tea. And his wife. I said I'd gladly get them fresh breakfasts if they liked. And I said to the girl, 'And yours,' I said, 'I'll get you another bowl of mix-it-yourself muesli.'

But she didn't even look at me. She just stared down at the table like she was all locked down inside herself now. And she said, 'Leave me alone. Just go away from me. Just go!'

And from the way she said it I knew that it was pointless trying to argue or persuade. And all I could do was just mumble that I was sorry.

And I turned and walked away then, wishing that I had a blanket to put over my head to conceal my shame and embarrassment. I got back to my table and snatched up my guitar and my bag, intending to just get out of the place and get away. But then I saw that the walking obscenity of a truck driver had got hold of my lyric book! He'd taken it out of my bag and he was reading my letter to you, Morrissey, reading it and laughing! I grabbed at it and tried to snatch it out of his hand but he was too quick for me and he held it away so that I couldn't reach. And all the time he kept saying to me, 'All right, Moby, calm down, Moby. What's up, Moby Dick, wouldn't she give you one?'

I kept trying to think of what Oscar Wilde would have done in a situation like that, what appropriately cutting epithet he would have coined to wound and deflate and defeat his adversary. But I couldn't think of nowt so I just grabbed up a fork and jabbed it into the fat bastard's hand. He screamed like a stuck pig then and dropped my book onto the floor. But as I bent down and reached for it, he brought up his knee and caught me right in the face. I didn't just see stars; I saw the Blackpool illuminations.

Apparently that's when the carpet fitters got involved and stopped him just as he was about to tread all over my head. When I came round, one of the carpet fitters was helping me towards the door and the other one was carrying my gear. As we approached the beautiful girl's table, the carpet fitter who was carrying my gear said to the carpet fitter who was carrying me, 'Hey, I could give that one a good seeing to,' and they both started laughing that horrible, nauseous laugh that only men can make. And as I passed her I saw the Girl with the Chestnut Eyes look up and give me a fleeting glance of bitter disappointment. That was when I stopped, stopped alongside her table. And I said to her, 'I don't share their thoughts or their deeds; you've got me all wrong. As a matter of fact,' I said to her, 'I happen to have taken a vow of celibacy!'

Well, that's how the carpet fitters got it into their heads that I'm a novice priest. As he was helping me into the back of the van the one who was carrying my gear apologised for all his coarseness and lasciviousness. So I'm sitting here now, on six rolls of floral-patterned shag pile, headed somewhere up the Pennine Chain. And the carpet fitters are on their best behaviour and calling me 'Father' all the time.

I feel a bit guilty now about saying I'd taken a vow of celibacy. Not on account of the carpet fitters but on account of the girl. You see, Morrissey, on top of everything else, I'd lied to her. It's not that I've taken a vow of celibacy, it's just that I am. Celibate! It's one of those facts. Like water's wet, like grass is green. Like Raymond is celibate. And as it's an incontrovertible fact I thought I might as well try and turn it into a sort of a virtue. I was in town one Saturday and I saw this graffiti written on the side of the Kentucky Fried Chicken. It said, 'Raymond Marks has never had it.' I went back that night with a spray can and I wrote, 'Raymond Marks doesn't want it actually!'

It was just after I'd read that article about you, Morrissey, and you'd told the interviewer that you were a 'lapsed celibate'. I thought it was brilliant, that. I wish I could say the same, but so far I've found that the 'celibate' bit is easier to achieve than the 'lapsing'. I don't think about it too much though. I've got my Morrissey records and my Smiths records and my book of Oscar Wilde quotes. And I've got my lyric writing and that's dead important to me. And something I've noticed, Morrissey, when I've been reading about other writers or listening to them being interviewed is that a lot of them say the same thing – that when it comes down to it, writing is better than sex. Well, if that's true, I'm having a great time.

Yours sincerely,
Raymond Marks

From the Lyric Book of Raymond James Marks

Down by the back of the shopping arcade
A big horse chestnut grows
Like a thing left over from another age
But refusing to decompose.
I threw a big stick at that chestnut tree
And waited for a conker to fall;
But the stick fell back and landed on me
And I ended up with sod all.
So I picked up my stick and I walked away
Mocked by the growling skies
Until I heard a voice calling, 'Ray!'
It was the Girl with the Chestnut Eyes.
She gently said, 'Give over,
You're seeking far too soon.
You get conkers in late October
And it's only the middle of June.'
I went to reach out for her
But my hands just grasped thin air
Although I know in my bones that I saw her.
I *know* that she was there.
So I waited till the swallows
Started nesting in the eaves
And the potholes, dips and hollows
Were stuffed with fallen leaves.
Then in bright anticipation
I went back to that chestnut tree;
But found nowt! Only desolation
Waiting there for me.
My heart just turned to parchment
I was sadder than a circus clown;
The men from the Parks Department
Had been and chopped the tree down.
I turned like the fighter who's won the fight
Then been denied the prize
And shouts out that it isn't right
As tears start to prick his eyes.
As narked as a bus conductor,

As pissed off as ice in the sun,
As Deirdre (when Ken Barlow chucked her),
I turned and I started to run.
And I ran till I came to the waters
That are known as the Rochdale Canal;
There was nothing now that could sort us.
I looked up and I said, 'Thanks, pal.'
There'd be no more tomorrows see
I'd soon be 'was' and no longer 'am':
I said my farewells to Morrissey,
To Oscar Wilde and to my Mam.
But as I slipped into that iced,
Bike-frame-infested pool,
I heard a voice that said, 'Oh Christ.
What's he doing now, the fool?'
Then it all went as quiet as tea in a cup.
I was sinking, the water grew darker
When some soft bastard started pulling me up
By grabbing the hood of my parka.

They put me to bed in a bright white place
Where the light was always on
And wrote on a card it was one more case
Of a lad with his marbles gone.
So I shouted out and tried to explain
And tell them I hadn't gone bonkers,
That it wasn't my marbles that had gone down
    the drain
And that all that I'd lost was my conkers.
But the more I said it the more they laughed
So the more I lost my patience
So the more they said I *must* be daft
And gave me more medications.
To calm me down, to help, they said
But they turned my brain to jelly
Till I just sat quietly by the bed
And watched game shows on the telly.
Or, with assistance, walked the grounds,
Adolescence prematurely departed,

23

Like a wino shuffling on his rounds
On the march of the broken-hearted.

Winter, spring and summer passed by
But I didn't hardly notice
With my brain baked as hard as a chip-shop pie
Then smothered in a kaolin poultice.
But then the leaves started falling
And as I shuffled along that day
I thought I heard them calling
'Look! This way, this way.'
My head felt as heavy as a sack of old pennies
As I lifted my eyes from the floor
But there, through the mist of the downers and
    bennies,
Standing before me I saw
The great golden bough of a galleon
In the form of a chestnut tree;
I thought, shit, is this just the Valium
Or can I believe what I see?
But then I *knew* I wasn't drugged or drunk
That it wasn't tricks or lies
Because stepping out from behind the trunk
Was the Girl with the Chestnut Eyes.
She wrapped her arms about me
And whispered, 'Do not be afraid.
Promise never to doubt me
And I promise you will be saved.'
I swore that oath, and immediately
The earth seemed to crack in two,
The sewers of hell rushed up at me;
It was like an acid house do.
The girl in my arms became a whip
That lashed and sliced my skin
But I could not, would not release my grip.
She became a jagged tin
That ripped and tore my flesh away
And gouged out both my eyes
But still I wouldn't, couldn't give way;

I had to hold on to the prize.
Then she became a scorpion
And stung the arms about her
But still I just kept holding on,
Still I refused to doubt her.
She became disease personified,
She became the atom bomb,
Became every soul that had ever died
But still I kept holding on.
Then finally she became the core
That burns white hot at the centre of the sun;
And just when I thought I could hold on no more
My ordeal was finally done.

We were walking along a street in town,
She was laughing at things I said,
I was smiling, not depressed, not down,
Not like one who'd come back from the dead,
Pill popped planted and plonkered.
I'd come through, I'd gained the prize.
And that was how I got conquered
By the Girl with the Chestnut Eyes.

RJM

Dear Morrissey,

The crackpot carpet fitters dropped me here. As I got out of the van they indicated the town and said, 'Here we are then, Father, this is as far as we go.'

I looked down the hill towards the plethora of pizza parlours, privately owned pebble-dashed prefabs and all the variously vulgarised Victoriana.

'This is Halifax,' the driver proudly announced.

'Thanks for telling us,' I said. 'I might just have mistaken it for Paris!'

They frowned at me. 'Is that where y' headed for?' one of them asked.

I shook my head. 'No,' I said, 'I'm headed for Grimsby.'

They looked at each other then, the carpet fitters. And then they looked at me with a considerable degree of pity and sympathy. Then one of them patted me on the shoulder and said, 'Never mind, Father, never mind!'

Before they drove off they told me I'd easily get a lift from here. I hope their carpet fitting is more accurate than their powers of prediction! I've been stuck at this shagging lay-by for more than two hours now and the nearest I've come to getting a lift was when a customised Ford Sierra slowed down and two hilarious bastards leaned out the windows, yockered all over me and told me to fuck off. A minibus carrying a clutch of nuns did begin to slow down for me but when I grabbed my gear and ran up to it, it started pulling away and the Hebden Bridge Sisters of Charity all started laughing out the windows and giving me the finger. I just gave up then and sat down at the foot of the road sign. I'm beginning to think I should have got the coach to Grimsby like I'd told my Mam I was doing. But hitch-hiking seemed more romantic somehow; a fitting tribute to my last few days of freedom. I'm beginning to suspect though that it might have been a mistake to abandon my customary cautiousness and flirt with the capricious nymph of adventure. I hate my Uncle Bastard Jason! I got out one of my felt-tip pens before and I wrote, right across the road sign, I wrote: 'My Uncle Jason is a bastard and a thief; he stole my Gran's satellite dish! And now he enjoys Sky TV while my Gran wallows in a lead-lined box, inside an ill-fitting and contentious grave!'

I hate my Uncle Bastard Jason. I wouldn't be going to a pox hole like Grimsby if it wasn't for him.

I know I said I was going to Grimsby because of you, Morrissey, but I wasn't blaming you when I said that. Your part in all this was merely incidental and I absolve you totally of any blame whatsoever in my enforced flight from Failsworth. That part of it was my fault, I know that. I just never should have played your records to my Mam. But my Mam was happy, you see. On that Saturday night my Mam was dead happy. I knew she was because she was making an apple pie from a Delia Smith recipe she'd copied down off Ceefax. It had cinnamon and cloves and the zest of lemons and things that my Mam normally wouldn't bother with in an ordinary apple pie. But my Mam was happy that night. When my Mam isn't happy she doesn't do any cooking at all. She just fetches something frozen from the freezer and microwaves it in an expedient but joyless ritual of perfunctory preparation. When she bothers with baking though, I know that my Mam's all right, I know that she's happy.

On that Saturday night she was even singing to herself as she pounded out the pastry on the kitchen table. 'I'm Not In Love' it was, that old song by 10 CC. My Mam adores that song. And I was happy that she was happy. When I went through to the kitchen to get a drink of water my Mam even picked up the rolling pin, pretending it was a microphone! It was the sort of stomach-clenching moment of acute embarrassment that mothers are prone to produce every once in an unfortunate while. But at least it was only in our kitchenette so there was nobody else around to witness my Mam's excruciating lapse. And I was happy that my Mam was happy and so I summoned up something of a smile.

She stopped singing then and looked at me all curious. 'Bloody hell, Raymond,' she said, 'is that you smiling? Or have you just got wind?'

I said, 'You know that song you're singing? It was recorded at Strawberry Studios, that was. The Smiths recorded there as well.'

'I love that song,' my Mam said and she got a sort of dreamy look in her eyes as she sighed and started singing again. Then she began laying the pastry over the dish and she said, 'It's not *your* sort of music though, is it, Raymond?'

I just shrugged. 'It's all right,' I said. 'I quite like it really.'

My Mam looked at me all surprised. 'Do you?' she said. 'Do you honestly?' And I could tell it was dead important to her to get my approval of a song that she loved.

'It's all right,' I said. 'It's all right. It's not brilliant but yeah, it's all right. It's sort of clever the way it says things backwards.'

28

My Mam's face lit up with a lovely smile and she closed her eyes and dead intensely she said, 'Oh I love that. I just love it so much that he's trying to say to her, he's trying to say that he's not in love with her but he's so . . . he's so deep in love he's almost drowning in it.'

When she said that, I saw that my Mam's eyes had gone all bright and glistening with the great happiness of such sadness. I thought for a minute that the tears she held just behind her eyes were about to spill down her cheek but she just sighed, a big deep sigh of sadness and satisfaction as she started brushing beaten egg all over the top of the apple pie.

'You know, Raymond,' she said, 'you know what it means when you start being able to appreciate the sort of music your parents listened to?'

I was beginning to regret that I'd said owt about the sodding 10 CC song; I might have said that that one was all right but I hoped she wasn't about to start asking me to listen to the bleeding Bee Gees or Leo sodding Sayer or any other such frivolity as my Mam was susceptible to.

'What it means, Raymond,' my Mam said, 'is that you . . . are beginning to grow up.'

She stood there looking at me all proud and smiling and gratified.

It was on the tip of my tongue to tell her that I didn't want to grow up. But I didn't want to blight her happiness by saying something like that. So I just said, 'Mam, I'm going back to my bedroom now.'

But I didn't make it to my bedroom because my Mam suddenly said, 'Hey! Why don't you bring some of your records out and play them for me. You only ever play them in your bedroom.'

I shrugged. I said, 'I just didn't think it was the sort of stuff you liked.'

'Well, how do I know whether I like it?' she said. 'You never let me hear any of it, not properly. All I ever hear is what drifts through the bedroom door. I might like your records if I heard them properly,' she said. 'I mean, you've started liking my music, why shouldn't I like yours? I'll tell you what, Raymond,' she said, 'let me get this pie in the oven and I'll sit down with you and listen to them . . . what are they called again?'

'The Smiths,' I said.

'The Smiths,' she said. 'We'll sit down together and we'll both listen to The Smiths.'

I was dubious; I was extremely dubious. But I could see that my Mam was dead delighted with this mother and son communion and wanted to make the effort to develop it further. And I didn't want to make her unhappy. So I disregarded my dubiousness and went through to my bedroom and got the cassettes.

My Mam sat on the edge of the sofa, smoothing her skirt and doing her best to be like the mothers on the TV advertisements, all alert and attentive in a perfect pose of enthusiastic expectation.

'Come on, Raymond,' she said, all beaming and bright, 'let's sample some sounds!'

I didn't say nowt. I just blushed all over inside for her. Then I pressed the play button and tried to look elsewhere as my Mam sat on the sofa, smiling and bobbing her head and tapping her fingers to 'This Charming Man'.

She said, 'Hey, it's nice, Raymond! It's nice guitar playing, isn't it?'

'You have to listen to the lyrics,' I told her.

'I am doing,' she said, 'I am doing.' She listened again for a minute. 'He's got a nice voice, hasn't he?' she said. 'The lead singer, it's different like, but it's quite a nice voice really.'

'That's Morrissey,' I said. 'He writes the lyrics. He's brilliant.'

'What's that he's saying?' my Mam said, cocking her ear to the cassette, ' "*I would go out tonight but*" . . . What's he saying?'

' "*I would go out tonight but I haven't got a stitch to wear,*" ' I told her.

'*I* feel like that sometimes,' my Mam said. 'It's

30

brilliant, isn't it? The way someone you've never met can write a song and it just . . . just like sums up the way you feel.'

'But that's Morrissey, Mam!' I said, feeling an uncharacteristic surge of excitement. 'That's what he does. Because he's a poet he can articulate things for all of us. Do you really like it,' I said, 'or are you just saying that?'

'I do like it, Raymond,' she said, getting up from the sofa as the track finished, 'I like it very much indeed.'

And because I could smell fresh apple pie baking in the oven and because I was glad, just glad that I had a Mam who could like The Smiths, I got enthusiastic about it and said, 'I'll play another track if you like.'

My Mam glanced towards the kitchen and then back at me. 'Go on then,' she said, sitting back down again, 'but I mustn't forget that apple pie.'

I played 'Barbarism Begins At Home' for her and 'Hairdresser On Fire', 'Heaven Knows I'm Miserable Now' and 'Girlfriend In A Coma'. And as the songs were playing I kept telling my Mam everything about The Smiths and about you, Morrissey, and about the songs and what they meant and how brilliant they were and what influenced them and where they were recorded and everything. And I kept saying, 'Listen to this bit, Mam, this bit's great, this is,' and 'Just listen to that lyric, Mam, isn't that brilliant?'

I suppose I'd got a bit carried away. I even played 'Vicar In A Tutu' without thinking. I was so carried away on the tide of my own evangelical zeal that I didn't even notice that my Mam had started to look at me in a worried, questioning sort of way and that her fingers no longer tapped out time but fiddled nervously with the cloth of her skirt. Then as I pressed fast forward and said, 'Wait till you hear this one, Mam, this is "Death Of A Disco Dancer",' my Mam said, 'I don't think I want to hear any more if you don't mind, Raymond.'

'No,' I said, 'you'll love this, Mam, it's "Death Of A Disco Dancer".'

But as I pressed the play button my Mam upped and ran through to the kitchen shouting, 'Oh bloody hell, Raymond, the apple pie!'

I switched off the tape player.

When I went through to the kitchen, my Mam was stood there staring down at the charred, charcoal remains of a Delia Smith disaster area. My Mam's head was bowed and I saw a tear fall from her eye. It landed on the charcoal crust and sizzled. I said, 'Mam, it's only an apple pie, it doesn't matter. We can just have a packet of Angel Delight instead.'

My Mam said, 'It's not the pie, Raymond!' She looked up at me and a sob shuddered through her. 'What are you doing, Raymond,' she said, 'listening to that sort of music?'

I said, 'I like it.'

She said, 'But it's morbid, Raymond, it's all morbid.'

'Morrissey's not morbid,' I told her. 'He's not *morbid* morbid.'

'Not morbid?' my Mam shouted. 'Not morbid? "*If a ten ton truck should kill the both of us . . . to die by your side, the privilege, the pleasure is mine*"! Not morbid, Raymond? Not mor— "*Oh Mother I can feel the soil falling over my head! Heaven knows how miserable I feel.*"'

' "*Heaven knows I'm miserable now!*" ' I corrected her.

'And no bleeding wonder, Raymond,' she said. 'I'm bloody miserable myself after listening to that. Not morbid? It's sodding suicidal. And not only morbid,' she said, 'it's bloody criminal: "*Lifting some lead off the roof of the Holy Name church!*" What sort of a song is that, Raymond?'

'A brilliant song!' I told her. 'You just don't understand,' I said. 'And it's not morbid like you think it is! Being morbid doesn't mean being unhappy. You can be dead happy being miserable, like Morrissey; like me!'

I went back into the front room and started gathering up all my cassettes and putting them back in their covers. When I turned round my Mam was stood there shaking her head as she looked at me with trembling lips and worry in her eyes.

'Raymond, son,' she said, 'I thought that phase was over; I thought we'd come through all that. I'd started to believe you were a normal boy; I thought you were normal now, Raymond.'

And it just brassed me off whenever my Mam said that. I knew it was my Mam's ambition for me to be normal. I knew it'd be her height of delight to see me correspond to conformity. My Mam was always hinting about that sort of stuff. Whenever the NatWest advert came on she'd look at that prat of a student and say, 'Isn't *his* hair nice, Raymond,' or 'That's the sort of jacket that would suit you, y' know, Raymond.'

My Mam's greatest ambition was that one day I would miraculously emerge from the chrysalis of my own self to become what is vomitingly known as a *young person*. But I'd never become a *young person*. I hate young persons; they've all got student railcards and high-pitched laughs, and listen to Steve Wright and his pathetic posse. I'd rather be a deceased person than a young person. On balance I don't think there's a great deal of difference either way.

So I said to my Mam, 'I'm not normal! I don't want to be normal,' I said, 'I hate normality! I'm going back to my bedroom.'

As I closed the door behind me I heard her shouting, 'You can't live your life in a bedroom, Raymond!'

But I was quite happy to live my life in my bedroom. I like my bedroom. And I might even have still been in my bedroom now if my Mam hadn't gone round to see my Bastard Uncle Jason. I would have been all right if she hadn't gone to see him. I would have come out of my bedroom later on and I would have asked my Mam if we were having toast and milky coffee. And although she would have given me one of those looks like a cheesed-off checkout girl, it would have been all right in the end. We would have finished up sitting in front of the telly eating toast and drinking milky coffee and everything would have been all right.

But it wasn't all right because when my Mam got back from my repulsive relatives she just stood there without even taking her coat off and looked at me with a glare of suspicion and deep dubiousness.

I said, 'Do you want some toast and milky coffee?'

She just looked straight through me. 'I had coffee at your Uncle Jason's,' she said. 'Raymond, are you a homosexual?'

I looked at her. 'Well, do you just want toast then?' I said.

'I don't want toast, Raymond!' she said. 'Your Aunty Paula did spam fritters for us all. On pitta bread. Now are you going to answer me? I want the truth, are you a homosexual?'

'Who said that about me?' I asked her.

'Never you mind who said it. I just want to know if it's the truth!'

I didn't say nowt. I just thought of my Mam and how she'd betrayed me by going and talking about me to my Uncle Bastard Jason, conversing with him even when she knew that he was the felonious one who'd appropriated my Gran's satellite dish. I could see my Mam sitting there on my Aunty Paula's brushed Dralon pouffe with my reprehensible reprobate Uncle on one side and my unspeakable Aunty Paula on the other as the three of them sat there eating spam fritter pitta and speculating on the nature of my sexuality.

I said, 'There's nothing wrong with homosexual people.'

She said, 'I never said there was, Raymond; I'm just asking you what you are.'

I said, 'Y' know what I am.'

'What's that?' she said. 'You tell me, Raymond. What are you?'

I just looked at her. I shrugged. And I was trying not to cry. I said, 'I'm just a boy,' I said, 'that's all. I'm just a boy with a thorn in his side!'

34

My Mam stood there looking at me like I was an inscrutable puzzle that would never be solved. And I stood looking back at her. I wanted her to put her arms around me. And hug me. And tell me that she never should have gone round to my Uncle Jason's and that he was a thieving bastard. I wanted her to make me laugh and tell me stories about my Aunty Paula's Venetian bathroom suite from Texas Homecare. I wanted my Mam to be on my side. I wanted to sit down with her and eat toast and drink milky coffee and even be a young person, and explain to her that I wasn't homosexual, just a lad who seemed to be having great difficulty in becoming hetero-bleeding-sexual. I wanted my Mam to hug me and understand. But she just kept looking at me; looking at me the way she'd looked at me all those years ago when everything had happened at the canal. And the little girl had gone missing.

I said, 'What y' staring at me like that for?'

But my Mam just shook her head all slow and sad like a woman of constant sorrow. 'Jesus,' she said, taking her coat off, 'Jesus, Jesus!'

And because I couldn't bear the pain of my Mam's despair, because regardless of owt I wanted her to be happy, I agreed. About going to Grimsby!

It was my Bastard Uncle Jason's idea. He came round the next day and told my Mam that he had a mate who was working in Grimsby building a thirty-two-screen cinema complex with ancillary services including major retail emporia, environmentally enhanced parking facilities, premier fast-food outlets and a themed public house with a seafaring ambience housed in an architect-designed reproduction trawler boat. And as a special favour to my Uncle Jason, his mate was willing to give me a start. Just a bit of labouring and making the tea at first. But if I showed real promise I could get promotion, go on the hod and have the chance of earning some real money. My Mam said it was the answer to everything, that what I'd always needed was a job,

35

something to get me out of the house, to get me mixing with people. I just stared at her, stricken dumb with incredulity. I didn't want a job. I didn't want to be out mixing with people. I don't like people. From what I've seen of them, people are a very overrated species; especially people on building sites. I hate building sites; it's a well-documented fact that building sites are crucibles of brutality with frivolous bastards full of sweat and epithet and 'I luv u mam' tattooed on their gnarled knuckles. I didn't want to go on a bleedin' building site. I didn't want a sodding job. I was perfectly happy being a failure in Failsworth. But my Mam glowed and beamed, as though she was imparting the news that I'd just been awarded the Nobel Prize for literature.

'It's a chance, Raymond,' she said. 'It's the chance you've always deserved. Come on,' she said, 'you get yourself dressed, I'm taking you out for Sunday dinner as a celebration.'

And that's when my Mam did hug me. And it was like all her sorrows had been assuaged and the balm of delight that was upon her brought back something of her girlish bloom. So that when she planted a big kiss on the side of my face and said, 'Aren't you just thrilled, Raymond? Aren't you thrilled?' I said, 'I am, Mam. Thrilled!'

And all that week, as the day for my departure drew nearer, my Mam continued to blossom and the house was filled with ever more delicious smells of gourmet cuisine created especially for me. Normally my Mam complained about me being a vegetarian and said I was dead awkward to cook for. But the week before I left was a week of vegetarian cornucopia and every dish was prepared and served with love and happiness and hope for the future. So I couldn't say nothin' and I couldn't do nowt. Apart from pray that the place that is Grimsby could be visited by a freak but benevolent tidal wave, or an earthquake or a nuclear bomb, obliterating that town and its embryonic thirty-two-screen picture palace. But as Grimsby didn't receive so much as a mere mention on this morning's news I must regretfully conclude that Gruesome Grimsby is still there, where Grimsby has always been (and that I'd better do something about getting there).

But I do remain, Morrissey,
Yours sincerely,
Raymond Marks

A bench,
The Railway Station
Concourse,
Halifax,
West Yorkshire

Dear Morrissey,

I asked the ticket clerk for a single to Grimsby.
   He said, 'That'll be fifteen pounds ninety please.'
   I said, 'Fifteen pounds ninety!'
   He just nodded.
   I said, 'But it's only nine pound fifty if you go by coach and that's from Manchester!'
   He said, 'Listen, do you want this ticket or don't y'?'
   I asked him if he'd got any cheaper tickets to Grimsby. I said I'd willingly travel in the guard's van if that'd be any cheaper.
   But he just said, 'Hey, mate! How many times? I don't care if you're riding in the guard's van, the toilets or even on the fucking roof, the cost is fifteen pounds ninety. Did you hear me? Fifteen pounds ninety!'
   I just looked at him. And said, 'I thought crime wasn't supposed to pay.'
   He said, 'What are you? A fuckin' comedian or what?'
   'Me?' I said. 'Fifteen pounds ninety just to get

to Grimsby! You're the one who's telling the jokes.'

He lowered his voice then and said, 'Hey! Do you want this fuckin' ticket or don't y'?'

I said, 'It's not a question of what I want!' I said, 'It's bad enough that a person has to go to Grimsby in the first place, let alone having to pay through the nose for the privilege of it!'

He got all huffy then and dismissively threw the ticket up in the air. 'So y' don't want it then?'

'I don't *want* it,' I said, 'but I've got to have it!'

He blew out a big sigh and picked up the ticket again and I bent down to get my wallet out of my bag. And that's when I discovered that it wasn't there. My wallet! It had gone! My wallet was missing! I checked my bag again then checked all my pockets then checked my bag once more. And then I remembered the Greasy-Gobbed Get of a truck driver in the service station. He'd been reading my lyric book, so he must have been in my bag.

'The bastard!' I said. 'The bastard, he's pinched all my money!'

The ticket clerk just looked at me, his eyebrows raised in a somewhat sceptical manner. 'For the last time,' he said, 'do you want this ticket?'

'The truck driver,' I said, 'the Incredible Bulk who gave me a lift, he's robbed all my money!'

'Right! You don't want it,' the ticket clerk said, and looking beyond me at the queue that was starting to build up he said, 'OK, who's next?'

'Look,' I said, 'look, I do want the ticket. It's just that all my money's gone!'

He nodded then, the ticket clerk. And adopting a disingenuous smile, he said, 'So what would you like me to do, son; present you the ticket with my compliments? Perhaps you'd like me to throw in a fiver as well? I mean, I'm already paying taxes as it is. Working my bollocks off and handing over half my fucking wages just so that loungers and scroungers and bone-idle scum like you can roam around the fuckin' country to your heart's content, never doing a tap from the cradle to the grave while poor bastards like me are working from morning till night just to end up with nowt but negative equity, three fuckin' whingein' teenagers who want seventy-pound training shoes every other fuckin' week, a wife who'd turned into a dog before the ink on the marriage certificate had dried and a clapped-out fuckin' Ford Escort that's just failed it's MO fuckin' T!'

I just looked at him.

'What about me?' he said. 'Don't you think I'd like to go to fuckin' Grimsby? Don't y' think I'd like to be an idle bastard student with a guitar, a hideous haircut and a stupid fuckin' tee shirt on his chest?'

I thought that was particularly unpleasant, that. So I told him, I said, 'Actually, I'm not a student!'

But he just looked at me and shook his head and then a person behind me in the queue announced that if I didn't get a move on he'd rip the strings off my guitar and gladly garrotte me with them. He had a number-one haircut and a violent glint in his eye and I could tell that he was one of those persons who ate beer bottles for breakfast. So I just picked up all my gear and went and stood over by the Tie Rack and pondered my predicament. All I had left was a couple of pound coins and a 20p piece and that wasn't going to get me anywhere. I thought about having a go at busking to see if I could raise the extra fare but the only songs I can play are my own and a few of yours, Morrissey. And looking at the station concourse I saw a panoply of shell suits, straights and Sunday morning refugees from the Saturday night before; all of which led me to conclude that this was not an audience that would be inclined to show its fiscal appreciation for 'Girlfriend In A Coma'. And anyroad, the only place I've ever played my guitar up to now is strictly within the confines of my bedroom.

So I just started hustling around and asking if anyone could spare us a few bob. But it wasn't a spectacular success; a feller in a suit said, 'By all means, my young friend. Let's discuss it further in the gents.'

I moved off quick, stood by the Sock Shop and asked a posh woman if she could spare us a couple of quid. She said I was a Welfare State parasite and whacked me over the head with a quality newspaper. I moved off again and stood under the clock. But my luck didn't change. When I asked if they could spare me some money to help me get to Grimsby, people just ignored me; apart from a clever bastard who asked me if I accepted American Express! Then after a bit a girl with short hair and pimples came over and started screaming at me to get off her patch or she'd kick me in the balls. She had very thick Air Ware boots on so I called it a day and decided to spend my last few bob on getting something to eat. I went looking round the station concourse but the ambience was considerably carnivorous and I doubted that I'd find food of a vegetarian variety in the various shrines to nutritionally neutered fast-food culture. But then, as I was walking past a place called the Burger Banquet, I saw a picture of something described as a Spicy Bean Burger.

I said, 'Is it vegetarian, the Spicy Bean Burger?'

She said, 'Of course it's vegetarian — that's why it's called the Spicy Bean Burger.'

'Oh, right,' I said. And I looked up at the pictorial display above the counter. But despite its allegedly vegetarian status, the Spicy Bean Burger looked about as appetising as pressed polystyrene. Concluding, though, that a beggar cannot be a chooser, I said, 'All right, I'll have the Spicy Bean Burger then.'

She said, 'You can't.'

I said, 'Why not?'

She said, 'Because it's Sunday. And we don't offer the Spicy Bean Burger on a Sunday. Or a Saturday for that matter. We only offer the Spicy Bean Burger on weekdays. It's not available at weekends.'

I frowned at her. I said, 'But that's cracked, that is!

41

You don't just stop being a vegetarian at the weekend, y' know.'

She just scowled at me. And she tutted very loudly and said, 'You're holding up the queue, you are.'

'I'm sorry about that,' I said, 'I didn't mean to hold up the queue,' I said. 'I was just making an enquiry apropos the Spicy Bean Burger and its apparent non-availability on a Saturday or Sunday.'

She sighed then and dropped her chip-scoop. And all slit-eyed and huffy she said, 'We don't offer the Spicy Bean Burger on a Saturday or a Sunday because the Spicy bleedin' Bean Burger is not a concept that's considered compatible with the appropriate ambience of the weekend leisure environment!'

We stared at each other.

'Have y' got that?' she said. 'Have y' got it or do y' want me to write it down for y'?'

I just shrugged. It was patently apparent that she was not the kind of person who'd read and taken heed of the Citizen's Charter.

I said, 'I'll just have chips then. On a bun.'

She said, 'You can't.'

I said, 'Why?'

She said, 'Because the Burger Banquet Experience does not recognise the concept of chips.'

I pointed up at the pictorial display. I said, 'Well, what are them up there?'

She said, 'Frits! They're the Frits.'

I looked up at the picture again. I said, 'They look like chips!'

'Well, they're not!' she said, leaning forward and glaring at me. 'They're Fried Frits, not chips.'

'All right then,' I said, 'I'll have the Fried Frits.' She blew out a long sigh and reached for her chip-scoop. And I said, 'Just a small portion please.'

She stopped and cocked her head to one side and stared at me with a warning glint in her eye. And pointing her chip-scoop at the hideously lurid pictorial display she said, 'Can you see the word "small" anywhere up there?'

She glared at me again and I shook my head.

'No, that's right!' she said. 'And why do y' think that is?'

I just shook my head again.

And with a hint of triumphant corporate pride in her tone she said, 'Because "small" . . . *small* is not a concept that is acknowledged within the Burger Banquet Experience! We offer the Modest Frit, the Medium Frit, the Major Frit and the MajorMega Frit.'

Somewhat defeated now by the Burger Banquet's pedantic semantics, I dutifully uttered the appropriate word and watched as she half-filled the chip-scoop and deposited my Modest Fried Frits into a waxed cardboard container. Then I ordered a Cautious Cappuccino and found myself a moulded plastic seat at a moulded plastic table where I sat eating my moulded plastic chips and looking around at all the other unfortunate souls who were undergoing a week-end leisure experience courtesy of the Burger Banquet.

Then a man in a knitted cardigan came up to the table where I was sat. And he said to his wife, 'Go on, you get in there where you'll be out the way.'

And she did as she was bid, his wife, and dutifully slid into the inside seat where she suspiciously picked at her portion of Fried Frits as her husband got to grips with his Double Topper Cheesey Whopper.

And then he suddenly looked up and asked me whose fault I thought it was.

'Whose fault was *what*?' I said.

He said, 'Halifax.'

'I don't know that it's anyone's fault,' I said. 'It's probably just one of them things like the San Andreas fault and nowt can be done about it.'

But he told me I was wrong there and started going on about how Halifax and the whole of Yorkshire used to be a real community but now it was on its knees and everyone was depressed on account of how

43

the government had closed all the mills and the mines and how the colliers can't collect coal no more. I didn't say nowt but from what I've seen of them, I can't imagine that people from Halifax went dancing in the streets even when the bastard mills and mines were still open. But it was pointless saying owt to him. Because he was one of those persons who never listens to nobody but himself. I looked at his wife who was just sat there, silently staring down at her frits. And she looked like a person who'd been taken hostage many many years earlier and had given up all chance of rescue now, or escape. And you could tell that she'd been crushed out of being by the weight of her opinionated and terminally boring husband who was no doubt something of a star on the local radio phone-ins where he'd probably talk for hours about all the graffiti these days and how there was never no graffiti when he was young and nobody never had to lock their doors because everybody was good and kind and swapping bowls of sugar in the olden days when they all wore clogs and shawls and there were no murderers or paedophiles or psychopathic serial killers because people were brought up to show respect and children knew right from wrong and they didn't have shoes to wear or videos to watch or pizzas to eat because they ate dripping-on-bread and gristle soup and succulent feet of pigs and were all the better for it and obeyed the rules in the schools where hymns were sung and poems recited and everybody knew how to read and do algebra by the time they were seven and loved it when they got a good six hard strokes of the cane because they knew it was doing them good and help-ing them to grow up to be the kind of decent, virtuous, moral-minded, community-spirited, sugar-swapping, shawl-wearing, saintly Samaritans that everybody was a few years ago in that world which is so fondly and so accurately remembered by so much of the sincere citizenship that is so compelled to share its profound and compelling insights via the local radio network.

I just sat there, staring into my coffee and thinking about my Gran. Because my Gran was the only old person I ever knew who said that all the stuff about the olden days was just a load of bollocks and bunkum. My Gran used to say the old days was just sentimental slop dreamed up by people who'd got scared of the nowadays.

But my Gran always said she loved the nowadays and wished that she'd been a girl in the nowadays because she would have burnt all her bras and gone on marches with Germaine Greer and lived in London in her own apartment where she and her friends would eat nouvelle cuisine, experiment with recreational drugs and talk about Simone de Beauvoir and things that mattered.

And I'd always say to my Gran, 'Well, perhaps you'll still do all that, Gran.'

But she'd just pat me on the head and tell me that time tricked everybody in the end. And she said, although she wished nothing but goodness for all the young folks with their lovely skin and their shiny hair, it probably was a bit late, at her time of life, to start going in for body-piercing and doing Ecstasy.

'But believe me, son,' she said, 'if I was a girl, nowadays, I wouldn't make the same mistakes that I did. I wouldn't have put up with him for a start. I wouldn't have married him, the fun-loving, philandering bastard that he was!'

My Gran hated my Grandad. Even after he'd died she still wouldn't show no sympathy for him. She said the lecherous old bastard fully deserved the dark demise that his lustful leanings had led him to: my Grandad had fell off the roof trying to fit a satellite dish so that he could watch lewd films and pornographic game shows beamed in from the continent. Everyone had said as how he shouldn't try and fit it himself, that he should get a qualified fitter on the job. But the earliest an aerial fitter could do it was the following Tuesday and my Grandad's libidinous longing to look

45

at continental pornography made him far too impatient for that and against all advice he decided to indulge in a bit of DIY. And he did manage to get the dish fitted onto the chimney. But as he did, he became so excited by lascivious thoughts of the European erotica that would soon be beaming down the dish, he missed his footing, fell off the roof and broke his neck. He'd done a good job with the satellite dish though; my Gran was sat there in the front room watching a Belgian documentary on food and sado-masochism under the impression that it was Welsh Channel 4. When my Grandad fell screaming from the roof, my Gran just ignored it, thinking it was from the soundtrack of the film where a feller was flagellating himself with a Jerusalem artichoke. By the time my Gran switched off, having learned a few tricks with chilli peppers and courgettes that Delia Smith never dreamed of, my Grandad was just a crapped-out cadaver on the patio.

'He lived by lust, he died by lust!' my Gran always said. 'You're too young to understand that now, Raymond,' she said, 'but you will do one day.'

I did understand though because when I'd been in the last year of the infants' school my Grandad had suddenly offered to walk me to school every day. My Mam thought he was just being nice in his old age and trying to get to know his grandchild. But he only did it because he wanted an excuse to get to know the lollipop lady who worked on the dual carriageway. He always stopped and talked to her and it always made me late for assembly. He was always cracking jokes with the lollipop lady, telling her that what she needed was a real lollipop and that he had just the very thing for her. In those days I was too young to know what a metaphor was. But I knew what a pigging lollipop was! I used to get dead embarrassed. Then after a bit the lollipop jokes stopped and whenever we got to the crossing point the two of them would just gaze longingly into each other's eyes. And instead of holding my hand to cross the road, the lollipop lady held my Grandad's hand instead and I had to find my own way through the bleeding traffic. Then one day we got to the crossing and instead of the lollipop lady gazing lovingly into my Grandad's eyes, she lifted up her lollipop and battered shite out of him. It seems that someone had apprised her of the fact that my Grandad was also sharing his lollipop with the bisexual dinner lady from St Bernadette of Perpetual Succour's Comprehensive. Me and my Grandad always had to walk up the hill and cross at the pelican lights after that. And then he fell off the roof and the vicar said to my Gran it was a tragedy.

But my Gran said, 'Tragedy, my arse!' she said. 'When he hit that patio it was the start of my life and my only regret is that we didn't have satellite television thirty bloody years earlier!'

The vicar blinked and said that perhaps they should move on and discuss which hymns my Gran would like to have at the funeral. My Gran said, 'Oh Happy Day' and 'Glad That I Live Am I'.

The vicar coughed and quietly said something about grief affecting people in peculiar ways. Then he told my Gran he had to be getting along now but before he did he wanted to know if my Gran would like to have my Grandad buried or cremated. My Gran said she'd prefer to have him quicklimed. The vicar looked confused and coughed again and hurried off.

'They don't understand, y' see, Raymond,' she said after she'd shown the vicar out. 'They don't understand what I've had to put up with for all these years. Tragic? I could tell that bloody vicar about tragedy. You know my tragedy, don't you, Raymond?'

'Yes, Gran,' I said. 'Your tragedy is that you were never a mediocre woman, but you were forced to lead a mediocre life.'

'That's right, Raymond,' she said, 'that's right. I lived a mediocre life. And all because of him. I met him, didn't I, I married him. Him, with his fun. "Let's go to

Blackpool, Vera. Let's go to Blackpool and have fun."
He loved fun. He always loved having fun. But I hated
bleeding *fun*. I hated candy floss and Arthur Askey
and the hoola-hoop and bastard bleeding Butlin's and
balloons and pratfalls and Charlie chuffin' Chaplin
and singalongs on charabancs and the hokey-sodding-
cokey. Fun? I never wanted fun. I wanted joy! But he
couldn't see it. And do you know, Raymond, son? Do
you know when I first found out about his fornicating
and philandering, when I found out what he was up to
with that Comptometer operator from Cheadle, do you
know what he said to me? Do you know what he said
when I asked him why? He said, "She's good fun, Vera.
She likes a bit of fun. And you're no fun at all any
more."'

My Gran carried on looking away into the distance
for a moment. Then she stubbed her fag out and started
collecting up the dishes from the table. 'You know
what Thomas Hardy said, don't you, Raymond,' my
Gran asked me. 'You know what Thomas Hardy said
about Tess of the d'Urbervilles, don't y'?'

I did know but I said I didn't because I knew that my
Gran liked to recite it so much.

'"*She was a victim of the most common tragedy of
all,*"' my Gran declared. '"*She married the wrong
man!*"'

My Gran stood there nodding solemnly with the
dishes in her hand. 'And when he wrote those words,
Raymond,' she said, 'Thomas Hardy could just as
easily have been talking about me!'

I picked up the cups and saucers and followed my
Gran through to the kitchen.

'You know who I should have married, don't you,
Raymond?' she said as she ran the water into the
washing-up bowl.

'Yes, Gran,' I said, 'you should have married Jean-
Paul Sartre.'

'That's right,' my Gran said, 'that's right. Jean-Paul
Sartre, that's who I should have married. I could never

read his books but y' could tell from his picture, there was nothing frivolous about Jean-Paul Sartre.'

My Gran started washing up the dishes and I got the tea towel and started drying.

'And I've always said, Raymond, I've always said, son, that you're a bit like Jean-Paul Sartre yourself. There's not a lot of frivolity about either one of you. That's why you understand me, son, that's why I can talk to you.'

And my Gran was right; I did understand her and I loved talking to her even though it was her who did all the talking.

My Gran doesn't talk at all any more. It was my Uncle Bastard Jason and my Aunty Pigging Paula; they wanted to get their hands on the satellite dish, and they wanted my Gran's house. And that's why they had my Gran put away, in the Stalybridge Sanctuary for Seasoned Citizens. It was all their fault. And none of it would have happened if I'd been able to keep on talking with my Gran; I never would have got into as much trouble and been such a worry to my Mam. My Gran always understood me. And she'd never let nobody say nothing bad about me. Even after what happened at the canal.

So most of it wouldn't have happened if my Gran had still been here.

I wouldn't be going to gruesome gobbing Grimsby if my Gran was still here.

It was thinking about Grimsby that made me look up and I saw that I was still sat there in the bleeding Burger Banquet. I must have been sat there ages. The man with the knitted cardigan had gone and taken his hostage wife back to captivity. And I realised that I'd have to get gone and all. I promised my Mam that I'd phone her tonight and tell her I'd got there safely. But it's nearly one o'clock now and I'm still stranded in Halifax. And that's why I've decided to take the chance. I feel nervous really, because normally I'd

49

never do what I'm about to do now. But I've got to get to Grimsby.

Wish me luck, Morrissey, wish me luck.

Yours sincerely,

Raymond Marks

Dear Morrissey,

It didn't work, Morrissey. As you can see from the above address, I've been somewhat detained.

I know now that I was a fool. I know that I should never have done it.

I thought I'd be clever and buy a platform ticket so that at least I'd have legitimate cause to be there on the platform. But when I went up to the window and asked for a platform ticket it was the same sodding ticket clerk as before. He looked at me all dead suspicious.

'I hope you realise,' he said, 'that boarding a train without a valid ticket is a serious offence.'

I said, 'I've got no intention of boarding a train.'

He said, 'So how come you wanted a ticket to Grimsby before?'

'I didn't want a ticket to Grimsby,' I said. 'I just wanted to know how much it'd be if I ever *did* want to go to Grimsby.'

He looked all dubious. 'So you're just going on the platform to meet someone, are y'?' he said.

'No,' I said. And I held up my lyric book. 'I'm a train-spotter!'

51

He looked at me and suddenly laughed. 'Well, that fuckin' explains everything,' he said as he took the 10p and threw the platform ticket at me.

I picked it up and walked towards the barrier, somewhat depressed now at the thought that I could convincingly be taken for a train-spotter.

I started to get all nervous when I got onto the platform. I just stood there looking at the train and the sticker on the window that said *Leeds*. It seemed as if everyone else on the platform was staring at me, that they all knew what I was about to do. I'd started perspiring and it was coming through my tee shirt so that the picture of Edith Sitwell looked like it had started growing a beard. I felt dead guilty and I'd not even done nowt yet! I thought about my Mam and how I'd promised her that I wouldn't get into no trouble. And there I was just about to commit a minor misdemeanour by availing myself of public transport without being in possession of a valid ticket. But then I thought about how much more worried my Mam'd be if I wasn't able to phone her tonight to tell her I'd got there. I looked all around me. And none of the legitimate commuters seemed to be staring at me no more. So I quickly pulled the carriage door open, threw my stuff on board and climbed in after it. I'd planned to lock myself in the toilet. But I tried the door and it was locked and there was a big yellow sticker on it, saying 'out of order'. I turned towards the toilet on the other side of the corridor but a young executive type got to the door ahead of me and locked it behind him. Then out of the window I saw two railway guards coming towards the train. And then I saw that the ticket clerk was with them and that he was pointing at the train and I knew then, I knew that he hadn't really taken me for a train-spotter and it must have just been a ploy so that he could catch me doing something wrong. I began to panic then and started legging it along the carriage towards the other set of toilets at the far end. But the carriage was packed and my guitar slung over my back kept banging and bonging on the seats and everyone was looking up at me. And then my guitar bonged against someone's head as he tried to get out of his seat. I turned around and said I was sorry. But then I saw it was the person with the number-one haircut who'd said he'd gladly garrotte me.

'You will be sorry,' he said, rubbing his head as he started to come after me, 'you'll be more than fuckin' sorry when I get hold of you!'

And then I heard the ticket clerk calling, 'That's him, that's the little bastard, catch him, mate.'

I managed to make it to the end of the carriage and went to get off the train but as I pulled down the window to open the door I saw one of the guards running alongside me on the platform. And there was nowt else for it; I had to jump out of the opposite door and try to scramble across the tracks and up onto the far platform. Halfway across though, I looked behind and I saw that the ticket clerk and the feller whose head I'd bonged were about to jump down onto the track and come after me. But just as the garrotter and the clerk were about to jump down, they were cut off by a 125 train that came hurtling through the station going so bleeding fast it almost sucked the pus out my pimples.

I clambered up onto the far platform and I thought I'd made it. I was running towards the exit sign. It was all right, I was going to get away, I'd be OK. But as I ran past the bottom of the footbridge an extremely fleet-footed guard came hurtling down it and managed to grab hold of my guitar from the back. And as I was still umbilically attached to my instrument, it was all up then and I was marched back across the footbridge. I kept saying that I'd only got onto the train to use the toilet facilities. I said I'd been suffering somewhat with my bowels and I hadn't intended to travel on the train. But they said I could tell that to the police. They brought me in here and handed me over to the Station Master. He locked the door and asked me what my name was and I thought about giving a false name and address. But then I knew it would just make everything even worse if I did. So I told him my proper name. And the Station Master phoned up the police then. And there was a pause and I knew that the police would be checking my name on the computer. And then the Station Master put the phone down and said the police would be here soon.

And I know that I'll never get to Grimsby now. Not now. Not now that they've read about me on the computer. I hate computers. They don't tell the truth. They just tell the facts. That's why I've decided to tell you, Morrissey, about the canal and everything. Because it was all just a mistake, Morrissey; everything was a mistake. And everything that happened to me after that was all because of that mistake. And I want you to know that, Morrissey. That it was all just something that got twisted into something else. If everybody had listened to me when it originally happened at the canal then it would have all been different. But no-one does listen to you when you're eleven years old. And I don't care what anyone says, I don't care, because I know even if no-one else does – we weren't wanking! None of us were. I know that we had our things out, all fifteen of us. But having your dick out doesn't mean that you're wanking. It doesn't necessarily. We always used to get our dicks out in summer, down by the canal. No-one could see. There was a big warehouse wall at the back and trees at the side, and if we did see anyone coming we used to put everything back in our pants till they'd gone. I don't even know how it started. No-one ever said, 'Let's get our dicks out.' We just did it. And we'd carry on talking about Lego or school or football or what had been on the telly the night before. And then this day, as we stood there talking about stamp collecting or *Star Wars* or something like that, this fly landed right on the end of mine and it was just an instinctive reaction really. Before the fly knew what had hit it, I'd pulled my foreskin over it and held it there for a minute. Then when I pulled it back this asphyxiated fly just dropped off the end of my dick. Well, all the other lads thought that was bloody brilliant, that. And that's how the flytrapping craze started. Every dinner hour we went down to the canal and it became a competition to see who could bag the most flies. I can't remember who scored the most, but whenever we went flytrapping Albert Goldberg always came in last. Even with the handicap we gave him, Albert couldn't do much to a fly with his circumcised diddler. Sometimes he'd try and flick the fly dead with his finger but more often than not he'd flick the end of his dick and make his eyes water. But one dinner-time we were at the canal and when we started flytrapping Albert had this big smug smile on his face and when we asked him what was up, he pulled out a small jar from his pocket. It had had honey in it and Albert told us how he'd worked out this plan for keeping the fly on the end of his dick long enough for him to give it an accurate flick. Well, he daubed honey all over the end of it and he was catching so many flies that some of the others said he was cheating and that honey wasn't allowed and it wasn't fair. That started an argument between Albert and Kevin Cowley and while Albert was shouting about the unfair advantage of the gentile, a wasp was attracted by the honey on the end of Albert's equipment. Albert didn't even look. He just thought it was another fly and still yelling at Kevin Cowley, he flicked what he thought was the fly. Well, the wasp was a bit pissed off at that. And it flew back. Only this time it stung Albert, right on the end of his honey stick, and Albert instinctively lashed out hard with his hand. But with the shock of the sting Albert missed his dick, bashed himself in the balls and fell headfirst into the canal. We were all screaming with laughter at first. Then we realised he hadn't come back up. And the laughter turned into fear and panic then, as we all remembered that Albert couldn't swim. I didn't think about anything, I just dived in. I couldn't see nothing at all, I just had to keep feeling about amongst the slimy weed and the bits of broken bike frame and supermarket trolleys. I thought my lungs were going to burst. But I didn't care because I couldn't bear the thought of Albert being dead. So I forced myself to keep trying. But I felt myself getting weak and tired and I knew that I'd have to go up for air. I got to the surface and I was just gulping in big lungfuls of air and I felt dead dizzy and I didn't think I had the strength to go back down again. But then I saw the faces of my friends on the bank. They were all looking frightened and Kevin Cowley and Geoffrey Weatherby had started crying. And I think I was crying by then and I didn't know what to do and I didn't know what to think. But I heard myself saying to the lads on the bank, 'I'll give it one more try.' And then I gulped in as much air as I could and I dived back down again. And when I felt about and my hand clutched hold of this clump of something I thought it was just more weeds at first and I was about to let go. But then I realised. It was Albert's hair that I was clutching onto. I don't know how I got him out, really; my lungs felt like balloons blown up beyond busting point. But I struggled and I struggled and I wouldn't give in until I'd pulled him up and up and up and out, beyond the surface, back into the air where the two of us just clutched hold of the bank as we gulped and gulped at the air. Soon there were hands reaching out and I could hear all the other lads shouting and cheering as they pulled us both up onto the bank. Albert was spluttering and coughing and shouting about the pain in his lungs and the pain in his dick but everyone just kept on cheering and clapping and saying I'd been really brave for rescuing Albert. The only one who didn't seem too happy about it was Albert himself because when we got him to his feet he started crying and shouting and said Kevin Cowley was a fucking bastard and none of it would have happened if it hadn't been for him. Kevin didn't even argue back. He just told

Albert he was sorry. And after a bit Albert and Kevin agreed to shake hands. We were all friends again then. And we walked back to school. Geoffrey Weatherby said we'd have to explain how me and Albert had got so soaked. And we all agreed we'd say that Albert had just missed his footing and fallen into the canal. And that I'd jumped in to save him. We all agreed on that. And every one of us knew that not a one of us would say nowt about flies.

Mr Donaldson was on playground duty that day. He said that we should never have been near the canal in the first place. And me and Albert just nodded our heads and said, we just forgot, sir, and we're dead sorry, sir. Mr Donaldson shook his head and said we'd been very lucky. And then he lowered his voice, Mr Donaldson, and he said, 'You're particularly lucky the Headmaster wasn't around.' We just nodded and Mr Donaldson found us some tee shirts and shorts and said, 'Here. Get dried off and put these on.'

He was dead nice, Mr Donaldson, and I thought everything was going to be all right. I thought then that we'd managed to get away with it. But when Mr Donaldson came back into the changing room, Albert suddenly started crying again and said he didn't feel very well. Mr Donaldson turned to me and he said, 'Listen, Raymond, you go back to your class. I think we'll keep Albert down here and ask the school doctor to come along and give him a check-up.'

I must have looked worried then because Mr Donaldson said, 'It's all right, Raymond, it's just a check-up. There's nothing to worry about, I'm sure it's just the shock and Albert will be as right as rain in half an hour.'

And perhaps I still looked worried because as I was going Mr Donaldson said, 'Well done, Raymond. And cheer up, will you? I think you've proved yourself to be something of a hero this afternoon.'

And that did cheer me up and I forgot all about the doctor then.

I'd never been called a hero before, and going back to my class it was like I was walking on air. And it got even better because when I walked into the classroom, Miss Barraclough even made me stand at the front for a minute as she told all the kids in my class what a very very brave boy I was and everyone cheered and patted me on the back as I walked towards my desk. And Rosemary Rainford smiled a big adoring smile at me. And she'd never looked at me before, even though I'd been in love with her ever since we'd both been jam-jar monitors. It was dead exciting, being a hero. I tried to concentrate on the geography we were doing but a note was passed back to me. It had a picture of a heart with the names Rosemary and Raymond inside it and after that I just gave up trying to put the names of the rivers by the names of the towns, and I just sat there instead and basked in my new-found status as school hero and Rosemary Rainford's official boyfriend.

But I'd forgotten all about the doctor!

I didn't know that back in the changing room there were certain discoveries being made. I didn't know that Albert had carried on crying and saying that he had an awful pain. And when the doctor asked him exactly where this awful pain was, Albert told him it was 'down there'. That's when the doctor told Albert to drop his shorts. And when he did, the doctor and Mr Donaldson just stood there speechless and staring at Albert's dick that was all swollen up now so that it looked as though he had a circumcised Cumberland sausage dangling between his legs.

And even then, we might just have got away with it. But then the worst thing happened – the doctor said that the Headmaster should come and take a look! Mr Donaldson looked anxious and wondered if that would really be necessary. But the doctor insisted.

If it had been the old headmaster, if it had still been Mr Kerney who was in charge of our school, everything would still have been all right. He would have found out, in the end, what had been going on. But Mr Kerney would have just sent for me and the others and got us all in his office. Then he would have looked at us, Mr Kerney, looked at us all sad and disappointed, the way he always did when we'd done something wrong and let him down. And he would have quietly told us how much we'd hurt him and made him sad in his heart because he'd always believed that we were trustworthy boys and good boys and there we were, all the time, going behind his back and sneaking off to the canal. And we would have all felt awful by then. Mr Kerney with his big sad eyes would have looked at us one by one and asked all of us to think about the danger of playing near the canal and think too about Albert's mum and dad and just consider for a moment what it would have done to those two particularly lovely persons if their son had drowned in the canal today.

And by that time, me and all the others would have been crying our eyes out and feeling really guilty and we'd never have gone back to the canal after that and it would have all been over and done with, the fly-trapping and all the fuss and everything.

But Mr Kerney wasn't in charge of our school any more. Mr Kerney had been sacked in the aftermath of the Transvestite Nativity Play Scandal. They called him a 'loony leftie', Mr Kerney. And Mrs Bradwick who was the Chair Person of the Governors was on the North West News and said she didn't blame it on Mr Kerney personally, but blamed it on the Sixties when teachers stopped caring about Janet and John and Nip the Dog and long division and the ten times table and all they ever did was finger-painting and dancing and the sort of poetry which made no sense and didn't even rhyme. That was when I was still in the lower juniors and it was boys like Norman Gorman and Twinky McDevitt who were in the top class then. But it wasn't true, what Mrs Bradwick said, about how we never learned about any of the proper things when Mr

Kerney was in charge, because we did! We learned how to read and write and do sums and history and geography and all those things. But we learned all sorts of other things too, when Mr Kerney was the head-master. Like we learned that it was all right to be different, like Terry McDevitt was different. But nobody ever called him Terry. Everybody called him Twinky, even Mr Kerney and the teachers, and 'Twinky' fitted him better than 'Terry' because he was always skipping with the girls and linking arms with them and doing concerts in the playground where he did his impressions of Petula Clark and Lulu and Dorothy from *The Wizard of Oz*. But Norman Gorman said his dad was getting him a pedigree pit-bull terrier for Christmas and then Twinky McDevitt better look out because it was a well-known fact that pit-bull terriers just went mad and couldn't be stopped when they picked up the scent of a queer! Twinky McDevitt just did another pirouette and told Norman Gorman he was so ugly that when he got his pit-bull terrier nobody would be able to tell which one was the dog and which was Norman Gorman. So Norman Gorman punched Twinky in the face then and Twinky ran off into school crying and telling the teachers that he'd probably be scarred for life now, which meant that his future was in serious jeopardy and he'd have to have plastic surgery right away or his career as a glittering star of the West End stage would be denied him. By the time the teachers had calmed Twinky down and reassured him that it was no more than a bruise and his skin remained unblemished, Mr Kerney had found out about the fracas and immediately called a special assembly. And Mr Kerney spoke to us all about differentness and being different and said that if it hadn't been for the Chinese people we'd still have chip shops where all you could get was fish and chips and pie and chips and perhaps some mushy peas. And he asked all us boys and girls to just think for a minute and consider what it would be like to live in such a world; where the

Failsworth chip shops had no chop suey rolls and no fried rice and no char sui and no such thing as piping hot beansprouts and steaming thick hot runny curry sauce for dipping your chips in and warming up your insides all yummy and lovely on cold and frosty winter nights. Mr Kerney looked down at us all and asked us would we *really* want to live in a world like that? And we all of us shook our heads and said, 'No, sir.'

And then Mr Kerney said something about Twinky McDevitt being different and how lucky we were to have somebody who brought such enthusiasm and glamour to the grey world of the playground. Mr Kerney said he'd like everybody to think about that as we stood in silence for a moment. So we all stood there in silence and tried our very best to think about differentness and about Twinky and his pirouettes. But really we couldn't think about nowt but piping hot chips and beansprouts with soy sauce and char sui foo yung and lovely runny curry sauce and whether we could persuade our mams to let us have our tea from the Garden of Confucius Cantonese Chip Shop tonight even though it wasn't yet Friday.

And then we all sang the song about the family of man and Mr Kerney asked Norman Gorman and Twinky McDevitt if they'd like to come up onto the stage and make their peace with one another. The two of them went up the steps and told each other they were very sorry and then they shook hands. And everybody in the hall applauded. So then Twinky did a big curtsy and everybody laughed, even the teachers and Mr Kerney. And that must have been an irresistible encouragement to Twinky because he started pirouetting around the stage then and doing his latest bit from *The Wizard of Oz*. Everybody was laughing and it was lovely and while Twinky went dancing and singing up the yellow brick road, Mr Kerney told everyone in the hall how he hoped that just like himself, we were all glad in the heart that the little world of our school had been made brighter and warmer by Norman and Twinky settling their quarrel.

And everybody went home feeling nice and happy (apart from Norman Gorman who said that Chinese people were all slant-eyed twats and it was a well-known fact that they wipe their bums with their bare hands) and none of us, not even Mr Kerney, knew that the bright little world of our school was a world which Mr Kerney would shortly have to depart in the wake of the Transvestite Nativity Play Scandal and Twinky McDevitt's notoriety as reported in the pages of the local gutter press.

Twinky had been given the part of one of the Three Kings. But Twinky wasn't too happy about that because he'd had his heart set on playing the part of the Virgin Mary. Miss Thompson told him not to be so stupid and how could he play the Virgin Mary which was a girl's part and that's why Samantha Hardcastle would be playing the Virgin Mary.

Twinky did a pirouette and said he could easily take the part of the Virgin Mary, especially as he was much prettier than Samantha Hardcastle.

Samantha Hardcastle started crying then and Miss Thompson shouted at Twinky and said if he didn't shut up he wouldn't even be playing one of the Three Kings and he'd have to be Sheep Number Twenty-Four instead!

Twinky shrugged philosophically and asked Miss Thompson would he be playing the King who brought the frankincense, the King who brought the myrrh or the King who brought the gold to Baby Jesus.

Miss Thompson, who was still preoccupied with stemming the sobs from Samantha Hardcastle, said, 'For God's sake, Twinky, I don't know.' And plucking the first thing that came into her head, she said, 'The gold. You can be the King who brings gold as a gift.'

Twinky cheered up and said, well, that was all right then, because the King who brought the gold to Baby

Jesus was the special King, the most important one and the other two Kings were just there to make up the numbers.

Twinky got their Cindy to make his costume and design his make-up for him. But he refused to let anybody get even a glimpse of it until the day of the first show.

Samantha Hardcastle didn't stand a chance.

Dressed from head to foot in velvet robes, wearing long false eyelashes, a golden crown and their Cindy's feather boa, Twinky McDevitt swept onto the stage looking like a cross between Shirley Bassey and the Pope. Even the mums and dads who normally only ever watched their own kids in the nativity said that you couldn't keep your eyes off Twinky McDevitt. They were all clicking their cameras – apart from Samantha Hardcastle's mother who was sat there quietly seething at seeing her daughter being totally eclipsed as Twinky McDevitt, flagrantly upstaging everything in sight, paraded around the stage as if it was his own private catwalk.

Not content with the moves that had been rehearsed Twinky started adding some of his own, and after he'd presented his gift of gold to the Baby Jesus, Twinky held out a regal hand to the Virgin Mary who was patently expected to kneel down and kiss it. But pulling a face and sticking out her bottom lip, Samantha Hardcastle sat there on her bale of straw, resolutely refusing to do any such thing.

So Twinky just patted the Virgin Mary on the head and told her the baby was looking a bit peaky and perhaps it wasn't getting enough milk.

That's when Samantha Hardcastle's mam had had enough, more than enough! She got up and stormed out of the hall in a huff, demanding to see the headmaster. She kicked up a big stink. She told Mr Kerney it wasn't right and it wasn't proper and everybody knew, everybody, that the proper nativity was where Baby Jesus got visited by the Three Kings, not by two

63

Kings and an effing little Queen in a pair of cut-down curtains.

Mr Kerney quietly explained that perhaps Mrs Hardcastle had failed to appreciate the progressive nature of the production which, personally, Mr Kerney had found rather bold and refreshing, reflecting as it did the question of gender ambiguity which was such an important issue in contemporary society. But the Virgin Mary's mother just told Mr Kerney to fuck off and said she'd never have sent their Samantha to this school in the first place if she'd known how bleeding crap it was and the kids never did nowt but weird nativity plays and learned more about sodding Chinese chip shops than they did about maths and geography and the Battle of Waterloo. And then she said she'd had enough of it and this nativity business was the last straw and she was taking their Samantha from the school forthwith and enrolling her in a private academy regardless of the financial sacrifices that would have to be made.

And that was how Twinky got to realise his dream and take over in the role of the Virgin Mary.

Some of the teachers were doubtful at first. And when Mr Kerney walked onto the stage the next day and announced that in today's performance the part of the Virgin Mary will be played by Twinky McDevitt there was murmuring and frowning and the raising of eyebrows amongst the mums and dads and the Governors and their guests. Mrs Bradwick got up out of her reserved seat in the front row, intending to go and have a word with the headmaster. But the hall lights were already dimming, the play was about to start and Mrs Bradwick had to sit down again as the spotlights came on. The infants held their silver-foil stars aloft, me and all the rest of us in the lower juniors began to softly croon 'O Little Town of Bethlehem', and there on a donkey sat a Virgin Mary so beautifully serene that there were gasps from the audience, spellbound now, as Twinky McDevitt in nothing more elaborate than a simple frock and knitted shawl exuded a palpable aura of spiritual calm and enigmatic femininity. Even Norman Gorman who was playing the part of Joseph the Carpenter seemed to be captivated by the fragile beauty of his leading lady and when he had to lift her down from the donkey and carry her across to the cattle shed he did it with a grace and an elegance that had never been seen in Norman Gorman before, scooping up Twinky in his big protective arms just like he was Rhett Butler carrying Scarlett O'Hara in *Gone with the Wind*. Twinky McDevitt's Virgin Mary seemed to have that same inspirational effect upon everybody who was in the play, even all the sheep who Miss Thompson said she'd given up on because they were more like a herd of Friesian heifers than innocent little lambs. But with Twinky McDevitt leading the cast, the little lambs were delicate and dainty and when Baby Jesus was born they all bleated and baaed in perfect unison the way that Miss Thompson had always wanted them to. And in Twinky's hands even the Baby Jesus, who was just a wrapped-up plastic doll that Miss Thompson had got from a car boot sale, now seemed to wriggle and stretch and kick its little legs beneath its swaddling clothes. And maybe that's what did it. Perhaps, like everybody in the audience, even Twinky himself had started to believe that instead of just a plastic doll from a car boot sale, there was a real live baby wrapped up in that bundle. Or perhaps it was Twinky just doing what he always did and never knowing when to stop. And if he had stopped there, if the curtain had come down and the hall lights had come on when everybody in that hall was still sat there, captivated, enraptured and in absolute thrall to the most magnificent Virgin Mary that Failsworth had ever seen, if Twinky had stopped there then Mr Kerney would have been a hero and probably got the MBE and still been the headmaster at our school. But Twinky didn't stop. Twinky stood up in the cattle shed and slowly stepped forward towards the front of the stage, all the time gazing lovingly down at Baby Jesus, tenderly cradling the infant and bestowing upon him a smile that seemed to embody the very essence of motherly love. And perhaps Twinky *was* just carried away by the moment. But as he stood there, gazing adoringly at the baby, Twinky slowly started to unfasten the top buttons of his dress. And two hundred jaws dropped into two hundred laps and two hundred pairs of eyes watched in stunned silence as Twinky put the baby's mouth onto his left nipple and said, 'You have a good suck on that, Baby Jesus. And when that one's empty there's another full one on the other side.'

Mr Kerney did his best.

He tried to pass it off as a sincere and dramatically effective attempt to promote the virtues of breastfeeding amongst the young mothers of Failsworth. But Mrs Bradwick said that was precisely the kind of so-called enlightened liberalism and progressive poppycock that had so seriously tarnished the reputation of the school, bringing it perilously close to the precipice of decadence and anarchy.

And interviewed for the pages of the *Failsworth Fanfare* under the headline '*Transvestite Virgin Mary in Nativity Shocker*', Mrs Bradwick sought to reassure all the parents and the community at large by announcing Mr Kerney's immediate departure from the school. She said that on behalf of the Governors she wished Mr Kerney well and hoped that he'd be happy in his new post as proprietor of the One World Vegetarian and Organic Foodstuffs Shop in Glossop.

And when we got back after the Christmas holidays there was a new headmaster in charge of our school. And he stood there, the New Headmaster, waiting at the door and staring at us all as we walked in. And as we went down the corridor he suddenly barked like a big dog and said, 'You! You, lad!'

And I didn't know that he was talking to me, because my name was Raymond and I'd never been called 'You, lad' before. So I carried on walking down the corridor and then he barked even louder and said, 'YOU!'

And that's when Geoffrey Weatherby nudged me and urgently whispered, 'Raymond, he means you.'

And I turned round then and he was pointing at me with a spiky finger, the New Headmaster. 'You!' he said. 'Yes, you! Come here!'

And I had to walk all the way back down the corridor and everyone was looking at me. When I got to where he was stood he just glared at me, the New Headmaster. And he said, 'What's your name, little boy?'

I told him it was Raymond James Marks and he just stood there slowly nodding his head.

Then he suddenly clicked his fingers dead loud and pointed at the comic I was carrying and said, 'What have you got in your hand, Raymond James Marks?'

I said, 'It's just a *Spiderman* comic, sir.'

He clicked his fingers again and said, 'Give!'

And he took hold of my *Spiderman* comic and stared at the front cover as if he was looking at something that made him sick. Then he flicked open the pages and said, 'Do you think this is suitable material to bring into school, Raymond Marks? In fact do you think this is suitable material at all for the eyes of a boy who's no more than, what . . .' He closed the comic and looked at me. '. . . eight years of age?'

I told him that I was nearly nine and he said, 'Oh! Nearly nine. And that makes it all right, does it, nearly-nine-year-old Raymond James Marks? That makes it all right, does it, to be looking at filth like this, bringing pictures such as this into school?'

I didn't know what he was talking about! It was only *Spiderman versus the Vulcan Vixens*. And the Vulcan Vixens did have dead long legs and big pointy bosoms and me and Geoffrey Weatherby used to say that they were dead sexy, weren't they. But we didn't even really know what we were talking about. We were only eight and barely beginning to understand what 'sexy' meant.

Sometimes, when I was in bed reading, I'd stare at the pictures of the Vulcan Vixens and they'd make me feel all nice and funny. And other times I'd look at them and I'd think how stupid they were, the Vulcan Vixens, always running round wearing nothing but knickers and brassieres. They certainly didn't have much chance of defeating Spiderman and taking over planet Earth, dressed like that! They definitely wouldn't be able to survive an Arctic winter!

'Well, Raymond Marks,' the New Headmaster said, 'are you going to explain yourself?'

And I thought then that the New Headmaster was doing what Mr Kerney used to do. Even when he didn't like what we'd been doing, Mr Kerney always used to give us the chance to offer an explanation. And sometimes Mr Kerney even changed his mind and said that we were right and he was wrong and he'd learned something from us.

So I explained to the New Headmaster and I said to him, 'Sir, I don't think that I am too young to be reading it, actually. Because if I was too young to be reading *Spiderman versus the Vulcan Vixens*, my Gran wouldn't have bought it for me.'

He took a step back and looked me up and down from head to toe, the New Headmaster. And then he leaned down very slowly until his face was facing mine and his eyes were all bulging as he said, 'I don't like precocious little boys, Raymond Marks. Is that what you are, a precocious little boy, or just a very rude little boy?'

I didn't even know what precocious meant. And I certainly didn't think that I'd been rude. So I just shrugged and said nothing. And the New Headmaster said, 'Let me tell you something, nearly-nine-year-old Raymond James Marks. There's been far too much precociousness in this school, far too much for far too long. But there's going to be a lot less from now on, a lot less old heads on young shoulders, a lot less nine and ten and eleven-year-olds behaving as though they

68

know better than their teachers, better than their headmaster.'

He held up my copy of *Spiderman versus the Vulcan Vixens* then and he said, 'In my school, Raymond Marks, little boys will behave like little boys. And I don't care a twopenny sausage what your grandmother says about what you can and cannot read. In my school, there will be no room for filth of any sort, Raymond Marks.'

And then he held out *Spiderman and the Vulcan Vixens* and he ripped it right down the middle! Then he told me to get to my classroom. And as I walked away, he said, 'Raymond James Marks! I don't doubt for a single second that Raymond James Marks is a name I will be hearing more of!'

It wasn't nice in our school, after the New Headmaster took over.

We never had special assemblies any more and the New Headmaster never ever talked about things like Chinese chippies or lovely runny curry sauce or the niceness of things being different. Twinky McDevitt got sent to see a psychotherapist and he didn't do his pirouettes or concert parties in the playground any more. And nativity plays were just nativity plays after that. And with the New Headmaster, our school became just a normal, ordinary, everyday sort of school. And gradually everybody forgot about the niceness of things being different.

But Mrs Bradwick was happy and the School Governors were happy. And the New Headmaster was happy. Because the Governors said they'd expected it would take years to put everything right in our school. But after only eighteen months in the job, the New Headmaster had performed miracles.

Such was Mrs Bradwick's delight at the spectacularly successful transformation of our school that she'd started to speculate openly about the possibility of the New Headmaster's efforts being recognised at a national level and rewarded with a summons to the

Palace and a CBE. The New Headmaster was very happy.

And on a beautifully balmy summer's day, Twinky McDevitt long gone now and moved on to the comprehensive and the latest in a long line of psychotherapists, the New Headmaster stood in his office, a sense of profound satisfaction in his stomach as he gazed from his window and surveyed the playground, empty now after dinner, empty and childless and tidy, not a bit of litter in sight, not a ball or a bag left lying where a ball or a bag shouldn't be, not one single syllable of gratuitous graffiti nor illicit patch of discarded hardened chewing gum to taint and mar the flat, grey perfectly pristine playground.

The New Headmaster was extremely happy.

And then! Out of the blue: Albert Goldberg and his swollen protuberance! Summoned by the school doctor, the New Headmaster stood in the changing room, stared, shook his head and wondered aloud as to the cause of Albert's current deformity. And when Albert explained that a wasp flew up the leg of his trousers and stung him in his private parts, the New Headmaster was tempted to leave it at that. The Headmaster was happy, it was a balmy, beautiful summer's day, the playground was immaculate and there were only two weeks left until the end of term. But try as he might, the New Headmaster could not avoid the keen whiff of bullshit that his headmasterly nose had detected in Albert Goldberg's account of the cause of his current condition.

And the New Headmaster did not like it when his intelligence was being insulted, when little children used their little minds to try to deceive a man of his wisdom and experience. So the Headmaster informed Albert Goldberg that he wasn't having any of that! And that being something of an international authority on insect behaviour, especially the common wasp, he quite failed to see how one of those poor maligned little creatures could have wormed its way up the inside of Albert's trouser leg and then managed to prise its way beneath the band of a tight pair of jockey shorts!

Albert, struggling now but valiant, still tried to tough it out, insisting that it was true about the wasp climbing up the inside of his trouser leg and probably what had happened was that the wasp had chewed its way through his jockey shorts!

The New Headmaster nodded and appeared to consider the matter as he bent down and retrieved a pair of discarded training shoes that had been left under one of the benches. 'Or perhaps,' he helpfully told Albert, 'perhaps it was a Scissor Wasp! One of that rare breed of wasps that is born with little sets of scissors on the end of its front legs.'

Albert nodded, saying, 'Yes, sir, you're right, sir. That was definitely it, sir, because I've seen them wasps on David Attenborough, sir, and now that I come to think about it, it was, it was one of them.'

The loud crack which whipped through the air as the Headmaster smacked one of the training shoes hard against the bench made even the school doctor jump with momentary fright.

And that's when the Headmaster, his eyes wide and glaring, told Albert Goldberg that unless the doctor gave him appropriate medication within the next three minutes, Albert Goldberg would have to go to the hospital! Albert Goldberg would probably have to have his swollen manhood amputated! Albert Goldberg would never get to do his bar mitzvah, never get married, never have a family when he grew up!

Looking at his watch, counting down the seconds, the New Headmaster let Albert believe that the crucial medication would most definitely not be forthcoming unless Albert cut out the bullshit and told the truth. The whole truth!

Albert finally crumbled and started to spill the beans.

Terrified that any omission, hidden detail or

glossing of the facts would result in permanent disfigurement, Albert spilt every single bean in the can.

And the New Headmaster, who'd previously been so happy, listened with a mounting sense of horror as Albert Goldberg tearfully narrated his account of the regular goings-on at the canal, of dicks and flies and fifteen boys and dirty doings that defied belief. Albert kept trying to tell the horrified Headmaster that the fly-trapping was just a game, just something like Lego or stamp collecting or Chinese burns. But the Headmaster was no longer paying much attention to Albert Goldberg. The New Headmaster was staring away into the distance, watching his CBE disappear and absently pulling at his left earlobe, which is what he always did when he believed that something bad had happened in our school. And from what he'd just heard, the New Headmaster was all too aware that something far worse than bad had been happening in our school, happening in *his* school, happening, and apparently happening repeatedly, under *his* headship and his very nose. The New Headmaster suddenly shivered as if someone had just walked over his grave. And in his mind's eye he saw a headline in the *Failsworth Fanfare*, a headline which proclaimed 'Second Head Rolls in Latest Failsworth Filth Fury.'

The doctor was asking if he could administer the antihistamine now.

But the New Headmaster couldn't speak. Fifteen of them! Fifteen, the Goldberg boy had said; a network, a chain of filth, an epidemic that had festered and flourished and gone unnoticed for God knows how long in *his* school. The New Headmaster was happy no more. The New Headmaster was frantically trying to assess his own chances of surviving a scandal that centred around mass alfresco masturbation sessions.

Desperately seeking a solution, the New Headmaster snatched at the idea of expulsion. But no sooner had he toyed with the idea than he ruefully conceded that dismissing fifteen pre-pubescent perverts at a single stroke would attract not only the attentions of the *Failsworth Fanfare* but probably the entire national news media as well. The New Headmaster tried to think. But thinking was difficult, especially with the Goldberg boy wailing and crying and constantly repeating that he hadn't been the one who'd started it, that he'd joined in with the flytrapping but he hadn't been the one who'd started it.

The New Headmaster turned, intending to tell Albert Goldberg to shut up. But as he did so, the New Headmaster suddenly realised what it was that Albert was saying. And suddenly he started to feel the first glimmer of hope.

His rational mind beginning to function again, the New Headmaster started to see that things might not be quite as horrifically bad as had first appeared. Fifteen perverts? The idea was ludicrous. That's when the New Headmaster almost laughed out loud at his own silly panicking. That's when the New Headmaster began to feel a surge of relief. There'd be no need for mass expulsion. *Fifteen* pre-pubescent perverts in the same school year! The simple law of averages said that it just wasn't possible. But what *was* possible, what was perfectly possible, was that a group of gullible lads had been led astray.

He hadn't started it! That's what the Goldberg lad had said, he hadn't started it. But somebody must have started it. One, just one, that's all it would have needed, one bad apple, just one warped and depraved and precociously sexual little beast who'd lured and led his impressionable peers into this rancid cesspit of insecticidal sexual torture.

The New Headmaster stopped tugging at his earlobe.

Albert Goldberg looked up, to see the New Headmaster smiling.

'Now, Albert,' he said, 'the doctor's going to give you that medication now. And while he's doing that I want you to think very hard, Albert. And I want you to tell me who it is who has been *forcing* you to do these things down at the canal.'

Albert didn't even cry when the doctor put the needle in his arm; because Albert couldn't believe his luck. Not only was he getting his manhood-saving injection but Albert could tell from the tone of the Headmaster's question that he was being offered the chance to get off the hook, to become the victim rather than the culprit.

'Tell me, Albert,' the New Headmaster purred. 'I know that you could never have dreamed up something like this, could you, Albert? As you rightly say, it wasn't your idea, was it? You didn't start it, did you?'

Albert Goldberg shook his head.

'So, Albert, who did?' the New Headmaster gently asked. 'Who did start it, Albert?'

Albert paused for a second and thought about how I'd saved him from drowning. But then he thought about the deep shit he was in and how he still had to face his mum and his dad and how somehow that shit wouldn't be half so deep if he accepted the victim status that was now on offer.

So Albert Goldberg swallowed and told the New Headmaster what was, after all, the truth, told him, 'Raymond Marks, sir. It was Raymond Marks who started it all.'

The New Headmaster smiled and slowly nodded. 'Raymond Marks,' he said, sighing a sort of satisfied sigh, 'Raymond Marks! I always knew the day would come when I'd hear that name again: Raymond James Marks.'

So you see, Morrissey, that's what started it. That's what started everything. That's how I began my rapid descent from being the new school hero to being the precocious pervert, the evil influence, the filthy little beast who'd forced innocent and reluctant children into sadistic mass masturbation sessions on the banks of the Rochdale Canal.

If the New Headmaster had never come to our school, if we'd never done the flytrapping, then I never would have ended up in the special school. I never would have become fat and done the shoplifting and made up Malcolm and been such a cross for my Mam to bear. All we were doing was playing a game. But nobody ever believed me. And if they had then none of the rest of it would have happened the way it did; not if they'd believed me. And if Paulette hadn't gone missing.

But I can't tell you any more about that at the minute, Morrissey. Because the Station Master has just told me to get all my gear together. He said the police have arrived. He said they're waiting for me at the front of the station. 'Come on,' he said, 'I'm just clocking off and on my way out I'm handing you over to the bobbies.'

They'll have read all the facts on the computer; about the canal and being in Swintonfield. And what happened to little Paulette. But facts aren't the truth, Morrissey. That's why I've told you the truth, or at least as much of it as I could. I know that you'll understand, Morrissey; not like the police. The police never understand. The police said I committed an act of gross indecency, Morrissey, but I never did, I never did at all. But once they read all that stuff on the computer they'll never believe me.

Yours sincerely,
Raymond Marks

Dear Morrissey,

I can hardly believe it! I've been reprieved! As you can
deduce from the above address I didn't get arrested and
incarcerated in Halifax after all. They weren't waiting
for me, the police. Because he never phoned them,
he'd never phoned the police at all. He'd just been pretending, the Station Master, he'd just pretended. He
said he'd just intended frightening me so that I
wouldn't ever do nowt so knob-headed ever again. He
said I looked like the sort of balsa-brained prat who
needed to be taught a lesson.

'Yeah, and you were shit-scared, weren't y',' he said.

I just nodded and said nowt, because I had been
scared.

'So you remember!' he said, pointing his finger at
me. 'Next time y' think about doing something so
fuckin' stupid, just remember how scared you were
sitting in my office, thinkin' you were gonna be taken
away by the bobbies and locked up.'

I said that I would remember and I explained that all
my money had been robbed off me and if that hadn't

happened I never would have tried to bunk onto the train in the first place.

We were stood outside the station and he was rolling up a ciggie from a tin of Golden Virginia. He offered the tin to me but I told him I didn't smoke. As he lit up he nodded at my tee shirt. And he said, 'So, how long have you been into Morrissey then?'

I said, 'A couple of years now.'

He nodded. Then he took a long drag on his roll-up and stared into the distance. He said, 'Yeah, he's not bad, Morrissey.' He laughed then. And he said, 'It's a fucking good job you weren't wearing a tee shirt with the Pet Shop Boys on it or I *would* have had you locked up.'

I said, 'If I'd been wearing a Pet Shop Boys tee shirt, I'd expect to be locked up!'

He took another drag on his ciggie then. He said, 'I don't suppose you're into Frank Zappa, are y'?'

'No,' I said, 'I've heard a bit of his stuff but I wouldn't say I was *into* it.'

The Station Master stared at me with what looked like a mixture of pity and contempt as he slowly shook his head and quietly intoned, 'Forgive them, Zappa. They are mere earthlings, in a world not yet ready for the genius that is yours.'

(From the deliberately limited amount I've heard of him, I've always considered Frank Zappa to be quite execrable really, but on balance I thought it was best to say nowt.)

'God wants Zappa, y' know!' the Station Master announced. I stared at him as he nodded. Then he said, 'D' y' know why? Why God wants Frank?'

I shook my head.

And in a relatively reverential hush, the Station Master said, 'Because God's lonely in heaven, without an intellect to match his own.'

The Station Master stared at me, his eyes all grave and full of solemnity, and I got the impression that he was somewhat cracked actually. But still I didn't say nowt. I just watched as he nodded and stubbed his ciggie out. Then he said, 'Can I ask y' summat?'

I said, 'Yeah.'

He said, 'What were you writing in that book?'

'Nothing,' I said, 'just some . . . some bits and pieces like.'

He nodded. 'Fancy yourself as a writer then do y'?'

'No,' I said, 'I just . . . it's just a book that I put my lyrics in and write letters and that.'

He turned on me all dead hard and mean then and he said, 'You're not a fuckin' writer!'

I started to look around me.

'Hey! Hey!' he said. 'I'm talking to you, Morrissey-man; you look at me when I'm talking to y'.'

So I did what he said and I looked at him. I was beginning to think I'd have been better off if the police *had* been waiting for me.

'You, sitting there in my fucking office,' he said, 'sitting there for hours and writing in that book. Writing,' he said. 'Fucking writing! I'm a writer! I write books, I do!'

His eyes were popping out at me and I could see a big angry vein beating on the side of his forehead. 'I'll write a book tonight!' he said. 'When I get home I'll write a book, I will. I might even write two books tonight.' He had hold of me then by the front of my tee shirt and he was glaring at me. 'A trilogy,' he said, 'three books. I might even write three books tonight. What do you say to that, Morrissey-man? What do you say to that?'

Well, I thought that was preposterously prolific really but I just shrugged. And I said, 'Well . . . Jeffrey Archer's probably shitting himself.'

He looked at me then, the Station Master, as if he was seeing me for the first time. 'Who?' he said. 'Who?' And he let go of my tee shirt then.

I grabbed up my gear quick from the pavement and I said, 'I've erm . . . listen,' I said, 'I've got to get off now. It's been quite nice really talking to y' and that,' I said, 'but I've got to get to Grimsby and it sounds as though you'll be rather busy yourself tonight.'

I started to move away then but he ran after me, grabbed hold of my arm and held me against a lamp-post and stared at me with his wild weird eyes and I thought he was going to hit me or murder me or something. But then he said, 'Here, mate.'

And I looked down and he was holding out a ten-pound note.

'Take it, Mr Morrissey-man,' he said. 'I didn't mean you no harm. Take this.'

I just looked at him all puzzled and shook my head.

'Take it, Morrissey-man,' he said. 'Take it to assist y' on your arduous journey.'

And he stuffed the tenner into the pocket of my jeans. 'Y' can get the coach with that,' he said. 'You'll have to get yourself to Huddersfield first. There's an express coach depot in Gibbet Street.'

And he just nodded at me then before he turned and started walking off towards his bus stop. And even though he'd frightened the shit out of me there was something about the Station Master that made me feel sorry for him. And I called out, 'I'll take it then, the money. And thanks for letting me go,' I said. 'I promise I'll read one of your books when they come out.'

He turned round then. And he called back, his voice all proud and princely, 'You won't be able to, Morrissey-man.' He laughed then, as he called out, 'I write them all up here,' and he tapped a finger to his head. 'All of them books,' he said, 'they're all written up here.'

And he must have seen his bus coming then because he ran across towards the bus stop and I never saw him no more.

I think he was a very sad person actually, the Station Master. They must have been brilliant books, the books inside the Station Master's head. But I knew, and I think the Station Master must have known really, that all those brilliant books of his would only ever exist up there in his head. And as I made my way up the street, looking for a bus that'd take me to the coach depot in Huddersfield, I wondered if that's what it had been like for my Dad. I wondered if my Dad had been a bit like the Station Master.

I don't think my Dad ever had books in his head. My Dad's head had just been full of melodies. That's what my Mam told me. She said it was the long-necked banjo that finished her. And before that it was the button-key chromatic accordion! Whenever she told me about my Dad, my Mam always said it was the long-necked banjo with the rosewood fretboard and the mother-of-pearl inlay that finally finished her off.

Apparently my Dad was always coming home with musical instruments that he could never ever play. And at first, my Mam said, she didn't mind.

'That was the reason I fell in love with him,' she said, 'because he was a man who had so much melody in his heart.'

But for all the melody that apparently hummed within the heart of my father and regardless of how fine the instruments he acquired, no matter how dedicated and determined his efforts, he could never wring a tune out of nowt.

'And it was bleeding us dry,' my Mam said. 'You were just a little baby then, still in your pram; and with me just doin' part time at the Kwiky we'd hardly a pair of pennies to knock together. We'd gas bills and electricity bills, hire-purchase bills and the rent to pay. But it never made any difference. We'd all the debts in the world but they were as nowt to your father. I'm not saying it was his fault. It was like a sickness that he had. Johnny just couldn't help himself. With whatever money we did manage to scrape together, he'd set off with the best of intentions in the world, telling me how he was off to the gas showroom or the electricity board to pay off the bills. And me,' my Mam said, 'I always believed Johnny, always believed your father because your father believed himself. But he'd never get to the showroom or the electricity board. He'd turn up back here with a big bass fiddle or a saxophone or flute. And he'd have that dreamy look in his eye again.'

And that's what started the rows between my Mam and my Dad. My Mam said that at first, after the shouting was over, she always found it in herself to forgive him for spending all the money on a Hammond Organ or a xylophone or a trumpet or a bass trombone.

'What you have to understand, Raymond,' my Mam explained to me, 'is that your Dad's delight was so disarming! Whenever he walked through the door with a freshly purchased instrument the delight that was upon your Dad would take your breath away. And in no time at all he'd have you believing he'd brought home ingots of gold. And because I knew how much melody he had in his heart I kept on making the same mistake, kept on believing that this time he'd brought home an instrument that he'd actually be able to play! And I wouldn't have cared about the money being spent; not if he could have unlocked even just a taste of that melody that was within him.'

But my Dad never could. No matter how passionately he tried, all my Dad's efforts to wring melody and harmony from any instrument whatever just resulted in a stubbornly discordant cacophony of excruciating atonality.

And then my Mam came home from the KwikSave one day and saw him with the Rickenbacker guitar that he'd said was an absolute steal at four hundred and thirty-four pounds; my Mam watched him as he stood there, in the middle of the parlour, the guitar strapped around his shoulders as he pretended to play, as he mimed along to an Eric Clapton record, his fingers skittering up and down the fretboard in a wildly haphazard but passionate frustrated frenzy. And my Mam said there were tears dropping down from my father's eyes. And she told him, 'You've got to give this up, Johnny; it's an obsession, it's an addiction and it's bleeding us dry.'

And my Dad did give up the guitar. But when he took it back to the shop he saw a button-key chromatic accordion. He said he got a fantastic part-exchange deal on it.

And that's when my Mam started seeing the holes in the carpet and the flaking paint on the window frames; and with each new instrument my Dad brought home, the flaky paint got flakier, the holes in the carpet grew and my Mam had to work harder and harder at the KwikSave just to keep us all standing still. And that's when my Mam first started to think; that a man with melody in his heart could also be a millstone around a person's neck.

She didn't want a lot, my Mam said. She didn't want jacuzzis or conservatories, didn't want curtains with electronic rails. She didn't want split-level cookers or showers; she said a bath's quite sufficient for keeping us clean. She said she wasn't asking for a tumble-drier or a big chest freezer stuffed full of pork. She said she wasn't asking for a garden with a fountain, or even a lawn with wide handsome stripes. Luxury, my Mam said, wasn't what she was seeking; 'Luxury's just a lot of what people don't need.'

But, she said, sometimes she would like to look around her and see something that said there was hope for the future, something that said they weren't just standing still; a lawn, my Mam said, nothing too fancy, just a plain square of grass, a small patch of green; where she could sit out if we had a nice summer, where the washing could billow without collecting no dust, where the blackbirds and sparrows could feed upon breadbits and she'd put out the pram on warm afternoons.

And my Dad was a man with the best of intentions and he promised my Mam that he'd get some nice turf. He saved up the money and he phoned up a farmer who said, 'Yes, I've got some fine turf y' can buy.' My Dad said he'd call round the next day and see it. And it wasn't my Dad's fault. He never intended going back on his word and upsetting my Mam. But stood in the farmhouse, talking turf with the farmer, my Dad's eye wandered; and there, on the wall, hung a long-necked, five-string Vega banjo with a pigskin vellum and silver-plated tension bars. The pegs for the tuning were carved from mahogany, the rosewood fretboard delicately inlaid with mother-of-pearl that glimmered and shimmered and dazzled my Dad who promptly forgot about turf being laid.

Elated, excited, bearing the banjo – but minus the turf – my Dad arrived home like the kid-with-the-candy, the cock-a-hoop-cowboy, the cat-with-the-cream. And he said to my Mam, 'Just look at the vellum, just feel that fretboard, it's smoother than silk; and watch, watch how the inlay just lights up and sparkles and dazzles your eyes as it catches the light. And look at the neck, it's . . .' But my Mam interrupted. And quietly said, 'Johnny, you went out to get turf.'

My Dad kissed my Mam and said not to worry. Because he'd finally found the instrument which would change all our fortunes and as soon as he'd cracked it (the tuning, the fingering, the picking and that) people would pay good money just to listen, then he'd get my Mam more than a plain patch of grass; he'd give her a lawn that ran down to a river, with big handsome stripes crisscrossing it all; my Mam would be living in marmalade and clover with all the nice things that she'd always deserved. And my Dad said the sun would shine down upon them and he'd make the long-necked, five-string banjo sing.

My Mam didn't shout, she didn't start yelling (she said she was far too weary for that). She just opened the door. And said, 'Tarar, Johnny! I'll pack up your bags an' send 'em round to y' mam's.'

My Dad stood there frowning, his face all a puzzle. But my Mam's mind was made up, there was no going back. My Mam said her heart was too tired to be broken, as the truth of the matter finally dawned on my Dad; and he started to plead and seek explanations and ask my Mam why, but my Mam shook her head. And said not a word because words would be wasted like words had been wasted so much in the past. And my Dad, mild of manner, mountains of melody still locked in his heart, just started to nod. And all that he said was, 'I'm sorry. I'm sorry. Tell the lad I'm sorry.' Then he picked up the banjo and crept out of the door.

My Mam said she cried for a very long time after she'd thrown my Dad out. But I don't remember any of that because I was just the baby in the pram when all that happened.

Look though, Morrissey, I don't want you thinking that I hold any sort of a grudge against my Dad for disappearing like he did. He wasn't bad, my Dad, or owt like that. He wasn't like Tony Perroni's dad who ran off with the Littlewoods catalogue woman and left Mrs Perroni destitute, having to bring up their Tony and all the other Perroni progeny on no maintenance money; and Mrs Perroni went around telling everybody she was taking Littlewoods to court on account of one of their agents had appropriated her husband. But in the end they sent Tony's mam a dinner service and a microwave oven with their compliments. And Mrs Perroni abandoned her litigious leanings, and said you've never tasted pork till you've tasted it done in a microwave. Everybody was glad that Mrs Perroni seemed to be all right after that. But whenever his name came up, everybody agreed he was a bastard, Mr Perroni, running off with the catalogue woman and leaving his wife with all those kids.

But it was never like that with my Dad because my Dad never walked out on anybody and it had been my Mam's decision. And although they all liked my Dad they could see it had been a trial for my Mam, putting up with all those instruments and never having a decent bit of lawn. But that's about the worst that anybody ever said about my Dad (apart from my Uncle Bastard Jason!). And there were even some as would just shake their heads in sympathy at the mere mention of my Dad's name. Like my Gran always did. And even though she was my Mam's mam and not my Dad's mam, my Gran always used to say, 'Agh, God love him. Poor Johnny. He had all the goodness of sun-ripened oranges about him. But still, I often wondered if he was even of this Earth.'

Which wasn't the same thing at all as saying that my Dad was mentally defective! Which is what my Uncle Bastard Jason always used to infer, making out that my Dad was two tracks short of a full CD and that was the reason that I'd turned out the way I had. But it was nowt to do with my Dad and I don't blame him for anything that happened to me because it wasn't my Dad's fault, none of it. My Mam always said it was better for us and better for my Dad that we'd gone our separate ways. And I never even really missed my Dad or got deprived or neglected or nowt like that because I had my Mam and I had my Gran and before I started school I didn't even realise that I was supposed to have a dad. Then even when I did start school there were loads of other kids like me and like Tony Perroni who didn't have dads and so it never really mattered. Until after the canal.

That was when my Mam first started saying that perhaps it would have been better after all if she hadn't thrown my Dad out. That's when she started to say that maybe all the trouble wouldn't have happened if there'd been a man around when I was growing up. She said that she blamed it all on herself for throwing my Dad out and leaving me without the benefit of a masculine role model. She even said that it might not be too late and that perhaps she should make the effort and go out more to pubs and clubs and places where she might meet a good man and get married again and then at least I'd have a stepfather. I started crying when my Mam said that because I didn't want her to go out to pubs and clubs and bring home a stepfather for me. I didn't want a stepfather.

But I couldn't say nowt because that was the day of the canal, the day I became the fallen hero, the day my Mam's supervisor in KwikSave had appeared at my Mam's check-out terminal and told her that she had to get down to the school immediately. That was the day my Mam was ushered into the Headmaster's office where she found herself facing the New Headmaster and Mrs Bradwick, both of whom sat there and stared solemnly at my Mam until she frowned and nervously asked of them, 'What is it?'

And that's when the Headmaster stood up and cleared his throat and informed my Mam that I was being suspended from school with immediate effect. That was when my Mam, perplexed and un-comprehending, frowned even more deeply as the New Headmaster advised my Mam that in his opinion she should seek professional help. Mrs Bradwick agreed with the Headmaster and said that with the right sort of therapy it might be possible to arrest the problem at an early age and avoid what could be even graver consequences in the future.

And my Mam, increasingly worried but still per-plexed and uncomprehending, asked the Headmaster, 'What is it he's done?'

The New Headmaster lifted a sheet of paper off his desk then and said to my Mam, 'In anticipation of that question, Mrs Marks, I've prepared a brief report which I'd like you to read. When you do, I'm sure you'll appreciate my reluctance to offend either your sensi-bilities or, indeed, my own or Madam Chairman's by putting into spoken word the appalling nature of what's gone on today.'

And the Hideous Headmaster sat behind his desk and watched as my Mam lowered her head and read the brief report in which her own son had exerted his guile and influence over less knowing and largely innocent lads who had stupidly (but, it must be said, naively) allowed themselves to become enmeshed in a web of sexual malpractice including exhibitionism, group masturbation, sado-bestiality and going out of bounds during the school dinner hour.

And my Mam just started shaking her head as she vacantly murmured, 'I don't believe it, I don't believe it, I just don't . . . I can't . . . I don't . . . But . . . it can't be true.'

'I'm sorry, Mrs Marks,' the Headmaster interrupted, 'but I don't deal in falsehoods. There are fourteen boys, Mrs Marks, fourteen of them who one way and another were drawn into this . . . farrago of filth. Fourteen! And each and every one of them testifies that the filth that's been going on at that canal is a filth that originated in the mind of one boy, Raymond James Marks! Your son!'

The Headmaster glared at my Mam. And all my Mam could do was stare at the foot of the Headmaster's desk and slowly, slowly shake her head.

'And it's because', the Headmaster said, 'he did at least admit to his responsibility in being the ringleader that I have prevailed upon Madam Chairman and the other school governors to exercise a degree of leniency in this matter. As you might expect, Mrs Marks, such a grave and grossly offensive business would normally warrant nothing less than expulsion. But, taking into account his admission of guilt and having regard for the problems you already face as a single parent, it has been decided that Raymond shall be suspended rather than expelled.'

My Mam, whose brain had become a ball of cotton wool, just mumbled some sort of a thank you.

'Effectively, however,' the Headmaster explained, 'with only two weeks until the end of term it means that we shall not be seeing Raymond James Marks back here at this school. Let us all hope that the disgraceful and disturbed behaviour he has exhibited in this school will be corrected before he starts at the comprehensive.'

My Mam started to mumble again but the Headmaster got up from behind his desk and told her, 'He's waiting in the deputy head's office, Mrs Marks.

I'd be grateful if you'd collect him now and remove him from the school premises without further delay.'

And my Mam did collect me. She walked into the deputy head's office where I'd been sat crying and waiting for my Mam. And now there she was still in her check-out clothes, stood in the doorway, looking at me like I was something strange and frightening. And I couldn't look back at my Mam.

'Is it true?' she said. 'What I've just been told, is it true?'

And I didn't know what to say because parts of it were true but none of it was true like the Hideous Headmaster had said. The Hideous Headmaster had made it sound wicked and dirty and disgusting. I wanted to explain it all to my Mam and make her understand that it was all right and I hadn't really been any of those things. But the Hideous Headmaster had already taken charge of the truth and he'd tangled it all up in badness and being dirty and disgusting goings-on. And even though I knew what the real truth was, he'd made me feel that I *was* dirty and wicked and disgusting. And I was only eleven and far too young to know how hard it is to rescue the truth when the truth's been tied up and tangled and turned into something that makes you burn with shame. So I didn't say anything. And finally my Mam just looked at the floor and said, 'Come on! I've got to take you away from here.'

And as me and my Mam left the school, the New Headmaster and Mrs Bradwick watched from the office window as my Mam and me walked across the empty playground, neither one of us saying a word. The New Headmaster and Mrs Bradwick glanced at each other as they saw me, my Mam and all their problems disappearing through the school gate.

But on the other side of that gate, my problems and my Mam's problems were only just beginning. Outside the school gate were Mrs Duckworth and Mrs Goldberg and Mrs Cowley and all the mothers of all the innocent children who'd been lured and led and corrupted.

And they shouted, the mothers, and called my Mam names and said that if I came anywhere near their children again they'd fuckin' well swing for me! But it was like my Mam was in some kind of trance because she just stared straight ahead and walked and said nowt.

It was only when we were halfway up the street and we'd left the shouting mothers behind that my Mam finally spoke. She didn't look at me, she still kept staring ahead, and she asked me again, 'Is it true?'

She stopped now and turned and looked at me and said, 'I want you to tell me, Raymond, is it true?'

I'd never told lies to my Mam. And I didn't want to start telling her lies. But I didn't want my Mam to think that I was dirty and disgusting and from the way she looked at me I knew that she was looking at me like I was somebody she didn't know any more.

And I said to my Mam, 'It is true but it isn't true!'

Then my Mam started shouting and she said, 'Don't you dare! Don't you start, with your words. You're not talking to your Grandmother now!' And she pointed at me and she said, 'It's a simple question. Now you just give me a simple answer! Is it true?'

I said, 'I was just playing, that's all.'

But my Mam didn't understand because she shouted again and said, 'I know you were bloody well playing! Playing with yourself in broad bloody daylight, I know that! And that's bad enough, but what's all this about bloody flies?'

'It was only a game!' I said, shouting like my Mam was shouting. 'It was just a game.'

And my Mam closed her eyes then and shook her head. Then she looked at me and she sighed and she said, 'A game? A game!' And now she was looking at me like she was seeing me for the first time. 'You get expelled from school,' she said, 'and you're telling me it was just a game!'

My Mam shook her head again. And then she turned

89

and told me, 'Come on!' and I just stood there watching as my Mam started walking off up the road. And I wanted her to turn round and look at me and tell me it was all right and to get a move on so that we'd be in time for *Blockbusters* and we could sit there on the settee, me and my Mam, eating toast and drinking milky coffee and shouting out the answers at the telly as Unbearable Bob and the Embarrassing *Blockbusters* carried on being unbearable and embarrassing and perfectly predictable and comforting and reassuringly ordinary; and a six-letter word, beginning with N, which means conventional and commonplace. Which is what I wanted to be, as I watched my Mam disappearing up the road. Normal. I wanted to go back to being normal again. I didn't want to be the boy who'd done bad things at the canal. I didn't want to be the boy who'd been turned out of his school. I didn't even want to be the hero no more or even Rosemary Rainford's boyfriend. I just wanted to be normal again, to be the ordinary, normal, commonplace boy I'd always been.

And I walked home dead slowly, just hoping that by the time I got there, somehow, everything would be all right and back to normal. But when I did get in, my Mam was just sat there, at the table, staring out the window. And the air in the house was cold and empty of toasty smells or coffee smells. But I wanted everything to be normal. So I went through to the kitchen and I did the toast and made the milky coffee and tried to do it exactly like my Mam did so that it would be perfectly normal. But when I brought it through, my Mam was still sat there staring at the window. I put her coffee and plate of toast on the table but she didn't even look at it. So I switched on the telly and Bob was there as usual with the *Blockbusters*, all of them doing what they always did, being reassuringly unbearable.

And I said to my Mam, 'Mam, it's *Blockbusters*.'

But my Mam didn't answer me. So I sat there on the settee and tried to be normal by myself. I even shouted out some of the answers, hoping that my Mam would join in. I even got some of the answers deliberately wrong, thinking it might nudge my Mam to come up with the right answer and then she'd start being normal again. But my Mam just sat there. And from start to finish she never shouted out a single answer. So I switched off the telly. And it was Cubs that night. So I carried on being normal and I went up to my bedroom and put my uniform on. And I went downstairs again. And I asked my Mam if I could have my two pound fifty, for subscriptions and summer camp. But my Mam just kept staring out the window. And I asked her again but then there was a knock at our back door and I went to answer it. But as I did, my Gran walked in, all normal like she always was, and just for a minute I forgot all about the canal and I was dead glad to see my Gran.

'Hiya love, how are y'?' she said. 'Are y' just off to your Cubs?'

But my Mam, still staring out the window, said, 'Of course he's not going to the bloody Cubs.'

I looked at my Gran and she pulled a face at me as if to say, what's the matter? And my Grandma said, 'Agh, Shelagh, what's he done? Don't stop him going to the Cubs.'

My Mam turned from the window then and said, 'What's he done? What's he done? Why don't you ask him yourself, Mother?' Then my Mam looked at me and she said, 'Go on! Tell your Gran, tell her what you've been doing. See if she still thinks you should be going to Cubs when she's heard what you've been up to.'

She got up from the table then, my Mam, and she said, 'Go on, Mother, you ask him yourself. He's always been the apple of your eye, hasn't he? Well, he was the apple of my eye once! But that's when I thought he was a nice boy, Mother. But he's not a nice boy any more! Apple of my eye? I can barely bloody bring myself to look at him any more.'

I turned and I looked at my Gran who was staring at me with big puzzled creases in her forehead.

And I felt all my face just crumple up as a big, wailing, terrified sob came up from somewhere deep within me and drowned me in the fear that my Mam would never love me no more. My Mam was shouting at me again and my Gran tried to calm her down but it only made my Mam worse and she screamed at me to get up them bloody stairs and get out of her sight. And I just ran out, screaming as my Mam shouted after me, 'And don't you worry! Even your Gran won't be sticking up for you when I tell her what you've been up to.'

I couldn't bear the thought of my Mam telling my Gran what it was I'd been doing and I lay there on my bed, crying into my pillow, with my hands over my ears so that I wouldn't hear the voices downstairs. And I must have been lying there for ages because when I finally took my hands away from my ears there was no more shouting going on downstairs and all I could hear was voices quietly murmuring. I crept out of my bedroom and sat at the top of the stairs and I knew, as soon as I heard my Gran, that even now she was still sticking up for me.

I heard her quietly telling my Mam, 'Shelagh, come on! So he was being a bit mucky. He's a lad! They're all mucky little beggars.'

'Mucky!' my Mam said. 'He's been expelled, Mother! They don't expel a lad just for being mucky. It was an orgy, that's what the report said, "an orgy of mutual masturbation"! That's not just "mucky". "Mucky" is what a lad might get up to under the sheets on his own. But fifteen of them, Mother, fifteen! All doing it together! That's not "mucky", that's unnatural!'

It went quiet for a minute then and all I heard was my Gran as she sighed. And then my Mam said, 'And there was coercion. I don't know how, but the Headmaster reckoned he had some kind of a hold over the rest of those lads. Every one of them, every single one of them testified that it was our Raymond who led them into it.'

'But what else would y' expect, Shelagh?' my Gran

said. 'It's very convenient for them, isn't it, putting all the blame onto our Raymond. What do y' mean, "some kind of hold over them"? What the hell's he supposed to have done, hypnotised them all, led them off to the canal like the Pied Piper of Hamelin and commanded them all to whip out their equipment an' start—'

But my Gran never got to finish because my Mam suddenly yelled, 'Mother, I don't want to hear it! D' y' understand, I don't want to hear! I know very well what he did. And I know that it was disgusting. You've not even heard the worst of it . . . something about flies . . . dead flies!'

There was a long pause. Then my Gran said, 'Dead flies? What do you mean, dead flies?'

And my Mam sighed a big sigh and said, 'I don't know! And I don't care about the bloody details.'

I heard a sob in my Mam's voice then. And she was crying as she said, 'I just know that he disgusts me!'

That made me start crying again and I thought I'd have to go back into my bedroom so that they wouldn't know I was sat there listening. But then I heard my Gran and her voice was all tender towards my Mam and I knew she must have her arm around her as she said, 'Shelagh, sweetheart, come on. Just listen to yourself. It's your own son you're talking about.'

But my Mam was still crying and said, 'Yes! *My* son. And you should have heard what those mothers were saying about my son as I walked out that sodding school. You think it'll stop there? I won't be able to walk down the street now without hearing the whispers and seeing the finger-pointing.'

'But Shelagh, Shelagh,' my Gran implored, 'when the hell did you start tryin' to live your life according to the values of your neighbours? Sod them, Shelagh. They're just idle-tongued skitter merchants who've suddenly got something to chew on. Neighbours! Don't be taken in by them. For all their cars and their conservatories and their foreign holidays in continental parts there's barely more than a modern light bulb between them and the dark ages.'

My Mam was marginally mollified at that but then there was another knocking at the door and it was apparent that news of what went on at the canal had started to spread faster than a shoe full of dog-shit, because our Cub-master walked in then, wearing his full regalia and looking apprehensive but resolute.

My Mam, all flustered and dabbing at her eyes with a hanky, thought he'd come to see where I was. And she said, 'I'm sorry, Akela, but . . . well we've had a bit of . . . well, it's a bit unfortunate but our Raymond can't come to Cubs tonight. I'm hoping he will be back next week but . . .'

And that's when Akela started to shake his head and said, 'I'm afraid not, Mrs Marks. Not next week. Or the week after. Or even . . .'

Akela said he hoped my Mam would appreciate and understand that it was not particularly pleasant to be the bearer of such news and that in a Scouting career spanning two decades this was the first and only occasion on which he'd had to inform a Tenderfoot that he no longer commanded the respect and the trust of the Pack. And that accordingly Raymond would no longer be welcome at the Cubs.

My Mam started crying again then. But my Gran didn't cry. My Gran just narrowed up her eyes and puckered her lips and said to the Akela, 'You what? You what? You're expelling our Raymond? You're expellin' my grandson, a slip of a lad, just because of a bit of business at the canal?'

And Akela, visibly wincing at the mere mention of the word 'canal', told my Gran, 'Forgive me, madam, but I don't think you've quite grasped the implications here.'

'And you forgive me,' my Gran interrupted, 'but I've been six decades on this Earth. And I am not about to put up with being patronised by a pillock in a pointed hat and a neckscarf!'

'Mother!' my Mam admonished.

And for my Mam's sake, my Gran momentarily reined in her wrath and just glared at Akela as he said, 'As their leader I am charged with responsibility for the moral well-being of my Cub Scouts. And, no matter how regretful, it has nevertheless become painfully apparent that I could no longer guarantee the moral welfare of the Pack if Raymond were to remain within the organisation.'

'Well, that takes the Garibaldi, that does,' my Gran declared. 'That takes the full bloody box!' And all her feathers ruffled now, she told the Cub-master, 'Akela? Akela! You're not worthy of the bloody name. Rudyard Kipling, he must be turning in his grave to think a spineless little gobshite like you could bear the name of the intrepid wolf, Akela!'

My Mam admonished my Gran again but Akela was already headed for the door declaring that he'd no longer tolerate such verbal venom, not to mention mockery of the Scouting regalia. But my Gran was up in arms now and impervious to protests and admonishments, she followed Akela to the door telling him, 'Moral welfare! I'll not heed no lessons in moral welfare from the representative of an organisation whose founder was a five-foot-nothing paedophile with crypto-fascist tendencies!'

That apparently got beneath the skin of the retreating Akela because he turned back then, faced my Gran and told her that the former Chief Scout and Founder of the Movement had led a life of impeccable propriety and that slanderous slurs such as my Gran had just uttered were merely the product of an irresponsible and malevolent media which was bent upon tarnishing the reputation of a great and gifted man.

My Gran just told him to piss off though. And warned him there'd be no more bob-a-jobbing at her house and from now on she'd be giving her money to the glue-sniffers and joyriders and the intravenous drug users, who might be the scum of society but at least they weren't spineless hypocrites in neckscarves.

And then my Gran slammed the door on him and it all went quiet.

And I just sat there, at the top of the stairs where I'd been listening to it all, where I'd learned that they didn't want me in the Cubs no more. And when all my friends went bob-a-jobbing and going to camp and playing their parts in the Gang Show I wouldn't be going with them no more; they'd be bob-a-jobbin' without me now and sleeping in tents without me now and having farting competitions without me now. All of them, they'd all still be riding along on a crest of a wave. And I'd just be stuck there on the shore, watching them from a distance.

I didn't want my Mam to hear me crying and know that I'd been listening on the stairs. So I went through to my bedroom. And I pulled off my Cub shirt. And I just held it in my hand and looked at all the badges, so many that you couldn't see any of the khaki shirt for all the badges that were there: Firefighter, Friend to the Elderly, Cycling Proficiency, Lifesaver . . .

And then I heard a noise and I turned round and my Gran was stood there in the doorway. And when she asked me was I all right I nodded. But I couldn't hold the crying back and my Gran came into my bedroom and sat on my bed and said, 'Come here.'

And she folded me into the big downy pillows of her bosom and kissed me on the hair of my head. And my Gran thought I was crying because of the Cubs but I told her that it was because my Mam said she didn't like me no more.

And my Gran even started crying then and hugged me harder and told me, 'Of course your Mam likes y'. She loves y' like I love y' and we'll always love y', Raymond son.'

And we just sat there then, on the bed, until the sobbing subsided. And my Gran said, 'Now listen. Take no notice of what your Mam said. She's upset at the minute but she didn't mean it. All sorts of things get said, Raymond, all sorts of utterings occur when a person's upset. And your Mam *is* upset. Any mother would be upset, getting called out of work and having to go down to the school and face what she had to face.'

I just nodded, because I knew how awful it had been for my Mam. And that made it all even worse.

'And don't forget,' my Gran said, 'your Mam's had it hard, y' know. Not like her brother; God forgive me but our Jason, he's as thick as a box of Mars bars. But that's been his blessing, y' see. He's just breezed through life, our Jason. And if he ever met a problem it never bothered him because he was so bloody thick he never saw the problem in the first place. But your Mam, she was always a good deal brighter than your Uncle Jason. She feels things, Raymond. She worries, y' Mam does. And she tries to do her best. She's never had it easy. He tried to be good to her, in his own way, your Dad. And he was as mild-mannered a man as you'd ever wish to meet. But for all the mildness of his manners and the goodness in his heart, Johnny would have tested the patience of a Mahatma Gandhi. And your mother tried her best, Raymond; but Mahatma Gandhi she was not and so she had to do what she had to do and bring you up on her own.'

My Gran took hold of my face and held it in her hands then, smiling at me as she said, 'And despite today and the goings-on down at that canal, I reckon your Mam's done a pretty good job so far.'

My Gran kissed me then and told me that she had to be getting off now or she'd be late for the Positive Pensioners' Party Night.

'And we're doin' philosophy this week,' my Gran said. 'Wittgenstein! Oh I'm lookin' forward to it. He was a very great thinker. And do you know what he said, son?'

I shook my head and my Gran pulled me to her. And whispered, ' "Boys with beautiful hair are just as important as philosophers!" '

My Gran nodded, and kissed me and said, 'Now come on, son, you get yourself into bed. Get yourself a good night's sleep and mark my words, everything'll look brighter in the morning.'

And even though it was still light and dead early I did what my Gran said and got into bed and my Gran tucked me in and whispered, 'There's nowt that tidies up like time. Just give it a couple of weeks, a month at the most and it'll all be forgotten. You'll be back in them Cubs and doing your reef knots and your dib-dib-dobs and your gooly-gooly-gan-gan-goos.'

My Gran kissed me goodnight then. And said, 'Don't you worry; it'll all blow over in the end.'

And it even seemed like it was starting to blow over. Because after my Gran left, my Mam came up to my bedroom and asked me if I wanted some milky coffee. I got out of bed, went downstairs with my Mam and sat on the settee while she was boiling the milk. But my Mam kept looking at me from the kitchen and she was still looking at me like she didn't know who I was any more. And I wanted to tell her and make her understand about everything. But I was only eleven and I didn't know how to explain it or what words to use or how I could make my Mam see that the badness wasn't half as bad as the badness she believed it to be. So I just sat there on the settee, not even aware that I'd started crying again. Then, suddenly, my Mam was there, hugging me to her. And we just sat there clinging hold of each other and crying together, with my Mam saying it was all her fault and if she hadn't kicked my dad out and become a single parent she wouldn't have had to be at work all the time and could have kept an eye on me.

In the end my Mam made me look at her and asked me if I could promise her that I'd never ever never do nothing again like I'd done down at the canal. I crossed my heart and told her that I promised. And my Mam managed a bit of a smile and said she'd finish making the milky coffee. And when she said did I want some toast as well with mushroom tasty topper on the top I started to feel that it would be all right now and that me and my Mam could go back to being normal. I sat there on the settee with her, drinking milky coffee, and watching *Blankety Blank*. I hated *Blankety Blank*. But I liked it that night when I sat in my pyjamas at the side of my Mam, drinking milky coffee and eating toast, that night when I heard my Mam start laughing at Les Dawson, that night when I thought my Gran had been right and that time had started to do its job and tidy up all the awful mess.

Only my Gran had got it all wrong. Sometimes time doesn't tidy up at all. Sometimes time just carries on making more of a mess. But my Gran didn't know that and so I don't blame her. Because my Gran didn't know and I didn't know and none of us knew that the mess had only just started.

Yours sincerely,
Raymond Marks

P.S. But listen, Morrissey, I want you to know that I don't regret any of it. Because regrets are no good to anybody, that's what my Gran said. She said the road to self-pity is paved with regrets. And self-pity never did nowt for nobody; that's what my Gran said. 'Self-pity, Raymond,' she said, 'self-pity never peeled a potato.'

And I always remembered that, Morrissey, always refused to walk down the street that is paved with regrets and leads up a cul-de-sac and into a place called self-pity. I know that you'll understand me, Morrissey, because, like me, I know that there was a day in your life when everything fell apart and you suddenly found that you'd got no friends. I know how hard it must have been for you when The Smiths just suddenly broke up like that and you and Johnny Marr weren't friends any more. Although you've said very little about it in the press, I do know that privately it must have been a particularly traumatic time and the cause of much grief. One minute you're part of a group and even though you might not like everybody in that group you've still all shared things together, grown together and developed together. And even if some-times you probably all hated each other and wanted to strangle each other, it doesn't alter the fact that amongst you all there exists a shared history. And I know that that night, when The Smiths suddenly broke up, it meant that a significant part of your own history got broken up as well. I know that all the fans were devastated and heartbroken. But no matter how much they loved The Smiths it could never be the same for them as it must have been for you. Because no matter how much they adored and mourned the passing of The Smiths, it wasn't their personal history that was being rent asunder. I know that I've never been in a group, Morrissey, and so you might think that I'm being presumptuous. But I know what it's like when all your personal history gets blown up and you have to start all over again. And I'm just so glad that you did that, Morrissey; I'm just so glad that you didn't sit there amidst the rubble of your own adversity, enfeebled and shell-shocked and absently picking through the broken bricks and mortar of your rudely blitzed recent history. I'm just so glad that you picked yourself up, walked away and left it all there, behind you. By the time I knew about The Smiths and the break-up, my Gran had already gone. But if she'd still been here I would have told her about it, Morrissey, and all about you and how you picked yourself up and carried on despite the shock of it all and the hurt you must have been feeling and all the snide things that got said and the sniping that started. And I know what my Gran would have said. She would have said, 'Good for him! Good for Morrissey. I've always admired a man with the kind of moral fibre it takes to resist the temptress of self-pity. Because all the self-pity in the world never peeled a bag of spuds. So good for Morrissey. And if you're talk-ing to him, Raymond, you just tell him from me, tell

Morrissey, your Gran said if he ever feels the need for a cup of tea and a talk about Oscar Wilde he'll be welcome at our house any time he likes.'

So I'm just passing that on, Morrissey. Because even though my Gran isn't here any more and so she can't invite you round for tea I know that she would have liked to do that. And I know that you would have liked my Gran. Just like I liked her.

Gibbet Street Coach Station,
Huddersfield,
West Yorks

Dear Morrissey,

So! Here I am, with all the other unfortunate refugees
awaiting deportation and permanent exile to Gulag
Grimsby. And I just hope that my Uncle Bastard Jason's
pleased with his pigging self! I bet he never would
have worked it so that his *own* kids got deported and
exiled to the bleak and arid wastes of northern
Lincolnshire. He said it would be good for me, going to
Grimsby; my hideous, horrible, sewer-minded, green-
eyed slimeball of a two-faced, felonious bastard of an
uncle. But he wouldn't be saying that if it was their
Moronic Mark or their Sickening Sonia who was being
forced to flee from Failsworth and become a slave
labourer in Gulag gobbing Grimsby! That would never
happen though; because he'd never do to his own
appalling progeny what he's done to me. He never
liked me, my Uncle Bastard Jason. Even when I was
little he never liked me because he knew that I
was always my Gran's favourite and my Gran could
never abide their Mark and Sonia. My Gran said Mark
and Sonia were the sort of children who'd make a
paedophile eat his own sweets. She said the pair of

102

them were too frivolous by half and always acted like children. And that's why she never took them out to any of her special places. My Gran said they had no gravity to them and of all her three grandchildren there was only me who had the appropriate temperament and the suitable sombreness of tone for such places as cemeteries and libraries and other such shrines to the dead. I loved it when my Gran used to take me to the library. She used to tell me dead interesting things about people like Thomas Hardy – the master of misery – and George Bernard Shaw and Daphne du Maurier.

But my Gran never took Mark and Sonia to the library or told them dead interesting things about Thomas Hardy. She said she did try it once, taking them to the library in the hope that the pair of them might be suitably moved by the palpable aura that prevailed in the majestic cathedral of words. But Moronic Mark kept saying he was bored and Sickening Sonia said it smelt in the library and it was a pooey horrible smell that made her feel sick and why couldn't they go to the My Little Pony shop instead. But my Gran persevered, telling the appalling pair of them about Robert Louis Stevenson who still managed to write his books even though his lungs were turning into slime and jelly because of the tuberculosis; and Karl Marx who never had no money and lived in a room that was barely a broom cupboard with his wife and all his children and every one of them died, one by one.

But Simpering Sonia said she still felt sick and Moronic Mark said why couldn't they go to the pictures instead! So my Gran tried to tell them all about the Brontë sisters who never got married and they all had spectacularly tragic early deaths because the pipe for the drinking water ran through the churchyard where all the bodies were buried so whenever they had a cup of tea or a glass of home-made gooseberry wine, the unsuspecting Brontë sisters were drinking bits of decomposing bodies. But Sonia and

Mark remained resolutely unimpressed and Sonia wandered off down the aisles of books as my Gran tried to tell Moronic Mark all the dead interesting stuff about Branwell Brontë being a drug addict and a drunkard and Mark might not think it but all sorts of writers were drunkards and drug addicts and all. But before she could get around to other substance abusers such as Robert Burns and Lord Byron my Gran heard the sound of vomiting and looked up to see Sickening Sonia being sick in the non-fiction section. And my Gran had to go rushing down the aisles saying, 'For God's sake, child, look at what you're doing all over *The Origin of Species*!'

My Gran never took Mark and Sonia to none of her special places after that. She only ever took me to those places. And she said to me once, my Gran, she said that I'd been more of a son to her than her own son had ever been. And so that's why he always hated me, my Uncle Bastard Jason; because he knew I was my Gran's favourite.

And that's why he's getting his own back all these years later; that's why he's worked it so that I've got to go to Grimsby.

He said I'd probably have a fantastic time in Grimsby! He said they do the best cod and chips in the world.

I said, 'Oh well that makes all the difference then, doesn't it? There was me thinking I might be somewhat bored and disenchanted, living in a downtrodden trawler town on the furthest frozen edges of the North Sea. But I'd forgotten about the cod and chips, hadn't I? I'd forgotten that if I ever became bored or frustrated or felt exiled, isolated, banished, forgotten and trapped in that tawdry trawler town, I could just get myself some cod and chips!'

I don't know why I wasted my breath. Impervious to such sarcasm, my Uncle Jason looked at me and said, 'That's right. Do y' a world of good, Grimsby cod.'

I just sighed and wished that he'd disappear back to

the living room and leave me alone. I was fed up as it was. It was Friday night. I'd already put off packing for as long as I could because I was still hoping that with the east coast being so notoriously fragile and prone to coastal erosion, Grimsby might have just suddenly slid off into the sea and so I wouldn't have to go. I was still hopeful even after I'd watched the news on the telly. They never mentioned Grimsby but I thought perhaps it might have slid into the sea anyway and they just considered that it wasn't very newsworthy. Then Michael Fish came on with the weather and his map. And there it was, Grimsby, implacable Grimsby, still stuck there beneath a band of low pressure and stubbornly clinging onto the rest of Britain.

I started to pack.

And every time I looked around my bedroom I was reminded of how I only had two more nights and then I'd be leaving Failsworth and I wouldn't be able to be in my bedroom no more. So I was doing my best to savour every last moment I spent in there. And then my bleeding Uncle Jason had arrived and he'd just walked into my bedroom unannounced and uninvited. He hadn't even knocked! And now, here he was, telling me about the life-enhancing qualities in a bit of battered cod!

I just sighed and carried on packing my bag as I said to him, 'I know that it's probably escaped your attention, Uncle Jason, but for almost two years now I've been a vegetarian. And vegetarians don't eat such things as cod even when it's the best cod in the whole wide world.'

I thought that might be an end to it then and he might go back into the front room with my Mam and my Aunty Paula. But he just snorted a derisive snort of disgust and said, 'For Christ's sake! You're bloody nineteen years of age, son! Don't y' think it's time you were growing out of that kind of bloody vegetarian malarkey by now!'

I just stared at him. 'Malarkey?' I said.

'Vegetarianism isn't malarkey. It isn't like Lego or *Play School* or the Rubik's cube, y' know. It's not a fad or an affliction that you grow out of. I doubt that you ever heard of him,' I said, 'but there was a man called George Bernard Shaw and he was a vegetarian all his life and he lived until he was ninety-something!'

He gave me a look then, my Uncle Bastard Jason. And I could tell that I'd got under his skin. But I was glad. He didn't belong in my bedroom and I didn't want him there, especially not him, dishing out his advice and his platitudes and going on about the glories of Grimsby. If Grimsby was so bleeding glorious why didn't he sod off there himself and take my Aunty Paula and his appalling progeny and leave me where I was; happy and doing exactly what I wanted to do, being miserable in Failsworth!

He eventually started moving back towards the bedroom door and I thought I'd finally got rid of him. But he stopped and suddenly turned round, taking a few paces back towards me. And he narrowed up his eyes as he said, 'You think you're such a clever little bastard, don't y'?'

He lifted up his finger and pointed at me then as he said, 'Don't you fuckin' try and tell me about George Bernard Shaw. I don't need you to tell me who George Bernard Shaw was. I had my own mother prattlin' on about stupid bastards like George Bernard fuckin' Shaw from one year's end to the next.'

He took another step towards me then and he said, 'Listen, clever arse! I came in here to try an' give you a bit of advice. George Bernard Shaw might have lived on fuckin' lettuce and lentils and lasted till he was ninety-summat. But George Bernard Shaw wasn't workin' on a fuckin' buildin' site in Grimsby. The only people he ever mixed with were ponces and fairies and fuckin' soft-handed bastards wavin' cigarette holders. Which was probably just as well because I doubt that a bearded bastard fuckin' vegetarian playwright would have cut much mustard with a hod on each shoulder

106

and a half-hundredweight of brick in each one! He would have been laughed off the soddin' site, George fuckin' Bernard Shaw!'

I just shrugged then and said, 'And I can't think of too many bricklayers who could have written *Pygmalion*!'

He just carried on glaring at me. And then he started looking around my bedroom, looking at the walls and all my Morrissey posters.

'Look!' he said. 'Just bloody look!' He nodded towards the wall, indicating that poster of you, Morrissey, where you've got all the flowers sticking out your back pocket.

'Is that how you want to turn out,' he said, 'like that morbid bastard? Look at him! Look at him, fuckin' stood there like a big ponce with a bunch of daffodils up his arse!'

(From which it was perfectly apparent that amongst my Uncle Bastard Jason's many other failings was a gross inability to appreciate the finer points of our native flora.)

'They're not daffodils,' I said, 'they're gladioli actually.'

He rolled his eyes then and he said, 'Does it matter? Does it fuckin' matter at all what kind of flowers they are?'

Of course it mattered! But on balance I thought I might just be wasting my breath, trying to explain the iconography of various flora to someone who thought he could assess the qualities of George Bernard Shaw on the principle of how good he was with a hod full of bricks.

He was looking at me, my Uncle Bastard Jason. He slowly started shaking his head. And then he said, 'All right! Listen! For your own good just try and listen for once. All right, perhaps we've never seen eye to eye, me and you. But I'm your uncle. And what I'm tryin' to make you understand, son, is that you're about to start work, working on a building site. And the lads you'll be working alongside, they're hard, rough and hard. Don't get me wrong; they're good lads too! Bloody smashers once y' get to know them. And if you'd just soddin' well shape yourself and make a bit of effort for once you'd find that they'd treat you like one of their own. This is an opportunity for you, this is. You could have a bloody crackin' time in Grimsby, you could, with all the lads. Grafters they are, good grafters, the Grimsby lads. They work hard. But they play hard an' all. Clubbin' it and pubbin' it every night they are. They have a bloody marvellous time over there. Laugh? They're out havin' a bloody laugh till all hours, them lads. And all it'd take from you is the right sort of attitude and you could be included, you could be part of all that.'

I just looked at him. And wondered if he had even the first glimmer of the fact that he'd just described hell on earth! Clubbin' it and pubbin' it with gnarled-knuckled, laughter-loving lager lads in the celebrated and sophisticated nightspots of Gulag Grimsby (all of it no doubt rounded off with a trip to the late night state-of-the-art chippy and a steaming bag of the best cod and chips in the world).

'But I'm telling you now, son,' he was saying, 'start going on about bloody vegetarian twaddle and boring everybody to fuckin' death talkin' all kinds of soft shite like my mother taught y' and playing that morbid bastard Morrison music and you'll never get to be part of nowt! Get it into your head, lad; they don't want that sort of thing in Grimsby!'

That's when I'd had enough. That's when I folded my arms and told him, 'Well, in that case I don't think I'll *fuckin'* bother going to *fuckin' fuckin'* Grimsby after *fuckin'* all!'

He looked at me for a second as if he was taken aback. But then there was a sliver of a smile appeared on his lips and a triumphant glint in his eyes.

'Oh, you're going all right,' he said. 'You're going to Grimsby, no matter what. I've made sure of that!'

The smile spread wider across his lips then and he said, 'Your Mam's sat there now, in the front room, talkin' to your Aunty Paula. An' she was just sayin', your Mam just saying that she's happier now than she's been in years.' He paused for a second and stood there looking at me. 'And why's that?' he said. 'Why's your Mam so happy?' He nodded. 'That's right,' he said, 'because at long, long last she thinks that you have started gettin' yourself sorted out. That's why our Shelagh's happy, because her daft son is doing something fuckin' normal for once, starting a job.'

He looked at me with that horrible smile hanging on his lips.

'So what y' gonna do?' he said. 'Go in there now and tell y' Mam that you're not going to Grimsby after all?'

He stared at me for a second and then he slowly shook his head. 'No! I didn't think so!'

The bastard! He was right, the bastard. He knew that I wouldn't disappoint my Mam like that.

'That's right, son,' he said. 'We don't want to upset your Mam, do we? You've already caused her enough upset, you have, enough to last a fuckin' lifetime. And that's why you're going to Grimsby, lad, for y' mother's sake. Y' think I did this for you? You think I called in a favour and got you fixed up with a job just to make you happy? No way, lad! You? You're a fuckin' waste of space, you, and y' always have been. But I'm not doin' this for you, I'm doin' it for y' Mam. Because I love that little sister of mine.'

I just closed my eyes. I couldn't bear it! I couldn't bear him and his cant, contaminating the room and creeping all over my skin and making me cringe.

'She's had her heart broken enough as it is,' he said. 'And left to your own devices I haven't got the slightest doubt that you'd carry on breaking her heart for ever!'

And that's when I hated him the most of all, when he pretended. When he pretended that he cared for my Mam. And he didn't and he never had and he never would and all he'd ever done was rob and cheat and thieve. And that's when I started to shake and clench my teeth and turn my hands into balls of fists as I shook with rage at his cant and putrid pretence and the sentimental slime that oozed from the bastard pores of him and I started quietly chanting, 'Thief thief thief, felon, cheat, swindler, thief thief thief, crook, robber, thief, thief thief thief.'

He started moving to the door but I kept on chanting and didn't stop, not till he'd got to the door itself and then I just stood there, still clenched and shaking and glaring out all the hatred I had for him. And I knew from the way he looked that he was frightened of me now. But he pretended that he wasn't and he just nodded his head at me and said, 'You want to get a grip on y'self, you do. Or I don't know about going to Grimsby; you might end up back in Swintonfield!'

'Thief!' I said. 'Thief, thief!'

And then he was gone. He was gone, he was gone! I rushed over to my window and opened it as wide as I could and stood there breathing in the air, letting it all into my room and letting out the sickening atmosphere of my rancid, repulsive Uncle Bastard Jason.

And that's when I heard my Mam calling me, telling me to come into the front room and say tarar because my Uncle and my Aunty were going now. I walked in there and my Uncle Bastard Jason was wearing his other face now, all smiling and chummy and unbearably uncle-ish. I just stood there in the doorway and watched the appalling pair of them as they said tarar to my Mam. And I thought to myself, it might be grim in Grimsby but at least I wouldn't have to suffer my Uncle Bastard Jason and my Appalling Aunty Paula no more.

But then he turned and looked at me as he was going out the door, that double-faced bastard uncle of mine. And he said, 'Hey, Raymond! Next week! I've got some dealings over there in Grimsby. I'll be at the site myself on Wednesday.'

My Aunty Paula clapped her hands together and said wasn't that nice and perhaps if I was feeling a bit homesick it'd cheer me up, seeing my favourite uncle.

'I'll call in at the site,' he said. 'See how y' gettin' on. You can even take me out for a pint and a codfish supper if you like.'

I just stared and said nowt and listened as my Mam said wasn't that lovely and it was the least I could do, buy my Uncle a pint and a codfish supper when he'd put himself out so much and gone to all that trouble to get me fixed up with a job.

'No trouble at all, Shelagh!' he said, beaming a big smile at my Mam.

'No, it's no trouble,' my Aunty Paula concurred, 'sorting out a little thing like that. It's nowt, not when you've got the kind of connections that Jason's got.'

They beamed at each other then, my patronising Aunty and my giblet-faced Uncle. And they might have stood there beaming at each other all night but my appalling Aunty suddenly remembered and said they'd better hurry up because it was time for their budgerigar to have its anti-depressants.

I just stood and watched as my Mam saw them out. And then my Mam came back into the front room, smiled a lovely warm smile at me and said, 'I'm so happy for y', son. So happy.'

And that's why I'm here, Morrissey, awaiting a coach that's bound for the cowing cod capital of the world; here because it's made my Mam happy, me doing this. But listen, Morrissey, what my Bastard Uncle said, about me breaking my Mam's heart, it's not true, that. I never broke my Mam's heart at all. I know that I caused her all sorts of upset but my Mam says herself now, she says it wasn't my fault. Sometimes things just happen and no matter how much you try and change things and make them better it just doesn't work. Like when I lost all my friends. I did my best to get them back. But my best just wasn't good enough.

It was the summer of the canal; the long summer holidays. And the weather was particularly balmy that summer when I was still only eleven and should have been out playing with all the others, swimming and footballing, hide-and-seeking, camping on the recreation ground and pretending to be all the Superheroes. But that was the summer holidays when I stayed at home every day instead and just read all my books and my comics and ate a lot and got depressed. I didn't want to be staying in or staying at my Gran's and eating sweets and pot noodles and pizzas and pies and all sorts. But all the mothers on our estate had told their kids that they couldn't play with me no more.

Even Geoffrey Weatherby wasn't allowed to play with me. And his mum and dad were very low-tech, high-fibre, recycled, stripped-pine sort of people who cared about global warming and Nelson Mandela. Geoffrey Weatherby's mam had even been on *Richard and Judy* as the spokesperson for all the newts and the toads and the frogs who couldn't safely cross Failsworth Boulevard since it had been turned into an urban expressway. And Mrs Weatherby said it was absolutely imperative that the newts and the frogs and the toads should be able to cross the road in safety so they could hatch their eggs and have their babies on the far side of the boulevard which was their traditional spawning ground. Mrs Weatherby told Richard and Judy it was a scandalous hypocrisy, the way the human beings had looked after their own safety and well-being by borrowing from the animal kingdom so that they could come up with things like *Cats*eyes to help them see the road at night, *panda* cars to help keep them safe and protected from burglars, *pelican* lights to help them cross the road and *zebra* crossings to do the same. But what about the poor animals themselves, Mrs Weatherby demanded. What about the pelicans, the zebras and the pandas and the cats? Where was there for those poor creatures to safely cross the road so they could have their babies in peace?

Richard and Judy looked at each other. And Richard

tried to inject a misjudged moment of levity by declaring that in his experience you didn't get many pandas or zebras or pelicans in the vicinity of Failsworth Boulevard.

But when it came to flattened frogs Mrs Weatherby was immune to humour. Ignoring Richard and Judy's chuckles, she said that everybody who drove a car, including Richard and Judy themselves, was a guilty party in the Failsworth frog genocide. Mrs Weatherby told them that they all had frog blood on their hands. Judy looked a bit disgusted at that and you could tell that Richard and her were getting a bit fed up with Mrs Weatherby because they tried to introduce the next item about the growing trend for cosmetic surgery amongst garage mechanics. But Mrs Weatherby interrupted and stuck her head in front of Judy's camera and began appealing directly to the conscience of the nation before studio security moved in and forcibly removed her from the set, where Richard and Judy looked visibly shaken but nevertheless agreed that Mrs Weatherby was obviously a deeply caring and highly committed person.

And she *was* caring, Mrs Weatherby. That's why my Mam said she found it so hard to understand why even Geoffrey Weatherby behaved like all the others and wouldn't come round to ours any more.

Geoffrey Weatherby had been my best friend since we were in the infants. We always did everything together, like we collected *Marvel* and *DC* comics together. And when we were eight, we'd got some invisible ink from the Comic Exchange and we'd made a secret document saying that no matter what happened and even when we grew up and perhaps even got married we'd still always be each other's best friend. We sealed the secret document in clingfilm then wrapped it up in a plastic sandwich-bag so it was waterproof. Then we buried it in a secret place by the foot of the railway bridge and swore that if we ever dug it up again we could only dig it up together. I think we

113

loved each other really, me and Geoffrey Weatherby. But after the 'incident' at the canal Geoffrey Weatherby wouldn't come near me. And in the end my Mam went round to see Mrs Weatherby to try and effect a reconciliation. Because, like my Mam said, Mrs Weatherby was a very humane and compassionate person and perhaps if she had a word with her son, then me and him could become friends again. But Mrs Weatherby just shook her head at my Mam. And said that when she'd first heard about the goings-on at the canal she'd treated the whole thing as a rather innocent and welcome return to the Bacchanalian tradition of fertility rites and phallus worship. But, she told my Mam, *then* . . . then she'd found out that it was not innocent at all. Tears welling up in her eyes now, Mrs Weatherby said it had been the *slaughter* of the innocent!

'The slaughter of innocent flies!' she said. 'Flies! Yes, flies! Don't flies have rights?'

My Mam just stood there looking at Mrs Weatherby, whose face was all contorted now in grief for the plight of the common fly.

'Don't flies deserve respect?' Mrs Weatherby demanded. 'Or were those poor, persecuted creatures put on this earth just so that the likes of your son could amuse himself at their expense, infecting others with his brutish disregard for their suffering and torment?'

My Mam sighed and she said, 'Mrs Weatherby, I've been upset about it myself! I wish it had never happened, none of it. But I've tried my best to be rational. And, after all, what we're talking about is just . . . common flies!'

But my Mam had said completely the wrong thing and Mrs Weatherby went loopy then and shrieked at my Mam, telling her that was exactly the sort of attitude that had led to the near extinction of the giant panda and the humpety-backed whale and no wonder her son behaved like he did when he'd been brought up knowing no respect for the sanctity of those with whom he had to share the finite resources of this threatened earth!

When my Mam got back to our house it was obvious that she hadn't been able to do any good. She just stood there shaking her head and said, 'I think that woman's ill!'

And I was sorry if Mrs Weatherby was ill. But I still wanted to be friends with Geoffrey. So I waited for him one night where I knew he had to go past on his paper round. And as soon as I spotted his bike coming round the corner I started walking along the other side of the street as if I just happened to be there. Then I pretended I'd suddenly seen him and I shouted out, 'Hiya Geoffrey!'

But he just looked embarrassed and busied himself with his magazines and newspapers, pulling out a *Failsworth Fanfare* and putting it through the letter box of number forty-seven. And all the time he wouldn't look at me. He was coming back down the path of forty-seven and I shouted, 'Geoffrey! You'll never guess what, Geoffrey: I went to ComicSwap and I found a first issue copy of *Plastic Man and the Purple Planet*. And my Mam says you can come to ours for tea tomorrow if y' want. And then we can look at it together, *Plastic Man and the Purple Planet*.'

Me and Geoffrey Weatherby, we both used to have dreams about finding a copy of *Plastic Man and the Purple Planet*. And we'd always said that if one of us ever did find a copy then we'd share it and own it between us. That's why I knew that Geoffrey Weatherby wouldn't be able to resist and he'd have to start talking to me again and being my friend. And I didn't care that it was like trying to buy his friendship. I didn't care that I hadn't even got a copy of *Plastic Man and the Purple Planet*. I just knew that if I could get Geoffrey Weatherby to come round to ours then we'd soon be friends again.

Only it never worked! Even *Plastic Man and the Purple Planet* didn't seem to be enough to make

Geoffrey Weatherby want to be my friend again. Because he just climbed onto his bike and never said a word. So I just stood there and watched as he pedalled past, his head down over his handlebars. And it was only when he got to the end of the road that he stopped and turned around. And I thought then that he was going to come back. Only he never. He just shouted something at me. I probably heard it wrong because he was so far away by then. It sounded something like 'Fatso!' but I knew it couldn't have been that because I wasn't fat. I'd never been fat!

So I walked off. And I thought that perhaps it'd been a bit stupid picking a comic like *Plastic Man and the Purple Planet* because everybody knew it was so rare and precious that you'd never ever find a copy of *Plastic Man and the Purple Planet* even if you lived in New York City. And Geoffrey Weatherby would certainly have known that, so that's why he'd just pedalled off. But it'd be all right because I could wait for him tomorrow night and I could just laugh and tell him it was only a joke, about *Plastic Man and the Purple Planet.* I just knew that it'd be all right. And I still thought that it'd be all right as I walked past the railway bridge. But then I saw it out the corner of my eye, the fresh soil dug up at the foot of the embankment. And I didn't want to look any further but I couldn't help myself. And I stood there, staring down at the dark, disturbed soil and the torn-up paper pieces of the secret, sacred document.

I didn't cry. Not then. I just walked home with this strange feeling that I'd never had before, this feeling that all the insides of me had been emptied out. I didn't even want to cry, not then. I didn't want to cry or talk or do nowt. I just wanted to disappear. But when I got to our house I couldn't disappear. Because when I got to our house, my Mam was in the kitchen making tea for my Uncle Jason and my Aunty Paula who'd just turned up with their appalling progeny. And I could tell that my Mam was cheesed off that they'd come round. My Mam had been cheesed off for weeks about my Uncle Jason because she knew that he'd borrowed money off my Gran. And he'd said the money was so that their pedigree Labrador could have a life-saving operation on its gall bladder; which would have been all right, my Mam said, even though you could tell just from looking at it that the dog was merely a mongrel with nothing more than Labrador pretensions. But still, my Mam said, pedigree or mongrel, a dog was still a dog and regardless of its ancestry she wouldn't like to see it denied a new gall bladder.

But then my Uncle Jason and my Aunty Paula and their kids had just disappeared. And my Mam had found out that they'd all gone on holiday to the Canary Islands. And now they were all back again, stood in our front room, all of them with suntans and, in the case of my Uncle Jason, a nose that was starting to peel and flake. My Mam told me to go through and talk to them while she made the tea.

When I walked into the front room they were all laughing at something. But then they saw me and the laughing stopped and they all stood there, my skin-fried Uncle with his barbecued brats and my chargrilled Aunty, the hideous quartet, all of them stood there looking at me like they were looking at something in the zoo.

I just ignored them. I went and switched on the telly and started watching the Open University programme about the intelligent traffic-light system in Pontin Le Frith.

I heard them whispering behind me. And then Moronic Mark whispering to his dad, asking him, 'Dad, why has our Raymond gone fat?'

My Aunty Paula laughed her appalling laugh and said, 'Mark! Don't be so rude.'

Then my Sickening cousin Sonia clutched hold of her mother's skirt and smiled a sly delighted smile as she whispered, 'Our Mark's right, Mummy. Look at Raymond.'

So they did. They all stood there looking at me as I just sat there looking at the telly and wishing they'd all go home.

But my Mam called through from the kitchen then and said, 'So Jason, how's that dog of yours doing with its new gall bladder?'

But if my Mam was hoping to shame my Uncle Bastard Jason she was wasting her breath because he just shook his head somewhat ruefully and pretended he was suddenly too choked to even talk. And it was left to my Aunty Paula who called out, 'Didn't you know, Shelagh? I thought you would have heard.' And then adopting a suitably sombre tone my Appalling Aunty Paula said, 'We lost him, love. We lost our beloved Benny.'

'Lost him?' my Mam called through, sounding all surprised. 'But I thought you were having him surgically seen to by a top veterinary surgeon.'

'That's right, we were,' my Aunty Paula explained, 'but you see, Shelagh, our Benny, he had such a rare pedigree that it was always going to be difficult, y' see. The vet said, if he hadn't been a dog of such exceptionally high breeding then he could have tolerated any number of gall bladders. But he was blue-blooded, y' see, our Benny. The vet said he had aristocratic organs, Shelagh. And that's why they couldn't find a suitable gall bladder. In the end we just had to have him painlessly put down.'

Simpering Sonia cuddled closer to her mother then and said, 'He's in Doggy Heaven now, isn't he, Mummy, our Benny.'

My Appalling Aunty nodded and adopting a suitably sombre tone, told her diabolical daughter, 'That's right, love. That's right. Benny's barking with the angels now.'

My Mam appeared from the kitchen then, carrying the tea. She stood in the doorway for a second and glared at the cruelly bereaved quartet.

'And so, with the money,' my Mam said, 'the money

that was supposed to be for a gall-bladder transplant, the money you borrowed off my mother, you just upped and buggered off to the Grand Canary Islands instead.'

My Mam just stood there, staring accusingly at my Aunty Paula and my swindling Uncle Jason who was looking narked and uncomfortable.

'What d' y' mean,' he said, 'just upped and buggered off? We never upped and buggered off at all.'

'Shelagh!' my Aunty Paula chipped in. 'It was a very distressing time after we lost our Benny, a very distressing time indeed. After what we went through with that poor dog, I don't think there's anybody, at least anybody who understands compassion, would begrudge us a few recuperative days in the sun, Shelagh.'

My Mam nodded, her eyes all wide and angry. 'That's right, Paula!' she said. 'Nobody would begrudge y' a *few days* away. But my understanding is you spent three weeks in the Canary Isles!'

My Aunty Paula looked peeved then and my Bastard Uncle Jason started shrugging and looking all huffy and picking at his peeling nose. My Mam had them trapped and wriggling though and she probably would have told them what she thought of them. But Mark the Moron, oblivious to the arctic atmosphere, started laughing and suddenly piped up, 'And guess what, Aunty Shelagh?'

Giggling and unable to contain the hilarity he was about to inflict upon us all, Moronic Mark said, 'Three weeks in the Canary Islands and all the time we was there we never saw one single canary! Ha ha ha. Ha ha ha. D' y' get it, Aunty Shelagh, d' y' get it?'

He tried to keep on laughing but then he saw that everybody was just staring at him. And it started to dawn upon Moronic Mark that the 'joke' which had been such a winner in fun-filled, sun-filled Tenerife had just fallen fatally flat in Failsworth.

'Hey! Enough!' his father commanded and Moronic Mark just started to scowl while his septic sister allowed herself a sly smile of sadistic delight at her sibling's slapping down. And then pouting and thrusting out her head from behind her mother's skirts she triumphantly told her brother, 'See! I said it wasn't funny.'

'Just leave our Mark alone,' my Aunty Paula appealed. 'He's only telling his little jokes.'

'Jokes!' my Uncle Jason exclaimed. And that gave him exactly the cue he needed because he turned and looked directly at me then. And he said, 'From what I've been hearing there's been enough bloody jokes while we've been away!'

My Mam put the teacups down on the table and said, 'What's that supposed to mean?'

My Uncle Bastard Jason just snorted a sort of laugh and he said, 'Hey, Shelagh, don't try and pretend with me. I've heard!' And pointing at me then he said, 'I bloody know! I know what's been going on!'

'Jason!' my Aunty Paula hissed. And with a tight little shake of her head she silently enunciated, 'Not in front of the children!'

My Mam sighed then and shook her head as she stirred the tea.

And Simpering Sonia announced, 'He's been expelled from school, hasn't he, Mummy?'

That's when my Mam told me to switch off the television and take Mark and Sonia up to my bedroom and let them play with my *Star Wars* figures. And before I could even start to protest, Moronic Mark and Simpering Sonia were halfway to the door and headed for the stairs. But then my Aunty Paula suddenly realised that the precious fruit of her womb was about to be left alone in an upstairs bedroom with an infamous corrupter of the innocent. My Aunty Paula managed to intercept her precious progeny and slammed shut the door, telling them, 'No no no! Not the bedroom! You're not playing in the bedroom. I don't want you playing inside when the weather's so nice. Go on, play out the back where I can keep an eye on y'.'

My Mam was staring at her but my Aunty Paula beamed a big false smile and said, 'They'll be better playing out the back, Shelagh. It's much healthier for them. I think it's rubbish, all this ozone layer!'

My Mam shrugged and looked baffled. But she handed out the tea and said, 'Go on then, Raymond. Bring your *Star Wars* stuff down here and you can all play together out the back.'

I just looked a horrified look at my Mam. She knew that I preferred not to be in the same universe as my cretinous cousins, let alone in the same backyard. But my Mam gave me one of those looks that said, don't argue!

So I did what I was told and went upstairs to my bedroom. I was fed up. I was fed up at my Mam because she'd had my Bastard Uncle Jason and my Acrid Aunty Paula on the ropes. But then she'd let them get away. And now I had to go and play *Star Wars* with the sickening twosome.

I pulled the box out from under my bed where I kept all my *Star Wars* figures. I grabbed some of the Stormtroopers and the Ewoks and the Wookies and picked up Han Solo and Obi-Wan Kenobi and Luke Skywalker. And I was just reaching out to pick up Princess Leia when I stopped and I changed my mind and left her lying there in the box. And I had a perfectly good reason for doing that; because it was a dead certainty that if I took Princess Leia back downstairs with me, Simpering Sonia would just get hold of her and try and treat her like a doll, carrying her around and stroking her hair, looking all dopey at her and singing stupid songs to try to get her to sleep. But Princess Leia didn't need to go to sleep because Princess Leia wasn't a dopey doll! Princess Leia was a Rebel Freedom Fighter in the war against the evil imperial forces! So nobody could have blamed me for not taking Princess Leia downstairs with me. I had very good reasons. But I knew. Even as I left Princess

Leia lying there in the box I knew that the real reason I was doing it was just to spite my cousin. And I knew that just because I felt horrible it didn't mean that I had to behave horrible and snidey. I could easily have taken Princess Leia with me and put up with her being pampered and smothered in saccharine by Sickening Sonia. But I didn't want to! And I didn't even care that I was being mean and horrible. I didn't care! And there was even a bit of me, a horrible nasty little bit of me, that felt delicious and glad! Because I was being so horrible and bad!

So I just left Princess Leia lying there in the box under the bed and I went downstairs. But halfway down the stairs I heard the voices of my Mam and my Aunty and my Uncle Jason. So I walked very, very slowly and listened as my Uncle Bastard Jason blew out a big sigh and said, 'I don't know! I just don't bloody know at all.'

Then I heard my Mam telling him, 'I've told y', Jason, it's done with, it's dealt with, it's all over now and he's promised me that he'll never ever do nowt like that again; so let's just bloody forget it, shall we? I mean if you really want to talk about funny goings-on, why don't we talk about your holidays in the Grand Canaries? Mm?'

But my brass-necked Uncle Jason just ignored the bait and he said, 'Holidays! I don't bloody know that I can even think about my holidays now. Sitting there in the sun thinking I'm having a well-deserved rest, while back here the family name's being bloody dragged into the mud. I get back home to learn that there's a piggin' pervert in the family, a pervert! And he's barely out of short trousers!'

Everything went quiet for a second. But then my Mam's voice was all low and full of warning as she said, 'Pervert? Don't you dare! Don't you even *dare* use a word like that about my son!'

It all went quiet again then until my Aunty Paula piped up and laughed a frivolous laugh as she said,

'Now come on, Shelagh, I'm sure he didn't intend any offence, did you, Jason?'

But my Bastard Uncle Jason said nowt and my Mam said, 'So just what *did* he intend?'

That made my Uncle Jason back off a bit then and he told my Mam, 'Now look, Shelagh. I know that you've never had it easy. And you've enough of a burden to bear as it is. But I'm your brother, Shelagh. And I bloody care about you, I do! And that's why I'm tellin' y', for your own good, Shelagh. You've got to face up to facts! You can't just push something like this under the carpet. I mean, we're not talking about a few lads getting up to normal mischief like robbing a few apples or doing a bit of bloody shoplifting or something like that. This is serious, this is, Shelagh. There's implications for the future in all this!'

And I knew then that my Mam had started to have all the stuffing knocked out of her because her voice was all worried as she said, 'Implications? What do y' mean?'

'Shelagh!' my Uncle Jason said. And he was talking like he was all concerned now. He wasn't shouting like he always did. And he said, 'Surely to God, Shelagh, you're not trying to tell me that it's just normal behaviour we're talking about. Flies? Doing *that* to flies! What sort of a mind, Shelagh, what sort of a mind is it that can dream up something like that?'

And I knew that my Mam didn't have any kind of answer for him then because it all went really quiet. And my Mam must have just started crying because I heard my Aunty Patronising Paula saying, 'Agh, Shelagh! Come on, love. I know you're upset and who can blame y'? My God, you've already had enough to put up with, haven't y', 'ey? What with your Johnny? And now this! Now his son turns out like this. There, there! Go on, love, you have a good cry.'

And I hated my Aunty Pigging Paula then. I hated her and my Uncle Bastard Jason for pretending that they were saying nice and kind things to my Mam when they weren't at all. When all they were really doing was making it worse for my Mam, and the bastard pair of them enjoying it. But I was even more angry at my Mam because she'd let them win and she'd given in. And my Mam was always giving in to my Bastard Uncle Jason and my Aunty Pigging Paula and she didn't need to because my Mam was much cleverer than the pair of them put together and my Mam never ever ripped nobody off and never went borrowing money and not giving it back. But now my Mam was crying. And instead of shouting at my Uncle Bastard Jason and my Aunty Pigging Paula for cheating my Gran out of her money and spending it in the Grand Canary Islands, my Mam was just getting all upset about me again. So I kicked the door open then and I kicked it so hard that it banged back against the wall and my Mam said, 'Raymond! For God's sake!'

But I didn't even look at my Mam. I didn't look at anybody. I just walked through the living room, went outside and sat down on the tarmac, playing with my *Star Wars* figures and wishing there was a real Luke Skywalker and that he could come to Failsworth with his light sabre and rid the world of all my rancid relatives.

Moronic Mark and his sister were down at the end of the garden and they didn't see me at first. But then I heard a shout and the two of them came running up to me, the pair of them pronouncing about which of the *Star Wars* figures they intended to play with. And Sonia was doing that stupid chanting that she always did, saying, 'I'm playing with Princess Leia. I love Princess Leia. I'm playing with Princess Leia.'

But then she got to where I was sat with all the figures spread out on the tarmac and she stopped her chanting and summoned up a surly scowl as she saw that there was no Princess Leia. Moronic Mark said could he please play with Obi-Wan Kenobi and some of the Wookies and I let him because at least he had said 'please'. But Simpering Sonia just stood there scowling and then she stamped her foot and said, 'And I want to play with Princess Leia!'

I said, 'You can't!'

She said, 'Why?' and she thrust her head forward and glared at me.

And it wasn't even Sonia's fault really. She couldn't help being seven and stupid. And I don't suppose she could help it that she had my Appalling Aunty Paula and my Bastard Uncle Jason for a mum and dad. But it wasn't my fault neither; it wasn't my fault that I'd got all the blame for what had happened at the canal. It wasn't my fault that I didn't have no friends any more and that my best friend had betrayed me and dug up and ripped up the secret document. It wasn't my fault that I'd been suspended from school and expelled from the Cubs. And when Simpering Sonia stamped her foot again and said, 'Why? Why can't I play with Princess Leia?' I said, 'Because Princess Leia's dead!'

Sickening Sonia just looked at me. Even Moronic Mark looked up; the pair of them suddenly worried. And I was even worried myself. I didn't know why I'd said something like that. I knew that I was being awful. But somehow I just couldn't stop myself from being awful. And when Simpering Sonia's bottom lip began to tremble and she said, 'You're just telling lies! Princess Leia's not dead because I love Princess Leia,' I should have just left it at that, perhaps even gone upstairs and brought Princess Leia down so that Sickening Sonia could play with her.

But I couldn't seem to stop myself and I said, 'I'm not telling lies at all, Sonia. Because when you see the next *Star Wars* film, Princess Leia won't be in it and she won't even be mentioned in it because that's what George Lucas has said!'

And Moronic Mark who was palpably dead delighted at his sister's discomfort said, 'So it must be true, Sonia! Because Raymond knows all about George Lucas and the *Star Wars* trilogy. Raymond's the

cleverest person in the world about *Star Wars*, aren't
y', Raymond?'

And even then I could have just left it. I could feel
that I was digging myself into more trouble. But that's
the thing about trouble; it's like quicksand and once
you've got yourself into it, it's dead easy then to just
keep getting deeper and deeper into more of it.

So I told Moronic Mark, 'I don't know everything
about George Lucas and the *Star Wars* trilogy but I do
know that Princess Leia just had to die, didn't she?'

Sonia was staring at me, her forehead all creased up
with the effort of trying not to believe me. Then
Moronic Mark asked me why, why Princess Leia had to
be killed. And I didn't even know what it was I was
about to tell him. Until I heard myself saying, 'Because
Han Solo found out about Princess Leia, didn't he? He
found out that she was really a prostitute! And all the
time Princess Leia was supposed to be fighting the evil
imperial forces she was shagging them all instead!'

Moronic Mark's eyes were out on stalks.

'That's right,' I said, 'she'd been shagging the
Stormtroopers for fifty pence a go! And so George
Lucas said he's not having any prostitutes in his films
and that's why she had to get killed.'

Moronic Mark just slowly shook his head and stared
at me in speechless wonder. Then Simpering Sonia
piped up in her whingey whiny voice and said, 'Tell
me what you're talking about. I don't know what y'
mean.'

Nodding contemptuously towards his little sister,
Mark said, 'She doesn't know what a prostitute is,
Raymond.'

'I do!' Simpering Sonia declared.

'What then?' Mark challenged her.

Sonia just scowled and said, 'I'm not tellin' y'.'

So Moronic Mark ignored her again and said, 'See,
Raymond, she doesn't know what me and you are
talkin' about.'

Sickening Sonia announced that she was going to

kick their Mark then unless he told her what we were talking about. But Mark just said, 'We're not tellin' y' because you're too young, isn't she, Raymond? You're too young to know what prostitutes and shagging is. All you need to know, Sonia, is that you can't play with Princess Leia no more because Princess Leia's dead!'

Sonia just stood there then with her bottom lip sticking out as she watched me and Mark playing with the other *Star Wars* figures. And I even started to feel sorry for her and wished that I hadn't said all that about Princess Leia. So I lifted up Luke Skywalker who was my second best *Star Wars* figure and I said, 'Come on. You can play with Luke Skywalker if you like.'

But Sonia just shook her head and stuck her bottom lip out even further. Then as she stood there watching me and Moronic Mark playing *Star Wars*, she suddenly said, 'Well, I know something that you don't know!'

We didn't even look at her. 'What?' Mark asked in a bored, older-brotherly sort of way.

'There's a Bad Boy!' I heard Sonia say. 'There's a bad boy down at the canal. A bad filthy boy. And he gets the little children and he makes them do wicked bad things.'

I looked up at Sonia then. But Mark just kept on playing and he told his sister, 'That's nowt new! Everybody knows about that, Sonia. Just about every little kid in Failsworth knows not to go near the canal.' Mark suddenly pointed at Sonia then as he said, 'And you better hadn't go near there or he'll get you, the Bad Boy. So don't you dare!'

'I wouldn't, I wouldn't,' Sonia scowled.

'Because the Filthy Bad Boy, he's got evil ways,' Mark said. 'It's not safe at the canal, not for any of the little children. That's why all the mums and dads have told all the kids. And little kids should always do what their mums and dads tell them, shouldn't they, Raymond?'

I looked at Mark. And then I just nodded. And he

said, 'You see, Sonia! Even Raymond wouldn't go near the canal, not when there's a Bad Boy lurking who makes y' do bad things. Raymond wouldn't go and he's eleven!'

Sonia scowled then and said, 'Well, I wouldn't go neither. My mummy said I'd be smacked if I went anywhere near the canal.'

Mark nodded at her and he told her, 'Yeah, you'd be smacked if you were lucky enough to get back in one piece. But a little girl like you, Sonia! If the Filthy Bad Boy at the canal gets hold of you, y' might never come back in one piece, never!'

Sonia shuddered then. And she shut up for a bit. And then Mark started asking me about *The Return of the Jedi* so I started telling him and gradually I forgot all about Simpering Sonia. And with talking about *Star Wars*, even to someone as moronic as Mark, I forgot about everything else; forgot about school and the canal and the Cubs and everything. And it was even nice just sitting there on the warm tarmac. But I didn't know that Simpering Sonia had gone back into the house. I didn't know that she'd walked into the living room and stood there in the doorway, tears welling up in her eyes and her bottom lip starting to quiver. And when her mother finally looked up and asked, 'What's up, love? Sonia, what's up?' I didn't know that Simpering Sonia had burst into shuddering sobs and announced the recent demise of Princess Leia. I didn't know that her dad had laughed at that and told her, 'Don't be stupid! How the hell can Princess Leia be dead, love? She's just a character in a bloody film!'

And I didn't know that Sonia had stamped her frustrated foot then and told her father that Princess Leia *was* dead! Because Raymond had said! About Princess Leia and how she'd been shagging all the Stormtroopers and being a prostitute for fifty pence a time.

I didn't know that the air in our front room had suddenly plunged to forty-five degrees below zero. Or that my Uncle Bastard Jason had momentarily lost the power of speech. I didn't know that my Aunty Paula's jaw had dropped into her teacup or that my Mam had slowly closed her eyes and lowered her head into her hands.

I didn't know any of that because I was sat on the warm tarmac, telling Mark about all the special effects it took to get the Ewoks flying through the Forest of Endor. And the first I knew of what had been going on was when my Uncle Jason appeared at our back door and said, 'Mark! Get in this fucking house, go on! Now!'

And as Mark dropped his Wookies and quickly did as he was bid, my Uncle Jason stood over me and pointed down at me with his big finger and said, 'And you, y' sick little bastard, I'll swing for you, I will!'

I just looked up at him and he glared down at me. And it was like I was looking up at Darth Vader himself. And I know that if he'd had a light sabre in his hand at that second he would gladly have obliterated me. As it was he lifted up his arm and he was going to smack me but my Aunty Paula appeared behind him then saying, 'Jason, for God's sake! What good will that do? Come on,' she said, 'let's just get Mark and Sonia home.'

And then she took my Uncle Bastard Jason by the arm and pulled him away as she said to me, 'You! You're disgusting, you are. Telling filthy, twisted things like that to a seven-year-old girl. Sobbing, she is, sobbing her heart out in there.'

Then my Aunty looked at me in downright disgust and slowly nodded as she said, 'I always thought your father was daft as a brush. But at least he wasn't dirty with it, not like you!' And then she just looked at me as if I was something septic.

And my Uncle Jason pointed at me again and he said, 'You're bloody weird, you are, weird! But I'll tell y' something, son, you'll not corrupt those children of mine with your bloody weirdness and your disgusting mind! Because I'll break your fucking little neck first, I'm warning you!'

And then they disappeared into the house. I just sat there on the tarmac until I heard the front door being slammed. I started collecting up all my *Star Wars* figures. And my Mam appeared at the back door and I'd never seen her so angry before. She looked at me like she could willingly kill me and she said, 'Are you doing all this just to hurt me? Are y', are y'?'

I shook my head and just stood there clutching hold of my *Star Wars* figures.

'Then why *are* y' doing it?' she shouted. 'Princess Leia's a prostit—! Are you out of your stupid mind or what? What have I done, Raymond? Go on, you tell me, son, you tell me what have I done to deserve any of this?'

I couldn't tell her though because I knew my Mam hadn't done anything to deserve it. But my Mam just thought I was being insolent and she suddenly ran up towards me and pointed her finger in my face and said, 'You're going to tell me . . . you're going to tell me now and I don't care if we have to wait out here all bloody night, you're going to tell me, Raymond!' She grabbed hold of my arm as she said, 'I've bloody had enough and I want to know what's going on! Why in the name of God would you say a thing like that, 'ey, 'ey, 'ey?'

My Mam started shaking me and she was shaking me so hard that all my *Star Wars* figures fell out of my hands and spilled all over the tarmac. And I pushed my Mam away and she looked at me all shocked as I shouted at her, 'I don't know why!'

And then all the tears that I hadn't cried since I'd found the ripped-up document at the foot of the railway bridge started streaming down my face as I carried on shouting at my Mam, telling her, 'I've got no friends! And everybody hates me and even you hate me because I'm fat and I'm horrible and I can't help it! I didn't mean to do it! I didn't mean to tell Sonia what I told her but it just came out of me and I couldn't do anything to stop it. I know that I'm horrible but I can't stop being horrible because there's something inside me that just makes me be horrible!'

My Mam stood there looking at me and she had a hand raised up to her mouth. She slowly started shaking her head then and she sounded frightened as she said, 'Dear Christ! Dear Christ, what are we going to do?'

Then my Mam turned away and went into the house.

And I just sat down in the middle of all my *Star Wars* figures and wished with all my heart that I could just find my way back to when I was a nice boy; just an ordinary, normal, everyday, unremarkable boy. I didn't want to be the boy I was being; the boy who was horrible and spiteful to his little cousin, the boy who caused his Mam to keep shouting at him all the time. I didn't want to be like that. I wanted to be nice again.

And perhaps that's all my Mam wanted as well.

Perhaps that's why she decided, that night, that something had to be done.

She sat there in the front room and she thought about things. She thought about the dread that she'd always carried with her but never ever told anybody about – the dread that my Dad had never quite been all there, in the head. My Mam had always been loyal to my Dad, loyal to the memory of him. And even though he had been worse than bleeding useless and he'd never laid the turf, my Mam had always refused to listen to my Uncle Jason who was too fond of declaring that my Dad had been demented and even a bit twisted, the way he kept falling in love with Gretsch guitars and long-necked banjos and keyboards he could never play. But my Mam wouldn't have it that my Dad was daft and she always defended the memory of him.

'Feckless,' my Mam had always said. 'Johnny was never daft. Feckless and soft, I'll give you that. But that's the worst that anybody could say about Johnny.'

131

That's what my Mam had always said. That's what she always said to anybody if they ever suggested that my Dad might have been a bit untoward in his facility for falling in love with musical instruments.

But secretly, in her heart, there was always a dread that would whisper to my Mam; the dread that my Dad really had been a bit daft. And the worst dreadful whisper, the whisper that really frightened my Mam, was the whisper that one day her son would start displaying some sign that he was taking after his father.

And as she sat there in the front room, the night that Princess Leia had died, my Mam started to acknowledge what she'd been refusing to acknowledge ever since that day she'd been summoned to the school and told the terrible facts about me. My Mam began to acknowledge that my recent behaviour, my inexplicable behaviour, was something bad coming out; something that had been there lying dormant all these years, giving no hint of its presence in the nice, normal boy that I had previously been. My Mam thought back to that day in the New Headmaster's room and recalled the words of that chairperson woman, that Mrs Bradwick who'd said that perhaps my Mam should seek professional help. She thought too about what my Bastard Uncle had said about 'implications for the future'.

My Mam thought for a long time. And that was the night she decided. The night she acknowledged that the dread whisper was coming true. And that something had to be done.

My Mam never said nowt, not to me, not to my Gran. The only person she spoke to was my Uncle Jason. But my Bastard Uncle Jason told her, 'I don't know if it'll do any good, Shelagh. Y' might just be wasting your money. A bad apple's a bad apple and polishing it up a bit won't make it any good.'

'For Christ's sake, Jason,' my Mam told him, 'I'm looking for a bit of support here!'

And my Uncle Jason had shrugged then and said,

'Well, you can try it, can't y'? You've certainly got to do something, Shelagh. I know it's definitely something not right, doing what he did down at that canal. And telling things like that to our Sonia; traumatised she was, Shelagh, traumatised.'

My Mam sighed and apologised again, telling her brother, 'That's why I'm trying to do something about it, Jason. If there is something wrong with him, if he's ill then he needs help, doesn't he?'

My Uncle Jason just shrugged again. And he said, 'If he *is* ill, aye. Y' could be right. But then again, Shelagh, it might be nothing to do with illness. You might have to face up to the fact that it's just the way he's inclined, Shelagh, and it's got nothing to do with illness at all!'

My Mam got a bit nowty with her brother then and as she got up to leave she told him, 'That's what I'm trying to find out, Jason, whether he *is* ill!'

Only I wasn't ill. I was never ill! I was fed up! That's what I was. Fed up because I had no friends; fed up and getting fatter all the time from doing nowt but sit in the house watching daytime telly and eating pizzas and pot noodles. I was fed up that my Mam was up to something and wouldn't tell me what it was; fed up because I'd sometimes look up and catch my Mam staring at me, looking at me like she didn't know who I was any more.

But I wasn't ill at all.

I just wanted my Mam to look at me like she loved me. And I wanted her to hug me and be friends with me again and tell me that everything was all right. But it was like there was a wall had been built between me and my Mam. My Mam still talked to me and watched *Blockbusters* with me. But she didn't sit beside me on the settee no more. She just sat on her own in the armchair. And I had this feeling that somehow my Mam had become frightened of me.

And then one day she didn't go to work like she should have done. And she told me then that she was taking me to town. And when I asked her what for she said she'd arranged for me to see somebody. I didn't want to see 'somebody'. I didn't want to see anybody, apart from my Gran. But I couldn't see my Gran because my Gran had gone to Grasmere on a rambling holiday with the Positive Pensioners who my Gran said were a particularly po-faced lot but it suited her because there was no frivolity and she could spend many a happy hour in the house of William Wordsworth.

I asked my Mam when my Gran was coming back. But my Mam just told me to get a move on or we'd be late. And when I asked late for what, my Mam said late for seeing the doctor.

'What doctor?' I said. 'I don't need to see a doctor. I'm not ill!'

'Not a *doctor* doctor,' my Mam said. 'He's a special doctor. A private doctor.'

I said, 'I don't want to see a private doctor! What do I need to see any kind of doctor for?'

'Come on,' she said, 'stop asking questions and just get ready.'

I started putting my shoes on. I said, 'Is this because you don't love me any more?'

My Mam looked shocked then and she said, 'Don't love y'? Of course I love y'.'

'Then why are you making me go and see a doctor,' I said, 'if you love me?'

My Mam sighed and closed her eyes then and she said, 'It's because I love you that I am taking y' to see a doctor. If I didn't love y' then I wouldn't bother, would I?'

I wanted to be glad and happy that my Mam had said she loved me. But it didn't really count because the way she said it, it was almost like she was shouting at me. I just carried on putting my shoes on. And my Mam said, 'There's nothing to be afraid of; nothing to be worried about at all.'

I looked up at my Mam. 'Well, if there's nothing to

be worried about,' I said, 'why are y' taking me to see this doctor in the first place?'

My Mam let some of her narkiness out then and she said, 'Look! I'm your mother and I'm trying to do the best for y'. I'm your mother! I wouldn't do anything to harm y', would I? Would I?'

I looked at my Mam and I shook my head.

'Right!' she said. 'So stop asking questions! You're just a little lad. You don't need to know every single detail of what's going on, Raymond. All you need to know is that I'm taking you to see the special doctor. He's nice. You'll probably like him. So just get a move on and stop asking questions.'

I followed my Mam out of the house. And as we were walking down our path I said, 'You think I'm stupid, don't y'?'

My Mam just sighed and rolled her eyes and said, 'God give me strength!'

She held the gate open for me and as I went through it, I said, 'Well, if you don't think I'm stupid, just stop calling him the "special" doctor. That's what's stupid,' I said, 'calling him that. You don't need to say that because I know what sort of a doctor it is.'

'What then?' my Mam said, sticking her head out towards me.

'A psychiatrist!' I said. And I stuck my head out too.

'Well, you're wrong!' my Mam declared, all triumphantly. 'Because it's not a psychiatrist! I wouldn't take y' to see a psychiatrist! Why would I take you to see one of those?'

I shrugged. And my Mam said, 'Oh come on, look, there's the bus. Run.'

We sat there in his room, me in front of his desk and my Mam sat on a chair behind me. And he wasn't a bit nice. He wasn't nice at all, like my Mam had said he was. He had a bald head and a big bushy beard so it looked as though his head was on upside down. And the first thing he said to me was, 'So, Raymond, do you know who I am?'

I just nodded. It was a stupid question. I didn't even answer it. I knew who he was and he must have known who he was so what was the point in answering him?

'So,' he said, like he was starting to get impatient with me and we'd only been there two minutes, 'who am I then?'

My Mam nudged me. And I didn't like her nudging me and I didn't like him. I said, 'Psycho The Rapist!'

When I said that he looked at me like he was all shocked and surprised and my Mam put her hand to her mouth and whispered, 'Oh my God!'

'Psycho The Rapist?' he said, frowning at me as if I'd just said something really stupid. 'What could possibly lead you to believe that I'm called Psycho The Rapist?'

I pointed at the card that was stood on his desk and I said, 'Because that's what it says on there!'

He lifted the card up then and turned it round and looked at it. Then he turned it back so it was facing me and he pointed at the word with his finger like he was an infants teacher teaching 'A' for Apple and 'B' for Ball.

'Raymond, this word,' he said, 'it says, "psycho . . . therapist". "Psychotherapist". You say it. You try it, "psychotherapist".'

I just shrugged and I said it, 'Psychotherapist.'

And he nodded then and he said, 'Good. Good.' But then he frowned and he said, 'But I'm wondering why it is, Raymond, that you erm . . . interpret such a word as reading "Psycho The Rapist"?'

He was getting on my nerves. And if he'd ever read any *Marvel* comics he would have known because in 'Fantastic Four' (issue 5) that's where Psycho-Man first appears and that's why I'd seen 'Psycho The Rapist' in 'psychotherapist'. And perhaps I shouldn't have said it but I was still mad at my Mam because she'd sort of lied to me. She said she wasn't taking me to see a psychiatrist but he was a psychotherapist anyway so that was like denying that the wallpaper wasn't red because what it really was was crimson!

He was looking at me. And he put his hands together with his fingers touching his nose as if he was saying his prayers as he said, 'I'm also wondering why it is that you seem rather ... obsessed really ... with matters of a sexual nature.'

I turned and I looked at my Mam. But my Mam wouldn't look at me. And when I turned back and looked at him, Psycho The Rapist, he said, 'Yes, I have spoken with your mother, Raymond. Your mum came to see me earlier in the week. So I do know a little bit about you, Raymond. I know something of your family history and ... about your father.'

I was really mad at my Mam then. Because my Mam hadn't told me she'd been to see anybody! And she'd told him about my Dad! She'd said things about my Dad.

I turned round to her again and I said, 'What sort of things about my Dad? What have you been saying about my Dad?'

'Raymond!' he said, Psycho The Rapist. 'Would you turn this way please?'

But I didn't turn round and I said to my Mam, 'He wasn't daft, my Dad. He wasn't daft at all! And there was never anything wrong with him and you should tell my Uncle Jason that when he tries to make out that my Dad was a bit demented because he wasn't demented at all!'

'Raymond!!' Psycho said again. 'Please. You're here to talk with me, Raymond, not with your mum.'

I turned back to face him again. And it was like they'd got together about it all, him and my Mam. It was like my Mam was more friends with him than she was with me! He tried to smile at me. But because his beard was so bushy you couldn't see his lips, so the smile was like suddenly seeing a set of dentures in a privet hedge.

'We can talk about your father later,' he said. 'For

now I think we should concentrate on matters such as
. . . the things you did at the canal, Raymond. And the
kind of things you've been saying to your little cousin.'

I couldn't believe it! I couldn't believe that my Mam
had told him about those things.

'Because . . .' he said, 'I think we may possibly have
the beginnings of a pattern here, don't you, Raymond?'

I didn't say nowt. I just sat there with my head
down, staring at the feet of his desk.

'You see, I'm rather intrigued, Raymond,' he said.
'Interested that . . . these things your mum's told me of
. . . they're . . . well, do you think there's any connection between those things?'

I just shrugged.

Then he said, 'And you walk in here today,
Raymond, and here you are, within seconds of meeting
me, you're referring to me as something called "Psycho
The Rapist". Now, come on. Don't you see any kind of
a connection there?'

I still didn't say anything. I couldn't believe that my
Mam had told him about the flytrapping! And he was
sitting there like he knew things about me now. But he
didn't! He didn't know anything about me! All he'd
heard were some facts. And they weren't even the right
facts.

'Come on, Raymond,' he said, sounding like he was
trying to be all pally and chummy, 'your Mum tells me
you're quite a bright lad. So surely a bright lad, an
intelligent lad like you, you'd have an opinion on
something like that, wouldn't you?'

I did have an opinion. And my opinion was that my
Mam had deceived me and betrayed me! My Mam had
gone talking to my Bastard Uncle Jason again and that's
probably why I'd been taken to see Psycho The Rapist
in the first place.

'Raymond!'

I suddenly realised he was talking to me again. He
said, 'Raymond, there's not a lot of point in you sitting
there and refusing to say anything at all. If I'm going to

be of any help to you, Raymond, then we have to talk; and even talk about things that you might not want to talk about. Like some of the things your mother's already told me.' Then he said, 'Do you have any idea why your mother has brought you here?'

'Yes!' I said, 'I've got a very good idea why I've been brought here. I've been brought here because of my Uncle Bastard Jason!'

My Mam shouted then, shouted, 'Raymond! Your poor uncle . . .'

But I didn't care and I said, 'Well, he *is* a bastard and I don't care because he always upsets you! And their dog never needed a new gall bladder in the first place! And he's always saying my Dad was daft and my Dad wasn't daft! And I'm not daft neither,' I said.

'Raymond,' Psycho interrupted, 'please!'

I just looked at him and he was holding up his hand. 'Raymond,' he said, 'nobody is suggesting that anybody is daft!'

'Apart from my Uncle Bastard Jason!' I said. 'He's always saying that my Dad was daft and my Dad wasn't daft, he just had all the sweetness of sun-ripened oranges about him, that's all! But my Uncle Jason was always jealous because he's only a grapefruit!'

He just looked at me, Psycho The Rapist. And he cleared his throat.

'My Dad wasn't daft!' I said. 'And I'm not daft neither.'

He said, 'Raymond, we don't believe in words such as "daft" here. None of this is about "daftness" or silly words like that,' he said. 'I'm just here to try and help you, Raymond.'

But I didn't need to be helped, not like he was trying to help me; asking his stupid questions and talking to me like I was an infant child. He said, 'Do you understand what it is that a psychotherapist does, Raymond?'

'Yes!' I said. 'I know exactly what a psychotherapist does. He neuters people!'

My Mam put her hand up to her mouth again then and said, 'Raymond, for God's sake.'

So I swivelled round in the chair and I told her, 'Well, they do! Because my Gran said! She said that when Twinky McDevitt got sent to see the psycho-therapist he got neutered and when she sees him in Sainsbury's now he never pirouettes past the pizzas no more. He just pushes the trolley passively for his mother.'

'Raymond!' my Mam said and she was talking through clenched teeth and glaring at me with her eyes. But it was true. Because my Gran said she always loved seeing little Twinky McDevitt foxtrotting down the aisles in Sainsbury's and doing his pirouettes. And my Gran said Twinky McDevitt should never have been sent to see a psychotherapist in the first place because he was just a homosexual, that's all, and what he really needed was a stage and a nice costume and some good bright lights, not sent to see a sodding psychotherapist! And my Mam had agreed when my Gran had said that! And here she was, taking me to see a psychotherapist now and apologising to him, shaking her head and saying, 'This is how he's become, doctor. He just . . . just comes out with these things. And does these things. I barely recognise him any more.'

But Psycho just nodded and lifted up his hand as if to calm my Mam down. And he said to me, 'You see, there we have it again, don't we, Raymond: "neutered".' He looked at me. 'And all these things, Raymond, these episodes and outbursts, the flies at the canal, the sort of things you've been saying to your little cousin about . . . sexual intercourse; things you've been saying to me, Raymond, "Rapist", "neutered". Do you see, do you see how these things might be connected?'

But they weren't connected! They weren't con-nected at all. The only thing that connected them was me. Because they were things that I'd said and things that I'd done. But all he was doing was just picking a few things out of all the hundreds of thousands of other things that I'd said and done. And anybody could connect things up like that if they wanted to. So I just picked out the first thing that came into my head.

'Water!' I said.

He frowned at me.

I said it again, I said, 'Water! I drink water. I get washed in water. When I wee, I wee water. And when it rains I get wet in water. Water!' I said. 'There's all them connections, but it doesn't mean I'm a goldfish, does it!'

I only said it because I thought it might shut him up and he might let me go home then. But he just nodded and he sort of smiled again and said, 'That's interesting, isn't it? That's extremely interesting, Raymond: water. The canal! That's where this all started, didn't it, Raymond, alongside a stretch of water!'

He was looking at me, waiting for me to answer him. He started saying something else but I wasn't listening any more. Because it was like my mind had suddenly slipped away somewhere. I wasn't in that room any more, with my Mam and Psycho The Rapist. I was back at the side of the canal; that day when Albert had fallen in and I'd dived down and rescued him. And then I was in the deputy head's room later that same day, after everything had been discovered and the New Headmaster had made it all turn bad and dirty. And I'd just had to sit there on my own and wait for my Mam while she was being summoned from the supermarket and told all about it. I'd had to wait for ages; ages and ages and ages, before the door had opened; and my Mam had stood there, looking at me. But looking at me with disappointment and disgust in her eyes. Looking at me like she didn't know who I was any more.

'Raymond!'

I looked up, at Psycho The Rapist. He was trying to tell me something about attending his clinic where he did his research. But I wasn't really listening. Because I knew now. I knew *why* my Mam had looked at me like she didn't know who I was any more. I knew why I'd sometimes catch her staring at me with a puzzled sort of look on her face. I understood it now.

Psycho The Rapist was showing us to the door and telling my Mam something about making the necessary appointment. Then we were walking down the road and back towards the bus stop and my Mam was really mad with me and saying she was disgusted at some of the things that I'd said to Psycho. But it didn't really matter any more because I knew now what I had to do; I knew how to make everything all right again. My Mam didn't need to worry any more. She didn't need to waste her hard-earned money taking me to see people like Psycho The Rapist. He was just stupid! He didn't know anything. I suppose it was good that we went to see him though because if I hadn't sat there and said what I'd said about the water then I might never have realised. And it was all so obvious now, as we got off the bus and walked up towards our house, with my Mam still all peeved and narked with me and saying that she didn't know what to do with me any more. But I knew exactly what to do. It suddenly seemed so easy and so straightforward. And I wondered why I hadn't thought of it before. It was all so simple, me being the wrong boy! That's who had come back up out of the canal, the wrong boy; and that's why my Mam was always looking at me like she didn't know who I was any more. Because I wasn't who I should be; I wasn't myself! I'd never been myself, not since that day; that day when I'd dived in and rescued Albert Goldberg. All I'd ever been before that was a nice boy, a perfectly ordinary nice young boy who'd never have done things like telling his little cousin about shagging and prostitutes and Princess Leia being dead when she wasn't. I'd never have done things like that; not if I was still the boy I'd once been. But he'd disappeared, the nice boy. And now I knew *where* he'd disappeared. He was still in the canal!

When we got into the house my Mam was still

142

narked and not speaking to me. She said she didn't know how she could face that poor doctor again after the sort of things that I'd been saying to him.

So I told my Mam, I said, 'It's all right, you won't have to face him because there's no need. And I don't have to go to his clinic.'

But my Mam started shouting then and said, 'Don't you bloody well dare! You're going! You're going to that clinic. I don't care what it costs, I don't care if I have to borrow to pay for it but we're going to get to the bottom of all this. I've had enough, I have.'

I thought it was funny really, my Mam saying that about getting to the bottom because she was right. And that's exactly what I was planning to do.

I told my Mam I was going to play out in the back because it was so hot. But she just ignored me. So I picked up a few of my *Star Wars* figures and went out there. I felt a bit awful really, about not telling my Mam. But I wanted it to be a sort of surprise. I couldn't wait to see her when I got back and she looked at me and saw I was the nice boy again.

I waited a few minutes. Then I got up off the tarmac and I knew it would all be all right now. I knew what I had to do. I went down to the bottom of our garden and climbed over the fence. I began to run, as fast as I could, up the street and down the cut, past the bread shop and through the gate and over the recreation ground, running past the allotments, into the lane and over the bridge, down to the cinder track and then into the high hay field, running through the long grass, running as fast as I could. It felt funny running because I could feel these bits wobbling on me. But it didn't matter because it wasn't really me, this fat boy, this horrible boy, this boy who couldn't even run properly and got out of breath dead easy, it wasn't me; it had never been me. I was going back to find me. And everything would be all right then, everything would be back to normal when the fat boy put himself back into the canal where he belonged; and then it'd be the nice

143

boy who came back up out of the water. And
everything would be normal again then. All my friends
would start to play with me again and I'd get back into
the Cubs and my Mam wouldn't have to shout at me no
more. And I almost laughed out loud when I thought
about my Mam and how I'd caught her looking at me
sometimes, staring at me in that puzzled sort of way
and looking at me like she didn't know who I was any
more. And it always upset me when I caught her looking at me like that. But I realised now, I realised that
she'd been right to look at me like that! Because it *was*
the wrong boy she'd been looking at. And I couldn't
wait to see my Mam's face tonight when she glanced
across at the settee and saw it was the right boy, the
nice boy, sitting there again. I ran, faster and faster, as
fast as I could, through the grass, laughing now, laughing out loud to myself as I thought about my Mam and
the delight that would be upon her when she saw the
nice boy had come back home again.

I didn't pay it any attention, not then, when I saw
the little girl running up ahead of me as I came out
of the high hay field and started running along the towpath, past the backs of the bungalow houses and up
towards the bridge where the old warehouses and the
derelict buildings start.

It was just a girl, that's all, just some little kid who
was running, running like she was playing tick or hide-
and-seek with the rest of her friends who were
probably hiding somewhere in the high hay field.

She just went running off and I started slowing
down, trying to get my breath back now as I walked up
to the edge of the canal, up to the exact same spot where
we'd done the flytrapping, exact same spot where I'd
dived in on that day when I'd disappeared. The water
was all lit up on its surface and sparkling golden in the
early evening sun; and I knew the water was happy
because the Wrong Boy was coming back to where he
belonged. And I knew that I was right and that once it
had the Wrong Boy back, the canal would gladly give

up its captive in return. I knew that the nice boy would soon be free, soon be coming back up again, smiling and normal and nice, from out of the canal.

And that's why I did it. I waited until I'd got all my breath back. I looked up and down the towpath to make sure nobody was coming and that the little girl and her friends weren't around any more.

And then I stepped back and I ran towards the canal, leaping up into the air and clutching hold of my knees like I was doing a depth charge. I heard the car coming over the canal bridge, heard it just before I hit the water. But then I couldn't hear anything any more as I hit the water and started sinking down into the silence; down, down, down . . .

And I knew I was right. I knew that I'd been right all along. Everything was just the same as I'd remembered it, beneath the waters of the canal, everything undisturbed and exactly as it was before. I reached out and there in the dark murky water, exactly where I knew it would be, was the rusted supermarket trolley and the weeds that had grown around it. I was right, everything was just the same. And even though I couldn't see anything, I kept my eyes wide open and then, just ahead of me, just where I knew he'd be, I saw something slowly coming into focus. And then he was there! There where I knew he would be, the nice boy, just sat there quietly on the bed of the canal, and smiling slightly like he'd just been sat there patiently waiting for me all this time. And I waved back at him then and I smiled as I started to swim towards him. And at first I thought there must be something holding me back because even though I was moving my arms and thrashing my legs and swimming towards the nice boy, I didn't seem to be moving at all. I pulled at my tee shirt and pulled at my pants but nothing seemed to be snagged or caught at all so I tried to swim even harder and made my strokes even stronger but still I wasn't getting any nearer to the Nice Boy. And then the worst thing happened because the Nice Boy slowly turned and he looked at me straight in the eyes. He smiled at first. But then he raised his hand and slowly waved at me; and he started to move away! Started to disappear like he was fading away, back into the darkness of the water. And I couldn't bear it then, I couldn't believe that I'd got so close only to lose him again. And I opened my mouth, trying to shout, trying to scream and let him know that I was there and that he could go back up to the surface and be set free for ever. But the more I tried to shout, the more the dark water rushed into my mouth and up my nose and into my belly and all around my head where it was swirling and swooshing and making my arms and legs lose all the life in them and start to feel like wobbly jelly. And the last I saw of him, the Nice Boy, he was gliding away effortlessly swimming like a silver fish, away into the further waters of the canal.

I can't really remember too much of what happened after that. I was vaguely aware of being in the open air again and a blue light flashing and being dragged and then carried, then something pushing down hard on my back and squeezing my chest into the ground. And I heard bits of voices with panic and urgency in them. And the next thing I knew was waking up and seeing white lights above me and smelling that smell which told me that I must be in a hospital. Then I saw a person in a uniform looking down at me and smiling as he shook his head and said something about I was bloody lucky that they'd been coming over the bridge at that very moment.

He was nice to me, that policeman. He said I could call him Dave. 'And my mate here,' he said, 'this is Eric.'

I turned my head and looked at him, Eric. All his uniform was saturated. He nodded at me and he said, 'That's right, I was the one who pulled y' out. So listen,' he said, 'that's the end of your pocket money for a while, isn't it? You're gonna have to buy me a new uniform, Raymond.'

He was smiling at me though; they were both smiling at me and I knew that it was just a joke. I tried to tell them then, but my voice was all croaky and my throat felt like it had just been sandpapered and Eric had to ask Dave what it was I'd said. The other one frowned and said, 'I don't know; something about the wrong boy?'

I started nodding my head then and trying to tell them that they'd rescued the wrong boy out of the canal. But they couldn't understand what I was trying to tell them because Eric said, 'Has someone been bullying you, Raymond?'

I just shook my head. And then the nurse came and told the policemen that there was a cup of tea for them in the nurses' room.

Dave reached out and ruffled my hair then and Eric winked at me. And they both said I'd be all right and then told me tarar. They were nice to me that night, Eric and Dave. Everybody was nice to me.

The nurse was smiling down at me and she said, 'Raymond. Hello, Raymond. Look who's come to see you, Raymond. Look who's here.'

And that's when I saw my Mam looking down at me and her face was all stricken with the grief of it. And all that she could say was 'Son! Son, son.'

And I didn't want her to be all upset and grieving about everything. I wanted to cheer her up. And even though it made my throat hurt, I managed to speak to her and I told her, 'It's all right . . . you don't have to worry . . . Mrs Marks.'

She looked like she'd been smacked across the face when I said that. But I told her, 'No, it's all right . . . don't worry. You don't have to worry, not about me . . . Because I'm not your son. Your son's still in the canal, Mrs Marks. And all I am . . . is the Wrong Boy!'

I tried to smile at her then but it didn't seem to cheer her up at all because she put her hand up to her mouth as she slowly staggered back and leaned there up against the wall. That was when I heard the nurse as

147

she comforted my Mam and sat her down and said something about me being slightly delirious and confused and it was to be expected because of what I'd been through and then they'd had to put tubes down my throat to get rid of all the putrid water. But everything would be better in the morning, the nurse said, because they were giving me something to help me sleep and then I'd be brighter and I wouldn't be confused no more.

But I wasn't confused in the first place. I knew exactly what was happening and what was going on. I knew that I was still fat and friendless. I knew that it hadn't worked. I knew that I was still the Wrong Boy!

But listen, Morrissey, I'm not able to tell you any more about that right now because the coach has just pulled in and I've got to get on board. I want you to know though, Morrissey, that that's all I was doing, that night when I went back to the canal; I was just looking for him, that's all. Just looking for the boy who'd got lost in the canal and never came back up. They tried to make out it was something else. But it wasn't, Morrissey. I know it must seem mad, believing that you're the Wrong Boy and jumping into the canal. But back then, back in that year when I got lost somewhere and couldn't find myself, it didn't seem like it was remotely mad at all. It just seemed perfect. And I was never doing what they said I was doing. I wasn't trying to dispose of myself at all. It was the opposite of that. I was trying to find myself, trying to release the boy who'd got trapped under the surface and had to stay there for four weeks or more, waiting, just waiting for the Wrong Boy to return so that the right boy could be free again.

They didn't believe me though.

They said I'd got frightened because of what I'd done to Paulette. They said I couldn't live with the guilt of it and that's why I'd tried to kill myself. But I didn't even know who she was. It'd just been some little girl, that's

148

all, just some little girl who I'd half noticed, running up ahead of me. I didn't know she'd been lost and frightened, her mind full of warnings and stories about the badness of the place in which she found herself, a place where there lurked a creature as terrifying as the Troll in the Three Billy Goats Gruff, a creature that she knew in her head as the Filthy Beast Boy. And in her panic, in her moment of dread, the little girl had heard a noise in the distance; and turning her head, looking down the towpath, she'd seen exactly what she knew she would see, seen something heading straight towards her, seen the Filthy Beast Boy pounding down the towpath, coming to get her, just like she'd been told he would in the hushed half-warnings and the whispers: the Filthy Beast Boy.

But I'd hardly even noticed her because all I'd been concerned about was trying to find my way back to being the nice boy. I never knew that she'd been running for her life. Because I never heard the whimpering sounds she made or saw the frantic terror in her face or the wild panic in her eyes and the tears that streamed down from them as she tried to escape the clutches of the Beast Boy.

As I found the spot I'd been looking for and prepared to leap into the dark waters of the canal, I didn't know that just a couple of hundred yards further up from me, a terrified little girl was crawling through a tiny gap in the boarded-up doorway of the disused warehouse in a frantic effort to find a hiding place from her tormentor. And as I was jumping into the water, I didn't hear the scream of the little girl as her foot found the place where the floorboards had been stripped away by various vandals or broken up and burnt by occasional homeless souls in search of some warmth in the winter.

I never knew, as I was sinking down into the murky waters of the canal, that a little girl was also sinking down, down into the dark vaults of the disused warehouse. I never knew a single thing about any of that.

Not till later. Not till I got out of the hospital; and heard, for the very first time, the name of Paulette Patterson.

Yours sincerely,
Raymond Marks

From the Lyric Book of Raymond James Marks

Paulette Patterson was only eight; but already
    she had sad and ancient eyes.
Though there were some who mistook the
    look, saying it came as no surprise
That 'poor little Paulette' was turning out like
    her brothers and sisters had done:
'A touch slow', 'a bit backward', 'a few
    currants short of a proper hot-cross bun'.
'Harmless!' they agreed, and 'pretty as a
    picture', 'polite', and 'always well-meant,
As if what God had denied her in wit, he'd
    made up for in temperament',
But Paulette Patterson wasn't 'backward'; just
    sad and a bit dreamy, that's all;
Sat at the table with her colouring book as her
    mam began yelling from the hall,
Warning their Darryl he'd be fuckin' dead if
    he didn't find his shoes,
And telling Paulette to stop arsin' about and
    be some soddin' use!
Paulette put down the blue crayon she'd
    pinched from the crayon box in school
As her mam began to scream at their Darryl,
    calling him a fucking fool
And saying if he didn't shape his stupid arse
    and get his shoes on, now!
She'd belt him into the back of next week.
    'And as for you, you stupid cow!'
She told Paulette, struggling to help her
    brother put his shoes on,
'Get his pushchair and get him strapped in.
    Come on, get a bloody move on.'
Paulette, as obedient as ever, went and fetched
    the pushchair,
Lifting her wriggling brother into it as she
    asked her mother where

She was going and would she be long and
    what time would she be back.
But Paulette's mother, deaf to her daughter,
    told Darryl he'd get another smack
If he carried on kicking and carrying on. She
    told Paulette to fasten his straps.
Doing up the buckles, as she'd been told,
    Paulette asked her mother if perhaps
She could come too. And then she could be a
    big help to her mother,
If she could come she could help with the
    shopping, help look after her brother.
But Paulette's mother shook her head, '*He*'ll
    be home soon. An' he's not got his key.'
Paulette looked up and told her mother, 'Why
    don't you leave our Darryl with me?
I could look after him; he'd be all right and
    you wouldn't have to bother with the pram.
You could leave him here, do the shopping on
    y' own. Why don't y' do that, mam?'
'Because, stupid!' her mother scorned, 'I'm
    takin' Darryl to town for a haircut.
So you just keep your nose out of it, you! Just
    keep your little mouth shut!'
Paulette watched in silence as her mam
    pushed the pushchair over the step and out
    of the door,
Telling their Darryl if he didn't stop crying
    she'd really give him what for.
And Paulette knew she had to do what her
    mam said and wait in the house for her
    dad;
She went and sat back at the kitchen table,
    picked up her crayons and her colouring
    pad.
But the chill in the house made her milk teeth
    chatter, her lips were blue and her fingers
    shook
Till Paulette could barely hold the blue crayon

against the page of the colouring book.
It was dark in the house but outside it was
    summer. It was cold in the house but
    outside in the sun
Bumble-bees bumbled and butterflies buttered
    the buttercups, cats napped and spiders
    spun.
Paulette got up and looked out of the window
    and decided it really wouldn't do much
    harm.
She could tell her mam she only went for a
    walk to make herself warm, just to get
    warm.
And she could tell her mam she'd not
    forgotten her father who'd gone off to work
    without his key,
And that's why she'd left the door on the
    latch, so her dad could still get in, you see?
And Paulette wouldn't stay out that long
    anyway. She only intended just walking
    around
Till the sun did its business and made her feel
    warmer, till her mam and their Darryl got
    back from town.

Paulette Patterson left the house between
    about three thirty and three forty-five
Or perhaps slightly later, said the neighbour
    who'd been polishing his car in the drive.
Mrs Machonochie who worked in the bread
    shop said definitely; and the reason she
    was sure
It couldn't possibly have been any later was
    that sharp, every day, she knocked off at
    four.
And it was her last customer who'd pointed
    and said, 'It takes me back, that, to when I
    was a girl,
Skipping down the cut in the long summer

holidays, not a worry in your head, not a
  care in the world.'
And the man with the corgi said he was
  certain it was her, she'd stopped to give the
  dog a stroke.
Yes, she was wearing a pale green dress and
  the strap on one of her sandals was broke.
Sandra Mitchell had stopped on the hill, she
  was jiggered with the heat and pushing the
  pram.
When she'd seen Paulette, asked where she
  was going, Paulette had said, 'The park to
  pick flowers for my mam.'
And Sandra says now she'll never forgive
  herself, leaving that child to go off on her
  own.
But it seemed such a nice day to do it, pick
  flowers. And like Sandra said, 'Who could
  have known?'

Paulette just thought it would be a good
  shortcut, through the allotments. She
  watched for a while.
There was no one about, no gardeners
  gardening. Paulette got up and over the
  stile.
Paulette was a good girl who kept to the path,
  not one of those kids who trampled the plots,
Pulled up the lettuces, stole the potatoes,
  smashed the hut windows and broke up the
  pots.
Paulette would never do anything so naughty;
  all she was doing was to take the shortcut.
But Paulette just stopped and stared and said
  nothing when the man with the fork came
  out of the hut.
He stood for a second and stared at the girl,
  his mouth puckered up and his eyes
  bulging out.

Then he started to growl and dropped the fork
     as he rushed towards her and started to
     shout
About vandals and brats and right little
     bastards and radishes ripped up, lettuces
     too.
'I'll get you,' he threatened; 'come here, you
     little bitch. Just wait till I get my hands on
     you!'
Paulette went running, skittering skeltering,
     zigzagging over the patchwork of plots,
Scrambling, stumbling on potato drills,
     treading through the leeks and the lettuce
     cloche;
Boots pounding, the Man from the Hut
     shouted, 'I'll get you!' as she ran for the
     hedge,
Tears stinging her eyes now and hot shameful
     water starting to trickle down her legs
As she scrambled in the tangle of privet,
     bindweed, bramble and thorn,
Her arms, her legs, her face scratched and
     bloodied, her green dress ripped and torn;
The Man from the Hut started laughing, as she
     thrashed and flailed to find a way through,
His gnarled-knuckle fingers reaching into the
     bushes telling the girl, 'Oh I'll soon have
     you.'
Snared in the thicket, Paulette pleaded,
     whimpered and cried as the Man from the
     Hut
Felt through the branches until his hard bony
     fingers found what they sought and seized
     the small foot,
Making Paulette start thrashing in vain,
     screaming and straining to get free of his
     grasp;
Tugging and trying to pull free from the
     fingers until the clapped-out rusted clasp

Of her sandal snapped free and she was
      falling out of the dark hedge and back into
      the sun.
Leaving the Man from the Hut with nowt but
      a sandal, she scuttled to her feet and began
      to run
Down the bank and through the nettles,
      scrambling across the railway track,
As the Man from the Hut shouted, 'Don't you
      worry! I'll be waiting for y' when you come
      back!'

Paulette Patterson kept on running, one shoe
      off and one shoe on,
Knickers wet, scratches stinging, dress all
      ripped and buttons gone.
But Paulette thought if she kept on running,
      she'd somehow manage to find her way
Back to the park, the swings, the sandpit,
      mothers watching their toddlers play.
But Paulette never turned up at the swings, all
      the mothers were absolutely sure.
Mrs McGann, who knew the girl well, said
      she'd been at the sandpit till half-past four
And she'd not seen hide nor hair of the child
      and she'd definitely remember if she had
Because Paulette always came to the sandpit
      and always played with her little lad.
But that afternoon, that hot afternoon, that
      afternoon they would never forget,
None of the mothers in the park could recall
      seeing hide nor hair of little Paulette.

Too tired, too hot to run any more, lost and
      wandering along a cinder track,
Paulette tried not to think about how she was
      ever going to find her way back.
She tried not to cry and not be afraid. But she
      was in bad trouble she knew;

Even if she managed to find her way home her
    mam would be sure to notice her shoe
Was missing, her dress was all torn. And,
    worst of all, her knickers were wet!
And the last time it had happened her mam
    had warned her, told her exactly what she'd
    get;
'Once more, just do it once more, wet your
    knickers again and I bloody well swear,
 I'm taking you to the hospital, I am! And then
    I'm fuckin' well leaving you there!'
Paulette was in very bad trouble, she'd tram-
    pled the vegetables down.
And her mam had told her to stay in the
    house while she took their Darryl to town.
And Paulette's mam would slap her legs, 'You
    downright defiant little cow.
And for leaving the house when you'd been
    told not to, you can get yourself to bed right
    now.'
And Paulette's dad would sneak in later and
    tell her, 'It's all right, love, it's all right.'
At first, she'd be glad that her dad still loved
    her. But then her dad would switch off the
    light
And . . . Paulette stopped thinking! Tried to
    concentrate instead on how to make things
    better
So her mam wouldn't take her to the hospital,
    so her mam wouldn't shout and hit her.

The grass at the side of the cinder track was
    thick and deep and tall
And the day so perfectly warm and windless,
    it wouldn't take much time at all
For her knickers to dry out. Paulette quickly
    decided and then slipped into the field;
And when she was sure she couldn't be seen,
    she ducked down and she peeled

Off her damp pants and laid them on the grass
  in the smoothed-out hollow she'd made.
And then knelt down, closed her eyes, put her
  hands together and prayed
That everything would be all right now. And
  as soon as the sun had dried her pants
She'd run back home as fast as she could; and
  with a bit of luck there was still a chance
She'd get back to the house before her mam
  and their Darryl got back from town.
And she wouldn't be in trouble then. It'd all
  be all right! Paulette sat herself down
In the grass, at the side of her knickers,
  waiting for them to dry;
And that was when she saw it fluttering above
  her: the capricious red butterfly.
It seemed as if it was waving at Paulette,
  inviting her to come and to play,
Gliding down, almost touching her nose and
  then soaring up and away
Before settling on a head of grass, fluttering its
  wings at the child in the hollow
As if waiting for her, its winged eyes winking,
  bidding Paulette to come follow.
It was the butterfly's fault, that's what caused
  it, the mischievous butterfly;
Whenever Paulette got to within a touch of it,
  off and up it would fly
Again, always just out of reach, just beyond
  the touch of the girl;
Seeming always to stop and to wait for her but
  then always to swirl
Up into the air once more, fluttering above her
  head
Before settling on another flower a few more
  yards up ahead.
And again Paulette crept up on the creature
  but again it took to the air
And, laughing now as she ran through the

grass, Paulette called out, 'It's not fair, not
    fair;
You're a cheat! Because you can fly and I can
    only run
And wings against legs, that's not fair; you can
    ask anyone.'
Paulette was right, wings versus legs, it was
    never an equal match.
And hot now, hot and bored and knowing
    she'd never be able to catch
The capricious butterfly, she turned and began
    to make her way back
To where she'd left her knickers drying, at the
    edge of the cinder track.
And Paulette was certain she knew the way;
    all she had to do was follow
Her footsteps back the way she'd come and
    she'd soon be back at the hollow
Where her knickers would be dry by now.
    She'd be able to put them back on
And then run right home as fast as she could
    before anyone realised she'd been gone;
And perhaps (if miracles were there for the
    taking) it might just be that her mam
Had brought her a present back from town, a
    doll or a skipping rope, a toy pram,
A new painting set, some felt-tip pens, the
    whitest of white school socks,
Or a pencil case, a proper satchel or a Winnie
    the Pooh luncheon box.
And then she'd be the girl that Miss Miller
    liked, the one who always got praise
For the neatness of her colouring in; the girl
    who got to put out the trays,
The books, the crayons, the water jars, the one
    who got to stay in at break,
The clever girl, the trusted girl, the one who
    was allowed to take
The hamster home in the holidays and whose

workbooks were proudly displayed
In the glass cabinet by the headmaster's room
   on parents' and governors' days.
And then she would be . . . Paulette stopped!
   Such sweet dreams instantly banished
As she reached the meadow's edge and saw
   that the cinder track had vanished!
It wasn't there. She'd walked the right way!
   But the cinder track wasn't there!
And in its place was a stretch of dank dark
   water that fouled and filled the air
With the scent of something gone bad. Gnats
   hovered and flies buzzed furiously.
And although she'd never been to this place
   before, Paulette knew instantly
This was the home of the Beast of a Boy. Time
   and again, along with every other kid,
She'd been told she was never to come to this
   place; how she'd be in trouble if she did.
Paulette had heard all the mothers, all of them
   talking, whispering at the swings,
About the Filthy Beast Boy down by the canal
   who did unspeakable things.
'And looking at him,' Mrs Kershall had said,
   'you'd think him an ordinary lad.'
'But just from looking,' Mrs Durney had
   replied, 'you can never tell good from bad!
They change, you see, when they're that way
   inclined; they look normal but they're not.
Something goes off, up here in the head and
   then . . . an animal, that's what you've got!
You mark my words; he might look normal, he
   might look like an ordinary kid.
But ask yourselves this, would an ordinary
   kid ever do what that kid did?'
And when Paulette had asked Mrs McGann
   what the Beast of a Boy had done,
Mrs McGann had looked sour and stern and
   said that very bad things had gone on.

And when Paulette asked her about it, asked
    what kind of bad things she meant,
Mrs McGann told her to shush and just make
    sure that she never ever went
Where the Filthy Bad Boy was lurking, 'Just
    waiting for little children like you!
He gets them under his spell, he blinds them
    he does; then he forces them to do
Things they don't want to, things that aren't
    nice. Things you're too young to know.
So you just remember, Paulette Patterson, if
    you're ever tempted to go
Anywhere near that canal, you just think on
    what you've been told.'
Paulette did remember; the hot summer's air
    suddenly chilled and fear's cold
Fingers caressing her skin as she imagined
    him lurking there in the canal,
The boy who had something that went off in
    his head; the boy who became an animal,
The Filthy Beast Boy, hidden below the
    water's surface, his eyes already fixed on
    her
As he prepared to spring up and out of his
    foul and fetid watery lair
To snatch her and catch her for daring to tread
In this dark foul place where all the mothers
    had said
Little children should never ever be foolish
    enough to go.
Slowly, Paulette edged back from the canal
    and turned towards the meadow
Where the sun still shone and the air was
    sweet and warm
And there was nothing there that could do a
    small child any harm;
In the cover of the long grass she'd be hidden
    and she'd be safe.
But Paulette faltered, stopped and stared at

the grass; the terrified waif
Suddenly aware of the silent swell, the shift-
ing motion,
The billowing rise and fall in the swaying
green ocean.
Paulette stood, convinced now that the merest
tremble of the smallest blade,
The softest tremor in the sea of grass was
being made
Not by sun or breeze or any normal process of
nature
But by him! The boy who turned into the
animal; the creature!
And then, she heard it! Coming towards her,
the unmistakable sound
Of something moving through the grass, running feet pounding the ground
And the noise of something gulping at the air,
gasping
As it scythed its way towards Paulette, its
limbs rasping
Through the grass as Paulette stood rigid with
fear, unable to run
As she watched it rising out of the grass, the
head silhouetted by the sun,
So that Paulette didn't see that what she was
seeing was just a young boy's head;
Just a young boy, running through the
meadow. What Paulette saw instead
Was a face that contorted as it bore down
upon her, its form and each feature
Bending and twisting until the face became
that of the Creature:
Its neck thickening, its head engorged, eyes
swollen and a bulbous pitted nose
Erupting as jowls of skin unfolded and large
leather-skinned ears rose
Like gnarled ancient mushrooms on the side
of the mutant creature's head;

A head that Paulette Patterson knew! Its face
   familiar. Paulette turned and, finally, fled
Along the towpath now, not knowing or
   caring where she was going,
As she fled from him, from the face she
   dreaded, running from knowing:
That in the face of the Filthy Bad Boy
   Creature
She'd seen the unmistakable face of her own
   father.
Not her nice daddy, the daddy she loved; the
   one who tried his best
To stand up for her when her mam kicked off;
   the daddy she'd never have guessed
Could turn into that other daddy, the one who
   told her she mustn't cry;
The one who said how special she was and
   tried to convince her that's why
Daddy does it. And when he does it, he only
   does it so she'll know
How precious she is and how much she
   means to him; does it to show
Just how much he really loves her (and a
   daddy's love is always the best).
And that's why she must never tell a soul –
   because some people, they're obsessed
With confusing things and twisting things,
   making them what they're not.
And that's why Paulette must never breathe a
   word. Because if those people got
Wind of how much her daddy loved her
   they'd twist it into something not nice,
Tampering with the truth and dressing it up in
   the poisonous slime of their lies:
'Wicked' and 'evil', 'disgusting' and 'wrong';
   that's what those people would say.
And Paulette wouldn't have a daddy then.
   Because they'd take her daddy away!
And though Paulette dreaded what her daddy

163

became whenever he found her alone
She dreaded it more to think of him gone, to
    think she might be left on her own
With her mam, who shouted and said she was
    stupid, and Darryl, her little brother.
If those people took her daddy away, then
    she'd have nobody to love her.
And when he was being her proper daddy, the
    daddy she loved so much,
She knew she had nothing to fear from him
    then, knew that his words, even his touch
Were those of the daddy who really loved her,
    loved her like a father should.
And Paulette could almost forget, then, the
    other daddy, the one who made her blood
Turn to iced water and caused a wave of
    sickness to swell through her
As the daddy she loved turned into the other
    daddy, the one who did bad things to her,
The one who crawled, uninvited, into her
    dreams; the one whose face she would
    suddenly see
Looking down at her from the platform in the
    hall at school as she stood in assembly
Or as she glanced up from the picture she was
    colouring in, to see it was no longer the
    teacher
She was looking at now but the sickening face
    of the Creature;
The Creature who was chasing her now, his
    feet drumming behind her
As she fled along the towpath at the edge of
    the field, frantically trying to find a
Way to escape the Creature, knowing now that
    he intended to kill her!
For what she'd hidden behind the skirting
    board, the story she'd written when Miss
    Miller
Had said they could write about anything they

164

wanted; and Paulette had spent ages and
    ages
Writing out the story about the girl called
    Lucy, the story that filled four whole pages
All about the girl who lived with a giant, a
    warm and lovely giant, who Lucy Brown
    adored.
But inside this giant was another giant, a cruel
    one who sometimes clawed
His way out and took the place of the lovely
    giant. This cruel giant, Lucy hated.
And every day, Lucy Brown would pray that
    the two could be separated.
So then Lucy could be with the giant she
    loved, the one she wanted to stay
The gentle giant who truly loved her. And
    then the other one could be taken away
By the people she mustn't talk to, the
    mothers, the dinner ladies, the teachers;
The people who knew how to rescue her and
    the nice giant from the awful creature's
Grasp. When she'd handed in the story of
    Lucy Brown, Paulette had waited each day
For Miss to look up from her desk and,
    smiling, ask Paulette to please stay
Behind after class. And then when all the
    other girls and boys had gone out,
Miss Miller would tell Paulette she knew just
    who the story was really about.
And Paulette would tell Miss Miller
    everything then. And Miss Miller would
    hug Paulette
And tell her she didn't need to be afraid any
    longer, she didn't need to worry or fret
Because Miss Miller would be able to make it
    all right. Miss Miller, so pretty and clever,
Would know exactly what to do to make the
    cruel giant disappear for ever.
And Paulette would have just her real daddy

then, her proper daddy, just the one;
When Miss Miller read the story of Lucy
    Brown, and the cruel giant was gone.
But Miss Miller had never got around to
    reading the story of Lucy Brown.
Paulette had watched her with the exercise
    book, watched her as she put it back down
On the desk again, as she sighed and asked
    out loud how she could possibly be
    expected
To mark a piece of work like this when its
    author had so obviously neglected
The basic rules of grammar, spelling and the
    need for clear handwriting;
Miss Miller held up the exercise book and
    said it looked like spiders had been
    fighting
All over the pages after dipping their feet in
    ink! The kids in the class had all laughed.
And Sarah Pugh had said that everybody
    knew that Paulette Patterson was daft!
Smiling through the scalding shame and
    shrugging at the spikes of embarrassment
Paulette picked up her exercise book. And
    that night when she got home, she went
Straight to her room and ripped the shameful
    pages from the book, the stupid story of
    Lucy Brown.
And finding the hole in the skirting board, she
    stuffed the scribbled pages down
Amongst the scrunched-up sheets of old
    newspaper that were meant to keep out the
    draught;
And tried to forget the shame and disgrace. To
    forget how everybody had laughed
As Miss Miller had betrayed her and held up
    the book; said it looked like spiders had
    been fighting;
And had never even noticed it was Paulette's

first try to write a story in joined-up
writing.

Paulette tried to forget! And what she couldn't
forget she pretended had never taken place.
Although something that couldn't be
pretended away were the pages stuffed in
the space
Behind the skirting boards and the danger that
they might be discovered
And read by her father. And Paulette knew
what would happen if he uncovered
The story and perhaps read a bit more closely
than Miss Miller had bothered to do;
Her father, seeing through the scrawly writing,
the thin disguise and realising who
The story was truly about. Her father who'd
told her never to talk about their special
game.
Because if she did, bad things would happen.
And she'd only have herself to blame.
He'd smile at her when he told her that. But
Paulette saw the threat behind the smile,
Heard the note of warning in the whispered
words; and thought about the pile
Of pages still stuffed behind the skirting
board, pages that swelled and multiplied
At night when she was in bed, in the dark.
And then when the wind outside
Began to stir, she'd hear the hideous chorus
start up, behind the alabaster;
The hidden pages rustling and scratching at
the wood and plaster,
The scrawly words coming to life, letters
sprouting spidery legs until a teeming
Army of ugly, inky insect words began
pouring off the pages, streaming
Up and down, this way and that behind the
wall, itching, scratching, the frenzied horde

Feverishly scrabbling till they found the gap
    and began to spill over the skirting board,
The torrent of misformed alphabetical bugs
    scattering out and over the floor,
The tittle-tattle, tell-tale words scurrying
    across the carpet and under the door,
Swarming down and through the house to
    spread the word of deceit and defiance;
And how Paulette Patterson had betrayed her
    father with tales of cruel giants.

Time after time she'd intended retrieving
    those sheets of paper,
To pull them back out from the skirting board
    and hide them somewhere safer.
Or better still, rip them into pieces and throw
    them down the grid,
Flush them down the toilet, bury them, burn
    them, get rid
Of the ruinous writing; but now she knew
    she'd left it too late.
And he'd warned her; warned her so many
    times how he wouldn't hesitate
To do what would have to be done if the
    meddlers and the snoopers got to know
Just how much he loved his little daughter.
    And it wouldn't be his fault. No,
Because he'd warned her! How many times
    had he said, daddy's love must be kept
A secret, just between the two of them. And
    he thought she was such a good girl!
    Except,
Look what she'd done now! With her
    sneakiness and slyness, cunning and
    invention,
Boiling the pot and meddling with what she'd
    been told she must never dare mention.
He'd warned her! Oh he'd warned her. And
    he'd believed that she'd understood;

When all the time she'd just been pretending,
    planning to deceive her own flesh and
    blood
With a fairy tale for the teacher; spidery
    letters, coded, crippled words betraying
Him to the interferers; the snoopers, meddlers.
    Oh they'd all start baying
For his blood now. The fools who'd be falling
    over themselves to damn and to brand him
A monster: all the godly, the good, the
    interfering who'd never understand him!
And he'd warned her, so many times, of what
    would happen if she ever dropped
Even the merest hint of how much her daddy
    loved her. Hadn't she stopped
And considered the consequences? The times
    she must have heard him say
There was nobody, nobody on this earth who
    could take her daddy away!
Nobody. Apart from himself! Had she thought
    it was some sort of joke
When he told her what he'd have to do if
    anyone found out? When he spoke
Of how nothing could ever separate them;
    when he made his solemn promise
Of what he'd do if the snoopers ever knew
    and tried to take him from his
Daughter: that they'd find he was beyond
    them now, where a daddy's love couldn't be
    defiled,
Where death had beaten them to it; uniting for
    ever and ever the father and the child.

Blind to all but the demons that danced inside
    her head, she went
Hurtling along the towpath, a hunted animal,
    nostrils thick with the scent
Of her own fear, ears deaf to all but the heavy
    thudding

Feet that beat upon the path behind her.
    Terror flooding
Her imagination, she ran without knowing
    that her only pursuer
Was nothing but the ghost of all that had
    happened to her;
The jagged fingernails scratching at her skin
    nothing more
Than the snagging of bramble branches as she
    frantically tore
Past the hedgerows; the incessant beat of the
    feet she heard,
Just the pounding of her own frightened heart
    as she hared
Along the path, under the bridge and out
    where rusted coal shutes and long-derelict
Grain hoppers sagged, propped up like weary
    old men against the solid soot-bricked
Wharfside walls where suddenly she saw her
    chance of sanctuary:
Leaving the towpath she clambered,
    scrambling over neglected machinery,
Stumbling over lumps of stone and shards of
    shattered roofing slate,
Trying to reach her refuge and hide herself
    before it was too late
And he emerged from under the bridge, able
    to see her again before she'd had chance
To reach the abandoned buildings. As she ran,
    she risked a quick glance
Behind her, seeing nothing but hearing still
    the relentless rumbling
Beat of feet against the earth; the beat beat
    beat, sending her stumbling
On, over the pock-marked cobbles of the
    disused wharf,
And across the derelict builders' yard, racing
    past the half
Built hulls of rotting barges, running for her

170

life until she reached
The gaping hole where the boundary wall had
    been breached.
Scrambling through the gap, she thought she'd
    be safe on the other side.
Thought that everything would be all right
    and that she could just hide
Behind the wall. But it wasn't all right!
    Glancing back there was nothing to see,
No-one running down the towpath, nobody
    coming under the bridge. Nobody!
Nobody's feet on the pock-marked cobbles,
    nobody running across the builders' yard,
Nobody treading across the wharfside, not a
    single soul to be seen in the scarred
And lifeless wasteland; no track or trace of
    her tormentor;
Just the sound! The stubborn, ceaseless,
    thudding sound that sent a
Wave of panic coursing through her veins; the
    numbing beat, beat of drumming
Dogged feet, sending out the message that
    still, he was coming!
The warehouse towered above her, vast
    cathedral walls blocking the sun,
Doors and windows battened, boarded up
    with sheets of corrugated iron,
Each sheet pasted with a message that warned
    of the consequences
For those who chose to disregard the
    'DANGER – KEEP OUT' notices.
But Paulette Patterson didn't stop to read and
    heed the warning signs,
The threat of possible prosecution and the
    maximum level of fines.
She was in enough danger as it was, to care
    about risks that awaited
Those who ignored the warning signs and
    went beyond the corrugated

Sheeting and ventured inside the building.
   Paulette found the loading bay
Where the rusting metal cover had been
   pulled and partly prised away
From the wall. Squeezing through the narrow
   gap, she faltered, hesitating,
Suddenly afraid of the deep black darkness
   that loomed beyond the grating.
But as she paused, she heard it again, coming
   closer, the dull thudding sound!
Hesitating no more, Paulette dropped and
   lying flat on the ground
She writhed and wriggled beneath the grating,
   stifling her fear of the dark within
As she pushed past the rusted iron doors,
   edging deeper into the darkness, the thin
Shaft of light from the entrance quickly fading
   as she crept forward, a careful hand placed
Against the dusty wall, fingertips guiding her
   in the blackness as blindly she traced
Her faltering way, floorboards creaking,
   whining, crying out beneath her tread
As if in complaint, the groaning wood, dry-
   boned, too tired and foul-tempered
To bear the bothersome step, the tiresome
   weight of the intruder; the rotten pock-
   marked timbers straining
To bear the burden as Paulette stood, leaning
   against the wall now, regaining
Her breath; the throbbing thud of feet behind
   her finally beginning to slow, to fade and
   disappear.
Safe now, safe in the pitch black cloak of
   darkness, the beating feet all gone; nothing
   more to fear;
Only the dark, as she waited; counting to a
   hundred, two hundred, three hundred,
   four;
Then those same hundreds counted again,

counted backwards, counted and recounted
   until she was sure
That she'd escaped him; that by now he'd
   have gone, given up, given in, forced to
   postpone
His plans. And now, now that she was no
   longer so afraid, now that the terror had
   gone,
Paulette told herself that perhaps, by the time
   she got back home, he might be himself
   again,
Might have turned back into her ordinary
   daddy, her proper daddy. And then perhaps
   she could still explain
Everything so that her mam would understand
   it wasn't Paulette's fault, losing her
   knickers like she had;
It wasn't her fault at all, because it was the
   butterfly. And the missing sandal? She
   hadn't been doing anything bad
At the allotments; it was the man's fault, the
   man who'd chased her, that horrible Man
   from the Hut.
And so really it was his fault, Paulette losing
   her sandal; because he'd grabbed hold of
   her foot,
Pulling at her in the spiky hedge; and *that's*
   why the buttons were missing, that's why
   her dress was ripped;
And that's why her knees were scratched and
   bleeding, from where she'd stumbled and
   slipped
As she was running away. So none of it was
   her fault, not really; and if she could just
   explain it to her mother,
Just like she could explain it now, in her
   head, then maybe she wouldn't be in any
   bother.
And maybe her mam and her dad had even

been worried out of their minds, wondering
  where she'd gone,
So that when she did get back, her mam might
  cry and say she loved her and promise that
  from now on
Everything would be different; so that instead
  of being slapped and called stupid and told
  she was a walking disgrace,
Her mother would hug her and hold and tell
  her there was no-one who would ever take
  the place
Of her precious little Paulette. And her mam
  would wipe all her tears away then and tell
  her not to be afraid;
Because from now on, her mam would always
  be there to love and look after her and
  make sure she stayed
Safe and sound. Then Paulette's mam would
  whisper that of all the girls in all of the
  world
There was none so bright and clever; and
  none so loved and cherished as Paulette,
  her treasure of a girl.

And perhaps Paulette believed her
  concoction, of the mother as a mother who
  cared;
And her father, a father whose love she could
  trust, one who gave her no cause to be
  scared
Of him. Perhaps she believed it; or just
  needed to believe something better than
  reality
As she started to retrace her steps in the
  darkness, holding onto the wall, holding
  onto her fantasy
Of the joyful reunion; of her mam and dad
  both thrilled to see her safely returned.
Impatient now to be back outside in the sun,

running home, Paulette stopped and turned
Away from the wall that had been her guide,
   choosing instead to strike out across the
   warehouse floor
Towards the sliver of light from the entrance.
   But Paulette never made it to the door.
In the blackness, Paulette couldn't possibly
   have seen the void; the gutted
Timbers; spars collapsed, fallen or flung into
   the vault below; joists jutted
Out, fractured floorboards splintered into
   emptiness, a yawning hollow
Hidden in the dark; a ravenous gaping mouth,
   insatiable, ready to swallow
And suck down into its bottomless black belly,
   those who deserved everything they got
For straying so far from home; straying and
   meddling where they should not.
Paulette Patterson lifted her foot, eyes fixed
   on the shard of light from the door
As she stepped forward. But where her step
   should have met the wooden floor
There was nowhere for a foot to fall; nothing
   but the space, into which she lunged,
Toppling from her feet, arms flailing, fingers
   grasping, snatching at the air as she
   plunged
Tumbling into the void, plummeting down
   through the lift-shaft; and thudding to a
   halt,
Amid the stinking raft of scrap and rubbish
   that lined the black belly of the brick vault.

She tried at first to find a way out. But in her
   terrified heart she knew she was trapped,
   entombed
In this shaft, where the only chance of escape
   was to scale the sheer walls that loomed
Above her. She tried at first; clawing at the

brick, scrambling to find a crevice or crack
Where tips of fingers could grip, a foot could
    fit; and she could begin to push and heave
    her way back
Out of this dark stinking tomb. She tried,
    again and again; feet slipping, sliding,
    fingers scraping;
And all her frantic effort mocked by the voice
    in her head that said this time there would
    be no escaping.

Outside, in the stillness of the early evening
    sun, any passer-by would have heard the
    calls,
The shouts, the whimpered cries for help from
    deep within the disused warehouse walls.
But that evening, no dog was walked, no
    lovers strolled, no bicycle boys came
    thereabouts,
No vandals, vagrants, stickleback hunters,
    mischief-seekers, no-one to hear the shouts
Of the child drifting up from the bowels of the
    building. Nobody came and nobody heard
The wasted cries, left hanging limp and feeble
    in the sultry air where nothing but the
    gnats stirred:
And the butterfly! The single crimson
    butterfly clinging to the face of the baked
    brick wall,
Where it basked in the sun, in its own brief
    glory, unaware, undisturbed, untouched by
    the call
Of the child, growing slowly weaker, fainter;
    fading till it was barely more than a
    bleating cry;
Than the beat of a wing in the air that bore the
    soaring crimson butterfly.

                                        RJM

176

The Pulse and Husk
Wholefood Cantina,
Rennet Street,
Huddersfield

Dear Morrissey,

They cancelled the coach! When it came on the tannoy
and they said that due to unforeseen circumstances the
three o'clock service to Grimsby had been cancelled, I
couldn't help feeling a massive, if momentary, surge of
relief. All the other passengers started groaning and
shaking their heads but I just sat there hoping that this
was the news I'd been waiting for and that Grimsby
had had to be sealed off from the outside world
because of blue asbestos or an outbreak of foot and
mouth; or even severe earth tremors or civil unrest and
cod riots or the invasion of the sodding body-
snatchers. I didn't care what it was as long as it was
something that meant I could just turn round and go
home to Failsworth without upsetting my Mam.

But the announcement just said the cancellation was
due to mechanical problems with the incoming
vehicle. And we'd have to wait for the five o'clock
service instead. They said they were issuing vouchers
so the delayed passengers could avail themselves of a
selection of sandwiches in the bus station cafeteria.

But as all the selected sandwiches were of a notably non-vegetarian variety, and some of them were positively cannibalistic, containing things like brisket and brawn and tongue, I gave my vouchers to this elderly couple in the queue.

'Don't you want them?' the man said to me.

'No,' I said, 'they're no good to me. I'm a vegetarian.'

His wife looked at me then, cocked her head all sympathetically and said, 'Agh,' as if I'd just informed her I only had three weeks left to live.

I went for a walk round. Even after paying for my coach ticket, I still had £1.65 left. So I saw this place and I came in here. I don't know about you, Morrissey, but despite my avowed vegetarian status I always find the atmosphere in wholefood cafés to be somewhat intimidating. They seem to attract the sort of vegetarians who give vegetarianism a bad name, all sat around looking ill, avoiding salt and getting wound up about E numbers and CFCs. And for such caring people they all seem so hostile. Even the food seems to have some kind of passive hostility to it. I ordered a homity pie. But it was all attitude and no flavour. I took it back and told him the potatoes were hard. He looked at me like he was too bored to breathe.

He said, '*Al dente*, not hard!'

'And what about the carrots?' I said.

'*Al dente*,' he said.

I just looked at him. 'And the pastry!' I said. 'It's like concrete. Or is that just *al dente* an' all?'

He said, 'It's organic stoneground flour, what d' y' expect?'

I said, 'Well, I expect to be able to eat it without losing all my fillings in the process.'

He affected a nonchalant shrug but it lacked conviction and tailed off in the middle as if even mere nonchalance was too taxing on his available energy. Then he just reached out for the concrete crusted pie, swapped it for another and said I should count myself lucky I wasn't in the Third World where a family of ten could live for a month on nothing but a few lentils and two cups of flour.

I said, 'What's their name?'

He frowned and he said, 'Who?'

I said, 'The family. Who live on nowt but the lentils and the two cups of flour.'

But he didn't know! And they never do know, the food fascists like him and all the designer Buddhists and the recreationally compassionate, always talking about *People from the Third World* as if they didn't have names. And I just hoped for their sake that some of those nameless Third World persons never had the misfortune of turning up in Huddersfield and asking for a homity pie. They'd probably end up rushing back to the Third World and organising relief supplies of flour and lentils to alleviate the suffering in West Yorkshire!

I just left it sitting on the table, the homity pie. And if it did nothing else it gave me the excuse to sit here out of the rain and write this to you, Morrissey. Because, you see, the thing is, Morrissey, I wanted to tell you about Dr Janice. Dr Janice knew I wasn't mad or bad and she was just dead nice to me. Not like the no-nonsense nurse who woke me up. I didn't like her at all. She told me I was a brat!

She said I'd been trying to drown myself. But that was just ridiculous! I hadn't been trying to drown myself at all and the only thing I had been doing was trying to bring the nice boy back again. She just ignored me though. And as she stuck the thermometer in my mouth she said, 'I've got a good mind to stick it somewhere else!'

She stood there, the not-nice nurse, giving me a sour look as she waited for the thermometer. And then she told me I should be ashamed of myself.

She said, 'I shouldn't have to be doing this! Wasting my time on a selfish little boy like you when there's proper sick children, genuinely sick children who'd be grateful for this bed. Children who need looking after through no fault of their own! Children needing trans-plants, children with leaking valves in their hearts, poor little mites with brittle bones and all sorts of things wrong with them. That's who I should be seeing to. Properly poorly children, not horrible healthy little brats like you who throw themselves into the canal just to get a bit of attention for themselves! And end up wasting my time, everybody else's time, denying a bed to a poor little soul who really needs it!'

She snatched the thermometer out of my mouth and I tried to explain to her again, about the Wrong Boy.

But she just looked at me like I was soft. Then she said she had no more time to waste on me and she had to see to the boy from Blackburn who had a new kidney and septic tonsillitis.

'That's what I call sick,' she said, the no-nonsense nurse. 'That's what I call properly poorly!'

She disappeared then. And I just had to lie there, waiting for my Mam and feeling really awful because everybody thought I'd been trying to kill myself when all I had been doing was trying to bring the nice boy back. But they didn't believe me and my Mam prob-ably wouldn't believe me now. And it'd all be even worse than it was before. I didn't know what to do any more.

And then this nurse was sitting there, on my bed. I think I must have been asleep. She was smiling at me and even though her eyes looked really tired, they were sparkling and looked lovely with her blond hair. She wasn't like the other nurse, the no-nonsense nurse. And she didn't wear a uniform like the other nurses; she had a white coat and a badge with her name on; Janice, she was called. She was asking me about my favourite things and what I liked to play with and all that. And I started telling her about *Star Wars* and my comic collections and the books I liked to read.

She asked me if I preferred *Marvel* comics or *DC* comics. I couldn't believe that! I don't think I'd ever met an adult person who knew about such things. She saw the look of surprise on my face and she laughed. She told me she'd been a collector herself when she was a girl. She even told me she'd still got her comic collection.

'Somewhere,' she said, 'in some attic or other. I'll have to get them all out again one day and have a look at them.' And she suddenly looked weary for a second then and said, 'If I ever manage to get a day off.'

But then she sort of shook her head and smiled at me again as she said, 'And football? A lad like you,' she said, 'I'll bet you love your football, don't y'.'

I told Janice that I did like football. 'But I don't play it any more,' I said.

Janice looked surprised, 'And why not?' she asked.

And I explained to her then, I said, 'I used to like playing football, when I was the nice boy. I liked playing football and being in the Cubs and swapping comics with my best friend, Geoffrey Weatherby. But he won't be my friend any more and they won't play football with me, my friends.'

I nodded and Janice was looking at me, all concerned. 'Well, why's that, Raymond?' she said. '*Why* won't they play with you?'

I just shrugged and I said, 'Because they all know, my friends, they all know that I'm not the nice boy any more. I'm the Wrong Boy now and they all know that. And that's why they won't play with me.'

She frowned then, Janice, and she said, 'Horrible little buggers.'

It made me laugh that, hearing a nurse swear. Janice laughed too. 'Well, they are!' she said. 'Not letting you play with them.'

'I know that,' I said, 'but it's not really their fault, you see. It's my fault. Because if I was the nice boy and I wasn't fat they would still play with me. But they know, you see, they know that I'm not really Raymond.'

Janice raised her eyebrows then.

181

'Well, I *am* Raymond,' I said, 'but I'm the bad Raymond. And the good Raymond's still in the canal.'

Janice looked at me for a minute then and she was smiling at me.

'And is that why you jumped in there last night?' she said. 'Is that the reason you jumped into the canal?'

I nodded and I said, 'Yes. That's right.'

She looked at me all sort of thoughtfully then, Janice. And she said, 'Well . . . you do know, don't you . . . that a number of people, including your mum . . . they think that what you were really trying to do last night was . . . commit suicide.'

I shook my head at Janice then. And I told her, 'I wasn't! I wasn't doing that at all. All I was trying to do was make it so that the nice boy could come back. I promise, nurse,' I said.

That's when Janice said to me, 'I'm a doctor, Raymond. Not a nurse.'

'Oh,' I said, 'I'm sorry. I didn't know that.'

'It's all right,' Janice said, 'you don't have to be sorry.'

I just shrugged. And then Janice said, 'You don't like to upset people, do you, Raymond?'

I didn't know what she meant.

'Like your mum,' she said. 'You don't like upsetting your mum, do you?'

I shook my head, because Janice was right. I said, 'No, I don't like upsetting my Mam. My Uncle Jason, he upsets her all the time,' I said, 'but I don't like upsetting her. And when I was the nice boy I never ever used to upset her.'

'Did you upset her yesterday?' Janice asked.

I nodded. 'I keep upsetting her all the time now,' I said, 'now that I'm the Wrong Boy. I just can't seem to stop upsetting her and she doesn't know what to do with me any more.'

'And is that the reason?' Janice said. 'Is that the reason you tried to do away with yourself last night?'

I shook my head again. 'I didn't!' I said. 'I told y' that. I wasn't trying to do away with myself at all.'

Janice just sat there for a minute, looking at me very closely. And then she said, 'No. I don't think you were, Raymond.'

And I was dead glad when Janice said that because I didn't want her thinking I was telling lies.

'Because if you'd been trying to do away with yourself,' she said, 'you could have picked *any* part of the canal, couldn't you? You could have picked the stretch of canal nearest your house, couldn't you?'

She looked at me. I didn't really know what she meant but I just nodded. And then Janice said, 'But the spot where you jumped in last night was a very particular spot, wasn't it?'

I nodded again and Janice said, 'Not too far from the school.' She just sat there looking at me. Then she said, 'And it had to be that particular place, didn't it? Where you jumped in?'

I nodded once more and Janice said, 'Because something had happened to you before, in that same place, hadn't it?'

I looked at her. And I was frowning and I said, 'You've been talking to my Mam, haven't y'?'

But Janice shook her head. 'No. I am going to have a talk with your mum later on,' she said. 'But up to now I haven't spoken so much as a word to your mum, Raymond.'

And I knew that she was telling the truth, Janice. But I couldn't work out how she knew about it, the 'something that happened to me before'.

She reached across and patted me on the arm and said, 'It's all right. You don't *have* to tell me about it.'

But I wanted to tell Janice because she was nice and I liked her. And I said, 'It had to be that particular part of the canal because that was the place where he got lost. That was where he disappeared.'

Janice sat there looking at me for a moment. Then she said, 'The nice boy?'

I nodded. And Janice said, 'That's where he fell in the canal, the nice boy?'

I shook my head. 'No, he didn't *fall* in,' I said. 'He dived in. Because Albert Goldberg was drowning and Albert would have died if the nice boy hadn't dived in and rescued him.'

Janice nodded then. 'Oh, I see,' she said. 'And what were they doing at the time, the nice boy and Albert . . . what's-his-name?'

I just looked at Janice. And then I looked down at the bedclothes. And Janice sort of laughed and said, 'My God, that's such a big sigh for such a small lad!'

I kept on looking down at the bedclothes and I said, 'It wasn't just them two who were down there, Albert and the nice boy. They were all there, everybody; Darren Duckworth and Kevin Cowley and even Geoffrey Weatherby and he pretends now that it was nothing to do with him and he calls me "Fatso" and he won't play with me no more. But he was doing it as well! They were all doing it, not just me. And I never *made* anybody do it.'

'Do what?' Janice asked.

'The flytrapping!' I said. 'Everybody was in on it. I know that I invented it but that was just by accident and everybody *wanted* to do it after that. I never *made* anybody join in with the flytrapping!'

Janice was looking at me with a puzzled sort of look on her face. 'Flytrapping?' she said. 'What the hell's flytrapping?'

I just shook my head then and kept my lips together and didn't say anything else.

Janice leaned her head down and she whispered to me, 'Is it something really, really, really bad, flytrapping?'

I nodded my head. 'It wasn't,' I said, 'but it is now.'

Janice sat back up again.

'And you're not going to tell me about it?' she said. She looked all upset. 'I thought you and me were mates,' she said. 'I thought we were friends.'

I didn't want her to be upset. And I even wanted to tell her about it all. Because she was nice, Janice, and

184

she was kind and I thought she might even understand. But I couldn't do it, I couldn't tell her about that. So in the end I shook my head and said, 'I can't!'

She patted my arm again then and just kept on stroking it. 'Hey! It's all right,' she said. 'We're still friends, even if you can't tell me about it. I understand,' she said, 'because I'm an adult, a grown-up person and a nice boy couldn't possibly talk about a thing like that to a grown-up, could he?'

I just shrugged. And then Janice said, 'But you're not the nice boy any more, are you, Raymond?'

I shook my head and she said, 'You're the Wrong Boy now. And so it wouldn't matter, would it? Because the Nice Boy wouldn't have anything to do with it, would he? It wouldn't matter how bad it was. Because it would be the Wrong Boy who was saying it.'

And that's when I knew that I was going to tell Janice all about it. And I didn't care about it being bad because I just wanted to tell somebody about it, just once. And I stared down at the bedclothes and started twisting the sheet in my fingers as I began telling her about the flies and having our dicks out and me catching a fly on the end of it and then the fly dropping off dead and then everybody doing it then and it all becoming a big competition. But as I told it to Janice I couldn't look up at her because the more I told her, the more I started to see that it did sound like something really, really bad. And I wished I hadn't even started telling Janice because she probably wouldn't even come and talk to me again now that she knew.

And then I heard it. The laughter!

And I looked up and Janice was leaning back on the bed with her hand up to her mouth and tears streaming down her eyes as she tried to stop herself laughing. And I thought she was being awful laughing so I just sat there frowning which seemed to make her laugh even more! Janice kept trying to say she was sorry but every time she did, she just started laughing again and then she was bent over and screaming so much with laughter that I couldn't help it and even though there was nothing funny I felt myself starting to grin. And we looked at each other, me and Janice, and I started laughing then. And I couldn't stop and the both of us were howling and screaming with laughter and the not-nice nurse who was passing asked what we were laughing at and that made it even worse and we couldn't stop and when we looked at each other it would just start the other one off again. And what made it all the more funny for me was that I didn't even know why I was laughing. Because it was terrible, laughing about something so serious that it had got me suspended from school and slung out of the Cubs and made all my friends ignore me now. But every time I tried to stop laughing it made me laugh even more. And Janice ended up lying across the foot of the bed and clutching onto her sides as she tried to get her breath back. And I said, 'I don't know why you're laughing, because it's not even funny at all!'

But Janice just lay there, groaning now and panting for breath as she said, 'Oh God! Oh God . . . I know . . . I know it's not . . . Ogh . . . !' And she was panting for breath and wiping at her eyes as she said things like, 'Dear God. Flytrapping! Oh my God. Flytrapping!'

And when Janice sat up again on the bed she just looked at me with a big smile on her face as she said, 'Raymond, how in the name of sweet Jesus did something so good get turned into something so bad?'

And then Janice shook her head and sighed and said, 'I don't know!'

And I didn't know, not then, not when it was all happening to me. So I just sat there. And I shrugged. Then Janice reached out and took hold of my hand and sort of whispered, 'Do you know something? Just between you and me . . . I don't think you're the Wrong Boy at all.'

She sighed then, Janice, and she said, 'I think that what you are, though, Raymond, is a very very fed-up little boy.'

186

Janice nodded at me. And I looked at her. And even though I was trying dead hard not to, I felt my face starting to crumple up and I was crying and telling Janice about how I'd got suspended from school and my Mam had been summoned from work and had to go to the headmaster's office. And I told Janice about Sonia and upsetting my Mam again and making her put up with all sorts of things so that she didn't love me any more and took me to see Psycho The Rapist. And in the end Janice just put her arms around me and told me it was all right and everything would be all right. That's what she kept saying to me, 'It's all right, Raymond. Don't worry, everything will be all right.'

And I started nodding and managed to stop crying because it was funny but when Janice said that, about it being all right, I believed her. Janice made me believe that somehow, in the end, it would all be all right.

She handed me a tissue. And she smiled at me and said, 'Would you like to go home?'

I nodded and Janice said, 'Well, I think we can arrange that. I've just got to talk to your mum for a while. All right?'

'Is my Mam still upset with me,' I said, 'because of what I did last night?'

'Well, she's bound to be upset, isn't she?' Janice said.

'Will you tell her?' I asked. 'Because I know that my Mam would believe you. Will you tell her that I wasn't trying to . . .'

Janice smiled at me as she got up off the bed. 'Yes,' she said, 'I'll tell your mum.'

She winked at me then, Janice. And I watched her as she walked down the ward.

And when she got to the end, she turned, and she waved to me.

Later on, my Mam told me how it was Dr Janice who'd made her start to see some sense. My Mam said she'd been out of her wits with all the worry. But it was Dr Janice who made her see that it was all the worrying that was doing her no good and doing me no good neither. And Dr Janice told my Mam that what she had to do was stop sticking together things that didn't fit together; things like the dread about my Dad being a bit mad. Dr Janice said that what my Mam was doing was sticking something like that onto something like what I'd done down at the canal.

'But such things don't belong together,' Dr Janice told my Mam.

My Mam said that Dr Janice got angry and even started swearing. She wasn't angry at my Mam. But when she mentioned the flytrapping, Dr Janice said, 'And what was it, Shelagh? In truth, what was it? Just a few lads playing with their plonkers and dreaming up a bit of disgusting business with a few flies. That's all it was. It was nothing, until an appallingly pathetic jerk of a headmaster got hold of it and managed to turn a splendidly ingenious if, admittedly, mildly mucky canalside game into an act of scandalous filth and obscenity.'

Janice nodded at my Mam. And Dr Janice's voice was really angry then as she told my Mam, 'But that's all just fucking bollocks, Shelagh!'

My Mam said she just sat there with her jaw dropped open. She'd never even heard a doctor say 'bloody' before, let alone 'bollocks' and the 'f' word.

'Total bollocks!' Janice said again. 'Just some fucked-up headmaster who might have been a damn sight better if he'd once waved his own dick around and caught a fly or two!'

My Mam said she was just sat there blushing all colours. But Dr Janice didn't seem to care. And she told my Mam, 'But you don't question that headmaster, do you, Shelagh? No!' she said, with the anger still in her voice. 'Because you have been living in dread! You've been waiting for exactly this kind of abomination. Because you've been walking round for years with the idea that Raymond's father was some kind of mental case. And all that time you've been waiting . . . waiting for some sign that Raymond himself might turn out to be . . . not quite all there. And when, finally, he gets into a bit of bother with this flytrapping business, it's almost some kind of relief to you because here at last is the confirmation of the dread you've been carrying around for all those years. It doesn't fit, of course. It doesn't fit remotely. But that doesn't matter to you, Shelagh, because you've got the fear and the sticky glue of fear can make anything fit together. So you take the flycatching' – Janice was holding up her hand as if there was something in it and my Mam sat there staring at the fist full of filthy goings-on – 'and what do you do with this flycatching business, Shelagh?' Janice lifted up her other hand and told my Mam, 'You put it with this. You put it where it doesn't belong, mashing and mixing it all up with the family fear, where it doesn't belong, with your ex-husband's eccentricity, where it doesn't belong! And the next thing is, Shelagh, you're sticking all kinds of things together. Your son comes out with a bit of smut in front of his cousin. It's nothing. What's that, kids and a bit of smut? When was it ever any different? But you don't see that, Shelagh. No, what you see is more of the same. You see a lad who suddenly needs to be taken to see a psycho-therapist. You see dirtiness and badness and you see a son who's shaping up to turn out much more seriously doolally than his dad ever was! And when he ends up back at that canal, you see a son who was intending to kill himself.'

They stared at each other, my Mam and Janice. My Mam sat there looking slightly bewildered and Dr Janice breathing heavily and staring at my Mam.

Until, very quietly, my Mam asked her, 'Wasn't he? Wasn't he trying to . . . do away with himself?'

Dr Janice shook her head. 'No,' she said, 'not in my opinion.'

My Mam said that that's when she started crying, with all the relief that flooded through her.

'It was an extremely dangerous thing that he did,' Dr

Janice said, 'and the end result could easily have been ... But if we're talking about intention, no. I don't think for a second that Raymond had any intention of trying to kill himself. In his own way it was a sort of ... rational thing, trying to find his way to being nice again.'

My Mam sighed and dabbed at her eyes with her hankie. And then she asked Dr Janice, 'Will he ever do something like that again?'

Dr Janice looked at my Mam and she said, 'Shelagh, I'm a psychiatrist, not a prophet.'

My Mam just nodded. And then Janice said, 'But ... well, as a psychiatrist, I shouldn't even be talking like this ... But, no, I don't think he will do it again. If ... if you can help him get it into his head that you're not ... blaming him any longer, then no. With a bit of luck I think you'll both be able to put all this behind you.'

'And all that weird stuff he was coming out with last night,' my Mam said, 'saying he wasn't really my son ... and he was the wrong boy ...'

Janice smiled then as she got to her feet and started leading my Mam out of the office and into the corridor. And as they walked along, Dr Janice said to my Mam, 'You know all those comics he's always got his nose stuck into, you know his *Marvel* comics, have you ever looked at them?'

My Mam shook her head.

'Well, you should take a look at one or two,' Janice said. 'Dual characters, they're full of that sort of stuff; characters who mutate, characters who become inhabited by different personalities, characters who have twin forces within them, the good and the bad. I'm not saying he's deliberately taken something from such a comic. But with the kind of imagination Raymond's got, it's not too difficult to see how he could have come up with a concept like the Wrong Boy.'

Janice put her arm around my Mam then and she said, 'Just take him home. Go on. Go and get him and take him home. And try to remember what we were saying, Shelagh, about sticking together things that don't belong.'

My Mam nodded. They'd got to the end of the corridor. My Mam said, 'It's all my fault this, isn't it? It's me that's caused all this.'

But Janice shook her head and told my Mam, 'Fault doesn't come into it, Shelagh. It's not your—'

'No, listen,' my Mam interrupted her. She nodded her head and said, 'You're right. What you told me before . . . about always having this . . . dread. You're right. I'm afraid. I've always been afraid. And being afraid is what's caused a lot of this, isn't it?'

Janice just shrugged. And my Mam said, 'Well, I'm promising you here and now, doctor. You've got my word that from now on, I'm going to do my best not to be afraid, because you're right and I'm grateful and I can see that I've been stupid about all sorts of things.'

My Mam said, later, that it was funny but as she watched Janice walking away down that hospital corridor she wanted to run after her and stay with her and keep Janice with her all the time. Because, my Mam said, there was something about Janice that made my Mam feel safe.

But my Mam knew it was a stupid thing, wanting to stop a person, a doctor person you didn't even really know, just so that you could still have that person near you.

So instead my Mam just stood there for a second and repeated the solemn promise she'd made to herself; the promise that she'd do what Janice had told her to do, and that from now on she was going to try not to be afraid and not to be worried and not to let all the things get glued together and made into something that lay heavy in the pit of her belly.

And when I turned around in my bed I thought it was one of the nurses come to see me. But it was my Mam. And she was carrying my clothes and smiling and looking at me like she loved me again.

And she said, 'Come on, son. We're going home.'

And that day, when we walked out of the hospital, it felt like it was a new beginning. My Mam told me that she understood everything now and that that head-master had been a bastard the way he'd put all the blame on me.

'And all those mothers and all those bloody kids of theirs,' my Mam said, 'all of them, treating me and you like dirt! And it wasn't even nowt worth talking about in the first place, the doctor said, Dr Janice. And if a young doctor like that can say it was just a bit of kids' malarkey, that's good enough for me. So they can all sod off, the Mrs Weatherbys and the Bradwicks and the bloody Donna Duckworths.'

My Mam linked her arm through mine then and pulled me close to her. 'Sod them, love,' she said. 'Sod them all. Me and you, we'll be all right, won't we?'

I looked up at my Mam and I nodded my head because I knew everything would be all right now because my Mam understood and she was my proper Mam again because she wasn't looking at me like I was a wrong boy any more.

I can remember exactly the way the sun was slanting through the trees that day when we walked down the hospital drive, and the shards of bright yellow that cut through the gaps in the avenue of trees were like shafts of light that shined down from heaven. I didn't really believe in heaven, not like it was in the Bible and RE lessons and assembly. But my Gran always said there *was* a kind of heaven and it was here on earth, even though that was sometimes difficult to imagine when you had to take account of the appalling fact of things like the Arndale Centre and organised religion and Rolf Harris.

'But if you're alert to it,' my Gran said, 'and all your vision doesn't get used up and wasted on the not-worth-botherin'-with, and doesn't get wearied and worn out by the capacity for cruelty that's in each and every one of us, if y' can keep y'self open to it, you'll find that there *is* a kind of heaven, Raymond; if you are alert to it and you're lucky enough, you might even be rewarded by the tiniest fleeting glimpse of it one day.'

And I did see it; I saw a kind of heaven, that day when I was with my Mam and we walked together through all the halos of the sycamore trees. And I think that my Mam must have seen it too; because as we got to the end of the hospital drive, I looked up at my Mam's face and she was smiling, as if her soul was all filled up with serenity. And I knew that the tears spilling down from her eyes were nothing to do with sadness or worry, but just some of all that serenity spilling out from her. She laughed when she saw me looking at her. And I laughed and all. Then she stopped and took out a hanky and said to me, 'Listen! How are you feeling?'

I told my Mam I was feeling all right.

'You're not too tired,' she said, 'or worn out with what's happened?'

I shook my head and my Mam linked her arm through mine again. 'Right then,' she said, 'come on! We're not going home yet! We'll go to town,' she said, sounding dead excited. 'Come on, we'll go to Pizza Pacino's and have the biggest pizza in the place, with twenty-five toppings if we want. And then we'll go to the pictures. And after that we'll go . . . we'll go . . . ten-pin bowling! And we'll have chantilly milk shakes and gooey doughnuts and splash out on a taxi ride home. Let's go,' she said. 'Me and you, we're giving ourselves a treat.'

It was lovely, the day out I had with my Mam. And the best part of it wasn't the pizza or the ten-pin bowling or even going to the pictures. Because the best part was just seeing my Mam being so happy. We stopped off at Urdu's so that she could have her hair done. And as we were heading up King Street towards Pizza Pacino's my Mam stopped for a second and glanced at a frock in a boutique window.

And I said, 'Why don't you go in an' buy it, Mam?'

But my Mam laughed and said, 'Listen to you!'

And she said women of her age didn't go buying dresses in boutiques full of deafening disco music and slips of girls as slender as summer. She said they'd all be wondering why such an ancient person as my Mam wasn't shopping in Dorothy Perkins where she belonged. I frowned at that because my Mam wasn't ancient at all. And when I had friends who came round to our house, they always used to say that my Mam didn't look like she was a mam at all because she was dead pretty and she could be a film star or a model or something. And even though it made me a bit embarrassed sometimes to hear my friends saying that, it made me feel dead proud and all, having a Mam who didn't look like a mam.

So I said to her as we stood outside the boutique, 'You're not ancient at all. You should buy that dress.'

But my Mam just smiled and shook her head and we started walking up King Street again. Then suddenly, without warning, my Mam just stopped, right in the middle of the pavement. And she looked at me and said, 'No! You're right, son! You and Dr Janice, you're right. We've had enough of being afraid, haven't we. Come on,' she said.

And she turned right round and marched back to the boutique.

She got new shoes as well as the new dress. And she asked the assistant to wrap up her old shoes and her old dress because she was leaving the new ones on. She looked fantastic, my Mam. She looked much better than all the slender girls as slim as summer. And when we were in Pizza Pacino's, the waiter with the pepper-grinder and the handlebar moustache kept winking at my Mam and saying, '*Ciao, bella,*' even though you could tell he came from Prestwick or Stockport or somewhere like that. My Mam said he was a bit too forward for her liking and she felt a bit uncomfortable. But you could tell she didn't really. And even though normally I'd be a bit fed up and frowning at somebody winking at my Mam and saying '*Ciao, bella,*' I wasn't that day. I was just glad that my Mam looked happy. And pretty. And as young as she truly was.

And when I asked her which film she wanted to see, my Mam looked at me like she was all shocked and said, '*The Return of the Jedi* of course!'

She surprised me, saying that. Because my Mam was always dead bored with all the *Star Wars* stuff and the last time we'd gone to see *Return of the Jedi* she'd even fallen asleep. And that was only the fifth time we'd seen it!

So I said it didn't matter and we didn't have to go and see a *Star Wars* film and my Mam could pick the picture if she liked. But my Mam wouldn't have it and she insisted and said, 'No! I want to go and see *Return of the Jedi*.'

I thought perhaps she was being nice and putting up with it because I'd just been in the hospital. But it was like she was really really interested and when we came out of the pictures and even all through the ten-pin bowling and the gooey doughnuts, my Mam kept asking me all sorts of questions about what you had to do to become a Jedi Warrior and why the Wookies and the Ewoks didn't have light sabres. And she never looked bored for a single minute. She even got Obi-Wan Kenobi's name right so I know she must have been really genuinely interested. Because before that, whenever I'd be talking about *Star Wars* to my Mam, she'd get it wrong and call him Obi *John* Kenobi or something stupid like that.

On that day though, the day she collected me from the hospital and took me out to town, the day she looked young and lovely and said that from now on she was going to be brave, on that day, there was nothing remotely stupid in anything my Mam did or said.

That day, all the stupidity was happening somewhere else; where things were going on; things that I didn't know about, not then. Things I'd only ever find out about years and years later.

I was in town with my Mam. And before that I'd been in hospital. So I'd never even heard about it. And the night before, my Mam had been so worried about me that she couldn't be doing with the television or the radio. So neither me nor my Mam had watched the North West News or heard the broadcasts on GMR. And so we never knew about the little girl who'd gone missing; about a search, in the park, about sheds and back alleys and garages being scoured. We never knew about the sandal that had been discovered at the side of the allotment, the scuffed brown sandal with the broken clasp.

Neither me nor my Mam had heard anything about that.

Just like we'd known nothing about the press conference and the parents, the father with his arm around his wife's shoulders as he appealed for anyone who had any kind of information to come forward and assist the police in their search for his beautiful, beloved, happy-go-lucky little daughter. He broke down crying then. His wife didn't cry though. His wife just sat there looking like she was a dead person. And, as the detective sergeant told the interviewer, that's what it does to you when you suddenly have to live a nightmare, like Mr and Mrs Patterson were living a nightmare; the worst kind of nightmare, the kind of nightmare that every parent dreads.

It cut to pictures of the vigil then; the neighbours, the mothers who knew the child, all of them gathered outside the house, holding candles in the dark and vowing they'd stay for as long as they had to, telling the lady from Granada News that they'd stay for ever if need be, staying and praying for the little girl who always had a smile on her face and was such a happy fun-loving child. And the lady with the microphone turned to Mrs Machonochie and asked her if there was one particular word with which she could sum up little Paulette for the viewers. Mrs Machonochie choked back a sob, wiped her eye with a tissue and told the viewers that there were so *many* lovely words which could be used to describe little Paulette. Then Mrs Machonochie broke down in tears and was comforted by Mrs Kershall as the lady with the microphone nodded her sympathetic understanding, and the camera tracked in, lingering on the anguished face of Mrs Machonochie as the interviewer handed back to the studio where they went into the commercial break with a picture of the little girl dressed in a sort of school uniform; smiling, slightly anxious perhaps, but smiling, doing her best to look like a nice little girl.

We never saw that picture though, my Mam and me.

We hadn't seen the telly or listened through the night, like the neighbours had, pursuing their candlelit vigil and listening in to the hourly news bulletins, feeling some kind of personal betrayal as, during the night, the lead story slid from pre-eminence, becoming merely another news item, jockeying to hold any kind of position at all as it competed with fresher tragedies, more up-to-the-minute dramas.

And then, when, as Mrs Keogh had said, 'It was starting to look like the bloody world out there had forgotten poor little Paulette,' on the 6 a.m. bulletin from GMR, the name of Paulette Patterson suddenly topping the news once more, the announcer's voice adopting a note of appropriate gravity as he reported 'new developments' in the search for the missing child.

Clustered around the radio, the neighbours closed their eyes and held their breath as the police spokesman told of the item of clothing discovered on a stretch of common ground at the side of a cinder track. It was too early to say exactly, the police spokesperson said, but yes, he could confirm that the item was an item of female underclothing. And yes, the size of the undergarment would indicate that such an item belonged to a child.

The neighbour women exchanged anguished glances; Mrs Machonochie started to cry.

But me and my Mam knew nothing about

neighbours; of prayers and of candles, of vigils that stretched from dusk until dawn.

Or of the reluctantly retired milkman from Gatley who, rather than lying in bed and pondering his predicament, said he'd rather be up and out and walking the dog, relishing the morning and the walk down the towpath, beneath the old bridges and along by the lock.

We didn't know about him. Or his dog, that was usually so obedient, suddenly running off that morning, off towards the sheds and derelict buildings where it barked and it yelped and despite its master's repeated calls, refused to give over and come back to heel.

We didn't know.

Didn't know that the milkman had had to leave the towpath and go across to the abandoned buildings, cursing the yapping dog and intending to put it back on its leash.

We knew nothing of that; or of the sudden shock, the milkman's disbelieving stare, the pounding of his heart as he looked again, down through the rusted metal grill, down into that darkness; and saw in the shadows the small face, the wide, terrified eyes staring back up at him.

My Mam and me were unaware.

At first they thanked God, the gaggle of neighbours, thanked God that the child had been found alive. There were hugs and smiles and tears and kisses as they wrapped themselves up in the wonderful news, the crowd growing bigger, swelled by the curious, the downright nosey, the aimless and bored. But as they stood waiting for the child's homecoming, making plans for the welcome home, the word went amongst them; of how someone said that when she'd been found, the girl's dress was in tatters, her underclothes missing, her legs scratched and bloodied, her arms badly bruised.

They stopped thanking God, the friends and the

neighbours, as the details emerged and the facts got around. According to police who'd been called to the scene, she was less like a child and more like an animal, terrified and trembling and, so far at least, too frightened to talk. Such was the trauma, the ordeal that she'd suffered, a police spokesman said she might not speak again.

But regardless of that, the same spokesman promised, the force would be doing everything in its power to find whoever it was who was responsible for this evil act and for the indescribable suffering of this helpless child.

And then someone asked someone if they knew the location, if they knew where it was that the girl had been found. Then someone told someone who'd heard it from someone who knew for a fact, it was at the canal!

Me and my Mam didn't know. Me and my Mam were eating pizzas, and we were best friends again. That's why my pizza tasted like it was the nicest pizza in the whole of the universe, because my Mam was friends with me again. And I felt safe and I felt happy – because I knew I never ever had anything to worry about in the whole of the world, as long as me and my Mam could keep on being best friends.

But I didn't know. And my Mam didn't know.

About the neighbours who'd given up thanking God; and instead remembered, back at the beginning of summer, something that had happened down by the canal. Tales that they'd heard about innocent children, grim goings-on, unmentionable things. And a boy! From over on the far side of the estate. A boy who was old in the head, they said, much older than his years; a boy not fit to be called a boy, a beast of a boy, a dirty boy.

And everyone had said back then, back at the beginning of summer, back when it had first started, when all those children from the other side of the estate had been lured down to the canal and forced to do unspeakable things, everybody had said that that wouldn't be the end of it; said that something should have been done. Because kids like that, kids who can exert their influence, who can lure away and snare the less clever ones, kids like that aren't kids at all; left unchecked, a kid like that is a tragedy waiting to pounce.

But me and my Mam didn't know.

My Mam and me, we were watching the Ewoks, the Wookies, Han Solo, Obi-Wan Kenobi and the rest of the gang.

And now it was the little girl who was in the hospital, with her mam and dad, the policeman and police lady at the back of the room as the lady doctor kneeled and dabbed at her bruises, put cream on her scratches, as she casually asked, 'Somebody did something to you, didn't they, Paulette?'

Paulette, at first, looked at the doctor. Then glanced up beyond her, to the back of the room, where her mam and her dad were stood with the police. Paulette stared, eyes wide, unblinking, at the face of her father who stared back at her, small beads of sweat on his upper lip glinting, as the doctor asked Paulette again, 'Can you tell us who it was, Paulette?'

Nobody was looking at the face of her father; nobody saw it, apart from Paulette, the glint of warning in his eyes, the threat.

'It's all right, Paulette,' the doctor said. 'You know we examined you when you first came in?' The doctor smiled and nodded, 'Well, that's how we know, Paulette; that's how we know about somebody having done something bad to you.'

Paulette stared beyond the doctor's shoulder, saw her mother staring down at the floor like a zombie; saw the tears running down the police lady's face.

'The person who did it,' the doctor asked, 'do you know that person, Paulette?'

Eyes still fixed on the face of her father, Paulette Patterson began to nod.

All that warning and all those threats in her daddy's eyes didn't count for anything now; not here. It was easy now, with the lady doctor being here and the policeman and the police lady.

'Can you tell me?' the doctor asked. 'Can you tell me the name of that person?'

Paulette Patterson nodded once more, *still staring at her father* as she quietly said, 'Him.'

Paulette watched her father, his head tilted back against the wall, mouth sagging open.

And if the doctor had followed the gaze of the girl, then the doctor might have known. If the policeman hadn't been so concerned with comforting his distraught companion then perhaps he might have seen.

But the doctor didn't follow the gaze of the girl. Her face creased in a puzzle, she looked at Paulette and said, 'Who? Paulette, who's *him*?'

And in that moment, Paulette's daddy came back; his head tilting forward from the wall, her proper daddy; the daddy in whose face there was no longer any threat or warning, no jaw clamped in anger, no quiet fury in the eyes; only silent desperation, fear and pleading; and helpless appeal.

And in that look Paulette saw what she needed to see; saw love, saw kindness and care, repentance, regret and remorse. Paulette saw love in the eyes of her father; the only love she'd ever known.

And when the lady doctor asked once more, 'Who, Paulette, who do you mean, *him*?' Paulette Patterson took a deep breath, turned her eyes from her daddy and looking directly at the doctor, said, 'The Beast Boy. The Filthy Boy who lives near the canal.'

But we never knew, me and my Mam.

We were ten-pin bowling and eating gooey doughnuts. And even on the way home in the taxi, we didn't know.

The taxi driver said to my Mam, 'Well, the pair of you look as if you've had a really good time.'

And my Mam told him, 'We've had a brilliant time.'

201

She hugged me and smiled at me and said, 'Haven't we, Raymond?'

I nodded as she told the taxi driver, 'We've had a really great day out together, me and my son.'

My Mam turned and smiled at me again. And then, as we pulled into our street and my Mam reached for her bag to get the money for the taxi, I heard the taxi driver saying, 'Aye aye! Wonder what the bizzies are up to?'

That's when I saw it, parked outside our house, the police car and the two policemen standing by it. Just for a second I thought there was something wrong. But then I heard my Mam saying, 'Oh it's them! Look, it's Eric! And . . . what's-his-name? His mate . . . Dave who took y' to the hospital. Look,' she told me. 'Ah! They've come round to see how y' are; isn't that nice of them? Come on,' my Mam said, as she paid the taxi driver, 'they'll be dead pleased to see y'.'

We got out the taxi, me and my Mam in her new shoes and her new dress and her Urdu hairdo.

'Hiya,' she called out as we walked the few steps towards them. 'Look,' she said, putting her arm around me and gently pulling me forward. 'Look, fit as a fiddle he is now and the doctor said there's nothing to worry about at all.'

As she reached into her bag and took out the door key, my Mam asked them, 'Have you both got time for a cup of tea?'

And it must have been then that she noticed, my Mam; noticed that the two nice policemen didn't have quite the same nice look about them as they'd had the night before. One of them looked away as if he was embarrassed. And the other one reached out and opened the back door of the police car.

'What's up?' my Mam asked.

But a man got out the back of the car then. And he said, 'Mrs Marks? I'm Detective Sergeant Culshaw. Do you think I could have a few words with you please?'

'He's all right,' my Mam said, pulling me closer

and beginning to look worried. 'He's right as rain now.'

The detective man cleared his throat and then nodded towards the house as he said, 'I think it might be better if we went inside.'

My Mam paused for a second. And then she noticed Mrs Caldicott from across the road gawping out through the window.

My Mam opened the door then. And let them in.

He told my Mam it might be better if they spoke in private. And then he looked at me. My Mam twigged and said why didn't I go upstairs and get ready for bed and she'd be up to see me in a minute. I didn't want to go to bed. I didn't want to leave my Mam. She still had her new dress on and her new hairdo and her new shoes. But it didn't feel the same any more. Because my Mam had started to look like a mam.

'Raymond!' she said, and she was being sharp with me. 'Go on, up to your room.'

I just went then. And I walked into my room so that my Mam would hear the creak of the floorboards and think I was just doing what she'd told me. But then I quietly crept back towards the door, making sure that I avoided the creaky bits until I got to the top of the stairs.

I heard my Mam's voice at first, all high-pitched and nonplussed as she said, 'What d' y' mean, where was he? He was at the canal. Ask these two! It was them who pulled him out.'

I crept down the stairs until I got to the third stair from the bottom and I could see over the banister into the front room. I saw the two ordinary policemen sat there on the settee, and the detective sergeant looking at his notebook.

'And that was at . . . six thirty-five p.m. when the officers found him and fished him out. But prior to that, Mrs Marks, can you say roughly what time it was when you last saw your son?'

'What d' y' mean?' my Mam asked. 'Last night?'

'That's right,' he said. 'We know his whereabouts from six thirty-five, because that's when the officers here came across him. But before that, what time would it have been when you last saw him?'

'Why are you asking me this?' my Mam said.

But nobody seemed interested in answering my Mam's questions and the detective man just said, 'Was it ten minutes, half an hour, an hour . . . what?'

It all fell silent and I knew that my Mam must be thinking back. 'I can't be definite,' she said, 'but I think it was about . . . it must have been some time round about half-past five. I know it wasn't long after we got back from seeing . . .'

The detective man just looked up at my Mam as she tailed off. He smiled at my Mam then. 'Seeing what, Mrs Marks?' he said.

My Mam nodded. 'Seeing the . . . psychotherapist,' my Mam said. He looked at her, the detective man. My Mam sort of laughed nervously and waved her hand. 'It was nothing,' she said, 'nothing. There was nothing wrong with him after all. Dr Janice has explained it all to me now.'

The detective just cleared his throat. And then he sniffed. But I saw him glance at the other two police-men. 'All right,' he said, 'but let's just get back to . . . so what time would it have been when you got back from seeing the . . . psychotherapist?'

My Mam thought really hard then. And she said, 'Well, it must have been about half-past five. I mean I can't be exact but—'

'Five thirty!' he said, interrupting my Mam and writing it down in his notebook. 'So you can't verify your son's whereabouts for that hour or so between five thirty and six thirty-five.'

'What d' y' mean?' my Mam said. 'Of course I can verify his whereabouts, I can tell you exactly where he was. He was sitting out there in the backyard!'

There was a pause then, as if the detective man didn't know what to say about that. And then I heard my Mam say, 'But why am I being asked all this? What the hell is this all about?'

'Would you mind,' the detective said, 'if I just took a look out of that window?'

'The window?' my Mam said. 'No, I don't mind if you look out the window. Why should I?'

It went quiet again for a second. And then I heard the detective's voice coming from further away down the front room. And he said, 'So while he was out in the backyard, Mrs Marks, you were out there with him, were you?'

'No,' my Mam told him, 'I never said that. I wasn't in the yard, I was in here.'

'The whole time?' he said. 'The whole time your son was in the yard, you were sat in here?'

'That's right,' my Mam said.

'So then how can you be so certain', he said, coming back up the room, 'that your son was definitely out there in the yard?'

'Because that's where he was!' my Mam said. 'Sitting out in the backyard playing with his *Star Wars* figures.'

I heard him sniff again. And then he said, 'But you can't be certain of that, can you, Mrs Marks? Because as you've just told me, you were sat here in this room. And even if you'd been sat at the window, Mrs Marks, you still couldn't be certain that your son was sat out there. Because as I've just discovered for myself, your backyard can't be seen from anywhere in this room.'

My Mam got narked then and I heard her say, 'Now listen! You come in here, asking all sorts of questions and looking out of my windows and I haven't even got the first clue of what this is all about. I don't know what business it is of yours,' she said, 'but I'm telling you now, window or no window, I know exactly where my son was: he was sat out there sulking in the yard and I was sat in here, and I can remember it exactly because we still weren't speaking properly because I was mad about the things he'd been saying! He just went off with his *Star Wars* figures and played in the yard. And I sat in here. But don't you come into this house,' she said, 'saying what did and what didn't happen, because, I'm telling you now, Raymond was in the yard.'

He changed then, the detective, suddenly sounding all soft and upset and telling my Mam he was sorry.

'Honestly, love,' he said, 'I really am. I'll tell you the truth, Mrs Marks,' he said, 'I hate it myself, having to bloody disturb people and go around asking all sorts of questions. It's not just you, love,' he said, 'I've got to go and interview all sorts of people. But believe me, Mrs Marks, I don't choose to do it. I'm just told to get out there and make certain enquiries. It's just like ticking people off a list, y' know. I'm just the dogsbody on this. I just have to establish the whereabouts of, y' know, a few people and then they're ticked off the list and that's that.'

As soon as my Mam began to speak, I knew that he'd managed to make her feel a bit sorry for him and all his difficulties.

'Well, I'm not trying to make your job any harder than it is,' my Mam said. 'But if I just knew what this was all about! I don't even know what it's to do with.'

He laughed then, the detective. And he said, 'Hey, Mrs Marks! *You* don't know what it's about? What about me? An enquiry like this; I'm just told to get out there and ask some questions. But that's all I'm told. I don't even know what it's about myself. It's probably nothing. Kids causing a bit of trouble in the neighbourhood and somebody's put in a complaint. Not even worth the bother. But we have to be seen to be doing something. So muggins here, I get sent out to make a few enquiries.'

My Mam started to sound really relieved then. 'Well, you can take it from me,' she said, 'our Raymond's not been involved in any trouble. In fact,' she said, 'he's barely been out the house this summer holidays.'

He nodded then, the detective. 'Well, like I say,' he told my Mam, 'me doing this, a bit of checking up, it keeps the public reassured. Lets the community see that we're doing something.'

And I started feeling relieved myself then. Partly. It's

just that there was a bit of me that couldn't help wondering; if it *was* just some kids who'd been messing in the street or something like that, how come there was a detective sergeant and two uniformed policemen sitting there in our front room?

Perhaps it was all right though. Because I could hear my Mam and she wasn't scared or worried or anything like that now. She just told the detective, 'I wish you'd explained that in the first place. Because with you saying you were a detective, you had me dead worried. I thought detectives were really important. I thought it must be something really serious. I didn't think detectives had to do things like this, making enquiries when it's just some kids who've been getting a bit out of hand.'

'Hey, you'd be surprised,' he said, laughing. 'It's not all action and glamour like they make out on the telly, y' know. Routine, Mrs Marks,' he said, 'most of it. Plodding, boring, bloody mind-numbing routine work, most of it.'

'Well, I can sympathise with that,' my Mam said. 'I work on the checkout in KwikSave.'

'Hey,' he said, all chummy like him and my Mam had been best mates for ages, 'count yourself lucky. Compared to a job like mine, a checkout seems like paradise.'

'Oh aye,' my Mam said, laughing as she did, 'all the glamour of baked beans and bar codes!'

He chuckled at that, the detective. 'Well, thanks for your time, Mrs Marks,' he said. 'If everybody was as helpful and straightforward as you, perhaps this wouldn't be quite the tedious job it is.'

He spoke to the other policemen then and told them, 'Come on, you two, let's be having you.'

I saw them getting up off the settee and so I crept back up the stairs quick then and crouched down on the landing, so they wouldn't see me when they came into the hall. And I was dead happy that it had all turned out to be about nothing in the end. I knew I hadn't done anything wrong. But when you've got three policemen at the door, you start to think you might have done something wrong without even knowing about it. But it was all right because they were leaving now, coming out the front room and into the hall and the detective telling the two policemen, 'I'm sure Mrs Marks has got enough to do without us wasting her time any further.'

My Mam laughed as she followed them towards the front door and she said, 'I have as a matter of fact. With being out all day today I haven't even put the washing machine on yet.'

'That's what I mean,' I heard the detective say, 'it's not all roses, is it, having to work and bring up a young lad at the same time. And they're not easy, are they, kids?'

'You can say that again!' my Mam laughed. And from where I was on the landing, I could just see them through the stair rails now, as my Mam reached forward and opened the front door for them.

Everything was all right. They'd be gone in a minute and I'd be in bed and my Mam'd be up to see me and say goodnight and remind me not to read for too long because it's not good for your eyes, reading under electric light for too long. I was just deciding which one of my books I was going to read or whether to read my comics when I heard him, the detective sergeant.

'Mind you,' he was saying to my Mam, 'you'll have made it up now, I expect.'

'I'm sorry?' my Mam said. 'Come again?'

'The row,' he said, 'or perhaps I misheard you. I thought you said you'd had a row, you and your son; you weren't speaking or something.'

'Oh that,' my Mam laughed. 'Yeah, we've more than made it up,' she said.

'Ah well, that's good to hear,' he said. 'Kids, eh! They'll bloody row about anything these days, won't they? The trouble they cause.'

'Oh, it was nothing like that,' my Mam said. 'I

couldn't describe it as "causing trouble". In fact it was me,' she said, 'I'd got all upset after because of some sort of, I don't know, just some sort of kids' mucky stuff that he'd come out with. And then, well, you get worried about them, don't y'? And I ended up taking him to see the doctor.'

'The psychotherapist?' he said.

'Yeah. But it was ridiculous,' my Mam said. 'I was just overreacting.'

'Oh I don't know,' he said, the detective man, still sounding like he was all chummy and dead sympathetic, 'I think you'd have a right to be upset. A lad as young as Raymond, coming out with mucky things to his mother.'

'Oh it wasn't to me,' my Mam said. 'He didn't say it to me. It was something he'd said to his little cousin, Sonia.'

My Mam didn't see it, but I did. The glance. The detective sergeant glancing at the two ordinary policemen. Then, still sounding like he was being all sympathetic to my Mam, he said to her, 'A bit near the knuckle was it, what he said to the little girl?'

'No, not really,' my Mam said. 'I was upset at the time because my brother was here and he'd make a meal out of anything, him. But it was just a bit of smut, really. The sort of thing that kids get up to all the time, Janice said. She agreed, Dr Janice, y' know, at the hospital.'

He nodded. 'Some people,' he said, 'they get upset a bit too easily, don't they?'

'Well, to tell y' the truth,' my Mam said, 'our Jason, my brother, I think he's always been a bit jealous. Y' see, their little Sonia's not got a lot upstairs really, God love her. And our Raymond's got such an imagination. Dr Janice agreed. And I just think Sonia and our Raymond, they're not a very good combination. Raymond might just have been telling her a joke for all I know.'

He laughed then, the detective policeman. He

chuckled and he said, 'Well, come on, put us out of our misery; we need a laugh now and then, doing a job like this; you're not going to send us away into the night without letting us in on what he said, are y'?' He chuckled again and said, 'Go on, you won't make us blush!'

My Mam even started laughing then. And she said, 'Well, it *was* a bit funny, looking back on it. If you'd seen the face on our Sonia when she came in here and announced that Princess Leia was dead. You see, he'd told her, Raymond, he'd said that Princess Leia, y' know from *Star Wars*, he'd told Sonia that the Princess had had to be killed because she was really a prostitute and she'd been doing it, y' know, with all the Stormtroopers.'

I could see the faces of the policemen, especially the detective sergeant. And nobody was laughing at all. My Mam tried to. But it just tailed off as she realised she was laughing all alone. She just sort of shrugged then and said, 'Well!'

'And how old would she be?' the detective sergeant said. 'The little girl he was telling this kind of thing to, what age is she?'

My Mam sort of looked a bit like she didn't know what to do with herself. 'Seven,' she said.

'And Raymond's . . . eleven,' he said. And he left that kind of hanging in the air as if it was important and my Mam just stood there, waiting for them to leave. The front door was still open. But now they were making no effort to go.

The detective man was frowning and he said, 'Is it something that happens on a regular basis, this "smutty" behaviour of his?'

'Of course not,' my Mam said, 'what are y' sayin'? That he does that sort of thing all the time? Well, you're wrong because to my knowledge that's the first time he's ever done anything like that. '

'Is that right?' the detective sergeant said. He frowned at my Mam as he said, 'You're trying to tell me that you take your son to see a psychotherapist just because of one isolated incident. Come on, Mrs Marks,' he said. 'That wasn't the first time he'd done something like that, was it?'

'I've told y',' my Mam said, 'he's never done anything like that before!'

She was looking at him like she was scandalised, my Mam. And she said, 'Anyway. I thought you'd asked all the questions you needed to ask and I've got to put the washing on, so if you wouldn't mind.'

My Mam stepped forward and held the door open. But the detective didn't move. He said, 'You've got a short memory, haven't y', Mrs Marks. If your son's never done anything like that before, then how come when he was at Binfield Junior School he was suspended for luring a whole load of other young boys into an act of gross indecency?'

My Mam stared at him, looking all shocked and appalled, her hand going up to her mouth without her even knowing it.

'Is this what . . . Is this what . . . all this is about?' she said. 'It wasn't gross . . . inde . . . It wasn't anything like that, Janice said, Dr Janice! Talk to Dr Janice at the hospital, she'll tell y'!'

'I don't need to talk to doctor anybody,' he said, 'I've talked to enough people as it is. Like I've talked to his former head teacher, Mrs Marks. And I've talked to other parents in this community. I've spent most of the day talking to a great many people, Mrs Marks. I know everything that went on down at that canal.'

'Look!' my Mam said, and she was almost shouting now. 'It was a bit of muckiness, that's all!' She shook her head like she couldn't believe what was happening. 'A bit of muckiness!' she said, her arms outstretched like she was appealing to him. But he just stood there staring at my Mam. 'And I'll tell you something,' she said, 'we've already paid the price and all. We've suffered enough as it is, all because of a bit of muckiness! That headmaster!' she said. 'That bastard, can't he leave us alone? What's he doing bringing in the bloody police over something like that? Something that's been done and dealt with and finished.'

The detective sergeant slowly shook his head. 'We're not here at the headmaster's bidding,' he said. 'We only talked to the headmaster as part of our general enquiries. We're not here because of him.' He paused then, before he said, 'The reason I'm here tonight, Mrs Marks, is because of that little girl.'

My Mam frowned as she asked, 'What little girl?'

He snorted a disbelieving laugh, telling my Mam, 'The little girl who was abducted!'

I could see my Mam staring and then her eyes suddenly growing wide with horror as something dawned upon her. 'Oh my God!' my Mam said, and she slumped against the side of the stairs. 'Our Sonia,' she said, 'is this about our Sonia?'

He shook his head. 'No,' he said, 'her name's not Sonia. It's Paulette as a matter of fact, Paulette Patterson. But she's barely older than your little niece, Mrs Marks. Somebody lured her into a disused warehouse. And when they'd finished with her, they left her there, trapped in the cellars. Eighteen hours she was there. And when we found her, she was in a terrible state, cut, bruised, scratched, various articles of clothing missing. We hardly needed the doctor's report to confirm it. But it did, of course, the examination. You see, before she'd been left trapped in that cellar, somebody had been . . . "at her", Mrs Marks.'

My Mam leaned there against the side of the stairs, staring at the sergeant and shaking her head in appalled sympathy at the plight of such a girl.

'And, you see, the thing is,' he said, 'that disused warehouse where we found Paulette, that warehouse, Mrs Marks, happens to be alongside the canal. Not more than fifty yards from where your son liked to take his little friends. Fifty yards from where these two officers found him floating in the canal last night.'

It all went silent. I didn't understand! I was up there

on the landing, watching my Mam like I was watching in slow motion as her face creased up and her mouth fell open and her eyes burned up with horror. I just couldn't believe it. I couldn't believe what was happening. And my Mam couldn't believe it either. When the sound came out of her, it was like the wailing of a wounded animal.

'Raymond?' she said. 'You think Raymond could have something to do with a thing like that? He's just a young lad!' she said, her voice getting higher with every wail. 'He's just a child himself!' My Mam pushed herself away from the side of the stairs and moved back from the detective and the police officers. Her face had become a distorted mask of horror. 'Just a young lad,' she whimpered, 'a child.'

The detective shook his head at my Mam. 'There's no such thing as children these days. Not any more.'

My Mam stared at him in disgust. And then she suddenly pointed to the door. 'Get out!' she said. 'All of y', get out of my house now!'

But they didn't get out! The despicable detective just walked towards my Mam and she backed away from him until she was up against the door that leads to the kitchen.

'Now you listen, love,' he said, 'you listen to me. It's a mother's instinct to protect her son. I understand that. But you know as well as me, love; you know what he did to his little friends, down at the canal. You've been worried about him yourself, haven't you, Mrs Marks? That's why you took him to see that psychiatrist, didn't you? Because a mother knows about these things, doesn't she, Mrs Marks? A mother knows her own son better than anybody. You've already told me the sort of imagination he's got, the sort of imagination that takes delight in telling little seven-year-old girls about prostitution and things that little seven-year-old girls shouldn't have to listen to.'

My Mam was stood there and I could see that she was refusing to listen, that she was just staring straight ahead and trying not to hear whatever it was he was saying.

'And I think you also know', he said, 'that he wasn't sat out in that yard for an hour or more. So you ask yourself, love; if he wasn't out in that yard, then where was he for that hour? Where was he? And what was he doing?'

That's when this cry just came out of me. And I didn't even know where it came from, I didn't even know it was me. I just heard this terrified, half-strangled sort of voice as it cried out, 'I was in the yard. I was in the yard.'

And I heard my Mam belting up the stairs and saw her rush across the landing and get hold of me and pull me to her, her voice all wailing and crying like mine as she said, 'I know you were, son. I know you were! I know. I know you'd never . . . I know you couldn't . . . What are they saying, Raymond?' she said. 'What are they saying?'

He appeared. At the top of our stairs. He stood there watching me and my Mam as we huddled together in the dark at the back of the landing.

'What we're saying, Raymond,' he said, 'is that if you love your mum, and I think you do, then the best thing you could do is just tell us what you did to little Paulette. I know that you felt guilty about it afterwards, didn't you, Raymond; because you threw yourself into the canal, didn't you? You tried to do away with your-self, didn't you, Raymond?'

'Come on, come on!' my Mam said, and suddenly she was leading me along the landing. 'Don't listen,' she said, 'take no notice. Come on, just come with me, son, just come with me.'

She pushed past the despicable detective and started leading me down the stairs, 'Don't say anything,' she said. 'Just come with me.'

'And where do you think you're going to, Mrs Marks?' I heard him calling from the top of the stairs.

But my Mam wouldn't answer him and when we got

to the bottom of the stairs she grabbed her coat and mine from off the banister. 'Come on,' she said to me, 'put this on.'

She started getting me into my coat. And I heard one of the ordinary policemen saying, 'What are y' doing, love? Where d' y' think you're going?'

'Don't worry, son,' she said, ignoring the policemen. 'They can't stop us, they can't.'

He was coming back down the stairs then, the detective, and he said, 'You can't run away from it, love. You think you're helping him? The best thing you could do, love, is face the truth and get him to admit it now. He'd be given help, proper help, not quack psychiatrists.'

'Come on,' my Mam said. And we left the house, left it with the policemen still in it. But my Mam didn't seem to care. She just kept telling me, 'Come on, quick, come on,' as she hurried up the street like a mad dervish woman, walking so fast that I had to run to keep up with her. And when we got to the main road she nearly got knocked over, rushing out into the road and waving at a taxi, standing right in front of it so the brakes were all screaming and squealing as it shuddered to a stop just before my Mam. The driver shouted something about my Mam being a mental woman but she ignored him and just pulled the door open and told him to take us to the hospital.

He said something nasty and sarcastic about it should be the effing mental hospital.

'Why?' I asked my Mam. 'Why are we going to the hospital?'

My Mam took hold of my hand, squeezing it dead tight.

'It's all right,' she said, 'it'll be all right. We're gonna see Janice. We're going to see Dr Janice and it'll be all right. It'll be all right then, it will, it will!' she said.

Then she just sat there, my Mam, staring straight in front of her. And nodding her head all the time like a little sparrow bird. And sometimes muttering under her breath, 'It'll be all right, it will . . . It'll be all right.'

Her voice sounded all desperate and she was clutching hold of my hand so hard I thought my fingers might break. I didn't try and take my hand away though. Because even though it was hurting, I was glad that my Mam was holding on to me. Because the only thing that seemed to be real any more was my Mam. And everything else was mixed up and stupid and mad like a senseless nightmare. But as long as I had my Mam, and my Mam believed me and knew that I hadn't done anything bad to the little girl, then it didn't matter, the rest of it. Because it was all stupid and it must be some mistake because I was only a boy. So how could I have done something which bad men do to little girls? And as long as my Mam believed me, as long as she was clutching hold of my hand and telling me it'd be all right, then I knew it would be all right. It didn't matter what he'd said, that disgusting detective man. I didn't care what any detective said about me because as long as I was with my Mam and my Mam believed me and knew that I hadn't done anything to the little girl, then nothing else mattered. I knew that my Mam had been dead brave the way she'd walked past those policemen, the way she'd just walked out of the house and left everything. And now she was sorting it all out, going back to the hospital and telling Dr Janice. And I knew that that was the right thing to do because Dr Janice understood. She knew that I hadn't done any of those things that the detective said I'd done, like 'doing things' to my 'little friends' or trying to kill myself or 'taking delight' in telling dirty things to my little cousin. And because she was a doctor, Dr Janice would be able to tell the police and they'd have to listen to her and they'd know then that I was just a boy; the sort of boy who could never have done the sort of thing that bad men do to little girls.

But Dr Janice wasn't there. And it was like my Mam didn't seem to understand at first.

'She's got to be here,' my Mam said.

I could see that the Sister was starting to get fed up. 'She's not here!' she said.

My Mam frowned. 'I'll have to come back tomorrow then?'

The Sister shook her head. 'Dr Barnes won't be here tomorrow!' she said. 'Dr Barnes isn't attached to this hospital. She's a locum. She was just filling in for somebody today.'

My Mam looked around her, as if she thought if she looked hard enough she'd see Dr Janice somewhere in the corridor.

'I'm sorry,' the Sister said, 'but I can't help you.'

She turned as if to walk away but my Mam said, 'Where is she? Where could I find her?'

The Sister turned back and sighed out loud. 'Look,' she said, 'even if I knew where to get hold of Dr Barnes I couldn't just give out information like that.'

'It's important,' my Mam said, 'it's very important. Couldn't you just phone her and tell her I've got to see her. Tell her it's Mrs Marks. And Raymond.'

'I can't do that!' the Sister said. 'Apart from anything else I wouldn't know how to get in touch with her. I've told you, Dr Barnes is a locum. I don't know where she's going to be working tomorrow. She could be in Leeds, London. For all I know she might have left here tonight and flown straight out to Canada or New Zealand or somewhere.'

My Mam stood there, frowning and staring all around her. 'Couldn't you just—'

'Look! If you don't mind,' the Sister said, 'I've got a ward to run here and I'm extremely busy tonight. And I'd appreciate it if you'd just leave now.'

It was like my Mam finally understood. And when she understood, it seemed as if she just crumpled up inside. She took a deep breath like it was one of those sobs that you make when you've been crying really hard. And when she breathed it out it was like it had just become a tiny whimpering sigh. 'I'm sorry,' she said.

But I don't think the Sister even heard her.

And my Mam turned around and started walking back along the corridor. I just walked along beside her. And I had to tell my Mam where to turn left to get back to reception because she just kept walking like she didn't know where she was; and didn't care.

And when we got to the entrance at reception, my Mam just stopped and stood there. And I stood there with her, waiting for her to tell me what we were going to do now.

But she didn't move.

And I had to say to her, 'Mam, what are we doing?'

She just looked at me like she was too far off in her head to see me. And a nurse who was walking past even stopped and said, 'Are you all right, son? Is your mum OK?'

I just nodded. And the nurse said, 'Are you sure?'

So I nodded again and the nurse went on her way.

And I don't even know why I told the nurse it was OK. Because it wasn't OK. Everything wasn't all right, the way my Mam had been convinced that everything would be all right once she'd spoken to Dr Janice. Dr Janice wasn't there any more. Dr Janice was in Leeds or somewhere in an aeroplane. And my Mam was just stood there, in the hospital reception, not knowing what to do next.

'Mam,' I said, 'what are we doing? Where are we going?'

But I knew that she couldn't answer me. I knew that she didn't know. And I knew that I had to do something.

'Come on.' I tugged at the sleeve of her coat. 'Come on,' I said, 'we can't stop here, Mam.'

My Mam slowly started shaking her head. And she said, 'Not there. Not back there. I'm not going back there, not to the house.'

'You don't have to,' I said. 'Come on, Mam.' I led my Mam outside and walked over to where the taxis were waiting.

*　*　*

My Gran could hardly believe it when she opened the door and it was half-past eleven and me and my Mam were stood there on the step. My Gran just took one look at my Mam and then put her arms around her and led her into the house. And my Gran didn't ask no questions at all, she just took my Mam through to the front room and told me to go upstairs and bring the duvet and some blankets down. My Mam was sitting curled up in the big comfy armchair and my Gran took the blankets and wrapped them all round her, tucking them in, under my Mam's feet and all along the sides of her. My Gran told me to go and make a hot-water bottle and when I brought it back, my Gran was sat on the arm of the chair with my Mam cradled in her arms. And it was the first time that I ever really understood that my Gran was my Mam's Mam. My Gran was being lovely with her child. And I knew it was doing my Mam good, all the loveliness that my Gran was giving her. And as I stood there, I started crying, silently crying because I didn't want to disturb my Mam who looked like she was dropping off to sleep now, in the arms of my Gran.

My Gran saw that I was crying. 'It's all right,' she whispered to me. 'It's all right.'

And it was. At least it was sort of all right. Now that we were with my Gran.

We crept through to the kitchen, me and my Gran, and left my Mam asleep in the big comfy chair. And after she'd quietly closed the kitchen door, my Gran said, 'Right!'

And I thought she was going to ask me about everything. But she just said, 'Are we having peanut crunchies or Garibaldis?'

We went for the Garibaldis in the end. And my Gran said she was glad about that because there was something uplifting about a biscuit named after the father of Italian unity. Whereas the peanut crunchie was a biscuit sadly lacking in significant history and what it lacked in heritage, the Americans had tried to make up for with too much sugar.

'But that's the Yanks!' my Gran said, as she put the kettle on and got the Garibaldis down from the cupboard. 'Very clever, some of them, very clever indeed. But too much sugar! And it's never good for a nation, y' know, Raymond, if it gets too much of a sweet tooth!'

I sat there at the table, nodding and just listening to my Gran as she talked about things like America and Mark Twain and they might not know how to make a biscuit but you couldn't entirely dismiss a nation that gave us Huckleberry Finn. And it was good, just sitting there listening to my Gran going on about things. She never asked me any questions at all. She just carried on making the tea and telling me about the Great Depression of the 1930s and all the rich people in California spraying the fruit with creosote so the poor people couldn't eat the oranges.

And only when she'd made the tea and we were sat there at the table dunking Garibaldis, did my Gran look at me and say, 'Right, son. I think I've done enough talking, don't you? But now I'm going to shut up. And I'm going to leave the talking to you, Raymond.'

She sat there staring at me. 'Now what's been going on?' she said.

Me and my Mam, we never went back to our house after that. My Gran said it would be too dangerous for us to go back there. I didn't know what she meant at first. But she said she didn't have time to explain and explaining would have to wait till later.

'Right now, son,' she said, 'there's things to be done and done quick, if you and your Mam don't want to lose everything.'

She phoned up my Uncle Jason then and told him to get his van and bring it round, quick!

I could hear my Uncle Jason yelling into the phone and saying it was middle of the bloody night and had my Gran finally gone doolally.

But my Gran just told him, 'Listen, from what I hear, Jason, you're used to working in the middle of the bloody night! And if you want to keep your more clandestine activities quiet, you'll get yourself round here with that van and a couple of those dubious associates of yours to help out.'

I could hear him, all outraged and protesting and saying he didn't have dubious associates or clandestine activities. But my Gran just said, 'Oh aye? So where did all the brick and slate and Readymix come from to build that new extension of yours?'

Then my Gran just put the phone down and told me to go and look in my Mam's bag and see if the house keys were there. When I came back with them, my Gran had her coat on. I asked her what was happening and where she was going.

My Gran sat down then. And she reached out and held my hands as she said, 'Listen, son. Sometimes there are things that happen and they're just not fair. Like this isn't fair, none of it! It's not fair at all, son. But sometimes, Raymond, there's nowt much you can do about it. I know what they tell y' at school. About how y' can trust policemen and how we live in a just society and if you're innocent then you've got nowt to fear.'

My Gran nodded and looked at me very closely.

'And fortunately, son,' she said, 'a good deal of the time, that is true. But sometimes, when it comes to certain matters, you can't rely on all that stuff they tell y' at school. Do you understand?' she said. 'Do you understand the sort of matters I'm talking about?'

I nodded. 'I think so,' I said.

My Gran nodded too. 'Matters to do with sex,' she said. 'Sexuality.'

I shook my head and I couldn't help it, I just started crying again. 'I didn't do it, Gran,' I said. 'I never touched the little girl.'

'I know that!' my Gran said, as she took my head in her arms and pressed me to her bosom. 'I know you didn't do it, son.' And my Gran was crying herself now

221

as she said, 'You? You're as soft and gentle as your own father was and I know you could never hurt a little girl.'

My Gran rocked me in her arms as she kept saying she knew I could never have done something like that. Then she took my head in her hands and looked at me with her watery eyes. 'I know that you're quite innocent, Raymond,' she said. 'But you see, son, sometimes just being accused of something – never mind whether you're innocent or guilty – just the accusation itself is enough to put civilised behaviour on the back burner and send common sense flying out the window. And unfortunately for you, son,' my Gran said, 'with what they've accused you of doing, all the innocence in the world might not be enough to protect y'. That's why it'll not be safe for you and y' Mam to go back home, son. When it comes to something such as a little girl being interfered with, it's not just the police that y' have to worry about. You've been accused, son. And in the eyes of some people, that's all they need to send them rushing to judgement.'

There was a knock at the door then. And my Gran let my Uncle Jason in. He came into the kitchen and when he saw me he scowled. I hadn't seen him since all the fuss over Princess Leia.

'What's *he* doing here?' he asked my Gran. 'Hasn't our Shelagh told y',' he said, 'what he's been getting up to? The sort of things he's been saying to our little Sonia?'

'He's told me about that himself,' my Gran said. 'So y' can stop spuddlin' on. Right now we've got a damn sight more to be worrying about than the delicate sensibilities of little Sonia. Come on,' she said, 'let's get a move on. I just hope we can get there and do what we have to do before the word's leaked out all over the estate.'

He frowned then, my Uncle. 'What word?' he said. 'What's going on?' Then he scowled at me again, and he said, 'What's the little bastard done this time?'

My Gran turned on him then and her voice was all low and growly and thick with warning. 'Hey,' she said, 'he's done nowt! Our Raymond hasn't done a thing! Did you hear me?'

My Uncle Jason shrugged and looked uncomfortable. 'All right!' he said, his voice becoming high-pitched. 'All right, all right. I never said nowt, did I?'

My Gran gave him the glare and she said, 'No! And that's exactly how it'll remain; with you saying nowt! There'll soon be far too many people with far too much to say. We'll have to put up with that. But I'm warning you now, Jason,' she said, frowning and fixing my Uncle with her glare, 'if I ever hear that you've joined in, if I get so much as a whisper that you have judged and condemned our Raymond, on the basis of nowt but malicious gossip and the word of a bullying police-man; if I ever hear that you've helped blacken the name of this lad, I'll see to it that you pay the price for every single scrap of Readymix that never quite got to where it should be going! Did you hear that?' my Gran said. 'Did you hear me?'

I didn't know what my Gran meant, about the Readymix. But my Uncle Jason obviously did because he got all huffy and shifty-eyed then and said, 'Come on, come on. I thought y' said you were in a bloody hurry to get going. Well, come on, get a sodding move on will y'!'

He marched out the kitchen then and down the hall.

'Right,' my Gran said to me, 'if your Mam wakes up before I get back, put her in my bed. All right? Y' can both sleep in there for tonight.'

I asked my Gran where she was going. But she just kissed me and said tarar. I went through to the front room, got some cushions and lay down on the sofa.

And I lay there watching my Mam who was still fast asleep in the big comfy chair.

And when we woke up in the morning, Morrissey, I knew where my Gran had been all night. Because the hall and the spare room and the back bedroom upstairs was full of all our furniture and stuff from our house. My Gran said they'd taken as much as they could. She pointed to a box and said she'd got all my comics and my books because she knew how important they were to me.

'And as much of the furniture as we could shift,' she told my Mam. 'I've put all your clothes in the spare room, Shelagh.'

My Mam just stood there frowning and looking at all our furniture in the wrong place. It was like my Mam couldn't take it in at all. And she said, 'What have y' done, Mother? What's happening?'

'We're going back there this afternoon,' my Gran said. 'As soon as Jason's had a few hours' sleep, we'll get the carpets and the odd bits that still need picking up.'

My Mam looked at my Gran. 'There's no need for all this,' my Mam said. 'We're not moving in with you.'

My Gran shot me a look. And then she said to my Mam, 'So where *are* y' gonna live, Shelagh?'

My Mam frowned. 'In our house!' she said.

'Is that right?' my Gran asked. 'And how long do you think it'll be, Shelagh, before that detective lets it be known that he's powerless to do anything about our Raymond?'

My Mam just stared at my Gran with a puzzled look on her face.

'And once that gets out, Shelagh,' my Gran said, 'once people round here start to learn that the police are certain who did it but still can't take any action, because of his age . . . because they've got no evidence, d' you really think people are just gonna shrug it off and forget about it, Shelagh? Because if you do, love, you've got more faith in mankind than I've ever had.'

My Gran went through to the kitchen and me and my Mam followed her. As my Gran put the kettle on, she stared out the window and she said, 'I know he's just a lad, Shelagh, just a lad who's done nowt to nobody and it's worse than wicked that it should have come to this. But come to this it has, love. And when you've got people who can only believe what it suits them to believe then it's a bloody sad do. This might be modern-day Failsworth, Shelagh; it might be the far end of the twentieth century, with everybody living in glass conservatories and purchasing pot plants from garden centres, going to worship in the air-conditioned shrines of the supermarkets. But don't be tricked by any of that. Civilisation! It's a thin veneer, Shelagh. There's still many a barbarous bugger behind a supermarket trolley. Take away their pot plants and their honeysuckle and there's many a sadist stalking the garden centres. Don't go putting too much faith in so-called civilisation, Shelagh; given the whiff of a chance there'd soon be routine hangings and regular floggings and the burning of witches in the car parks at Asda and Tesco and Sainsbury's PLC. And they'd all be there, in their Armani suits and their Head and Shoulders hairdos, with their pot plants and Perrier water and chargrilled marinated Mediterranean tuna ready to be popped on the barbecue and savoured outside the conservatory after a sunny Saturday morning's beheading at the KwikSave car park.'

My Mam suddenly screamed at my Gran and told her to stop going on for Christ's sake and weren't things bad enough as it was without my Gran bleeding well banging on about sodding sadists in the supermarket?

'But that's what you're gonna be up against, Shelagh,' my Gran said. 'Mob mentality. And that's why you're gonna have to stay here, with me. Until we can get something else sorted out.'

My Gran poured the water into the teapot. And my Mam told her she was sorry for shouting at her and she knew my Gran was trying to do her best.

'But this isn't necessary,' my Mam said. 'We don't have to stay here. I'll give Jason a ring and ask him if he'll move all this stuff back for us this afternoon.'

But we never did move back. And we never even got

our carpets. Because just before dinnertime that same day, somebody poured petrol through the letter box of our house. And then threw a match in after it.

My Gran did her best. She said we could stay with her as long as we wanted. But we had to move in the end. It was awful, Morrissey, those weeks when we were living at my Gran's and I couldn't go out anywhere because my Gran said it wouldn't be safe. It was awful for my Mam. Because even though she tried to tell my Gran about it without me hearing, sometimes she'd forget that I was sat there in the cubby hole under the stairs and I'd hear her, telling my Gran about being spat at in the street. Or when she was at work and the customers would move to another checkout even though the other checkouts had long queues at them and my Mam's was empty. And the supervisor told my Mam she was really, really sorry but she'd have to put my Mam back on packing. I knew it was awful for my Mam. And sometimes I'd hear her asking my Gran, 'What are we going to do, Mother?'

But it was like even my Gran didn't know what we were going to do and she'd just sigh and sound all weary as she said, 'Christ knows, love, Christ knows.'

Then my Mam'd remember about school starting again in September and she'd say, 'He can't start there. There's no way I can let him start at that comprehensive.'

It was awful, Morrissey. My Gran's house was just filled with gloom from morning till night. Sometimes my Gran tried to cheer things up, asking me if I wanted to watch the Spanish news on the satellite with her. But I didn't want to do anything. I just wanted to stay in the cubby hole where it was all closed in and no-one could see me and I could just get on with cataloguing my comics all day.

My Gran knew and my Mam knew and I knew; that I hadn't done anything to the little girl. That's what I kept reminding myself as I went through my comic collection, making sure that everything was all right and that every comic was in its proper plastic bag with its title neatly printed on the front. And before, before they'd said it was me who'd done the bad things to the little girl, before that it was one of the nicest feelings in the world, cataloguing my comics and loving the look of the shiny covers and the nice neatness of them in their plastic bags and all their names on the front. Only . . . I couldn't feel it any more, all the lovely niceness of my comic collection. Nothing felt nice any more, not after they'd said it was me who'd done the bad things to the little girl. I tried to remind myself; all the time I tried to remind myself that I hadn't done anything wrong or bad. But no matter how much I tried to remind myself of that, I still couldn't stop myself from feeling that I was a soiled sort of person. It was like I'd been dirtied. And as if to prove it, there were these patches of dark hair that had started sprouting underneath my arms and between my legs. And it was like I knew now that I'd never ever be a nice boy again, not now. He was gone for ever, the boy with the smooth skin and a love of the loveliness of cataloguing comics. I really *had* become the Wrong Boy now.

Yours sincerely,
Raymond Marks

Gibbet Street Coach Station,
Huddersfield,
West Yorks

Dear Morrissey,

I'm still here! I'd been sat there in that café *al dente* writing to you, and when I realised the time I went running as fast as I could, all the way from the café back to the bus depot. But when I got there, it was too late. The five o'clock to Grimsby was just pulling out of the depot and accelerating away up the dual carriageway.

The lady in the ticket office said it was the last scheduled service today, the five o'clock to Grimsby. I just stood there and wondered what to do. She was nice though, the ticket lady. I think she sort of took pity on me.

'Are you all right?' she said.

'I've got to get to Grimsby,' I said. 'My Mam'll be dead worried about me because I promised I'd phone her when I got there and if I don't get there and don't phone her she'll be all worried and wary and think something's happened to me.'

The ticket lady shook her head in sympathy. 'Well, I'm sorry,' she said, 'but the next scheduled service to Grimsby doesn't leave till tomorrow morning.'

I just stood there and nodded and wondered what to do.

Then she said, 'Are you trying to get home? Is that where you come from, Grimsby?'

I shook my head. And if she hadn't been such a pleasant person I would have been gravely insulted by such a suggestion.

'No,' I said, 'but I've got to get there though because I'm starting a job and my Mam was dead happy about that because it's the first job I've ever had.'

The ticket lady tut-tutted and said, 'You lads! You're all the same. Break your mothers' hearts, the lot of y'. Why don't you telephone your mam now?' she said. 'Let her know that you're all right.'

'I would do that,' I said, 'but my wallet got robbed and I haven't got any money.'

The ticket lady shook her head and she said, 'I don't know! You youngsters, if it's not one problem it's another. Here!' she said. And she was holding out 50p. 'Go on,' she said, 'go 'n' phone your mam and let her know you're all right.'

I felt dead embarrassed. 'No! Look,' I said, 'I wasn't trying to scrounge money. I was just . . .'

'Take it,' she said, 'go on. There's a phone booth on the corner. And you can pay me back when you get famous with that guitar of yours. What sort of stuff do y' sing?' she said. 'Simon and Garfunkel? Do you like them?'

I stared at her. And wondered how such a kind and pleasant person could harbour such sick and sinister thoughts.

' "Bridge Over Troubled Water" ,' she said, 'can you sing that one?'

I shook my head and hoped she couldn't see the look of vomit that was written all over my face.

I think it must be very difficult being a nice person; they all seem to have something seriously wrong with them! It's like they're all immune to embarrassment and that's why they can happily walk around quite untroubled by their unnatural attachment to excrementally excruciating songs.

'And the Eagles,' the ticket lady said, 'they're another favourite of mine. "Tequila Sunrise", can you play that?'

I was tempted to hand back the 50p!

But I just shook my head and the ticket lady smiled sympathetically and said, 'Ah well, you just keep practising, son, and I'm sure you'll get there in the end.'

She sort of sighed then, the ticket lady, and she looked a bit sad and wistful. 'I wish my lad was a bit more like you,' she said. 'I wish my son could shape himself and get out and get a job. But no!' she said. 'Not our Derek, not him! No. Our Derek, he sits there, in his bedroom day in, day out, listening to that morbid monstrosity of a what's-his-name. Oh he gets on my nerves!' she said. 'Do y' know him, the one I mean, that Morrissey?'

The ticket lady shuddered and said, 'How could anybody choose to listen to morbid caterwaulin' like that?'

She sighed and shook her head at the apparent injustice of it all.

And I just stood there, wondering how I was going to get to the phone without having to turn around and let her see the back of my tee shirt with *Morrissey* written all over it.

And I knew it shouldn't have mattered to me and I wasn't being disloyal to you or anything like that, Morrissey. But I didn't want to upset the ticket lady because I knew that she couldn't help it really. She was just like my Mam, that's all; and older people, they just can't help it but they never understand, not about Morrissey. My Gran would have understood though, Morrissey. My Gran would have said you were marvellously mordant. And her eyes would have twinkled with a sort of conspiratorial delight if she'd ever had the chance to hear the lyrics of 'Cemetery

Gates' or 'Headmaster Ritual' or 'Barbarism Begins At Home'.

But ordinary older people, they never understand.

At least, though, the ticket lady had been very nice, lending me the 50p. As I was backing away from the ticket counter, making sure she didn't see my tee shirt, she was even nicer and she called me back. She was leafing through a book and she said, 'I've just thought on! There's a charter going out at six thirty tonight!'

She told me about the special coach and said it had been chartered by the North Lincolnshire Trades Association. 'They've been here for the conference,' the ticket lady said. 'But they're all going back tonight.'

'Isn't that a private coach though?' I said.

The ticket lady tapped her nose and winked at me. And she said, 'You come back here after you've phoned your mam and I'll see what I can do for y'.'

I felt a bit cheered up by that.

So when I phoned my Mam I thought it'd probably be best if I didn't bother her with the specific details of my journey thus far.

I felt a bit awful, letting my Mam believe I'd already arrived in Grimsby and was phoning her from there. But it would have been even more awful for my Mam if she knew I'd had all my money robbed, nearly been arrested in Halifax and still hadn't got further than Huddersfield.

That's why I pretended I was phoning from Grimsby.

My Mam was dead excited when she heard my voice on the phone.

She said, 'Oh son, I'm so glad you've got there safely. Is everything all right? What's it like? Is it lovely? Can you see the harbour from where you are?'

I was in the phone box at the end of Gibbet Street, looking out at the plethora of pizza parlours, burger bars, amusement arcades and the heavy-shouldered horde of city-centre citizens haggard and wearied by the endless dance of normality.

I didn't tell my Mam any of that though!

I told my Mam I was gazing out from a phone box overlooking a harbour where the boats were bobbing gently and balmy breezes blew.

And my Mam said, 'Oh son, son, it all sounds so lovely.'

And I was so glad then that my Mam sounded all happy and delighted, I even told her I could see warm-eyed fishermen with silvery beards sitting on the cobblestone quayside, soaking up the sun and savouring the tang of the salty air as they sat there mending their nets, spinning their yarns and softly singing sea shanties in rough but honest voices.

My Mam just cooed with delight and said it sounded like Shangri-la. 'Raymond, I'm just so glad for y',' she said. 'I'm just so thrilled that you've finally landed on your feet.'

She started to ask me about my digs then and what it was like, where I was staying. And I was just starting to tell her about the guesthouse on the cliff top, all covered in roses and ivy and how my room had a panoramic view of the dazzling blue ocean and the lovely woman who ran the guesthouse was like a cross between Mary Poppins and Mother Theresa and said I had to tell my Mam that she shouldn't be worried about me because Mrs Hovis would look after me like I was her own son.

And that's when I knew I must have got a bit carried away because I heard my Mam's voice become a bit solemn and suspicious as she said, 'Who? Mrs who?'

But the pips had started going and I told my Mam I'd call her again in a few days. And the last thing I heard was my Mam saying, 'Raymond! This isn't Malcolm all over again, is it, son?'

But then we were cut off and so I couldn't tell my Mam no more. And I felt awful. Because I'd phoned my Mam so that she'd be happy. And now she was worried about me again. She hadn't even mentioned Malcolm or the Wrong Boy or anything like that for ages.

I'd made him up, Malcolm. It was after we'd left my Gran's house in Failsworth and we'd moved to the maisonette in Wythenshawe.

In those days, Morrissey, I'd never heard of you or Johnny Marr. So I never knew that your great musical collaborator was a native of Wythenshawe. But even if I had known that, Morrissey, I don't think it would have made much difference; because I just hated Wythenshawe. It was like it had been built by a particularly brutalist town planner from the Soviet bloc and then half knocked down again by a variety of vandals.

I hated it. And my Mam hated it too. But she put a brave face on it at first. She said at least I'd be able to take up my place in secondary school and start catching up with all the education I'd missed. And she said I'd probably soon make some new friends now that we were out of Failsworth and nobody knew anything about us. I knew my Mam was trying really hard to make the best of it and I tried really hard as well. But with all the fuss and all the time I'd spent sitting in my Gran's house doing nowt before we finally moved to Wythenshawe, I'd grown even fatter than I was before. So when I started school I was just this fat oddity who hadn't even begun at the beginning of term and didn't know anybody and didn't even know his way around the school. And that's why I was late on my first day. And when I finally found the classroom and opened the door, Barry Tucknott shouted out and said, 'Fuckin' hell, look at that fat fucker!'

And everybody in the classroom started laughing. And the teacher had to shout at Tucknott and tell him off for using the 'f' word. But I could see that the teacher wanted to laugh himself. He told the others to get on with some work as he waved me over to his desk.

'You're late, lad! First day and you're late, lad. Why?'

But before I could say anything, Steven Spanswick

said, 'He probably got stuck trying to get through the school gates, sir.'

The teacher just glared at him and Spanswick laughed and went back to his work.

The teacher looked at me then. 'Right!' he said. 'Never mind. But if you're late tomorrow, son, there'll be trouble. OK, so what do we call you?'

And that's when Spanswick shouted out again and said, 'Moby Dick!' Everyone started laughing and even the teacher laughed out loud this time.

And it never got any better. I never even tried to make any friends because I hated them all, Spanswick and Tucknott and Mustapha Golightly. They said I had tits! I never had tits! I was just a bit fat, that's all. But they said I had more on top than Irene Broadbent did. And that's when they started calling me queer. They said I had the HIV. And if they had to sit by me or pair up with me for games they'd moan about it dead loud so that the teacher would have to give them a bollocking and make them sit by me or have me on their team. So they hated me even more then. And I hated them. Then one day I was in the playground, just keeping myself to myself, when Spanswick and Tucknott and Mustapha Golightly came up to me. They just stood there staring at first. And then Golightly said, 'Hey, Moby Dick! You used to live in Failsworth, didn't y'?'

I just looked at him. Then I said, 'What if I did?'

He looked at the other two then and he said, 'I told y'.' Then he turned back to me and he said, 'I've got a cousin who lives in Failsworth.'

I just shrugged. I didn't care where his stupid cousin lived. But then he said, 'I'm gonna fuckin' kill you, Marks!'

I tried to move away then but Spanswick pushed me back and he said, 'Stay where y' are, you fat twat!'

And Tucknott said, 'You fuckin' pervert!'

And I knew then! I knew it wasn't just one of the brainless insults that they were always coming out

234

with. I looked across the playground to see if there was a teacher on duty, but it was just kids everywhere and not a teacher in sight. Then Golightly jabbed his finger into me dead hard and pointed it at my face as he said, 'My cousin told me about you, Moby Dick! And what you did to that girl, that little girl!'

I just shook my head and I said, 'Well, your cousin must be as thick and stupid as you because I never did anything to any little girl.'

'You fuckin' liar!' Tucknott said.

And Golightly grabbed me by the shirt-front then and said, 'Don't you fuckin' call me thick! Y' twisted bastard.'

And that's when he slammed me up against the wall and it nearly knocked all the breath out of me. But it made something snap inside of me as well! And I almost felt the shape of this sound that started coming up from my stomach, mixed with bile and anger and fury. And when I opened my mouth and this sound just came out, a sound like a wounded, wild animal, it was such an awful noise that it frightened even me. But it frightened them too. And Golightly let go and moved back a bit with the others, all of them staring at me with their eyes like saucers, as I stood there and bayed at them! Bayed and wailed at them and their taunting and their stupidity and all the crude cruelness of them. And as they stood there, stopped in their tracks and momentarily unsure of what to do in the face of a sort of madness that they'd unleashed, I growled and heard myself telling them, 'See! SEE! Y' think I'm just Raymond Marks, don't y'! Just Raymond who you can laugh at and spit at and make fun of. But you better remember, if you ever try to mess with me again: because I'm not just Raymond Marks.'

They were still staring at me like they didn't know what to do. And that's when I should have walked away and not said anything further. And it was stupid really and I don't even know why I said it. But with them all looking at me like they were still shocked and unsure, I said, 'You better be careful in future, because I . . . am the Wrong Boy!'

It was Tucknott who started laughing first. Then the others joined in. And I did walk away then. But they kept following me, all of them screaming with laughter as they kept saying, 'The Wrong Boy! The fuckin' Wrong Boy!' And then Golightly said, 'He thinks he's Clark fuckin' Kent . . .' And that made them all even more hysterical as they followed me, saying things like, 'Show us your wrong boy, Raymond!'

I know I shouldn't have said it. But I had. And at least it seemed to keep them amused and made them forget about bashing me up for being a pervert. But I knew they wouldn't forget for long. And by the next day everybody in the school would have heard about it.

So that's why I stopped going to school.

I didn't want to tell lies to my Mam and be the sort of deeply devious boy who pretended he was going to school when I was just going down town every day instead and hanging about till it was time to go home again. And every night, when I did go home, my Mam would ask me if I'd made any friends in school today. But I'd just shake my head and watch the telly and wish my Mam would shut up about me making friends. It seemed dead important to her. But I didn't care. It seemed better not to care. Because if I didn't care then it didn't matter. But it mattered to my Mam. And one night my Mam was crying and said it broke her heart, the thought that I didn't have a friend in all the world. But I didn't want my Mam crying and having a broken heart. And that's why I invented Malcolm. The only reason I ever invented him was so that I could make my Mam happy.

He was fantastic, Malcolm. I made him an American and told my Mam that he'd been born in Baton Rouge. I said his dad was a professional bass guitarist who was playing over here, and he'd brought Malcolm with him and got him in at our school. My Mam was made up. And me and Malcolm were best mates right from the very first day he came and joined us in the English class. I told my Mam that I'd had to read out one of my essays to the class that day and then we'd had to discuss it. And when Mr Fuller asked Malcolm for his comments on my essay Malcolm had said, 'Well, gee, sir, I just wanna say straight off that Raymond's essay was neater than the stitches in the Turin Shroud. Wow! That's totally chilled me out, Raymond.'

My Mam beamed a big smile when I told her that. And when Malcolm was my friend, she sort of got younger and happier again and said that after everything we'd gone through perhaps things were finally looking up at last. My Mam started to do things like proper cooking again, with real vegetables, and we didn't have stuff like pies and pasties bought from the shop or frozen freezer food no more. My Mam would ask me all about the things me and Malcolm had done. And I'd tell her about the American games that me and him played in the playground; and how Malcolm had to wear two sweatshirts under his shirt because he couldn't get used to the English weather after living in Baton Rouge where it was always so steamy hot and sunny. And Malcolm had said, 'Gee, Ray, this Wythenshawe weather! It'd freeze the nuts off a polar bear!'

My Mam laughed for ages when I told her that. She said it was a bit rude.

'But I suppose that's just Malcolm's way,' she said, smiling. 'And really it must be terrible, putting up with weather like this when you've been used to the sort of temperatures that Malcolm was brought up in. Ah,' she said, 'I feel real sorry for him. Poor Malcolm, I hate the thought of him freezing to bits in that perishin' playground.'

That's why she bought him the jumper! The big thick chunky jumper. She brought it home from Marks and Spencer's the next night and wrapped it up all nicely. And I was supposed to take it into school with me the next day and give it to Malcolm. I didn't know what to do with it. I had to carry it round town with me all day. In the end I gave it to a homeless person who was sat outside the Arndale, asking people for money because he had a brain tumour and wanted to buy some Pedigree Pal for his starving dog.

I said, 'I haven't got any money but y' can have this if y' want.'

He snatched the parcel off me and ripped the paper open. Then he just looked at the jumper and said he wouldn't be fuckin' seen dead wearing something from Marks and Spencer's. He threw it back at me then and told me to fuck off back to Blue Peter or Oxfam or fuckin' Unicef or something. And I don't think he did have a brain tumour really.

In the end I just dropped the jumper in a bin and felt dead guilty about doing that. Because it was brand new and my Mam had paid good money for it. It wasn't my fault though. It was Malcolm's. I was starting to get a bit fed up with Malcolm. And when my Mam asked me what Malcolm had thought about his jumper, I toyed with the idea of telling my Mam that Malcolm had had to go back to America. But she was looking at me with such eager anticipation in her eyes and so I told her how Malcolm had been all delighted with his present and how his face had lit up when he'd seen it and he'd said, 'Wow! Ray! Your mom bought this for me?' And then his eyes had filled up with tears and he'd said, 'Just for me?' And Malcolm could hardly speak then because he was too choked and he had to lower his head for a minute and then shake it and pull himself together. And clutching the jumper to him like it was already his favourite thing in the world, he said, 'Ray ... your mom ... I guess she's ... a real special person.'

But I didn't tell my Mam any more of what Malcolm had said about the jumper because there were tears streaming down *her* face now and she had to run to the kitchenette and get some kitchen roll for her eyes.

When she'd stopped crying, my Mam said, 'Isn't it

nice to think that there's someone as lovely as Malcolm in the world. When you hear about all these young people nowadays,' she said, 'always in trouble, out of control, dragged up so they don't know the first thing about manners or respect; skipping school and hanging around town all day, shouting abuse and shoplifting, getting into trouble.'

My Mam shook her head and I looked at her, wondering if she knew, if she'd somehow found out about me not going to school. And about the shop-lifting. It wasn't bad shoplifting, not really. It had started with just a couple of packets of Super Noodles. And it was stupid really, because I couldn't even boil them up and make them into proper noodles. But I found that if you kept them in your mouth, made enough spit and chewed them for long enough, they did eventually become sort of soft. And in the end I quite liked them like that really. Only I didn't like being a shoplifter. I felt really guilty. And when my Mam said that about young persons, hanging around town and shoplifting, I thought it was all up and that my Mam had found out. And I was going to have to tell her about everything now and own up. But I was glad. Because I didn't want to be a shoplifter and I didn't want to be bunking off school and telling lies to my Mam. I knew she'd shout and get upset about it at first. But then she'd understand and help me and it'd all be all right again. And that was why I was glad when she said that about kids who get into trouble.

But when I looked at my Mam, I realised she wasn't talking about me at all. She wasn't even thinking about me because she had this faraway look in her eyes and she said, 'Isn't it wonderful, when a boy like Malcolm comes along. And he's such a good boy, such a nice boy, it restores your faith in kids today.'

My Mam just sat there with the dreamy look in her eyes. And that's when the jealousy started. Because it was like she *loved* Malcolm; loved him more than she loved me! And I said, 'Well, he's not always good, y' know!'

My Mam turned and stared at me with a disbelieving frown on her face. 'What d' y' mean?' she said.

I shrugged. 'Sometimes,' I said, 'sometimes . . . he cheats in school.'

My Mam looked really disgusted. 'Cheats?' she said. 'What d' y' mean, Raymond, *cheats*?'

'Cheats!' I said. 'Like when we have to do a test in English. Instead of finding his own answers, Malcolm always looks over my shoulder and copies down the answers from me.'

My Mam looked really offended. And I was glad because I thought it was Malcolm's behaviour that was causing her such offence. But then she said, 'Don't be so stupid, Raymond! Malcolm, a cheat?' she said. 'Malcolm wouldn't cheat! A boy like Malcolm doesn't need to cheat.'

I just stared at her. How the bleeding hell did she know? She'd never even met Malcolm!

'He does!' I said. 'He's always cheating because he—'

'Now look,' my Mam interrupted me, 'I think you should be very careful what you're saying, Raymond Marks! There's cheating and there's cheating. But just checking your answers against somebody else's, that's not cheating.'

She was glaring at me like she was defying me to say anything more about it. But I did say more because it was stupid her saying Malcolm didn't cheat when I was the one who sat next to him! I was the one who'd invented him in the first place. And if I wanted to make him into someone who cheated in English then that was up to me and it was nothing to do with her.

'Well, he wasn't just *checking* his answers,' I said. 'He was copying the answers and pretending they were his own; so that is cheating!'

My Mam sat there glaring at me with her mouth all puckered up like she was sucking on a sherbet lemon. And then she started nodding and said, 'Just listen to you! Just listen to yourself, Raymond! I thought I'd brought you up to show a bit of concern for those less fortunate than ourselves. But it seems I've been wasting my time. There's poor Malcolm speaking American English all his life and then he's suddenly plonked down in the middle of Greater Manchester where everything's different; it's freezing cold, the traffic goes the wrong way, there's only four channels on the television and if he wanted a game of baseball he'd be hard put. And on top of all that he's got to start thinking in a new language; he's got to forget about faucets and diapers and sidewalks. He's suddenly having to think in terms of taps, nappies and pavements, lifts instead of elevators and a thousand and one other strange things. But when he needs a little help, when all he wants is to just check that he's using the right words in a strange new language, what happens, what does he get? He gets you, his friend, begrudging him; begrudging him and calling him a cheat. Well, let me tell you something, Raymond Marks, Malcolm is not a cheat! And I think you should be deeply ashamed of yourself for coming out with something like that!'

It was ridiculous! My Mam was getting all narked with me and I hadn't done anything wrong. It was Malcolm! He was the one who'd done all the bleeding cheating, not me. I started to get narked myself then. And I looked over at my Mam who was just sitting staring at the telly even though it wasn't on.

'He swears an' all!' I said. 'He's always swearing, Malcolm is.'

My Mam shook her head and ignored me, staring at the telly like she wouldn't even listen to me no more.

'He even swears at the teachers,' I said, 'because yesterday Mr Fuller caught Malcolm cheating and told him he had to do detention for that. And Malcolm threw his exercise book at the wall and said, "Call this goddamned dump a school? It's more like a fuckin' penitentiary!" '

My Mam turned round and looked at me then. And

she got to her feet, all sort of huffy and swollen up. And she said, 'Well, perhaps Malcolm does swear now and then. But maybe with friends like you and teachers who don't understand him and want to put him in detention, who can blame him if he does come out with the odd salty phrase now and then?'

I couldn't believe it! If it was me who'd said the 'f' word, my Mam would have gone ballistic and hit the roof and wiped the floor and all sorts. But because it was *marvellous* Malcolm, because it was my *fabulous* friend who was doing the effing and blinding, my Mam was making all kinds of excuses for him. She stood there glaring at me as if I'd done something really really awful. And she said, 'I don't know what's got into you, trying to blacken the name of your best friend. All right, perhaps Malcolm does have one or two small faults but I don't see what cause you've got to be so high and mighty. Malcolm might come out with the odd swear word now and then. But you can bet that he'd never have got up to the sort of things you got up to down at that canal. Malcolm would never have done things that caused him and his mother to have to leave Failsworth and end up in a godforsaken hole like Wythenshawe.'

I couldn't believe my Mam saying that. She'd said. She'd told me it wasn't my fault and I wasn't to blame. But now she was blaming me. And secretly she'd probably always blamed me for having to leave Failsworth and move to Wythenshawe. And that's what got me so mad and I said, 'You blame me for everything, don't y'? You said it wasn't my fault but you were only lying when you said that, because you do think it's my fault, all of it, everything. An' I'll bet you're just like all the others in Failsworth and you even think that it was me who did something bad to Paulette!'

My Mam started to protest and say that she didn't think that at all. But I wouldn't listen to her and I said, 'That's why you don't love me any more. I know that you don't love me and you'd rather have a son like Malcolm than a son like me. Whatever he does, you never ever blame Malcolm but you're always blaming me!'

My Mam was looking at me, all upset now, and she started to move towards me saying, 'Look, look . . . come on, come on.' And I knew that she was coming across to try and hug me but I didn't want her to hug me and I looked her straight in the eyes as I said, 'Well, you're gonna have to forget about Malcolm from now on, aren't y'? Because Malcolm's dad's had an offer to join the Beach Boys in America and he's taking Malcolm back there with him!'

It was like my Mam had been hit with a bucket of cold water. The look of shock and hurt on her face was terrible. But that only made it even worse for me; because it wasn't me she was upset about! It was Malcolm. And if it had been me that she'd been upset about then I never would have run away in the first place.

I knew that I wasn't properly running away because I didn't try and go to Liverpool or London or anywhere like that. All I did was get the bus back to Failsworth and go to my Gran's house. And when I got there I wished I hadn't because when I rang the bell it was my Uncle Bastard Jason who opened the door. And straight away I knew the reason he was there because as I walked down the hall I heard my Appalling Aunty Paula in the front room, telling my Gran, 'But look Vera, forty-eight channels of international broadcasting! It's such a waste, Vera. I don't know what you want with all that media when you hardly ever even watch the ordinary television.'

They never gave up! My Bastard Uncle and my Appalling Aunty Paula. Right from the very beginning they'd had their eyes on that satellite dish. Even on the very day that my Grandad had fell off the roof and he was still a slightly warm cadaver on the patio, the first thing that my Uncle Bastard Jason had said to my Gran was, 'Well, you won't be needing all that media now, will y'!'

243

But my Gran had told him in no uncertain terms that she was keeping her satellite facility because the media was the future and whether she chose to watch it or not, it was a particular comfort to know that she had satellite capability and was electronically linked to the richness and diversity of continental Europe.

My Uncle Jason told her she was talking shite. But my Gran just ignored him and wondered aloud, as she'd wondered so many times before, why the first fruit of her womb had turned out to be a thick-skinned, sour and bitter grapefruit. My Uncle Jason had got narked then and my Aunty Paula called my Gran a wicked old bitch. And as a protest, my Aunty Paula said, her and my Uncle Jason might not even attend my Grandad's funeral now.

'Makes no difference to me,' my Gran had told them as they'd flounced out the house, 'because I certainly won't be going.'

And my Gran never did go to my Grandad's funeral. While my Grandad was being buried, my Gran went to the Progressive Pensioners' meeting instead and took part in a lively and sometimes heated discussion about the effects of marijuana on the over-sixties.

My Uncle Jason and my Aunty Paula wouldn't even talk to my Gran for ages after that. They said she was a callous old cow and uncaring and unnatural. But in the end their moral outrage and indignation were outweighed by their overwhelming lust to acquire the satellite dish. And they started going round to my Gran's again, dropping hints about the satellite dish all the time and trying different strategies like they were doing on the night I arrived from Wythenshawe. And it was lucky that I had arrived because I think my Gran was gradually getting worn down by the pair of them. And when she saw me stood there in the doorway she said, 'Ah, it's our Raymond, come to gladden my heart. Come here, son,' she said, 'come here and give your Gran a kiss.'

And as I did as I was bid and moved towards my

Gran to give her a kiss, I saw my Acidic Aunty and Unbearable Uncle swapping dark looks of peeved disapproval. And as I kissed my Gran, my Uncle said, 'I don't know what the bloody hell you're doing back here! I wouldn't have thought you'd have the neck to show your face in these parts, not after what you did.'

'Hey! He did nothing!' my Gran declared. And pointing her sharp finger straight at my Uncle Jason's nauseous nose, she said, 'He's done nowt wrong to nobody. So you just leave him alone! This is my house,' she declared, 'and our Raymond's welcome here any time he likes, day or night.'

My Gran glared at my Unspeakable Uncle and he couldn't say nowt no more because my Gran's glare was legendary; a glare from my Gran could stop the tongue of many a man and many a man much bigger than my Uncle Grapefruit Jason. He stood there chewing on his chewy and looking at my Aunty Paula who was staring at me like she was scrutinising the contents of a paper handkerchief she'd just blown into. My Gran ignored them both then and smiled at me as she held my hand, holding on to it dead tight.

'Now what do *you* think, son?' she said to me. 'What do you think about all this business with my satellite dish?'

'I don't know, Gran,' I said.

'Well, I want your opinion,' she told me, 'because to be honest I'm beginning to wonder if it's worth all the bother. At my age I might be better off forgetting about all this new media and the technological revolution.'

I saw them out the corner of my eye, my Aunty Paula and my Uncle Jason glancing at each other with the glint of possibility and potential triumph in their eyes. I could hardly believe my Gran was considering giving in to the pair of them.

I shrugged again and my Aunty Paula said, 'You tell her, Raymond. You tell her how much electricity it takes, running all those channels. It's not like watching the BBC, y' know. The BBC takes up hardly any electricity at all, because it only has to come from London. But when you've got channels which have to be beamed in all the way from abroad, it costs a fortune in electricity. And you see, my big worry is the hypothermia! You know what the old people are like. If we have a cold snap it could be the end for her. She could be sitting here frozen to death because all the electricity's being used up by the satellite channels and there's none left for the electric fire!'

My Aunty nodded a nod of significant solemnity; and my Gran sighed and said, 'Well, I don't want that. I don't want to be sat here dead and frozen solid like a leg of lamb out the deep freeze.'

What was wrong with my Gran? I couldn't work out why she was even bothering to listen to my addle-brained Aunty.

'Gran, you wouldn't have to be frozen like a leg of lamb out the freezer,' I said, 'because it doesn't use any extra electricity at all, watching the satellite telly.'

My Uncle Jason got noticeably narked at my intervention and he said, 'Hey! What would you know about it? You know nowt about owt so just keep out of it.'

But I ignored him and I said to my Gran, 'And another thing, Gran, how will you be able to keep on learning Spanish if y' have to go back to watching *The Nine O'Clock News* in English?'

And I thought that'd do it then because the one thing my Gran did watch on satellite was the news in Spanish. She'd never bothered with ITV and she said the BBC was full of frivolity nowadays and where had all the gravity gone? But then she'd discovered the news in Spanish and she was made up because the Spanish newscaster had a particularly sombre demeanour and a marvellously morbid face; and he delivered his nightly litany of tragedy, death and disaster as if it had all happened to him personally. My Gran said it restored her faith in broadcast news, and encouraged her to learn a bit of Spanish at the same time. And I thought it was really good that my Gran was trying to learn Spanish, even though she'd never got further than *Buenas noches, señor.*

But my Unbearable Uncle said, 'Spanish! Learning Spanish! I don't bleedin' believe I'm hearing this.' He glanced at his septic spouse then and shook his head as he said, 'With a mother like her I sometimes wonder how the hell I grew up with my sanity intact.'

I looked at my Gran then because I was expecting her to give him the glare again. But it was like my Gran hadn't even heard him and she was still clutching hold of my hand and looking up at me, smiling but like she was a bit puddled and all. And I said to her, 'So you'll want to keep your satellite dish, won't y', Gran?'

She sort of blinked as she looked at me. And then she beamed a big proper smile as if she was just seeing me for the first time and she said, 'Hello, son! Ah,' she said, telling my Aunty and Uncle, 'look who's here. It's Raymond, come to gladden my heart. Come on,' she said, 'give your Gran a big kiss.'

And I wondered at first. I wondered if it was just my Gran's way of outsmarting my Uncle and my Aunty and putting an end to any further satellite dish manoeuvring. And it even seemed to work because my Aunty Paula got up out the chair and said, 'Come on, Jason, the budgie's probably fretting for us by now.' She turned and looked at my Gran as she buttoned up her coat and said, 'We've done our best, Vera. A lot of good it's going to do you, learning Spanish, when you're sitting here getting frostbite and gangrene and having your legs amputated. But that's up to you, Vera. There's nobody can say that me and Jason didn't warn y'. That satellite dish, it's already been the death of one in this family. And I'm just praying, Vera, for your sake, love, I'm just praying that we can get through the winter without it claiming another victim.'

And then they were gone. And I said to my Gran, 'Are you all right, Gran?'

'I am now,' she said, 'now that they've buggered off.'

And that's why I thought there was nothing really wrong with my Gran. I thought she'd just been pretending to be a bit puddled so that she could get rid of the satellite-seeking pair of them.

'But what about you?' my Gran said. 'Are you all right? What are you doing coming out here on y' own, all the way from Wythenshawe?'

So I told my Gran. I told her about the row I'd had with my Mam. And I told her about Malcolm. I said, 'I've made up this boy, Gran. And it was all right at first but it's all sort of gone wrong now because my Mam won't talk about anything else; it's Malcolm this and Malcolm that and Malcolm morning noon and night. And my Mam loves Malcolm now and it's made me dead jealous and I know that's stupid because Malcolm's just an invention. He's just a figment of my imagination. He's sort of . . . apart from the American accent, he's sort of . . . the boy that I used to be, before the canal. And before everything happened to the little girl.'

My Gran stared at me and nodded. And I thought she was listening carefully to me and thinking about what I was telling her. I said, 'So I know it's stupid, getting jealous of him when all he is is who I once was. But I do get jealous, Gran. Because I can't *really* be him, not any more. I can't be the boy that I used to be. I keep trying, Gran. I keep trying not to be bad. But I can't seem to help it.'

My Gran was staring at me really hard now and I knew that it might shock and upset her if I told her about the other things. But I had to tell her, I had to tell someone. And I knew that even if she did get upset, my Gran would still understand and she'd probably say something that might help me make sense of it all. So I told her, I said, 'I haven't been to school for months, Gran. I've been bunking off and hanging round town and I've binned all the letters the school keep sending to my Mam.'

Then I told my Gran the worst thing of all. I couldn't

really look at her. I just stared at the mantelpiece and I said, 'I've turned into a thief, Gran. I've started shoplifting and I keep trying not to do it but I can't help it and if I get caught I know it's going to be just terrible, just really really terrible for my Mam.'

I kept staring at the mantelpiece and waiting for my Gran to say something to me. But she didn't say a word and I thought she must be so shocked that for the first time in her life she was speechless. So I turned round and looked at her. But she was smiling. And she said, 'Do you like Kentucky Fried Chicken, son?'

I just stared at her. That was before I'd seen the light and become a vegetarian. And as appalling as it seems to me now, I did like Kentucky Fried Chicken back then. But why the hell was my Gran going on about bleeding Kentucky Fried Chicken? I'd just told her the things that I couldn't tell to another single soul in all the world. But all my Gran said was, 'Ooh, I love it, I do. I love it, that crispy Kentucky Fried Chicken.'

And I really should have known then. I should have known that there was something starting to go wrong with my Gran. Because my Gran was the sort of person who normally would have frowned profoundly at the frivolousness of fast-food fried chicken coated in breadcrumbs and served in a waxy tub. But I never ever wanted anything to be wrong with my Gran. And I think that's why I ignored the bits and pieces of stuff that didn't seem to make no sense; because I just wanted my Gran to be all right like she'd always been. And when she said, 'Come on, get us my coat from the hall and we'll go and have some Kentucky Fried Chicken tonight, just me and you,' I did as I was bid and me and my Gran went down to the KFC. And apart from her bizarre change of eating habits, my Gran just seemed normal again. She told me about Wilfred Pickles who used to read the news during the war so that the Germans wouldn't understand him because he had a Yorkshire accent. She told me about the Asian flu epidemic in the 1950s and how they couldn't cope with all the corpses and had to put some of the bodies in the butchers' big freezers because all the mortuaries were full to overflowing. She told me about the blizzards that caused much suffering and a great many deaths in 1947 and the contaminated cans of corned beef that killed off thousands in the 1960s. And because it was dead interesting, like my Gran was always dead interesting, I never really noticed that the only things she was telling me about were things that had happened in the distant past. And she never once mentioned Malcolm or me bunking off school. Or becoming a shoplifter. It was like she hadn't heard a word that I'd said about any of that.

And riding back on the bus to Wythenshawe I even thought that perhaps my Gran had just refused to believe what I'd tried to tell her. Because perhaps she couldn't bear the thought of her favourite grandchild turning into a person who played truant from school and intercepted letters that were meant for his Mam. And went shoplifting in town. I didn't want my Gran to be ashamed of me. And I didn't want to get caught shoplifting and cause my Mam to feel really really terrible. So I promised myself that night, as I rode home on the bus, that from now on I wouldn't ever go shoplifting again. I'd even try and go back to school and just put up with them calling me queer and saying that I had the HIV. And if they did bash me up for being a pervert I'd just have to put up with it. Malcolm would have to go back to America and stay there, where he belonged. My Mam'd get over it in the end and then everything would be all right between me and her. That's what I decided as I rode home on the bus. By the time I did get home I felt much better. And when I walked into the front room and saw my Mam sitting there, staring at the blank telly, I told her, 'It's all right, Mam. I'm sorry that I ran away but I've come back now and everything'll be all right now, Mam, I promise you it will.'

Only it wasn't all right. Because my Mam just slowly

turned her head and looked at me. And I knew then! I knew that she hadn't even realised I'd been gone!

'When?' That's all she said. 'When?'

'When what?' I asked her.

'When are they going back?' she said. 'Malcolm and his dad?'

I just looked at my Mam. And I wanted to tell her. I wanted to tell her it was all rubbish and there was no Malcolm or his dad and there never had been. But I knew that'd be even worse for her than having the pair of them sent back to the US. So I just shrugged and shook my head and told my Mam I didn't know when they were going back exactly. My Mam got up from the chair then and said she was having an early night and going to bed. And I watched her as she walked to the door. She looked all weary like a woman without bones. As she got to the door she turned round and she said, 'I'd like to meet Malcolm . . . just once, before he goes back. Ask him if him and his dad would like to come round for tea one night . . . before they go back.'

I couldn't stand it! I couldn't stand my Mam being so upset. I know I shouldn't have done it. I should have stuck to it and sent Malcolm back to Baton Rouge. And I should have just gone back to school the next day like I'd promised myself that I would. But I had to think and I knew that I wouldn't be able to think if I had to spend the day putting up with the likes of Spanswick and Tucknott and Golightly telling me I was a fat twat queer pervert with the HIV. So I just went down town again but I didn't do any shoplifting. I walked around all day and I couldn't wait for it to be four o' clock so that I could go back home and tell my Mam that the Beach Boys had unexpectedly broken up because of artistic differences and so they wouldn't be needing a bass player now.

My Mam could hardly believe her ears when I rushed in and told her that Malcolm wasn't going back to America after all. She leapt to her feet and hugged me and I told her I was sorry for saying that Malcolm had been cheating and swearing and I'd only said all that because I'd been so upset myself, about my friend going back to America. My Mam hugged me even more then and it felt lovely. And she said she was sorry too and she shouldn't have shouted at me like she had. She said it was wonderful, wasn't it just the most wonderful news? And it *was* wonderful that night with my Mam hugging me. It didn't matter that we were living in a poxy maisonette in Wythenshawe. It didn't even matter that I was a fat and friendless shoplifter who hadn't been to school in ages. None of it mattered because Malcolm was back and my Mam was happy. So I didn't give a stuff that Malcolm wasn't real. What did it matter? My Gran always said that God wasn't real. But there were trillions of people all over the world who needed to believe that he was. So why shouldn't my Mam have Malcolm to believe in? It didn't do any harm. It was a bit difficult later that night when my Mam suddenly said, 'Raymond, listen. I know they're not going back to America now but it'd still be nice, wouldn't it, if Malcolm and his dad would come and have tea with us one night.' She looked all dead happy and hopeful. And as I sat there trying to work out what to do, I saw this sort of wistful look appear on her face as she said, 'He must get lonely, mustn't he, Malcolm's dad. I wonder what he's like? I wonder if he's blond like Malcolm.'

And it was the look in my Mam's eye, that sort of longing look, that made me frown. She caught me looking at her and she laughed like she was a bit embarrassed as she said, 'What? What?' But I just shook my head and my Mam really started laughing then and said, 'What's wrong? I'm only saying I'd like to *meet* him.'

But I knew. And my Mam knew that I knew. Because she suddenly pounced on me and started tickling me as she said, 'I'm just inviting him for tea, y' silly bugger; not asking him to marry me.'

She sat there on the couch with me, after the tickling

had stopped. And I looked at her as she stared at the wall. I could see that she was miles away. And despite her denying it, I knew that my Mam was sat there fantasising about being married to a blond-haired bass player from Baton Rouge. And if he'd been real I probably would have got all upset about that. But as he was just a figment of my imagination I didn't mind at all about my Mam being besotted by a bogus blond bass player.

I couldn't have him and Malcolm coming round for tea though!

So I explained to my Mam about Malcolm and his dad both being born-again Muslims and it was strictly against their religion for them to eat in non-Muslim houses. My Mam pulled a face and said that that was a shame. But then she brightened up again and said that strange as it must be to us, we must respect other people's religions. We had to count our blessings and all, she said. They might not be able to come to tea but the important thing was that Malcolm and his dad were no longer going back to Baton Rouge. My Mam got up then and went through to the kitchenette, singing as she did so. And all the bones were back in her again then, as she sang her song and reached for the bread and danced a few steps on the kitchenette tiles.

So I kept Malcolm going then and kept on telling my Mam about all the things that Malcolm did and all the things that Malcolm said. And if I ever started to feel guilty about it all, I'd just look at my Mam and see her smiling at me or singing to herself. And I'd think, well, it can't do any harm.

And it didn't.

Until just before my birthday.

I should have known that my Mam was up to something. But I didn't. Not until it was too late. I didn't know that my Mam had dreamed up this marvellous surprise and she'd gone to see Mrs Babu Daruwalla who ran the Eight Till Late in the precinct. My Mam asked her if she could recommend a Muslim restaurant in town. Mrs Babu Daruwalla was happy to oblige and gave my Mam the telephone number of the Vindaloo Village. My Mam booked a table for four people on my birthday. She even asked them if they could do a special birthday cake. And then she phoned the school!

And when Mr Wilson came on the line, my Mam said she was sorry for bothering him but she was planning a surprise birthday party and she'd be really grateful if Mr Wilson could have a confidential word with my American friend Malcolm and ask him and his dad to join us at the Vindaloo Village, seven thirty prompt on Wednesday. But it had to be kept secret, my Mam stressed, because it was a surprise. So would Mr Wilson make sure that Raymond didn't overhear when he talked to Malcolm?

There was a pause. And then my Mam heard Mr Wilson say, 'I'm sorry, who did you say it was speaking?'

'Mrs Marks,' my Mam said, 'Raymond's mother.'

There was another pause. Until my Mam heard Mr Wilson saying, 'Mrs Marks, could you come down to the school straight away please?'

My Mam asked him why.

And Mr Wilson cleared his throat then. And said he'd prefer to discuss it personally with my Mam when she got to the school.

'But I've got a shift this afternoon,' my Mam said. 'There's nothing wrong, is there, Mr Wilson? Our Raymond's all right, isn't he?'

'How could I possibly answer that,' Mr Wilson asked my Mam, 'when Raymond hasn't been near the school for the best part of two months!'

And as my Mam stood there, trying to take in what she'd just heard, Mr Wilson told her the worst part. Told her, 'And I don't know what you mean by an American boy, Mrs Marks. To my knowledge, there are no American boys at this school.'

* * *

I knew. Even before I saw Mr Wilson sat there on the settee, I knew that the shit had hit the fan, because it was still hanging in the air. My Mam was stood there, staring out of the window with her back to me, like she couldn't even bear to look at me. The telly was on with the sound turned down and I just stood there staring at it. I heard my Mam start crying. And then she turned and pushed past me and went into the kitchenette, slamming the door behind her. I just carried on staring at *Blue Peter*. If it had been a normal night we'd have been turning over to ITV by now and watching *Blockbusters*. And we'd be having milky coffee and toast with grilled cheese on top, all hot and bubbling up like the tarmac on the road at the height of an Indian summer. And I'd be telling my Mam all about the things that Malcolm had done today. And if *Blockbusters* turned out to be a bit boring or Bob was being particularly unbearable, I'd be telling my Mam about the really funny things that Malcolm had done. And my Mam would be laughing now. And delighted. If it had been a normal night. But nothing was normal. My Mam was crying in the kitchen. Mr Wilson was sat there on our settee, with a folder on his lap. The toast was still just bread, in the breadbin, the coffee still powder in the jar. And over on ITV, the Blockbusters and Bob were all Blockbusting away without us, doing the hand-jive and being unbearable. And doing it all without me and my Mam.

'Raymond,' I heard him say, 'nobody's going to shout at you.'

I carried on staring at the telly. My Mam came and stood in the doorway of the kitchenette and dabbed at her eyes with some kitchen roll.

'How could you?' she said. 'How could you do that to me? I loved him, I did. I loved that lad!'

She started crying again. And I wished I could cry myself. But I couldn't.

'Raymond, I've been having a long chat with your mum,' Mr Wilson said. 'She's been telling me about some of the things that went on before you moved here to Wythenshawe.'

I just nodded and carried on staring at the soundless *Blue Peter*.

'Like the . . . like the time the policemen pulled you out of the canal,' he said. 'Do you remember that, Raymond?'

I nodded again.

'And this, erm . . . thing about you being . . . what was it, Raymond . . . the *wrong boy*, was it?'

I just shrugged. It was funny on *Blue Peter* because they were launching another appeal, getting the kids to send in their jumble so that the homeless persons would be warm in winter. I hoped they didn't end up with too much jumble from Marks and Spencer's or the homeless persons would all be telling the *Blue Peter* presenters to fuck off. And they don't like homeless persons doing that sort of thing, not on *Blue Peter*.

'I was very interested, you know, Raymond,' he said. 'Yes. Very interested indeed when your mum told me about that, erm . . . wrong boy episode. And this, erm, this . . . Malcolm character, Raymond. I find that, erm . . . intriguing, Raymond. Very intriguing.'

I just carried on staring at the telly. But my Mam said, 'If you'd heard him, Mr Wilson! If you'd heard the way that he did Malcolm's voice . . . I swear to God, Mr Wilson, you would have believed him yourself. You would have sworn that Malcolm really was real.'

Mr Wilson put up his hand in a placatory sort of way and told my Mam, 'Shelagh, don't worry. Believe me, I know exactly how plausible a person can be in such, erm . . . circumstances. I don't doubt for a second that you were completely taken in, Shelagh. I know from the case histories I've studied. You see, if I'm right, Shelagh, then Raymond probably thought he *was* telling the truth. Isn't that correct, Raymond?' he said. 'When you were telling your mum all about this . . . Malcolm, you weren't telling lies to her, were you?'

I just looked at him. Was he soft or what? Of course

256

I'd been telling bleeding lies! Great big massive monster lies! He was stupid. I didn't like him. I certainly didn't like him calling my Mam 'Shelagh'.

I just turned back and stared at the telly again. And he said, 'As far as you were concerned, he was real, wasn't he, Raymond, this Malcolm figure . . . he was real, wasn't he?'

I stared at the credits coming up on *Blue Peter*.

'Am I right about that, Raymond?' he said. 'Didn't you believe that he was a real person, this American lad?'

I just nodded. Because in a way he had been real, Malcolm. 'He *was* real,' I said.

But that started my Mam crying again and she said, 'You! You. How can you say that? It's wicked what you did, it was wicked!'

Wilson calmed my Mam down then. And told her it was pointless, using words like 'wicked'. My Mam said she was sorry and she was doing her best to be understanding but when you've been tricked and cheated and made a fool of, it's not always easy to be so understanding. Mr Wilson said he knew perfectly well how my Mam must be feeling.

'But still, that shouldn't deflect us from pursuing this matter in as non-emotive a manner as possible,' he told my Mam. And turning back to me then he said, 'In what way, Raymond? In what way was this Malcolm a real boy?'

'He was,' I said, as I watched the beginning of *John Craven's Newsround*. 'Malcolm *was* real. Because he was me.'

I could see Mr Wilson's reflection in the television screen and I saw him glance at my Mam and slowly nod at her as if he'd just had something confirmed.

'How do you mean, Raymond,' he asked, 'that Malcolm was you?'

I just shrugged. 'Because he was,' I said. 'Malcolm was the boy I used to be.'

He nodded again, Mr Wilson. And he said, 'Oh, I

see. So you used to be an American boy, did you, Raymond?'

I just shook my head. And watched John Craven being nice in Africa or somewhere.

'No,' I said, 'I made that bit up, about him being American. And about his dad.'

I heard my Mam start crying again. 'And being born-again Muslims,' she said. 'They could have come round for tea after all.' And then she thought of something else and said, 'The jumper! I bought Malcolm a jumper and I don't even know what happened to it. And you,' she said, 'you stand there and have the gall to tell me that you were Malcolm!' She was shouting now, shouting and crying at the same time. 'I bloody well know now that it was just you, that it was only you! It's a bit late now though, isn't it? A bit late in the day, telling me that it was just you all along, just you pretending!'

Mr Wilson got up off the settee and went across to my Mam, telling her it'd be better for all concerned if she could just try and remain calm and rational. My Mam nodded and told Mr Wilson she was sorry again.

And then he said, 'It's all right, Shelagh, it's all right.'

And I didn't want him talking to my Mam. That's when I turned round to her then and I said, 'You don't have to say you're sorry. Because you've got nothing to be sorry about. It's me,' I said, 'I'm the one who's sorry. But I wasn't just pretending,' I said, 'I made up Malcolm because I knew that you'd love him. Like you used to love me. And if I could have sent me back to America and left Malcolm here with you, I would have done that.'

I saw the look on my Mam's face when I told her that. And then her face began to crumple up into a different sort of crying. And I know it would have been all right then, if it had just been me and my Mam and she'd been able to talk to me and tell me that whatever problems we had she'd never swap me, not even for a boy as marvellous as Malcolm.

258

But it wasn't my Mam who talked to me. It was Wilson. And he said, 'Raymond . . . Raymond, it's all right. You see, your mum understands. She's upset, of course. Any mother would be. But as I've already pointed out, your mother is an intelligent woman. And while she might have been shouting a bit, she knows, underneath it all, that we have to approach this problem in as mature a way as possible.'

I wanted him to just shut up! I wanted him to go and leave me and my Mam alone. But it looked like he was never going because he went back and perched himself on the arm of our settee and said, 'Raymond, I want you to listen to me. Will you do that for me?'

I don't know why he bothered asking because you couldn't help listening to him. He never stopped!

'Will you do that for me?' he said.

I just nodded.

'You see, the thing is, Raymond,' he said, 'I don't know how much of this you'll understand but I want to try and explain something to you. Now I've been telling your mum,' he said, 'I can't claim to be an expert in such matters. But as well as having many years of teaching experience, I'm also something of a student, Raymond. Now you're probably surprised about that, aren't you?'

I wasn't surprised at all. The only thing I was surprised at was how they let people like him loose in society!

'Now,' he said, 'I don't know if you've heard of the Open University, Raymond.'

He sort of paused as if he was waiting for me to say something. But I wasn't going to say anything, not to him. I didn't like him. I didn't like people who perched themselves on the arm of our settee and called my Mam 'Shelagh' when they didn't hardly know her. And I didn't like him making out that I'd never heard of the Open University. Everybody knew about the Open University. I was always watching it with my Gran and learning about things like Prometheus who got tied to a rock and the intelligent traffic-light system in Pontin Le Frith.

'Psychology,' he said. 'As well as being a teacher I'm also a student of psychology, Raymond. Now that's a big word,' he said, 'and you don't have to bother your-self with trying to understand what it means. But my studies, Raymond, along with my years of teaching experience, have given me an insight. You could say, Raymond, that I'm alert.'

And he was dead right about that! Because that's exactly what he was, a *Lert*! A big boring Lert who was lounging all over our maisonette. I stopped listening to him. He was just going on about me being the wrong boy and being Malcolm and what all that might in-dicate. But I wasn't listening because I was thinking about how there could be this film called *The Lerts Have Landed* or *The Onslaught of the Lerts* and it'd be all about these mutant Lerts who invade the Earth and suddenly start turning up in small-town America. But all the Lerts go undetected at first because they've disguised themselves as Open University teachers so everybody thinks it's normal that they seem a bit odd. But then the inhabitants of the town start dying in-explicably, the barber and the mailman and the soda jerk, and nobody can work out what they've died from. And soon there's so many bodies that there isn't room in the cemetery for them and the people who aren't yet dead have to keep the cadavers of their deceased neighbours and relatives in their freezer cabinets. But the strange thing is that none of the Lerts ever die. The Lerts just carry on as normal, walking round in their kipper ties and funny haircuts and talking about town planning in Preston and the Peloponnesian Wars. And the only person who starts to get suspicious about the Lerts is the Shoeshine Boy who's got a stammer and a limp but everybody loves him because he's so cute and he can shine a shoe so the shoe can shine like the sun-shine shining on the loco line. But one morning the Shoeshine Boy overhears one of the Lerts talking to another Lert while he's having his shoes shined. And just because he's got a stammer and a limp, the Lerts think the Shoeshine Boy's stupid and deaf as well and so they just talk as if he's not there. But the Shoeshine Boy can hear everything and he knows then, knows it's the Lerts who've been doing all the killing and it isn't just town planning in Preston and advanced hydroponics that they've got in mind, but total world domination! The Shoeshine Boy tries to just keep on polishing the shoes and not show how nervous he is. But one of the Lerts notices that his hands have started to tremble as he tries to polish the shoes. The Lert looks at the other Lert. And they both know then that the Shoeshine Boy's heard everything and so they'll have to kill him. They drag him round to the back of the saloon and while one of the Lerts pins back his arms, the other Lert begins a lecture about soil erosion in Snowdonia. And the Shoeshine Boy feels his eyes starting to glaze over and rapidly starts to lose the will to go on living. And he knows, the Shoeshine Boy, he knows now the secret weapon that the Lerts have been using to kill off all the townsfolk. It's boredom. The Lerts have been boring everybody to death. And now they're about to bore the Shoeshine Boy to death. He's already weak and wounded from the soil erosion in Snowdonia and now the Lerts are about to finish him off with a short module on Neo Vernacular Tendencies in Contemporary Supermarket Design. The Shoeshine Boy's just on the point of losing consciousness and it looks like the Lerts have claimed their latest victim. But then! The Sheriff suddenly appears from around the side of the saloon. The Lerts turn and try to bore him into oblivion with a devastating account of Victorian sewage systems. But the Sheriff just stands there and grins as he slowly lifts his gun from his holster and tells the Lerts, 'Save it for the judge, fellers!' And then the Sheriff points to his ears. And the Lerts can see then that it's useless and they can't even begin to bore the Sheriff to death, because the Sheriff is wearing earmuffs!

After he's locked up the Lerts, the Sheriff goes to see the Shoeshine Boy in the hospital. And although he was nearly killed and bored to death by the Lerts, he's made a miraculous recovery, he doesn't stutter any more and he's even lost his limp. And as he comes out of the hospital, all the people from the town start to cheer and clap and tell him he's a hero and then . . .

But I never quite got to the final credits of the film and what happened to the rest of the Lerts because I suddenly became aware of him again, the real Lert, Mr Wilson in our front room.

And I realised he'd started talking about me going back to school in the morning. So I just kept on staring at the telly and John Craven who was still being nice somewhere in Africa. And I said, 'I'm not going back! I'm not going back to that school. I don't care what you say, I'm never going back to that school!'

And that started my Mam screaming and shouting at me again but I didn't care. Because I wasn't going back and nobody was going to make me go back there. Wilson calmed my Mam down and suggested that she pour out the tea. And while she was doing it, he said to me, 'Raymond, could you explain to me, just to me, *why* you don't want to go back to school?'

And I nodded and kept staring at the telly and told him, 'Because they hate me.'

He asked me who it was who hated me.

I said, 'All of them.'

And Wilson repeated it, 'All of them?'

I just nodded, and he looked at me then and kept saying, 'Mmm, mmm,' and nodding his head. Then he said, 'Is it just the people at school who hate you, Raymond?'

I said, 'No, everyone! Everybody hates me.'

He sighed a big breathy sigh then and nodded his head in deep concern. And then he smiled his benignest smile again and he said, 'What about me, Raymond? You don't think that I hate you?'

I knew he didn't. Wilson was the sort who'd refuse to hate you even if your life depended on it. But I hated him! I didn't want him in our house, sitting on our settee and calling my Mam Shelagh.

So I said, 'I know that you hate me, just like everybody else hates me!' I just glared at him as he sat there staring back at me. And I didn't know, not then; I didn't know that that was when it first entered his head; as he sat there on the arm of our settee, staring at me; and the word 'paranoid' came into his caring, calm, considerate mind.

I didn't know that when he sat there looking at me and slowly nodding his head, that he was looking at something he considered to be 'a fascinating case', a boy who sometimes thought he was the Wrong Boy; a boy who readily testified to paranoid tendencies and already had what appeared to be one suicide attempt behind him; a boy who sometimes heard voices; a boy who may very well have been involved with the abduction of another, younger child; a boy who had so completely and convincingly created a fantasy world and a phantom friend that his mother was almost in a state of grief for the American boy that never was!

But I didn't know that the Lert was thinking anything like that. I just thought he was sitting there working out how he was going to get me back to school. So I told him, I said, 'I don't care what you do to me! I'm not going back to that school.'

My Mam started shouting again. But Wilson held up his hands and appealed for calm.

Then, smiling at me, he said, 'Raymond, Raymond! Have I mentioned anything about you having to go back to school?'

I just stared at him, wondering what he meant as I felt this small flicker of hope.

But my Mam said, 'Of course he's going back to school! He's got to go back to school.'

Wilson shook his head though. And he explained to my Mam that that was not necessarily the case.

I just stood there, barely able to believe my ears, feeling this real sense of relief now as he told my Mam, 'It's in everybody's interests, Shelagh, if we can spend a little time and effort trying to get beyond this ... truanting. And perhaps identify exactly what's at the back of it.'

That's when he said to me we could make a deal. He said that for the next fortnight the question of school could be left in abeyance.

'But a deal is a deal, Raymond,' he said, 'and so you'd have to play your part in it. Now do you think you could do that?'

I nodded quickly. I would have done almost anything to get out of going back to that school.

'All right then, Raymond,' he said. 'Now your part in this deal is that you would have to agree to a period of assessment and that would include attending the assessment centre for two or three afternoons each week.'

'Why?' I said, suddenly suspicious. 'Why would I have to do that?'

He looked at me. And then he suddenly laughed. 'Raymond, Raymond!' he said. 'You're not very trusting of adults, are you?'

I just shrugged.

'But you *can* trust me, Raymond,' he said. 'You've got my guarantee on that. You see, I can understand how you must have come across teachers, Raymond, people in authority who've let you down; perhaps even blamed you for things that weren't your fault. Well, I want you to know, Raymond, that you won't get that from me. I don't believe in blame, Raymond. I know there are all sorts of people, when they see a child with problems they're only too happy to blame the child. But that's not me, Raymond; that's not my way. In most cases, when a pupil is having problems at a particular school, people will blame that pupil, say it's all his fault. But I don't take that approach, Raymond.' He nodded at me. 'Do you know why?'

I shook my head. And he said, 'Because the problem, Raymond, might be the school and not the pupil at all!'

He stood there looking a bit pleased with himself at that. I've got to admit though, I was even pleased myself. Because he was right. If it was a decent school and I liked going there then I never would have stayed off.

'And that's the only reason', he said, 'that I want you to be assessed; because I think that what we might just find is that your academic needs might be better fulfilled in a different, more pertinent educational environment.'

'A different school?' my Mam said.

Wilson nodded. 'Possibly, Shelagh,' he said, 'possibly.'

My Mam looked at me then. 'What do you think about that then?' she asked me.

I nodded. 'I think it'd be good,' I said.

'So will you do it?' she said. 'Will you do what Mr Wilson says and go to that assessment centre?'

I nodded again. And then my Mam asked me to promise her and promise Mr Wilson I'd turn up like I was supposed to and not go truanting from there.

So I did, I promised them both.

Then my Mam said, 'And I think you should thank Mr Wilson, don't you?'

And when I did thank him, I really meant it and I even felt a bit guilty about calling him a Lert; because even though he was boring and patronising and went lerting on too much, I was dead grateful that I wouldn't be going back to that school. My Mam thanked him too and said she didn't know what she would have done without his help and his kindness.

He smiled at my Mam then and as he walked across towards the door, he said, 'Shelagh, if I'm able to provide a little help to a woman like you then really it's my privilege.'

I didn't understand what he meant, 'a woman like you'. And it was funny, but my Mam blurted out this dismissive sort of laugh as she shrugged and lowered her eyes. I didn't know what was wrong with her. It was like she'd suddenly gone girlish.

But then he was talking to me again, Wilson. And he said, 'Raymond, I wonder if . . .' But then he just tailed off and shook his head, saying, 'No! No, maybe not.'

And he was about to leave then but my Mam said, 'What, Mr Wilson? Go on, what were you going to say?'

He started scratching his head and he said, 'Well . . . I was just . . . I suddenly thought, well, you know I mentioned the course I'm doing, psychology? Well, as part of the course I've got to mentor a young person. It's sort of a case study. And I was just wondering if Raymond would like to participate. It wouldn't involve a great deal. I'd just have to meet with Raymond now and then, ask a few questions, sort of build up a profile really.'

He must have seen the scowl on my face though.

'Well, perhaps not,' he said. 'I can see Raymond's not too keen on the idea.'

He was dead right! Raymond wasn't remotely keen on the bleeding idea. But then I heard my Mam saying, 'No! Not at all, Mr Wilson. Raymond wouldn't mind doing that for you, would you, Raymond?' she said, turning and looking at me. 'You wouldn't mind doin' that, helping Mr Wilson with his studies?'

Then, without waiting for an answer from me, she turned back to him and said, 'Raymond would be delighted to help, Mr Wilson. After all the kindness you've shown to us,' she said, 'he'd be delighted. We both would. And if it's a help to you with your studies, then it's the least we can do.'

Then she turned back to me and said, 'Isn't it, Raymond?'

I just stood there, boxed off, stitched up, tied and tethered, a sickly sort of smile on my face as I dutifully nodded my head.

And that's how the Invasion of the Lerts began, Morrissey; with Wilson, the Lert of all Lerts, inveigling

266

himself into my life and into my Mam's. That night, after she'd shown him out, my Mam told me I was very very lucky indeed, having a man like Mr Wilson take an interest in me. And because I was just so glad not to be going back to school I agreed with her. Then my Mam said he seemed to be a very very nice person indeed. And I suppose I should have heard the warning bell right then, right from the very start. But he was the sort of person who wore a cardigan, corduroy trousers and brown suede shoes! And he seemed much much older than my Mam. So I wasn't really listening that much when my Mam said he didn't have any children of his own, Mr Wilson.

'He was just telling me,' my Mam said, 'how he lost his wife, just before the last Olympics. She was only young. Food poisoning. Mussels apparently. On holiday in the Dordogne. They used to go every year.' My Mam shook her head in sympathy. 'It's terrible, isn't it,' she said.

I just nodded. And saw a picture in my mind, of this woman keeled over at a table as her Lert husband sat opposite, still talking, lerting on and on and on, unaware that his own wife was now keeled over in front of him, brutally bored to death, her lifeless head lying face down in a bowl of mussels.

'I think that must be why he's doing this course, this psychology,' my Mam said. 'I think he's trying to fill the void.'

And maybe my Mam was right; maybe that's what he was doing, just 'filling a void'. But I didn't know that part of filling that void meant that I'd have to go to Sunny Pines. And then end up in Swintonfield. I didn't know that already I was being written up on Wilson's computer; that later that night, in discussion with all the other psychology-studying Open University Lerts, he'd tell them about 'a fascinating case'; a boy he knew, a boy in whom he'd taken a personal interest; a boy who exhibited many of the classic signs of emotional disturbance, resulting,

267

probably, from a latent functional psychosis which might very well become increasingly pronounced as time went on!

But I knew none of that, Morrissey; not then.

Yours sincerely,

Raymond Marks

Dear Morrissey,

I always knew it would be particularly grim in
Grimsby. But if this coach journey is anything to go by
then it's patently and painfully apparent that even in
my worst nightmares I have seriously underestimated
the true grossness of the grimness that lies ahead. I
know I should be grateful, with this being a private
coach; and if they hadn't agreed to give me a lift then I
would have been stranded in Huddersfield for the
night. But hideous as Huddersfield is, it might have
been preferable to being cooped up for five and a half
hours with the cream of Grimsby's retail traders. With
them all being shopkeepers and such I'd expected they
might effect a certain degree of that refinement and
sobriety which is apparently so esteemed amongst the
petit bourgeois Rotarian type of person. But they were
all as pissed as rats! They were mostly middle-aged
persons but as soon as the coach set off they started
cheering like they were a load of school kids going off
on a trip. And we hadn't even reached the M62 before
they were singing things like 'My Way' and 'New York,
New York'. Then things got seriously worse because a

woman with a big bosom and a bouffant hairdo stood up and started singing 'Lady In Red' and everybody joined in and even started waving their arms above their heads. I just sat there huddled up against the window, trying to make myself as small as I could and distance myself from such excruciating embarrassment. But then another lady, the one sat in front of me, turned round and said, 'Come on, join in. You'll easily pick it up.'

I was just about to tell her I didn't want to pick it up! I'd rather pick up hepatitis! But then I remembered that they were giving me a lift so I just sort of shrugged and sat there and said nowt. And I hadn't noticed that the big-bosomed bouffant lady had started wandering up the aisle of the coach, still singing as she went. And the first I knew of it was being grabbed by the hand and pulled out of my seat. And before I knew what had happened, she'd got her arms locked around me and I was in the indescribably appalling position of being trapped in the arms of a woman with a bouffant hairdo who was pressing her bosoms and her thighs against me and singing in my ear as we slow-danced in the aisle to that excrementally sentimental ballad by Chris de Burgh! And that wasn't even the worst of it because she stopped singing the lyrics and she started whispering other things. I couldn't believe it at first: she said she had the distinct impression that I was 'fit as a butcher's dog'! I just coughed! But she smiled and pushed herself tighter up against me. I was trying to back away but she had me pinned up against a seat. I looked round hoping there might be someone who could help me. But nobody was taking any notice; they were all just crooning away to 'Lady In Red' and waving their arms like they were in an anthemic trance. Then she whispered in my ear again and her voice was all husky as she said, 'I'll bet you're just dying to play with my chuff button, aren't y'?'

I just stared at her in appalled horror at what such a thing as a 'chuff button' might be. But to be on the safe side I said, 'I'm sorry, but I don't know anything about computers actually!'

She just laughed, a dusky dark laugh in my ear. And then she started running her tongue between her lips as she looked straight at me. Then she whispered in my ear again and she said, 'Have you ever made love . . . with Chris de Burgh . . . in the background?'

And I thought that was the most spectacularly disgusting thing of all! I said, 'I wouldn't even make toast with Chris de Burgh in the background!'

But I don't think she heard me because a man stood up at the front and he shouted, 'Beryl!'

She suddenly let go of me quick, and I scrambled back into my seat and sat there trying not to feel traumatised. I think if I'd been there any longer she might have tried to fondle my genitals! I just sat there, huddled up against the window, hoping I wouldn't have to suffer any such further encounters on Planet Embarrassment. But I'd barely begun to recover when I looked up and saw that the lady sat in front of me had turned round and was kneeling up on her seat, smiling and staring at me.

I just nodded at her cautiously. Then she said, 'Now I could be wrong, I might be wrong; but something tells me . . . you're not a Grimsby lad, are y'?'

I shook my head and she looked at me with her eyes all sparkling and excited. 'Ooh,' she said, 'this is not your first time, is it? Ooh! Is this the first time you've ever journeyed to the Cod Basket of the East?'

I just looked at her and frowned. And wondered if I'd be stuck on Planet Embarrassment for ever.

She was nudging her husband and telling him, 'Walter! Walter! This young man behind us, first timer! Never seen Great Grimsby before in his life!'

I thought that perhaps Walter might be somewhat underwhelmed by a fact of such staggering insignificance. But Walter was suddenly up on his knees beside his wife, his hand stretched out towards me as he said, 'Put it there, young man, put it there!'

It was embarrassing enough, just having to do that bluff blokey sort of stuff like shaking hands; but then he wouldn't even let go and he was crushing my fingers and shaking my arm so hard I was almost bouncing up and down in my seat.

'Walter Walmsley!' he said, beaming a big-toothed smile at me. And then he sort of puffed himself up as he said, 'Otherwise known as "the Codfather"!'

I think I was expected to say something but the power of speech had suddenly been denied me as the two of them sat there beaming with delight and staring at me as if I was some kind of exotic curiosity.

'Ogh, young pup,' Walter said, 'young pup, how I envy you! And do you know why?'

I just shook my head and gawped in incredulity, wondering how anyone who could address an innocent person as a 'young pup' wasn't securely locked up somewhere away from the rest of society.

'What I wouldn't give, young pup,' he said, 'to be in your position; to have in my head such virgin eyes as have yet to first gaze upon the glory that is Grimsby! Ogh . . .' he said, 'you'll never be the same again! You know what they say, don't y', young pup? Know what they say about Grimsby?'

I shook my head again. And Walter and his wife chanted in unison, telling me, 'Once a man gets to Grimsby, Grimsby gets to the man.'

They both roared with delight at that. And then Walter's wife said, 'Now then, come on, there's no need to be shy, you're amongst good Grimsby folk here and we don't stand on ceremony. Come on,' she said, 'get that guitar out of the bag and give us a song.'

And before I could say anything, the Codfather stood up and he told everybody else on the coach to shuttup because 'There's a young pup sat back here and he'd like to give us all a song.'

I was shaking my head and saying, 'I don't, I don't I don't, honest I don't.'

But Walter was oblivious and he'd grabbed my guitar

and he was taking it out of the case and everybody was clapping and turning round in their seats to see who it was who was going to give them a song. I wanted to die! I'd never ever played the guitar anywhere but my bedroom! And now there were fifty-odd people from Grimsby and thereabouts staring at me; and Walter the Codfather was pulling me up from my seat and thrusting the guitar into my hands. Everybody was suddenly clapping and cheering and whistling and Walter held up his hands and quietened them down as he asked, 'What's your name, son? What do they call y'?'

I mumbled my name and tried to tell him that I didn't want to do a song. But he wasn't listening and he was telling the 'audience', 'Ladies and gentlemen, a young lad, a young pup here who is making his very first journey to the Cod Basket of the East.' Everybody cheered and clapped again and Walter said, 'Now let's make him feel like he's one of the family; let's make him feel at home, before he even gets there. Ladies and gentlemen, let's have a real Grimsby greeting for RAYMOND MARKS!'

And then it was like there was this explosion sound in my ears and it was only when it was fading away that I realised it was applause. I looked down the coach and all these eyes were staring back at me. And so I did the only thing I could do: I shut my eyes and pretended I wasn't there, pretended I was back in my bedroom. I started to pick out the first chords that came into my head. I thought I was going to die at first. But then I heard this voice and I realised it was my own voice and I was singing. And here's the weird thing, Morrissey, the really really weird thing is that as I carried on, as I managed to get to the end of the first verse and started to go into the chorus, I realised I was doing all right! And even more than that, I felt myself relaxing and starting to enjoy it. I even opened my eyes! And there was something that was just . . . brilliant, about doing it, playing and singing, not just in my bedroom, not just in front of my mirror but doing it in front of other

people; it felt . . . fantastic. It felt . . . natural . . . it felt
. . . divine, Morrissey; it was like I'd become this other
person. And I could see him, stood in the aisle of a
coach with the guitar and his fingers moving effortlessly along the neck of the instrument, fingering the
chords without hesitation and his voice sounding
strong and even . . . even sort of lyrical. And I was
amazed, Morrissey, amazed at this person and who he
was. It was almost like I was on drugs; not the sort of
drugs they'd made me take when I was in
Swintonfield, drugs which dulled my head and made
me feel like cotton wool. This was like the opposite of
that, like there was something brimful of life coursing
through my veins, like I was the centre of the universe;
like I was immortal.

And then, all too soon, it was over and the final
chord reverberated down the coach, hanging there for
a few seconds like a magical mist before slowly evapor-
ating. And that's when I noticed it, the deafening roar
of absolute silence.

Just for a second I thought that everybody might
have been as similarly awestruck as myself and considered mere applause to be inappropriate for such a
breathtaking performance. But then I looked down the
coach and I realised that people were glaring at me
with palpable hostility. And that's when it started to
dawn on me, what I'd been singing. I just stood there
and stared back at an audience of retail traders, small
shopkeepers, upright Rotarians and their spouses, all
of whom had just been subjected to the lyrics of
'Shoplifters Of The World Unite!'

I started mumbling and I said I'd do them another
song, perhaps something more appropriate this time,
but that seemed to galvanise Walter who was out of his
seat quick and saying, 'You will not! I think we've
heard quite enough, son, quite enough.'

And I sort of felt awful that I'd upset them all. If I
hadn't been so nervous and I'd realised, I never would
have sung that particular song in that particular

environment. I tried to soften the blow a bit and I said, 'I didn't mean to cause any offence. In fact, that lyric,' I said, 'I think it's intended to be seen with a certain sense of satire and irony.'

But Walter just shook his head and said they didn't need satire and irony, not in Grimsby. 'To my ears,' he said, 'it's nothing more than incitement to theft. No wonder,' he said, 'no wonder my members are struggling against an increasing tide of public pilfering when there's degenerates like you condoning theft and robbery.'

'Honestly,' I told him, 'I wasn't doing that at all!'

But he took no notice and somebody piped up from the front, saying they should stop the coach and throw me off. Then I heard somebody else saying they should throw me off without bothering to stop the coach!

And I think they might have done it and all but Walter lifted up his hand and he said, 'Now now! Let's not stoop! Come on, ladies and gents,' he said, 'just because there's some folk who don't know how to behave, let's not lower ourselves to their level! Let's not forget, we're Grimsby folk. And Grimsby folk can rise above such provocation.'

He looked at me like I was something he'd just stepped into. And then he said, 'Come on, Janine.' And he left me standing there as him and his wife moved to a pair of empty seats further down the coach. As they were changing seats he called out to Beryl the Bouffant, saying that after such a distressing interlude he was sure it would be much appreciated by one and all if Beryl could lead the singing of something positive and uplifting as a reminder of the true Grimsby spirit.

And I just started putting my guitar back in its case as Beryl the Bouffant led a fervent rendition of 'Abide With Me' and I slunk into my seat and sat there as if I'd suddenly become the Son of Satan.

The only good thing was that nobody bothered me no more after that. And at least I was able to get my lyric book out, Morrissey, and start writing to you. And it was funny, but even though it felt uncomfortable, being there on that coach with all that hostility around me, it still didn't take away the feeling and the sort of warm glow that I'd got, Morrissey, when I'd been singing your song. I know that me doing one song on a coach and doing it to an increasingly outraged and pissed-off audience of shopkeepers and retail traders is hardly what you could call a performance. And even mentioning it in the same breath as your own astonishing performances is probably a major impertinence. But the thing is, Morrissey, I felt it! I felt what it was liké to stand there and do it. And there was something about it, Morrissey, that made me understand what it must be like for you, what it feels like when *you* stand there on the stage and you become this other person and it's like you just shed the skin of the person you really are and become someone and something else instead. It's like I've seen the disabled people at the baths, Morrissey. And they're all jerky and stiff and out of place in their bodies. And the first time I saw them being pushed to the pool in their wheelchairs I thought it was stupid and cruel. They looked frightened and I was frightened for them and I thought they'd hate it, being put into all that water. But once they were in it, Morrissey, they smiled and they beamed and they shimmered with the beauty of how they felt and who they were in the water that washed all the jerkiness out of them and released the real people inside of them.

And sometimes things are like that, aren't they, Morrissey? Sometimes it's the things you're most frightened of that turn out to be all right; and you find that you can float and swim and not get drowned in the deep and frightening water. Like I was frightened of going to the special school.

My Mam said, 'It's *not* a special school. They don't have special schools nowadays. Mr Wilson explained it all to me. It's a *progress* school, Raymond.'

I just scowled at my Mam; scowled at the sound of Wilson's name. He'd never said, never mentioned anything about any special school. I'd thought I was just being assessed to go to a different ordinary school. If I'd known they were thinking about sending me to a sodding special school I'd never have gone to the bleeding assessment centre or seen the sodding So Shall Worker. And if he hadn't turned up in the middle of *Blockbusters*, he might have got a completely different idea of who I was and what I was like. My Mam thought he was the window cleaner at first. He was wearing jeans and the sort of sweater that gets rejected by the Oxfam shop. But he said he was the Educational Social Worker. He said it might be a good idea if he could speak to me in private. So my Mam took the hint and went to the shops. I wish I'd gone to the bleeding shops as well. He just stood there in the middle of the room and then he said, 'So! Shall we switch the television off now, Raymond?'

Only I don't know why he bothered asking because before I could say owt he'd picked up the remote and obliterated Unbearable Bob and the Blockbusters.

He said, 'It is rude, you know, Raymond, watching television when you have a visitor.'

I said, 'It's not half as rude as walking into a person's front room and switching off their telly.'

But he just ignored me and said, 'So! Shall we introduce ourselves, Raymond? I'm Neville.'

I just looked at him! He nodded though, like he was trying to prompt me. 'And?' he said. 'And?'

'And what?' I said.

'And what's your name?' he said.

I just frowned at him.

'Come on,' he said, 'aren't you going to introduce yourself to me, Raymond?'

I was starting to get worried! He seemed like a lunatic person.

'Come on,' he said, 'tell me who you are.'

'You already know who I am!' I said.

But he was grinning and shaking his head and said, 'No, Raymond. I don't think I do.'

'Well, I think you do!' I said. 'Because you've said my name three times already.'

But he was shaking his head and still grinning his gormless grin.

'Did you know, Raymond,' he said, 'that the Native Americans of North Dakota believe that the giving of one's name is the giving of a gift. Did you know that?' he said.

I just gawped at him.

He nodded. 'Well, it's true,' he said, 'and in giving his name a person is giving the gift of friendship; he's declaring that he bears no hostility. And that's why I think it would be very good, Raymond, if you could introduce yourself to me. So, shall we try again?' he said. 'I'm Neville.'

I shrugged.

'And I'm pissed off!' I said.

I thought that might shut him up but he seemed delighted. He sat down and opened up his file as he said, 'You see, Raymond, hostility. You feel a hostility towards me, don't you?'

I nodded.

Then he nodded too and said, 'So shall we try and explore this a little further, Raymond? Have you any idea what's causing you to have these feelings of aggression towards me?'

'Yes!' I said. 'I wanted to watch *Blockbusters* but you've switched off the bleeding telly!'

He looked at me and nodded. 'So shall we explore this a little further?' he said. 'You see, what you're really saying here, Raymond, is that given the choice between interacting with an inanimate box or with a human being, your preference would be for the television. Is that right?'

I nodded.

'And . . . do you have any idea why that might be?' he asked.

'Yeah,' I said, 'because the telly's not boring.'

He looked at me. 'But me,' he said, 'a fellow human being, you find me boring?'

'Extremely,' I said.

He nodded. 'Well, that's intriguing, isn't it, Raymond,' he said, 'because you've only just met me whereas many, many people who've known me much longer than you consider me to be quite the opposite of boring.'

'Well, why don't you go and talk to one of them?' I said. 'And then I can watch *Blockbusters*.'

But he just opened up his pad instead and started writing things down in it. While he was doing that, I said, 'Can we have the telly back on now?'

He ignored me though and said, 'So! Shall we talk about this hostility, Raymond?'

But I ignored him then, like he'd ignored me. I didn't even know what he was talking about. I just sat there staring at the blank telly.

'So shall we, Raymond?' he insisted.

I looked at him. I said, 'Is that why they call you the So Shall Worker?'

He looked puzzled then. 'What do you mean?' he asked.

'*So shall*,' I said, 'so shall, so shall, so shall. You're always sayin' it!'

He just stared at me. Then he said, 'Does this happen a lot, Raymond?'

'Does what happen?' I said.

'Getting your words mixed up,' he said, 'confusing them.'

I said, 'They're not mixed up. I haven't confused them at all.' I said, 'It's you, you keep saying it! *So shall* we explore this? *So shall* we talk about that? *So shall* we do this? So shall, so shall, so shall!' I said. 'So that's why you're the So Shall Worker.'

He looked a bit peeved.

But I just shrugged and said, 'So! Shall we put the telly back on now?'

He ignored me again. Then he looked through his file and he said, 'Now you've spoken with Mr Wilson, haven't you?'

'Yeah,' I said, 'the Lert!'

'What?' he said.

'The Lert!' I told him. 'Wilson, the Lert!'

He frowned at me. 'Why do you call him that?' he asked.

I just shrugged. 'Because that's what he told me,' I said. 'He told me he was a Lert.'

The So Shall Worker frowned again. 'Do you mean', he said, 'that Mr Wilson said he was . . . *alert*?'

I nodded. 'That's right,' I said, 'a Lert! And they're threatening to take over the world, the Lerts. Mind you,' I said, 'you probably know that!'

He stared at me, the So Shall Worker. Then he looked down into his file again and he said, 'When you were younger, your mum took you to see a doctor, didn't she, a special sort of doctor.'

I nodded. 'That's right,' I said, 'Psycho The Rapist.'

He looked at me all squinty-eyed, the So Shall Worker. He said, 'Say that again.'

I said, 'Psycho! Psycho The Rapist.'

He just carried on looking at me.

I said, 'What's up?'

He said, 'Have you always done this?'

'Done what?' I said.

'Taken words,' he said, 'and twisted them into other things.'

I shrugged. 'It's just something that happens,' I said, 'like the witch on the beach.'

He sat there frowning and looking puzzled.

'The evil witch, on the beach!' I told him. 'Like when you're first learning to read and you have to put the words together by sounding out the different parts of the word. And that was the first really big word I ever had to read out loud. I had to sound it out for the teacher. And then I was dead frightened when I did because I thought Peter and Jane might get caught by the evil witch and then we'd never be able to read about Peter and Jane no more.'

He was just staring at me, the So Shall Worker.

280

So I told him, 'It was all right though, in the end; because the Sand Witch wasn't a witch who lived on the beach at all. So Peter and Jane had never really been in any sort of danger of being captured by the evil witch. And as soon as I'd got used to putting the two parts of the word into one, it was just two pieces of bread with some jam in the middle.'

He was staring at me with his mouth open and his forehead all creased up. He said, 'What was?'

I said, 'The sandwich!'

He stared at me for a bit longer. Then he started writing in his file again. He suddenly looked up though. And he said, 'So even when you were very young you were seeing things like evil and fear and blackness, this ... *blackness* in something as ... innocuous as a sandwich?'

I frowned at him. 'What do you mean,' I said, 'what *blackness*?'

But he just shook his head and he wouldn't say anything more about it. But I knew then, I knew he must have been talking about me with Wilson; the So Shall Worker and the chief Lert, comparing notes. But nobody had ever asked *me* about the blackness!

It was at the assessment centre; we had to do things like stupid art therapy classes. Wilson used to turn up there to see how I was doing. He always looked at my pictures. He'd stand at the back of me, looking over my shoulder and saying nowt. Sometimes he'd pick up my drawing and take it over to the art therapist and the two of them would stand there quietly talking about it, with one of them occasionally looking over at me and the other one nodding. But no-one ever asked *me* about it. Nobody ever came over and asked me, 'Raymond, why do you only ever use the colour *black* in your pictures?'

They just kept nodding and looking at all the black things I drew – the black sun, the black moon, the black trees, black snow – and concluded that it was me demonstrating all the blackness I felt inside of me. But

I wasn't at all bloody black inside and if someone had bothered to ask me I would have told them that with me sitting at the back of the art therapy room and all the other kids being bigger than me, by the time I got to the crayon box, the only bleeding colour left was sodding *black*. But nobody ever bothered to ask.

All they ever did, all of them, was just keep looking for what they wanted to see. And when it was all over, the assessment, and they'd got their profile, Wilson explained to my Mam that I'd be much better suited to the dedicated and sympathetic environment of the progress school.

Sunny Pines, my Mam said it was called. She said, 'It sounds nice, doesn't it, Sunny Pines?'

But I didn't think it sounded nice at all; it sounded like something you put in the toilet to try and hide the smell. I didn't want to go there.

I'd seen kids from the special school. You could always tell the kids who went there because they didn't get the ordinary bus and they had to stand at the lay-by instead and wait for the private minibus. And they always got picked on, the special school kids; spat at and called four-eyed twats and window-lickers and told to get back to fuckin' looney school, by all the nice, normal, ordinary kids who went to the nice, normal, ordinary schools. And even when you were inside the special school it was horrible because all the teachers were dead hard and they had to be hard and nasty because there were really big lads in there who'd even fight with the teachers, let alone the little first-year kids who got made to do awful things or got picked on and battered up at playtime. I didn't want to get picked on and battered up. I didn't want to go anywhere near a place like that. And I never would have gone there; I would have just refused to go, if my Gran hadn't got ill and become such a big worry to my Mam. It was after my Gran came back from Scotland. And I'd been waiting for her to come back because I knew that when my Gran found out my Mam was sending me to a special school, my Gran'd go mad and tell my Mam she must be out of her mind, sending me to a school with all the dyslexics, the disturbed and the don't-know-what-to-do-withs. My Gran wouldn't be impressed by the fact that they were called 'progress' schools nowadays. My Gran would just say, 'Yes! And water's called Perrier nowadays. But giving it a bit of fizz and calling it by a fancy French name doesn't stop it being wet!'

But my Gran never got to say anything like that; because when my Gran did get back from Scotland she was never really the same again. Mr McGough who was in charge of the Progressive Pensioners came round to see my Mam. And he said they'd had a terrible time with my Gran. They'd all gone on a two-week coach excursion called Scotland's Suffering: The Sites of Caledonian Misery. And at first my Gran had been having a marvellous time, seeing all the sites of suffering and slaughter and the catacombs in Edinburgh where the streets had been sealed shut and all the people with the bubonic plague left to die. My Gran was made up and said it was a real tonic, being in a country where there'd been so much misery and all the people seemed so suitably sombre.

But then the coach had stopped near Dumfries so the pensioners could visit the house where Robert Burns had suffered such hardship and penury before he died his tragically early death from overwork and rheuma-toid arthritis and the stupid doctor who made him drink mercury then stand up to his neck in the freezing waters of the Solway Firth. And Mr McGough said he knew my Gran had been particularly looking forward to that part of the excursion which was generally con-sidered to be the tragic high spot of the whole trip. Only, when they got there, my Gran said she was feeling a bit weary and didn't think she was up to the excitement of all that misery. She said she'd just sit on the coach. And Mr McGough didn't think any more about it. He went off with the other pensioners, believing my Gran had just got a bit overwhelmed by the wealth of such sustained Scottish suffering. But when him and the other pensioners returned to the coach, they found my Gran was sat there with a sheep. They all stopped and stared at my Gran. But she just patted the sheep on the head and told the pensioners, 'Come on, he's a good dog. He's very placid, he won't bite.'

All the pensioners looked at each other. Then Mr McGough said, 'Now then, Vera, what's this?'

'It's Rex!' my Gran said. 'Rex, my dog.'

And that's when Sylvia Mortimer told my Gran, 'Don't talk tripe, Vera! How can it be your Rex? You told me yourself, your Rex died, didn't he? Didn't he get run over by a trolley bus in Trafford Park when you were only twelve?'

And apparently my Gran frowned then. She turned and looked at the sheep. Then she slowly put her fingers up to her mouth as her eyes filled up with tears and she asked, 'What have I done?'

My Gran was all embarrassed after that and said she didn't know what had possessed her to do such a stupid thing. But everybody on the coach was dead nice to her. And Mr McGough (who'd always been particularly fond of my Gran) said, 'Vera, forget about it. It's just a bit of a lapse, that's all. It happens at our age, Vera; we all have our little lapses.'

But my Gran told him to stop being a patronising pillock. And Mr McGough was made up then because he knew that my Gran was all right again. Only my Gran wasn't all right. Because when they got to Galashiels, my Gran went missing and they had to get the police. They found my Gran outside the gates of the local junior school, where she was stood crying and saying that she'd get the cane because she'd forgotten her homework.

And after that it went from bad to worse, Mr McGough said. In the end, he decided the best thing was to bring my Gran back home and leave the rest of the Positive Pensioners to enjoy the remaining Scottish misery without them.

My Mam went straight round to my Gran's. But when she got there, my Gran seemed like she was just her normal self, complaining about being brought back from Scotland and saying Mr McGough was a mithering tit!

My Mam was dead relieved. And because she didn't want my Gran to be ill, she told herself it probably *was* Mr McGough making a lot of fuss over nowt. It was only as she was leaving my Gran's that she saw the three tins of Pedigree Chum on the sideboard. And my Mam said, 'What's this, Mother? Whose is the dog food?'

My Gran looked at it and frowned. 'It's not mine!' she told my Mam.

'Then whose is it?' my Mam asked.

'Don't be stupid!' my Gran said. 'It's Rex's.'

The doctor said it was hard to say. He said you could never be sure. He said sometimes just a lack of oxygen could cause that sort of behaviour. Physically, he said, my Gran was doing very well for a woman of her years. And when he asked my Gran the questions, like what her name was, when she was born, what was the name of the present prime minister, my Gran just gave him a look and said if he wanted to sit there playing silly bugger quizmasters, he could at least ask her a few decent questions. The doctor smiled at that and said, 'All right then, Vera . . . let's see . . . right . . the chap who was in charge of public health at the time of the Crimean War . . .'

'Aye aye,' my Gran said, 'that's going back a bit, isn't it?'

'Come on,' the doctor said, 'you wanted a difficult question so I'm giving you one. What was his name and what was particularly noteworthy about him?'

My Gran just glared at the doctor. Then she suddenly smiled and said, 'Easy. J. M. Barry! Different spelling but same name as the little Scottish feller who wrote *Peter Pan*. And when he died, it was only then

285

that they discovered that the J. M. Barry of the Crimea was really a woman who'd been passing herself off as a man.'

The doctor was impressed. He smiled at my Mam and as he put his stethoscope away he said, 'Well, I can't see there's much wrong with a mind like that.'

And as he was going, the doctor told my Mam, 'She seems fine. Just keep an eye on her.'

My Mam was overjoyed. And she said it was all a false alarm and probably it was just a lack of oxygen from being cooped up in that coach for a week. But my Mam's relief was short-lived because on Sunday night my Uncle Jason and my Aunty Paula turned up at ours. I was trying to watch *The Antiques Roadshow* but I couldn't hear anything because as soon as he walked in, my Uncle Bastard Jason started kicking off about my Gran. He said he'd been called out by the police who'd found my Gran stood outside the Kentucky Fried Chicken at six o'clock on a Sunday morning. And when they'd asked her what she was doing, my Gran had said, 'Waiting for my finger-lickin' chicken wings and my barrel of barbecued beans!'

My Uncle Bastard Jason said him and my Aunty Paula had had to take my Gran back to theirs for the day and all their Sunday dinner had been disrupted because my Gran wouldn't eat the sirloin of beef and kept asking what had happened to her barbecued beans and her finger-lickin' chicken.

My Uncle Jason told my Mam it couldn't go on like this and they'd have to think about putting my Gran in a nursing home. But my Mam was horrified when she heard that.

'Don't be stupid!' she said. 'There's no need for that. It's just a lack of oxygen. There's nothing wrong with my mother's mind. She's just a bit confused at present, that's all.'

But my Uncle Jason started growling and said, 'Yes and I'm bloody confused, Shelagh! I'm confused by your stubborn bloody refusal to accept what's right in front of your nose. Whether you like it or not, the fact is that our mother is no longer all there. She was never fully there in the bloody first place if y' ask me. But lately, she's gone dafter than a day out in Blackpool! And something's got to be done! It's all right for you,' he said, 'living out here in Wythenshawe. But we're on the bloody doorstep. We're the ones who have to pick up the pieces.'

My Mam just looked at the bombastic bastard. 'I don't care what you say, Jason,' my Mam said, 'I don't agree with y'. I don't think there's that much wrong with her at all.'

'Not much wrong with her?' my Uncle bellowed. 'A seventy-bloody-odd-year-old woman goes wanderin' off in the dead of night, trying to buy a bucket of chicken wings and barbecued beans and you say there's nothing wrong with her!'

'She could have been hungry!' my Mam snapped.

'Yes, and she could have been bloody well mugged an' all,' my Uncle said. 'Wanderin' the streets at that hour when y' don't know who the bloody hell's about – intravenous drug users and young persons who've turned their backs on society. She's bloody lucky not to have been gang-raped and left for dead.'

'For Christ's sake,' my Mam snapped, 'will you shut up! Don't y' think I'm worried enough without you bloody well sounding off like a sodding Sunday newspaper?'

And even he could see then, my stupid Uncle, he could see that my Mam was almost at the end of her tether. So he affected his tone of reasonableness and worldly wisdom then and he said, 'Now look, Shelagh. We're upset. We're all upset. I'm gutted I am, Shelagh, I'm bloody gutted to think that my mother's started going Alka-Seltzer! But she has, Shelagh. And we've got to accept it, love. She's gonna need looking after. We can't do it, not with two young kids and a sick budgerigar, we can't. And you can't, can y'? You've got your own cross to bear, haven't y'?'

I knew he meant me when he said that. But I didn't even look at him. I just carried on trying to watch the telly where the woman with the ormolu clock was trying to appear interested as Hugh Scully kept lerting on about the delicate detail and the marvellous movement when all she wanted was Hugh Scully to get to the good bit and tell her how much the clock was worth. But I heard my Mam start crying then and saying that everything was getting on top of her and she didn't know how she could cope any more. My Aunty Paula went and put her arms around my Mam then and said, 'Agh . . . poor love, poor love. We know how hard it must be for y', Shelagh; don't we, Jason? Don't we always say, she's a martyr, our Shelagh, she really is, a martyr that girl.'

She sickened me, my Appalling Aunty Paula. So I just turned back and looked at the telly. And Hugh Scully was asking the woman with the ormolu clock if she had it insured; so I knew then that it probably was worth a fortune. Only I never got to find out because that's when I heard my Aunty Paula asking my Mam if she'd like to go round to theirs next Saturday, share a fondue supper and watch *Sky Movie of the Week*.

I shot round in my chair and looked at her. And my Mam was looking at her as well.

'I didn't know you could get Sky,' my Mam said, wiping her nose and putting her handkerchief away.

My Aunty Paula and my Uncle Jason looked at each other.

'Oh yes. Yes,' my Aunty Paula said, 'didn't I mention that we'd gone satellite?'

'No,' my Mam said, 'you didn't actually.'

'Oh it's bloody marvellous,' my Uncle Jason said. 'We've got choice now, y' see, Shelagh. We've got choice coming out of our ears, haven't we, Paula?'

'Oh we can watch anything we like, whenever we like, can't we?' my Aunty Paula said. 'Do you know, Shelagh, there's one night, Tuesday I think it is, when we can choose, just listen to this, Shelagh, we can choose from twenty-nine different game shows. Twenty-nine; think about that!'

My Mam just stared at the two of them until my Uncle Jason said, 'Is there summat the matter, Shelagh?'

'Where did y' get it from?' my Mam asked.

'What?' my Aunty Paula said.

'Your satellite system,' my Mam said, 'where did it come from?'

'Well, where do you bloody think it came from?' my Uncle Jason said.

'That's what I'm asking you,' my Mam declared.

My Uncle Jason looked at her but my Mam didn't flinch from his gaze. My Mam got to her feet then and she said, 'Have you taken my mother's satellite dish?'

That brought my Aunty Paula to her feet too as she said, 'Shelagh!'

'Well?' my Mam insisted. 'Your twenty-nine different game shows, are they courtesy of my mother's satellite dish?'

'I've told you!' my Uncle Jason barked, 'Dixons! We got our system from Dixons in the bloody high street!'

'Right!' my Mam said. 'So when I go round to my mother's tomorrow, I'll still see it up there on the roof, will I, *her* satellite dish?'

My Uncle Jason just stared for a second like he'd had the wind taken out of him. But then he rallied again and he said, 'Of course you bloody won't! Because she flogged it, didn't she? Her satellite system. Flogged it through the classifieds. Let it go for peanuts and all! Sold for next to nowt to a Pakistani paediatrician from Prestwick pleading poverty. She said she wanted him to have the satellite dish so he could keep up with his Gujarati. Isn't that right, Paula?'

My Aunty Paula nodded quickly.

'I see!' my Mam said. 'And when I see my mother tomorrow, she'll confirm this, will she, Jason?'

My Uncle Jason and my Aunty Paula looked at each other again. Then my Aunty Paula said, 'Shelagh,

289

we've been trying to tell y', love, your mother's not well. And, you see, once the mind starts to go, Shelagh, they start imagining all sorts of things. Like when your mother was at ours today, it didn't matter how many times we tried to tell her that ours was a brand new satellite system, fresh from Dixons; but your mother couldn't take it in, Shelagh. All afternoon she sat there staring at our decoder box, saying, "That's mine, that's mine." And it didn't matter how many times we explained it to her, Shelagh, she's got it into that puddled head of hers that we've taken *her* satellite dish! Now as if, Shelagh, as if we'd do something like that to a poor old lady who's all enfeebled and suddenly presenting all the signs of Alka-Seltzers.'

'And that's why,' my Uncle Jason said, jumping in dead quick, 'we've got to sort something out, Shelagh. She needs professional care and you've got to start facing up to it.'

And I could tell then that he'd got my Mam where it hurt and she was about to give up on the satellite dish. So I jumped in quick too and I said, 'What was his name?'

They all turned and looked at me.

'His name, Uncle Jason,' I said, 'what was his name?'

He screwed up his face. '*Whose* bloody name?' he said.

'The paediatrician from Prestwick,' I told him.

He looked at me like I'd just crawled out from under a rancid rasher.

'How would I know his bloody name?' he said.

I just shrugged. 'Well, you seem to know everything else about him,' I said, 'including his profession, his native language, his ethnic origin and his current place of residence. I thought perhaps you might be writing his biography.'

My Uncle Bastard Jason and my Acidic Aunty Paula both looked at me with the sort of slit-eyed look that you could cut fresh bread with. But I just stared back at them.

Then my Aunty Paula turned to my Mam like I wasn't there and she said, 'I believe he's starting at the special school, isn't he, Shelagh?'

'It's *not* a special school!' my Mam declared. 'It's a *progress* school, Paula. A progress school.'

My Aunty Paula started nodding. 'Oh, of course,' she said, 'progress school, that's right.'

Then she turned and looked at me with the sort of smile the Queen puts on when she's in Africa. And she said, 'And do they think he will make some progress there, Shelagh?'

'There's no stigma,' my Mam said. 'There's no stigma these days, Mr Wilson told me; in fact, he said, some of those children who go to Sunny Pines, they're some of the most highly intelligent children in the whole of the county.'

My Acrid Aunty raised an eyebrow and slowly nodded her head. 'Is that right, Shelagh?' she said.

And my Mam tried to tell her how I'd probably do much better in Sunny Pines because, like Mr Wilson said, it was a more pertinent educational environment. But I could tell from her voice that my Mam had no more fight left in her. Because once it got onto schools and education, my Mam knew she couldn't even begin to compete and she'd just have to stand there and get battered with reports of how my Aunty Paula had recently put down the names of her appalling progeny at Manchester Grammar. So my Mam just said, 'Look, I'm a bit jiggered at the minute and I've still got a lot of . . .'

But my Aunty Paula and my Uncle were already headed for the door, telling my Mam they had no intention of outstaying their welcome. Then as they got to the door, my Aunty Paula paused and said, 'So we'll see y' next, Shelagh, for a fondue supper and *Movie of the Week.*'

'I'll see,' my Mam told them.

And as he was leaving, my Repulsive Uncle said, 'And y' better put your mind to it, Shelagh: we're gonna have to do something about my mother.'

When they'd gone I just looked at my Mam and I could see that she was all preoccupied and nearly at the end of her tether. And that's why I didn't kick up any fuss any more, about going to Sunny Pines; because my Uncle Bastard Jason had robbed the satellite dish; because my Gran was coming down with the Alka-Seltzers; and because my Mam had all the worries of the world on her shoulders and was nearly at the end of her tether.

I hated it! I hated having to get the stupid minibus and having to drive for ages, picking up kids from here, there and everywhere. It should have been better, because the classes were dead small at Sunny Pines. But you'd be sitting there in the classroom doing your work and it'd all be fairly quiet; then the next thing there'd suddenly be this high-pitched scream or something being smashed and you'd shit yourself before you realised it was just someone like Elvis Fitzsimmons going into one of his fits or Deborah Johnstone smashing her chair into the radiator because it wasn't the right chair, it wasn't her chair, it was the wrong fucking chair and all the bastards had hidden her chair, her special chair. By the time the teacher had dealt with Deborah, calmed her down and convinced her that there wasn't really a chair con-spiracy, the bleeding lesson would be over. And nobody really seemed to give a toss about learning any-thing. I felt sorry for them really, people like Deborah and Elvis Fitzsimmons and Ambrose McFadden. But even though I did really feel sorry for them, they got on my nerves, them and Chantelle Smith and all the others who had things wrong with them and were always kicking off and messing up all the lessons, so you couldn't really get on with anything. It was like being in some sort of a prison, being at Sunny Pines. And the Wednesday of that first week, when I found out about us having to do gardening, that's when I decided enough was enough; and tomorrow the Sunny

Pines minibus would be leaving Wythenshawe with-out me.

Gardening! I couldn't believe it! I thought it was just a stupid joke at first. But me and all the other boys in my year were trotted out to these patches of soil where there was this man who looked like a fat scarecrow. But he was the teacher! He had big wellies and a beard which looked as though it had birds nesting in it.

He kicked off when he saw me. 'They didn't tell me!' he said. 'Nobody told me there was a new lad starting! What am I supposed to do? There's no spare plots. I haven't got any spare plots for new lads who just turn up without me being informed about any new lad. What am I meant to do when there's no spare plots?'

I just looked at him and shrugged. I didn't have the first bleeding idea of what he was meant to do. He was supposed to be the teacher, not me! I didn't care a toss about any sodding spare plots anyway. I didn't want to do any stupid bleeding gardening in the first place. So I just stood there while he handed out the spades and things to the other boys and they all went off to their various bits of garden. I thought I was going to get out of having to do anything at all. But then he suddenly handed me this gardening thing and said, 'Here, take this hoe. You can work on one of the third years' plots for now.'

And then he pointed to a patch of soil and said, 'You get on with weeding that.'

But he didn't even tell me how to do weeding because all the other lads from my class had started fighting and throwing soil at each other so he had to rush over and give them a bollocking. Then, while he was doing that, Ambrose McFadden, who had an un-fortunate twitch and an even more unfortunate haircut, started crying and saying the handle on his spade was blue and he was supposed to have a green-handled spade, not a blue one. All the others started laughing at him which made him even worse until he flung the offending spade as far as he could and sat down in

293

the middle of his plot, crying his eyes out and telling everyone to fuck off.

It was just like being at the bleeding infants' school again! All you could hear was Ambrose screaming and all the others laughing. I was glad to be on my own. I just carried on doing what the teacher had told me, chopping off all these long green weeds and being dead pissed off because if my Gran hadn't been ill she would have been able to save me from all this. I knew it wasn't really my Gran's fault and I shouldn't have been mad at her. But I was mad at everything, at my Gran and my Mam and Wilson and my Uncle Bastard Jason; and mad at being there, in a special school and in a class with a load of stupid lads who thought it was the height of hilarity to tease Ambrose McFadden and then, when they got bored with that, spend the rest of the lesson doing nowt but throw soil at each other. So the more I had to hoe those weeds, the more mad I got about being in a place like this. In the end I was just chopping and hacking at them all and sending bits of them flying all over the place till there were barely any more weeds left to chop down.

I didn't know! Not till he came running over, the fat scarecrow of a teacher, and he was shouting, saying, 'Jesus Christ, lad, Jesus Christ . . . what the bloody hell are y' up to at all?'

'I'm chopping down the weeds,' I said, 'that's all; just doin' what you told me!'

But he looked like he was going to pass out. His face was all red and he said, 'Weeds! They're not weeds, y' senseless little bugger!'

Then he snatched the hoe out of my hand and all the other lads started crowding round and laughing as he said, 'They're bloody turnips, lad! You've chopped off an entire bloody crop of turnip tops!'

Everybody was staring down at the decimated plot and chopped-off turnip tops. And then the boy with the twitch and the unfortunate haircut said, 'That's Gonzo's plot!'

And Elvis Fitzsimmons had this excited, blood-thirsty look in his eye as he said, 'Ogh! Just wait! Wait till Gonzo finds out about this!'

And I heard somebody else saying, 'It's that new lad, the fat one. He's killed all Gonzo's turnips!'

Then Elvis Fitzsimmons started running towards the school building, saying, 'I'm gonna tell. I'm gonna get Gonzo now an' tell him!'

I looked up at the teacher and I said, 'It's not my fault! How am I supposed to know about gardening? I live in a maisonette! You didn't tell me,' I said, 'you didn't tell me which were the weeds!'

But he just ignored me and started collecting up all the hoes and spades from the others, mumbling something about early retirement and kids who get thicker and thicker with every passing year. Then he just walked off towards the school as the bell for dinner-time started ringing.

And the word about the turnip tragedy must have spread around the school faster than dog-shit on a shoe because as all the kids streamed out into the play-ground, loads of them came running across to the gardening plots until it seemed like there were hundreds of them around me and all of them were staring at the turnip tops and exclaiming, saying things like 'Fuckin' hell!' and 'Shiiiiiiittttt!' and 'Someone's gonna well fuckin' get it off Gonzo!'

That's when I started to try and get away. I just tried to walk away at first. But none of them would let me through and they stood there, all around me, staring at me and blocking my way. So then I tried to push my way through but some of the big lads pushed me back and sent me stumbling onto one of the other plots. And one of them said, 'Stay where y' are, you! Blubber Boy.' Some of them started laughing at that, laughing like hyenas. And some of them started chanting, saying, 'Blubber Boy, Blubber Boy, Blubber Boy.'

I just stood there, trying not to cry, doing my best not to cry; knowing that I was done for for ever at Sunny

Shitty Pines if I began crying in front of everybody. And instead of crying it was just like something snapped, really. Suddenly, all the madness started coming out of me and I didn't care and it didn't matter if I got bashed up or flattened and beaten up; I didn't ... fucking well care. And I didn't want to be in the stupid fucking school with the stupid fucking kids doing stupid fucking gardening. And I snarled at them all and I said, 'So where the fuck is he then, this gormless fuckin' Gonzo?'

And that's when I heard it, the voice from the back of the crowd, the voice that said, 'Right fuckin' here!'

And suddenly all my madness and anger just evaporated and I stood there, silently shitting myself as the crowd parted. And walking towards me was this big, ugly, curly-haired lad, with flared nostrils and his eyes fixed on me as he walked up and then stopped in front of me. He just looked at me. And then slowly he turned his head and quietly said, 'Move!' Some of the kids scattered quick, and stood back, revealing the chopped-off turnip tops in all their wilting glory. Then he turned and looked at me again and all I could do was stand there, staring back, waiting for it to happen, waiting for him to hit me. And that's when I started to realise, when we were stood there facing each other on the vegetable plots, surrounded by half the school; that's when I started to see someone who wasn't quite so tall or as big as this Gonzo, somebody with the same curly hair but without the beginning of bristles on his cheeks; someone who once had a pit-bull terrier and used to say the Chinese people were all slant-eyed twats; someone who'd always looked nowty and churlish and dead angry all the time; apart from one day, one day a long time ago, when I'd been a little kid, holding a silver-foil star aloft crooning the words to 'Little Town of Bethlehem'. And I'd watched him then, this Gonzo person, as he'd preciously picked up Twinky McDevitt from a donkey and tenderly cradled the makeshift Madonna in his big thick boyish arms.

And now, staring up at his scowling face, I said to him, 'Joseph the Carpenter!'

His eyes suddenly narrowed up as he squinted and stared in bewilderment.

I said, 'You're not Gonzo! You're just Norman Gorman from Failsworth!'

He cocked his head to one side, looking a bit wary now as he said, 'And who the fuck are you?'

'Raymond Marks!' I said. 'I used to live in Failsworth. You were in the top class at Binfield Road Juniors when I was in class eight.'

He stared at me for what seemed ages. Then some of the other kids started getting impatient and urging him to gob me one and reminding him about his traumatised turnips. But Norman Gorman just kept staring at me, like he was trying to work something out. Then this look started to spread across his face, like he'd just solved something. And he pointed at me then as he said, 'You're him, aren't y'? After me an' Twink had left Binfield fuckin' Road. You're that fuckin' kid! With the flies an' that! The flytrapping kid! That was fuckin' you, wasn't it?'

He was still pointing at me. I didn't know what to say! I didn't want anybody to know, not about the fly-trapping. But then Norman Gorman said, 'The flytrappin' game! That was fuckin' brilliant that was!'

I just looked at him. But he was smiling now and staring at me with a sort of awestruck admiration. And he said, 'Fuckin' hell, man! When me an' Twink heard about that, we couldn't fuckin' move. Twink was jealous as shit when he heard about that flytrapping. He said why didn't he think of it because it was fuckin' brilliant, man, solid fuckin' brilliant. Twinky said, "The kid who thought that up, they should have given him the Duke of Fuckin' Edinburgh Award."'

Norman Gorman shook his head. 'And that was you, wasn't it?' he said.

That's when I cautiously began to nod. But then

Ambrose McFadden said, 'So aren't y' gonna gob him one then, Gonzo?'

Norman Gorman looked at me. And then he said, 'Gob him?' He smiled then. And turning to Ambrose McFadden he said, 'Course I'm not gonna gob him, y' fuckin' window-licker!'

He pointed at me and he said, 'Raymond Marks! Fuckin' legend! I'm not gonna gob a legend just for a few fuckin' turnips. And not when he didn't get the Duke of Edinburgh Award or nowt, did y'?'

I shook my head. And Norman said, 'No, that's fuckin' right!' And then he turned to the others and he said, 'Got bounced, right. Got bounced out that fuckin' junior school, he did.'

Norman turned to me then and he said, 'Didn't y', Raymond?'

I nodded again. And that's when Norman took a step towards me, put his arm around my shoulder and started telling everybody, 'Me and Raymond here, we're fuckin' soul brothers. We both got fuckin' griefed up by that bastard new headmaster at Binfield Road. That's why I ended up here with all you fuckin' plant-pots and window-lickers, because of that fuckin' headmaster. Me and fuckin' Raymond here. We both of us got bollocksed by that same bastard.'

It was funny, standing there in the middle of that crowd with Norman Gorman telling all the others about it as if him and me had been oppressed people who'd suffered at the hands of the same regime. It felt sort of nice really. But then some kid at the back said, 'So what the fuck was it then, this flytrappin'?'

But fortunately I didn't have to answer because Norman Gorman said, 'Flytrappin'! Fuckin' brilliant, right. You get your knob out, OK, somewhere outside. And it's sort of like fuckin' fishin', right. But instead of a fuckin' fishing rod, you're using your knob!'

I couldn't believe Norman Gorman was saying this! There were even a few girls there and some of them were shrieking and screaming with scandalised laughter. But Norman just took no notice and carried on, telling everybody, 'Right! So you've got your knob out, all right. And what you do, right, is fuckin' hold back the skin, the foreskin, so it's just your knob-end sticking out.'

One of the more sceptical kids in the crowd piped up then and said, 'Aah, that's just wanking!'

'It fuckin' isn't!' Norman declared. 'Because if it was wankin', you fuckin' window-licker, you'd be moving your fuckin' hand up and down, wouldn't y'? But y' fuckin' don't move your hand, that's the fuckin' point. You've gotta be dead fuckin' still! Like a fuckin' bomb-disposal fucker. Y' daren't fuckin' move a muscle because if there's the slightest fuckin' tremor in your knob, the fly knows and it's fuckin' off then, quick, before y' can trap it. So y' wait there, like a fuckin' statue, not moving, dead fuckin' still, waitin', knob in hand, waitin'.'

Norman Gorman was sort of acting it out for them all now, stood there dead still like he was a statue himself. And all the kids were staring at him just like little kids, spellbound and listening like it was *Jackanory* or something. Norman Gorman lowered his voice almost to a whisper then as he told them, 'Then . . . y' fuckin' hear it, don't y' . . .' He started looking at the air all around him and some of the other kids even looked as well as he said, 'Dead fuckin' faint at first . . . but it's fuckin' there all right, it's coming, because y' can hear it . . . bzzzzz . . . bzzzzz . . . bzzzz and it's fuckin' get-tin' nearer now an' y' can fuckin' see it so y' all fuckin' excited but still y' can't move or it'll be off again. Bzzzz . . . bzzzz . . . bzzzzzz . . . it's fuckin' getting louder because it's getting nearer. And y' can even see it now, that fuckin' fly, buzzin' in the air, coming towards y'; and all y' can fuckin' do is stand there, still not moving an inch, but praying, all the time fucking praying and coaxing it with your mind, using all your fucking powers to attract it. And then . . . then . . . it looks as though the fuckin' fly's moving off again . . .'

Norman Gorman's face was a picture of thwarted endeavour and all around him lads began to groan and moan with disappointment.

'But then,' Norman suddenly said, his voice all excited now, 'it fuckin' turns back. The fly turns back! It's fuckin' headed straight for y', like a bullet and then: FUCK OFF! It lands! Right fuckin' smack perfect dead centre on the end of your knob! And that's when y' fuckin' strike! WHACK! Fuckin' foreskin over it! Wallop! The fuckin' fucker's fucked! Flytrappin'!'

Everyone started cheering and loads of lads were shouting out then and saying it sounded brilliant and Norman put his arm around my shoulder again and pointed at me as he said, 'And Raymond fuckin' invented that!'

They were all looking at me differently now. And some of them had started saying things like, 'I'm gonna fuckin' do it. I'm gonna play that game. Come on, let's fuckin' go 'n' do it. Let's go fuckin' flytrapping.'

They started running off in all directions and some of them shouted, telling Norman Gorman, 'Come on, Gonzo! Let's hunt fly!'

But Norman just said, 'Fuck off. I'm taking Raymond to see Twink.'

I just looked at him but he started leading me through what was left of the crowd as I said, 'Twinky McDevitt?'

Norman nodded. 'Yeah,' he said, 'Twinky got fuckin' sent here an' all. It was him again, wasn't it, that New Headmaster. It was fuckin' him who got Twink sent here.'

Norman Gorman paused for a minute. Then he said, 'But I fuckin' got *him*, didn't I?'

'Who?' I said.

'That fuckin' New Headmaster at Binfield Road!'

I looked up at Norman Gorman. 'What did you do?'

Norman shrugged and he said, 'Fuckin' chain-sawed his conservatory to bits. Had the fuckin' lot down inside a minute, with the bastard stood there in the middle of all the wreckage and shitting himself because he thought I was gonna start on him next and fuckin' bacon-slice him to bits an' all.'

I just stared at Norman Gorman. And wondered what I was doing, letting myself become involved with an extremely expletively challenged psychopath person! But I think Norman must have sensed something of what I was thinking because a frown came across his face and his eyes looked really sheepish as we got to the school doors and he said, 'But I wouldn't fuckin' ever do nowt like that now, y' know. I fuckin' wouldn't, y' know, Raymond,' he said.

And it seemed dead important to Norman Gorman that I believed him. So I nodded and he said, 'See, I wasn't fuckin' in touch with my feelings then, was I, Raymond? I was all fuckin' confused and aggressive and violent an' all that shit. But that was before I'd learned to get in touch with my feelings and start to fuckin' explore my true self and fuckin' get in touch with the child within and that, so that I didn't just kick off an' start going fuckin' mental. And that's why I'm dead fuckin' non-confrontational nowadays,' he said. 'Because I'm fuckin' empowered now! I've got all my strategies an' I'm developing my fuckin' people skills an' conflict fuckin' resolution an' all that sort of shit, an' being dead like fuckin' articulate now; y' know what I mean?'

I went on staring at Norman Gorman. And he was beaming a big proud smile as he pulled open the door, saying, 'Come on then, Raymond. Fuckin' Twink's gonna pirouette himself stupid when he sees it's you.'

I recognised him straight away, Twinky McDevitt. He was dancing with all the girls who did the dinnertime dancing class. Me and Norman were peeping through the door, looking through the gap in the curtains because boys weren't allowed to go into the hall when the girls were practising their dancing. I whispered to Norman, 'Well, how come Twinky's allowed in there?'

Norman just shrugged and he said, 'That's Twink, isn't it? If he's gonna do something, he's fuckin' gonna do it. He just turned up every fuckin' dinner hour in his tutu and his trainers and fuckin' Miss Coppleshaw just gave up in the end and let him join in. And she was fuckin' made up anyway because he's the best dancer by fuckin' miles, look.'

And Norman Gorman was right. All the girls were doing their best and some of them looked really nice, the way they moved and danced across the hall. But when you looked at Twinky McDevitt it was like you were looking at someone who belonged to the air through which he glided. Me and Norman Gorman just crouched there behind the door, peeping through the gap, watching Twinky McDevitt cutting through the air as if it were water and he a fish gliding through it.

I whispered to Norman again, 'I thought Twinky got sent to see a psychiatrist and he wouldn't ever dance no more after that?'

Norman nodded and kept on looking through the gap in the curtain. And it was funny really but he sniffed and quickly wiped at his eye with his hand. And just for a second I thought he might have been wiping away a tear. But then I realised that was ridiculous because this was Norman Gorman, this was Gonzo! But then he turned to me with a sort of sheepish smile on his face and he said, 'It was me.'

'What was?' I said.

'Gettin' Twink dancin' again,' Norman said. 'I fuckin' made him do it. When I ended up here and I found him, his head all shagged up and everything by that fuckin' psycho, it was me who made him start dancing again. Just doin' his pirouettes at first. But then proper dancin', fuckin' full dancin', look, like that.'

We both looked through the gap again.

And Norman Gorman whispered almost to himself, saying, 'Isn't that . . . fuckin' . . . beautiful?'

And I knew then! I knew it *was* a tear that Norman

Gorman had been wiping away. And I knew that Norman Gorman must be in love with Twinky McDevitt. It was like Norman must have guessed what I was thinking, because he turned and looked at me and sort of nodded. And then I did see tears in his eyes as he said, 'I fuckin' can't help it. I just fuckin' can't.'

And that's when I said to Norman Gorman, 'It's all right, Norman. In fact I think that's very nice actually.'

And Norman beamed a big smile at me through his tears and he said, 'I think you're fuckin' *mint*, you are, Raymond. Fuckin' mint, mate.'

And Norman reached out and sort of cuffed me across the head all affectionately. And I almost started crying myself then; because I suddenly realised, I had a friend!

And just seconds later I had *two* friends. Because Twinky McDevitt was stood there, in his leotard, with a towel around his neck, his eyes all twinkling with increasing delight as Norman Gorman excitedly (and effingly) introduced me as the legendary genius flytrapping kid from Failsworth. And Twinky McDevitt just slowly shook his head as he stared in amazement and then said, 'Sublimely sordid, disgustingly divine, outrageously outré.' Then this big lovely smile just lit up his face as he said, 'Hello, Fly!'

And it was just brilliant because in the space of only a couple of minutes I'd acquired two friends *and* a nickname. I'd never had a nickname before. But when Twinky christened me that, it just stuck and everybody called me Fly after that. And I loved it, being called Fly. Because it made me feel special. And I know that I *was* special when I was at Sunny Pines, when Twinky and Norman were my best friends and we were so inseparable that we became known as the Failsworth Three. Some people even got jealous and one day when me and Norman were waiting for Twinky to finish his embroidery class, Peter Pollock came past and he said, 'Fuckin' hell, it's Noreen and Doreen, waiting for Maureen.' But me and Norman just ignored him. Then Pollock said we only stuck together because we all came from Failsworth and it was well known that they were all snobby shits, people who came from Failsworth. Norman just told him to fuck off then and said the reason we did stick together was because unlike Pollock and all the other plantpots and window-lickers we were the only ones in Sunny Pines who had nowt wrong with us.

And then Pollock said, 'Yeah! Apart from all being queers!'

And the only reason Peter Pollock thought he could get away with something like that was because he knew that Norman had been working dead hard in his group sessions, doing things like Articulate Your Anger and Temper Your Temper. And so instead of gobbing Peter Pollock one, Norman just thought very very hard for a minute and then said, 'Fuck off, you dyslexic twat!'

And we walked away then. But I knew Norman was dead upset. And after a bit, he said, 'I'm not a fuckin' queer, y' know, Fly.'

I said, 'I know that, Norman, I know you're not.'

'They just fuckin' say that,' Norman said, 'because I just fuckin' love Twinky. But I can't help it, I just fuckin' love him, Fly. Picked him up off that fuckin' donkey when I was eleven and that was it; couldn't fuckin' stick him before that! Twinky McDevitt. Little fuckin' fairy. An' I hate queers; I can't fuckin' stand them. I didn't know I was gonna fuckin' fall in love with him, did I? But I just picked him up off that fuckin' donkey and that was it; gone, man. Head over heels and I've been the same ever since. I just fuckin' love him, Fly, I love him to bits.'

'I know that,' I said, 'I know you do, Norman!'

Norman nodded then. And he said, 'Like I fuckin' love you and all, Fly. I mean, not like I love Twink. Because that's fuckin', y' know what I mean, like fuckin' special an' that. But I love you too, Fly; y' know what I mean?'

304

I nodded. 'Yeah,' I said, 'I think I do know what y' mean, Norman. Because I'm the same really and I love you and Twink.'

Norman put his arm around my shoulders then. And he said, 'Isn't it . . . fuckin' . . . *brilliant*, Fly? That we all fuckin' love each other. Isn't that just . . . Isn't that the best fuckin' feeling in all the world?'

And it *was* the best feeling in all the world, having lovely friends. We all looked out for each other and looked after each other. And that's why Twinky said I had to go on the diet and start the exercises. He said it was pointless, the three of us running away to London and going to the auditions while I was still so 'portly'. Twinky said he was making it his mission to get me to be the boy I really was. I'd told them, Norman and Twinky, I'd told them all about everything and about being the Wrong Boy. I wasn't even a bit embarrassed or shy about telling them either because I could tell Norman and Twinky anything and they'd always understand. Like when I told them all about being the Wrong Boy. And Norman just shrugged and said, 'Fuckin' hell, Fly, that's nowt; you wanna be at some of the fuckin' group sessions with me. Make your fuckin' hair stand on end. There's some fuckin' plantpots and window-lickers in there, they think they're all sorts. One fuckin' kid, he's convinced he's Trevor McDonald off *News at* fuckin' *Ten*; he keeps going, "*Bong . . . bong . . . bong*. And now the news with me, Trevor McDonald." Fuckin' mental, man. And there's one girl, she's fuckin' convinced she's a sideboard. A fuckin' sideboard. I thought she was just jokin' when she came out with that. I fuckin' said to her, "Is that why your drawers are hanging out then?" But I got fuckin' bollocked for saying that and she never opened her mouth again for the next two months, the fuckin' stupid sideboard. So that's fuckin' nowt, Fly, what you thought. Fuckin' Wrong Boy, that's nowt, is it, compared with a fuckin' sideboard.'

And Twinky said, 'Fly, it's obvious, sweetheart,

when you can't bear to be yourself it's the most natural thing in the world to hide yourself away. That's why you've allowed yourself to become so corpulent, Fly. But what you've got to understand, treasure, is that you're not a bona fide fat person at all. You're just falsely fat, Raymond. And false, Raymond, false is never attractive on the stage. Now if you're *truly* a bona fide fat person then it's different. But to be attractively fat, you have to be fat inside; look,' he said, 'like them.'

Twinky pointed at the picture of the voluptuous ladies and said they were brilliantly beautiful because they were truly bona fide fat persons and comfortable with their corpulence.

We shouldn't have been in the art gallery really. We were supposed to be outside with all the others who'd been picked to participate in the human geography project. But Twinky had said he was pissed off and he'd only volunteered for the project in the first place because he'd thought human geography was something to do with studying handsome and highly attractive people. But it turned out it was just standing in the city centre with a clipboard and a questionnaire, asking passers-by whether they wanted the trams to come back. So Twinky just said he wasn't doing it. Mr McKenzie tried to argue with him at first but Twinky just flounced off and said he had absolutely no intention of standing in a scabby street talking to ugly people about an ugly and outmoded form of transport. Mr McKenzie told him to come back but Twinky ignored him and said he was going to the art gallery where there was beauty in abundance so it was a far more fitting environment for a person of his refined sensibilities. Mr McKenzie sighed and shook his head and called out after Twinky, telling him not to go anywhere else *but* the art gallery and make sure he was back in time for the minibus. But then Norman, who'd been dead quiet all day, started walking off as well and Mr McKenzie said, 'Gorman, where the hell do you think you're going?'

'The art gallery!' Norman said. 'With Twinky.'

'No!' Mr McKenzie told him. 'You're staying here.'

'I'm fuckin' not!' Norman said. 'Who's gonna look after Twink if I'm here and he's in the art gallery?'

'I'm quite sure that Twinky can look after himself,' Mr McKenzie insisted.

'He fuckin' can't,' Norman said. 'The skins'll get him, won't they? There's fuckin' skinheads everywhere and they're always on the lookout for queers so I'm not fuckin' standing here wankin' on about trams and shit when Twink could be gettin' griefed up by a fuckin' posse of crack-brained slapheads.'

Mr McKenzie just closed his eyes and sighed and said, 'Norman, Norman. I thought we were working on the swearing, Norman!'

But Norman obviously wasn't in the mood for working on the swearing because he just said, 'Oh fuck off, sir, you're doin' my head in!'

Mr McKenzie went to say something else but Elvis Fitzsimmons and Chantelle Smith had started a fight about which one of them was doing the interview with the pensioner lady who'd stopped and said she'd worked on trams in the olden days so she could provide particularly pertinent insights to help the survey. And while Mr McKenzie was deflected, dealing with the fracas between Chantelle and Elvis, Norman started walking off. But then he stopped and he called out to me. He said, 'Come on, Fly! Come the fuckin' art gallery. Y' can perv the nudes with me an' Twink.'

I didn't particularly want to go perving the nudes. But neither did I particularly want to talk about trams in a freezing cold street while my two best friends were in the art gallery without me.

So I looked at Mr McKenzie and I knew he wouldn't notice because Chantelle Smith had started holding her breath and going into a fit which is what she always did when she didn't get her own way. I ran off and caught up with Norman. I thought Norman might have cheered up a bit by now; but as we walked along

307

towards the gallery he was still dead quiet and seemed to be miles away. I started to think it might be me and I might have upset him in some way. So I said, 'Are you all right, Norman?'

But he just nodded and kept staring straight ahead. He still didn't say anything, not till we were going up the steps of the art gallery. And that's when he said, 'Y' know your mam and dad, Fly, are they like . . . still together?'

I shook my head and I told Norman, 'No. My dad went away when I was just a little baby.'

Norman stopped walking up the steps then and sat down instead and stared out. I sat down beside him. And we both sat there for a while, saying nowt and just staring out at the traffic and the people passing by. And then Norman sighed this big deep sigh and he said, 'I wish mine would just fuckin' go away!'

I looked at him. 'Your dad?' I said.

Norman nodded.

'Isn't he a nice person, Norman?' I said.

'He's one big fuckin' bastard!' Norman said.

'What's he done, Norman?' I asked.

Norman looked at me. Then he untucked a bit of his shirt from out of his trousers and said, 'Look!'

I just stared at the big angry bruise on the side of Norman's ribcage. Then I looked at Norman and there were tears filling up his eyes.

'This mornin',' Norman said. 'Fuckin' got me while I wasn't lookin' an' punched me off my feet, the fuckin' bastard.'

I stared at the horrible bruise and I said, 'Why did he do that?'

Norman shook his head, like he couldn't understand it. Then as he started tucking his shirt back in and blinking back his tears he said, 'Because he fuckin' knows I hang round with Twink.' Norman shrugged then as he said, 'But if he wasn't beltin' me for that he'd be fuckin' beltin' me for something else. He's always belted me. And I could fuckin' drop him, y' know, Fly. Even if he is a big fuckin' bastard, I could have dropped him any time from when I was about thirteen. An' if it wasn't for my strategies an' my fuckin' conflict skills I would have done him by now. But that's what worries me, Fly; he fuckin' hurt me this morning, the bastard. And I fuckin' nearly went, Fly, fuckin' nearly lost it an' stuck one on him.'

Norman just stared out across the street. And the tears he was trying to hold back began leaking down his face. That's when I reached out and took hold of his hand. And we both just sat there on the steps of the art gallery. And Norman squeezed my hand dead tight and said, 'But I'm not gonna fuckin' let him win, Fly! And that's what I'll be doing, won't I, if I fuckin' let him make me lose my rag an' I go for him, that's what I'll be fuckin' doin', just throwin' it all away, every fuckin' thing that I've learned, an' all the things I'm dead proud of now, like keeping my fuckin' head cool and not kickin' off, an' fuckin' controllin' it, Fly, controllin' it. And that's what I'd be throwin' away, wouldn't I, every fuckin' thing I've gained. If I stuck one on him I'd just be throwin' all that away, wouldn't I, Fly?'

Norman was looking at me, his eyes all wet and fierce with appeal. And I nodded my head and said, 'I think you're being really brave, Norman. I think you're a particularly admirable person.'

That made Norman smile. And even laugh a bit then. And wiping his eyes with the back of his arm, he said, 'Fuckin' hell, Fly, you don't half come out with some shite!'

But he put his arm around my shoulder then and we just sat there for a bit longer, me and my battered best friend.

And it made me think about how lucky I was, not having to put up with something like that, with a father who bashed me up. That was round about the time when I'd started thinking more and more about my own father and wondering if perhaps all the things that

309

had happened to me wouldn't have happened if my Dad had stayed at home and he hadn't been in love with all the musical instruments and he'd laid the turf and made a lawn and just been ordinary. But when Norman told me that, about his dad and being bashed up by him, I started to think it might have been better that my Dad had gone away. Because he might have become the sort of person who battered me up. Or battered my Mam up. And I didn't need a dad anyway. Because I had my Mam; and even though my Gran had started going a bit Alka-Seltzer, I still had her as well. And on top of all that, I had my two fantastic friends. But knowing all that, it made me feel a bit awful, sat there next to Norman, knowing that I was so lucky while my friend was so sad.

But then Norman said, 'Fuck it, eh Fly!' and he hugged me dead hard as he said, 'Fuck it! We'll be goin' to London soon, won't we? An' he won't be able to punch me then, will he? Will he fuck because we'll be in London and Twinky'll be a dead famous fuckin' star in the wonderful world of the West End. And I'll be his bodyguard and his chef. And you, Fly, you'll be his . . . fuckin' agent or something clever like that. And the three of us, Fly, we'll all just be together and no fucker'll ever punch none of us, never ever again.'

Norman looked at me and he was smiling now. And he said, 'Come on, let's go an' find Twink.'

We got up then and started up the last few steps to the gallery doors. But Norman stopped just before we got to them and he said, 'Don't tell him though, will y', Fly? Don't fuckin' tell Twink what I've just told you.'

'Cross my heart, Norman,' I said, 'I won't.'

'I don't want him fuckin' gettin' upset,' Norman said. 'Twink's got enough to put up with already, hasn't he, with being a gay boy and all that?'

I just nodded. And I thought he was really lovely, Norman, the way he cared about Twinky even more than he cared about himself.

But that's how it was, we all looked out for each

other when we were the Failsworth Three. I couldn't do anything about Norman's dad. But I still had 50p left over from my dinner money. And as we went through the shop you have to go through to get into the gallery, I saw this card. And I bought it.

When I gave it to him, Norman looked all surprised. He said, 'What's this?'

I said, 'Look.' And I showed him the picture. I said, 'It's Mahatma Gandhi.'

Norman just stared at it, frowning. And he said, 'Is he a fuckin' Paki?'

'No,' I said, 'he was an Indian. My Gran told me all about him. He was a hero and he never hurt anybody in all his life.'

Norman looked at me.

I said, 'That's why I bought it for you, Norman.'

'For me?' Norman said.

I nodded. 'Yeah,' I said, 'because I think you're a hero too.'

I could tell Norman didn't know what to say. He sort of swallowed a bit. Then he looked around him like he didn't know what to say or do. And in the end he just shrugged and said, 'Fuckin' hell, Fly! Come on, let's go 'n' perv the nudes!'

But I could tell he was glad. Because he put the post-card into his pocket dead carefully. And kept looking to make sure it was still there.

When we found Twinky, he was looking at the picture of the voluptuous ladies. But Norman said they were all too fat for him and the nudes next door were miles better.

But Twinky said, 'No, Norman. Just look at them. Look at those ladies.'

Norman looked at the picture again. Then he said, 'But they are, Twink. They're fuckin' fat.'

Twinky nodded at the picture. 'Fat,' he said, 'but lovely. Look, Norman. Look at their eyes. Look, Fly.'

The three of us just stood there then, looking at the eyes of the big nude ladies. And Norman said, 'Fuckin'

hell, it's like they're alive, isn't it? It's like they're looking at us as much as we're fuckin' lookin' at them.'

Twinky said, 'That's because they *are* alive,
Norman.'

Norman frowned a bit then. But Twinky said,
'They're alive with all the life that's inside of them.
And that's what's flowing out of them, Norman, all the
life, flowing out and cascading and tumbling down all
the marvellous massive mountainness of them. They're
lovely,' Twinky said, 'and they're all proud and
delighted to be up there in that frame, showing off all
the expansive excess of all their corpulence.'

And when you looked at the voluptuous ladies like
that, Twinky was right, they didn't just look like fat
ladies at all any more; they looked delicious.

And Norman said, 'You know what I'd like to do
with them ladies? I'd like to put my tongue on them
and lick them all over their skin.'

We all started laughing at that. And then, when it
had died down and we were just stood there, I said,
'*I*'m fat!'

Norman and Twink turned and looked at me. And
Norman said, 'Well, y' fuckin' might be, Fly, but I don't
wanna lick *you* all over.'

'I know,' I said, 'but I am, I'm fat.' I turned and
looked back at the picture and I said, 'But I don't feel
like those ladies feel.'

Twinky nodded then. And he said, 'You know why
that is, Raymond?'

I shook my head and Twinky said, 'Because you're
not *really* a fat person at all, Fly.'

I just looked at him and he said, 'You're not, Fly!
You're just a very slim person really. But you've hidden
him, haven't y'? This slim person. You've hidden him
behind all that flab.'

I just nodded. I said, 'It's all the pasties an' pies and
the pot noodles an' everything like that. I just got
into the habit. And now it feels like it's dead hard to
stop.'

Twinky looked at me. And he shook his head.

I said, 'It is, Twink. Honest, you don't know because you don't . . .'

'Norman!' Twinky interrupted. 'What was I like?'

Norman shook his head and said, 'Fuckin' couldn't believe it, man. Didn't even fuckin' recognise y', did I, Twink?'

I didn't understand what they were on about. But Twinky linked my arm then and he said, 'You never saw me, did you, Fly? You never saw me all that time when I'd stopped dancing, did you?'

I shook my head.

And Twinky said, 'Tell him, Norman, go on, tell Fly.'

Norman stretched out his arms as wide as he could and said, 'Fuckin' like that, he was! Fuckin' massive, man; weren't y', Twink?'

Twinky nodded, still staring at me.

'I couldn't believe it,' Norman said. 'When I fuckin' turned up at Sunny Pines, man, and I saw the state of him, I fuckin' cried, didn't I, Twink, cried my fuckin' eyes out. There he was, last time I'd seen him, this fuckin' slip of nowt; I could have picked him up off that donkey with one fuckin' hand. Year and a half later, I get to Sunny Pines an' I couldn't have picked him up with a fork-lift fuckin' truck.'

I frowned, looking at Twinky. But Twinky just nodded at me. 'That's right, Fly.'

I frowned again. 'But why?' I asked him.

Twinky shrugged. 'I just lost it, Fly,' he said. 'After all that shit over the Virgin Mary, I just lost it. It was like I didn't know who I was any more.' Twinky was staring at me dead intently. Then he nodded and said, 'You know what I mean, Fly?'

I nodded back at him. And he said, 'There was this big empty space inside of me. And the more I tried to fill it with food, the bigger it got. Till, in the end, I was nothing but a lardy ball of flab.'

I stared at Twinky and shook my head. 'I never knew,' I said, 'I never knew that, Twink.'

313

Twinky nodded at me. And he said, 'Well, it's true, Fly.'

And then this lovely shy smile broke out all over Twinky's face as he turned and looked at Norman and said, 'And I'd still be the same today and getting fatter by the minute, if it hadn't been for Norman.'

Norman almost began to blush at that but you could tell he was dead chuffed.

'What did you do, Norman?' I asked him.

Norman just shrugged and said, 'Agh, it was fuckin' nowt really.'

But Twinky said, 'Go on. Tell him. Tell Fly what you did, Norman.'

And Norman couldn't hide the proud little look he had on his face then as he said, 'I fuckin' wrote, didn't I? I didn't tell Twinky or nobody. But I fuckin' found where to write. And I fuckin' wrote the letter, didn't I, all on my own, wrote the letter to Petula fuckin' Clark and told her everything, about Twinky and how he'd always loved her an' admired her an' always danced and did his pirouettes to her songs. But he'd fuckin' had it now an' he couldn't dance no more and he'd become a right fat twat with his head all shagged up.'

Norman nodded and he said, 'An' y' know summat, Fly, Petula, she fuckin' wrote back the fuckin' very next day. Not just one letter neither, two fuckin' letters she wrote; one to me, "My dear Norman . . ." *My dear fuckin' Norman*, it said. And one to Twink, a fuckin' big long letter it was and she said how dead fuckin' sorry she was to hear what had happened to him and how he wasn't dancin' no more. And she said loads of other things, didn't she, fuckin' dead nice things because she's fuckin' brilliant, Petula, fuckin' top she is. And she said she didn't know if it would help Twink but regarding the weight problem she was enclosing a diet plan that she'd personally used and found dead fuckin' effective when she'd had her own "little problem with the pounds". An' in the PS, y' know what she said, Fly? She said she wanted to be kept informed about Twink and how he was gettin' on. And that's why we still fuckin' write to her, don't we?' Twink nodded. 'And she always writes back, y' know, Fly. Never fuckin' misses. An' we're gonna go an' see her, aren't we?' Norman said to Twink. 'When we run away to London we're gonna go an' fuckin' see Petula.'

Twinky was staring at me. Then he said, 'So come on, Fly. Are y' gonna give it a go? Or are y' gonna go on for ever, hiding those lovely cheekbones and pretending to be happy when you're not even a proper bona fide fat person in the first place?'

'I'll fuckin' help y', Fly,' Norman said. 'We can work out every dinner hour, while Twink's doing his dancin' or his fuckin' embroidery.'

I just stood there, looking at my two friends. And then Twinky said, 'Come on, Raymond; you can't go on being the wrong boy for ever.'

When I told her I didn't want it, my Mam just stood there looking at me with a face like a cheesed-off checkout girl.

She said, 'But you always have it! It's milky coffee and cheese on toast, with all the cheese bubbling up like you like it.'

I shook my head. 'But I don't want it,' I said. 'I'm not eatin' stuff like that any more. I'm on a diet. Twinky and Norman are helping me to . . .'

But she wasn't listening then because she just turned round and went back into the kitchenette. I heard her throwing the toast into the pedal bin as she said, 'Twinky and Norman! Twin— I'm sick of them. Sick of the bloody pair of them!'

'But you don't even know them,' I said, 'not properly, so how can you be sick of them?'

She came back into the doorway then, her eyes flashing at me as she said, 'I'll tell y' why! Because every other word you come out with these days is Twinky and Norman. Twinky says this, Norman does that, Twinky and Norman think this! I'm sick of it,' she

315

said. 'The world according to Twinky and Norman, I'm sick of it!'

'But they're my friends,' I said. 'I thought you'd be happy because I'd made friends.'

'Normal friends, Raymond!' she said. 'Normal friends, lads your own age and I would be happy. But you couldn't do that, could y', find a couple of nice normal friends. Oh no, not you, you have to start going round with a pair of maladjusted misfits.'

'They're *not* misfits!' I told her. 'And they're not maladjusted.'

'Not misfits! Not . . .' my Mam said. 'Do you think I'm daft? I remember them when we lived in Failsworth. That Gorman lad, he's an animal!'

'He's not,' I said.

'Don't talk rubbish,' my Mam insisted. 'Before Sunny Pines he was in an approved school!'

'But Norman's not like that now,' I said, 'he's not. Because Norman's got his strategies now and he works on his anger. He's my friend and he's a very nice person and if you'd let him and Twinky come to our house, you'd realise that.'

'I've told y',' my Mam said, 'I don't want them comin' to the house! I don't need to see them; I know from what Ted's told me, they're a right pair.'

And that got me really riled then. It was bad enough that she called him Ted nowadays, Wilson, the Lert. But now he was telling her things about my friends when he didn't even know anything about them.

'What does he know?' I said to my Mam. 'He doesn't even teach at Sunny Pines so how the hell does he know what Twinky and Norman are like?'

'Because!' she said. 'Because Ted makes it his business to find out! Because he promised me he'd take an interest in your welfare, that's why.'

I just looked at her. I said, 'He's not interested in *me* at all.'

She looked at me like she was disgusted. 'How have you got the gall to come out with something like that?'

316

she said. 'How can you say that about Ted when he's always dropping in to see that you're doing all right, phoning up to check how you're going on. Can you deny that?'

I just shook my head. And my Mam said, 'So how the hell can you say he's not interested in you?'

I shrugged. I was fed up with her. Fed up with her having a go at my friends. And having a go at me. So I said, 'Because it's not me he's interested in, it's you!'

Her eyes went all narrowed up and she cocked her head to one side as she took a step towards me. 'What are you trying to say?' she said. 'What are you trying to say?'

I shrugged again. 'Nothing,' I said. 'Just the truth, that's all. He fancies you!'

She just looked. Stood there looking at me. And then she said, 'Don't be so stupid! Fancies me!' she said. 'Fancies me? Look at me! Wrecked and hairless, trying to cope with my mother, cope with you. Fancies me? Chance'd be a fine thing,' she said. 'He's an educated man. And he's just trying to do his best for you. Don't talk so stupid! Fancies . . . ! Christ almighty!'

She just stared at me for a bit longer. And then she said, 'The only thing Ted's interested in is making sure that you're all right. You should be grateful. He's taken a personal interest in you. And if Ted says he thinks you'd be better off with more normal friends then I agree with him; and I think you should do something about it instead of spending all your time hanging round with a young thug and that McDevitt lad who can't make up his mind whether he's supposed to be a girl or a boy.'

I hated it when she said things like that. I hated it when she was being stupid, because my Mam wasn't a stupid person at all. I knew she was at the end of her tether and nearly worn out with looking after my Gran, going over there every day and seeing that she was all right and making sure my Gran wouldn't have to go into a nursing home. I knew my Mam had a lot to put up with. But that wasn't what was making my Mam stupid; it was him, Wilson the Lert. My Mam always said stupid things after she'd been talking to him; like she said about Twinky not knowing if he was a girl or a boy.

And I said to her, I said, 'Of course Twinky's a boy! And he's perfectly well aware that he's a boy. But he just happens to be a homosexual boy, that's all.'

She just looked at me. 'Listen to you!' she said. 'Listen to you, coming out with things like that, a lad of your age!'

I asked her what age had to do with it. But she said she wasn't arguing and she had to get her coat and get to the bus stop or she'd be late getting to my Gran's. Then she went. And we didn't even say tarar to each other or anything like that. And it was awful really, arguing with my Mam all the time. I didn't want to be arguing with her. But it was like my Mam didn't want to think for herself any more. It was like she'd sort of left me and gone over to Wilson instead, just spouting things that he said. And if that's what she was doing then that was up to her. She was on one side of the road, with the Lert. And I was on the other side, with Norman and Twinky. And I loved it, being with my friends. Even if my Mam wasn't interested and didn't even seem to care about me going on a diet and getting back to being the person I really was, Twinky and Norman cared. And with my friends helping me, that's how I did it, Morrissey, started getting back to being the person I really was, with Norman as my own personal fitness trainer taking me running every day and Twinky giving me all his encouragement and making me stick to the Petula Clark Petite Person Plan. It wasn't easy, Morrissey, not at first. But as the weeks and the months went by it all got easier and I got leaner, shunning the pasties, shedding the pounds. And one dinner hour, when Twinky didn't have a class and he came with us as well, me, Twink and Norman went running through all the fields that surround

Sunny Pines, all running together, breathing together, laughing together, across the field and over the brook, along the path beneath the trees where the sun shone through and speckled us all and made me think that my Gran was right, and there *was* a kind of heaven.

And if time could be stopped just by wishing, that's exactly where I would have stopped it, Morrissey; when I was lean and thirteen, in a kind of heaven with Norman and Twink; believing that happiness, once it's been found, is a thing that lasts for ever.

Yours sincerely,
Raymond Marks

The Grassy Bit,
By the Shell Shop
And Filling Station,
Ferrybridge Services,
M62

Dear Morrissey,

They abandoned me! The people on the coach. They
could have said! They could have just told me they
didn't want me on their cowing coach! They said it
was a toilet stop. Only when I came out of the toilet,
the bleeding coach had gone. And there was just my
gear and my guitar, left there in the middle of the car
park; abandoned, like me. I didn't care anyway. I didn't
want to be on a coach where everybody hated me.

I know it means I've still got to get another lift. But I
don't care. Sometimes it feels as though I'm bleeding
well beyond caring. Scott of the Sodding Antarctic had
less trouble getting to the South pigging Pole than I'm
having just getting to Grimsby! I can't even try and start
hitchhiking, not yet. Because when I walked over here
to start hitching there were already about six other
people queued up before me; student-looking persons,
all of them bearing pieces of cardboard with the names
of their destinations, universally unfortunate places
like Hull and Doncaster and Goole.

When I walked up and stuck my thumb out though, they all turned and looked at me like I'd just farted or something.

I said, 'What's up?'

And this girl with a shaved head and a major amount of body metal said, 'Do you mind! There is a stacking system in operation here.'

I said, 'What do you mean?'

But she just gave me a sour look and sucked on her tongue-stud as the lad in front of her said, 'Get to the back of the queue and wait your fucking turn! That's what she means!'

I just shrugged. 'I'm sorry,' I said, 'I didn't realise hitchhiking had become subject to the same principles as air traffic control.'

But they all just glared at me. And concluding that student anarchy was in no danger of making any kind of a comeback, I moved down here and took my proper place at the back of the queue. I think I might be stuck here for hours though. The person in front of me is clutching a piece of cardboard with a very strange destination written on it. I'd never begrudge a person his religious beliefs, Morrissey, but if I've got to wait for him to get a lift before I can finally get to the top of the queue, I think I might be stuck here for ever; because instead of Goole or Hull or Nottingham or somewhere like that, he's just got the word 'SALVATION' written on his destination card. He started talking to me before and asked me where I was headed. I told him Grimsby. But he shook his head and said, 'Then I'm sorry, my friend, but you are on the wrong road!'

I got worried for a minute and thought perhaps I'd wound up on the wrong side of the motorway. But then he said, 'No, my friend, there is only *one* destination. And those who want to reach it are those who journey with the Lord.'

So I'm just hoping, Morrissey, that the Lord's out driving tonight. And preferably on this side of the

M62, because if he isn't then I'm just going to be stuck here, behind this salvation-seeker, with all his certainty. I wouldn't mind, but seeing as he was supposed to be such a Christian sort of person I thought he might be a good Samaritan and let me take his place in the queue. I explained that I still had to get all the way to Grimsby and would he mind swapping places and letting me go ahead of him in the queue.

But he shook his head and said, 'My friend, it wouldn't matter how much further up the queue you got. Because your true destination, my friend, you will never reach. Not while you continue to worship a false idol.'

I told him I didn't worship any kind of idol actually.

But he nodded at my tee shirt and stood there smiling like he'd caught me out and was really pleased with himself. 'So!' he said. 'So? Will Morrissey get you to Grimsby?'

I said I didn't expect Morrissey to get me to Grimsby.

But he said, 'Oh yes you do!' And then he just stood there staring at me with this big certain smile on his face.

I decided to shut up and say nowt then; because, like my Gran always said, one of the few certainties in life is that persons of certainty should certainly be avoided. I couldn't avoid him though because he was just stood there saying, 'You see, my friend, I too have been where you are now.' He nodded and smirked and said, 'I too once put my faith in an empty vessel. I too had the tee shirts, the records, the posters, the LPs, the twelve-inch singles.'

I shot him a look of surprise. '*You* were into Morrissey?' I said.

But he shook his head and said, 'No. Not Morrissey. The pot into which I mistakenly poured my faith was a vessel known as Billy Bragg.'

That's when I started to feel somewhat sorry for him. If I'd been into Billy Bragg I think I might have ended up going over to the church! At least the music's better!

'They're everywhere,' he said, 'those cheap and leaking vessels: the Billy Braggs, the Morrisseys, the Michael Jacksons, all of them with their beguiling but empty promises. Where will they lead you, my friend? Will Mr Morrissey lead you to salvation?'

'Listen,' I said, 'it's hard enough just trying to get to Grimsby; so I'm not that bothered about salvation right at the minute.'

He stared at me. Then he nodded all smug and knowingly as he said, 'I see, my friend, that you are not yet ready for the word of the Lord.'

'That's right,' I said, 'I don't think I am actually.'

I thought he might give up then and go back to the queue of hitchhikers. But he just stood there, his finger pointed at me, as he said, 'But that day will come, my friend; that day will surely dawn for you as once it dawned for me; and on that day you will know that you are on the wrong road, with the wrong guide. Mr Morrissey is leading you into a cul-de-sac. Salvation lies elsewhere!'

He was really starting to make me feel pissed off. 'Well, listen,' I said, 'seeing as you obviously do know where salvation is why don't you just sod off there and leave me alone?'

And he did sod off then, back to the queue. And I wished he'd never left the bleeding queue in the first place. He was spooky. And I didn't like him talking about you, Morrissey. Because he didn't know what he was talking about. And he'd never understand anyway, a person like that. That's why I hadn't even tried to tell him; that you *were* my salvation, Morrissey. And if it hadn't been for you, I might never have got better. Even my Mam says; my Mam says that the day I really started improving was the day I started playing the guitar. But I'd never have played that guitar, Morrissey, if it hadn't been for you. That's what brought me back to life, hearing you, Morrissey; when I'd got out of Swintonfield, and I was still only half a person.

I never should have ended up in Swintonfield in the first place. I know it all started off because of Norman and Twinky but it wasn't their fault. I don't care what anyone says, I know that Twinky and Norman had nothing to do with it. They had to do what they did, I know that. So I don't blame them at all. Who I blame is Wilson, the Lert! Him; and Paulette Patterson's father. That's who I blame: them. And my Uncle Bastard Jason; my Uncle Bastard Jason and my Poisonous Aunty Paula. Because if it hadn't been for them, my Gran might not have ended up with a red nose and she might even have been able to help me on the night that it all happened. Only my Gran couldn't help me at all. Because my Uncle and my Aunty, the appalling pair of them, had just turned up at my Gran's house one Sunday morning when they knew my Mam wouldn't be there. And the two of them told my Gran it was such a nice sunny summer's day, they'd decided to take her out for a drive in the country. If my Gran had been herself she never would have gone with them, not in the summer. My Gran never liked the summer. She said everything was too full of frivolity in the summer, especially the countryside because it was all too green and gaudy and the birds made too much fuss. And the proper time for visiting the countryside, my Gran said, was in winter when the trees were dark and melancholy and the birds knew how to behave themselves. But my Gran had forgotten; forgotten that buttercups, dandelions and daisies are all such frivolous flowers, forgotten that she couldn't stick my Aunty Paula, forgotten that she hated being taken out for 'nice Sunday drives'; forgotten who she was any more. That's why she went with the traitorous two of them.

When the car pulled into the driveway of the big country house, my Gran looked a bit puzzled and said, 'What's this? I thought we were going out to the country.'

'We are,' my Aunty Paula said. 'But we thought we'd

just drop in here for an hour, Vera. We thought you'd like it, visiting a stately home.'

'Will I?' my Gran asked.

'Of course you will!' my Uncle Jason insisted as they pulled into the car park. 'Look at them lovely grounds, those nice lawns. Come on,' he said, 'let's get out and take a stroll.'

And if my Gran hadn't forgotten who she was, she would have realised, the minute they got out the car and went walking across the lawns, where there were many persons of considerable antiquity, their hands welded onto Zimmer frames and some of them in wheelchairs being pushed and paraded by nurses. But my Gran didn't realise. So she dutifully strolled the grounds of the 'stately home'. And it was only when she looked up and saw my Uncle and my Aunty were no longer with her that my Gran started to get a bit puzzled. And then she saw the two of them, in the distance, hurrying back towards the car park. And that's when she began to panic a bit then, my Gran. Because even though she couldn't quite remember who they were, my Gran knew that she was supposed to be with those two persons who were diving into the car and speeding off without her. That's why she began to panic and cry and shout out a bit. And she was grateful when the two nice nurses came and comforted her and took her inside and gave her a cup of tea. And the nice nurses even seemed to know my Gran's name. Then one of them asked if she'd like to see her room now. My Gran said that that would be very nice. And it was only in those bits of moments, in the tiny flashes of memory when my Gran still knew who she was, that she realised that this 'stately home' was the Stalybridge Sanctuary for Seasoned Citizens.

My Mam kicked up a big stink at first. She said she was going straight over to Stalybridge and bringing my Gran out of there. But my Aunty Paula and my Uncle

Jason got to work and the lying, conniving, treacherous two of them made it sound as if the Stalybridge Sanctuary for Seasoned Citizens was a sort of pensioners' paradise where my Gran would be happy in the evening of her years, being tended and cared for by angelic nurses, amused and entertained by the lively programme of daily events including water-colour painting, flower arranging, line-dancing classes and stimulating visits from local performing artists such as magicians, storytellers and folk-singing groups. And my Mam should have known that that would be hell on earth as far as my Gran was concerned.

But my Mam was weary and worn out with all her own efforts at looking after my Gran. So she reluctantly agreed that perhaps it might, after all, be better for my Gran if she had the care and attention of proper pro-fessionals. My Uncle Jason and my Aunty Paula could barely hide their satisfied smirks. And I know, Morrissey, I know I should have been paying more attention when all that was going on.

I know that if I'd been less concerned with myself, I might have seen exactly what my rancid relatives were up to and how they'd had my Gran put in a nursing home just so that they could get their hands on my Gran's house; so they could sell it and keep the money and go on a Thomson's Four Plus winter holiday to the silver sands of the Seychelles. If I'd been paying more attention I would have seen what the traitorous two of them were up to and I would have been able to warn my Mam.

But I wasn't paying attention, Morrissey. I wasn't paying attention to all sorts of things. Because I was no longer interested, Morrissey. And I feel terrible saying it now but back then, when I was still in Sunny Pines and just coming up to fourteen, I wasn't really inter-ested in my Mam's problems. My Mam, my Aunty Paula, my Uncle Jason, they were just . . . *there*, really; like the wallpaper's there and the carpet's there and the three-piece suite is there. And just like you never pay much attention to the wallpaper or the carpet, I didn't pay that much attention to what was going on at home. I didn't even pay that much attention to him, the Lert. He was always round at ours; just dropping in for a cup of tea and a chat. Or giving my Mam a lift over to see my Gran at Stalybridge. And sometimes just taking my Mam out for a drive. 'Just to give your mum a break, Raymond,' he said. And then asking my Mam if she'd like to come to one of his meetings with him; because that might give her a bit of a break and all. And I know now that I should have paid some attention to all that.

But none of that was exciting, Morrissey. Not like being with my friends was exciting, being with Norman and Twink. And that's where I wanted to be all the time really, with Norman and Twink, talking like we did and making all our plans and making each other laugh; and loving it, being together. My Gran understood that. Even when she was a doolally woman, my Gran could see what special friends me and Twinky and Norman were.

We went to see her.

We got the bus to Stalybridge. And before we got to the Sanctuary for Seasoned Citizens we stopped at the shop and I bought a packet of Garibaldi biscuits. I didn't even know if my Gran would remember that she liked Garibaldi biscuits but I bought them anyway.

The nurse said weren't we good boys, coming all this way just to visit a poor old lady.

I didn't like it, the nurse talking about my Gran like that. My Gran wasn't a poor old lady at all; she was my Gran!

'Now then,' the nurse said, running her finger down a list of names, 'it's Vera, isn't it? Vera Bradwell.'

I nodded and the nurse said, 'That's right. Vera Bradwell.' But then she laughed and winked as she said, 'We call her Vera Madeira.' She laughed again. 'We give them all pet names,' she said. 'They love it.'

I just looked at her. And tried to imagine it, my Gran

being addressed as Vera Madeira; and supposedly loving it.

'She's at the concert party,' the nurse said. 'Come on, I'll show you where the day room is and you can squeeze in at the back till it's finished and then you'll be able to see your Gran.'

We started walking down the corridors, past all these rooms, some of them with the doors open so you could see the old people sitting there or lying in their beds.

'Most of these,' the nurse said, half whispering, 'they're too far gone to appreciate the entertainment. They prefer the comfort of their own rooms. We try and have a laugh with them, like we do with all the guests. But these, they're too far gone.'

They didn't look far gone, the old people sat there in their rooms; they just looked sad and shrivelled up. I felt sorry for them. And I know that Twinky must have felt the same because he kept waving at the old persons and beaming his big lovely smile at them.

Norman wasn't smiling at anybody though. Norman was just walking along all hunched up, his head bent down, a scowl on his face and his eyebrows all furrowed up together.

'What's up?' I whispered.

But Norman shook his head and scowled even more as he whispered back, 'They fuckin' frighten me, Fly!'

'Who?' I whispered.

Norman shook his head again and said, 'Old people! They fuckin' frighten me. I wanna go home.'

'Norman, you'll be all right,' I told him. 'Don't worry. My Gran's not like an old person. In fact, my Gran's not really an old person at all.'

And that was true, because I never even thought of my Gran as an old person; not like all these old persons that Twinky kept waving at and offering his greetings to like he was a visiting celebrity. And I think the nurse who was showing us the way to the day room was getting a bit brassed off because when one old lady smiled and waved back at Twinky, he just waltzed straight into her room and started going into raptures about how beautifully embroidered her bedspread was. By the time the nurse realised there was one of us missing and went back to fetch him, Twinky was talking embroidery with the old lady and telling her he'd never seen such an exquisite example in all his life. And you could tell she was really made up, the lady, because her eyes were all ablaze with delight as she sat there, tightly clutching Twinky's hand in her sparrow-bird fingers and telling him how every single stitch was the work of her own, once nimble hands.

But the nurse coughed and spoke to the embroidery lady like she was a deaf person, or a daft person, telling her, 'Come on now, Margaret. These visitors aren't here for you. They've come to see Vera Madeira.'

And when we were walking down the corridor again, the nurse told Twinky, 'You don't want to be getting yourself trapped with Margaret! She's never been a bit of fun, that one. Margaret *Thatcher*, that's what we call her, Maggie Thatcher. She'd bore you to death with her embroidery.'

'I wasn't bored a bit,' Twinky told the nurse. 'In fact I could have happily talked to that lady for hours. I do embroidery myself,' he said.

'Oh do y'?' she said, the nurse, nodding and looking Twinky up and down like he was something that had just been gobbed up on the pavement. 'Well! I suppose it takes all sorts.'

But Twinky just lifted up his head, stuck his chin right out and executed a perfect pirouette. She ignored him then, turned to me and said, 'Come on, I'll show y' where your grandma is.'

She pushed open the door and showed us into this big room.

I couldn't see my Gran anywhere because we were stuck at the back, behind all the seasoned citizens who were stuffed into the day room, all of them sitting around on seats or in wheelchairs, each one of them clutching hold of a piece of string that had a balloon on the end of it. And up at the front on a small platform was one of those musical groups where the men have big beards and the ladies have stringy hair and don't wear any make-up and they're all very hearty people. The boss of the group was talking to the old people, telling them, 'Well now, lads and lasses, we're having some top fun this afternoon, aren't we? Come on, let's hear a big cheer for all the top fun we're having today.'

Only I don't think they were having much 'top fun' really. Because the only ones who cheered were the various nurses. The seasoned citizens who weren't asleep just sat there staring blankly back at the bearded singer. Not that he seemed to be that put out though because he raised a triumphant fist as he declared, 'Yes! That's right! We are! We're having a right party this afternoon, aren't we, lads and lasses? And just to show how much fabulous fun we're having today, I want to see everybody giving those balloons a really good shake. Come on now, lads and lasses: one, two, three, now shake those balloons.'

I don't know why he bothered! Most of the seasoned citizens had such trembling hands that they couldn't help but shake the bleeding balloons. But he didn't even seem to notice that and he kept saying, 'Yes, that's right! Let's see those balloons really shaking now, shaking for all the fun that we're having today.'

And with that, him and his group launched into an appalling song about somebody called Wild Rover who never wanted to go wild roving no more.

Twinky just looked at me as we stood there. And he said, 'Fly! I think I'm gonna vom!'

And glaring at the hairy hearties, who seemed to get hairier and heartier as the song went on, Norman said, 'Why is it that you never have a fuckin' machine gun when y' need one!?'

And then, just for a startled second, I thought that perhaps somebody did have a gun because there was a sudden loud bang and everybody jumped. Only it turned out to be just a balloon that had burst and I saw one of the nurses going down to the front to sort it out.

Then I heard her, talking like she was chastising a naughty child, saying, 'Vera! Did you do that on purpose? Now that's not very pleasant, is it? Look what you've done to your nice balloon.'

And that's when I heard my Gran's voice, heard her as she told the nurse, 'Bugger the bloody balloon!'

And that's when I saw her, my Gran; saw her standing up at the front and then picking her way through the chairs, with the nurse following her, saying things like, 'Vera! Where do you think you're going? The concert's not over yet, Vera.'

But it was perfectly apparent that my Gran had very different ideas about that and as far as she was concerned the concert was well and truly over. A thunderous look on her face, she was headed straight for the doors, telling the nurse, 'I told you. I told y' before, I said I didn't want to come here. Bloody balloons! Silly sodding singing. I'm not stopping here. I'm not. I'm not stopping!'

Me, Twinky and Norman were stood in front of the doors. And as my Gran got to them, Twinky and Norman moved aside to let my Gran past. But I just stood there, until my Gran looked up and was staring straight at me. I was smiling at her. I said, 'Hiya, Gran!'

But my Gran just looked at me. Stood there, all stooped over, looking like an old person now and staring suspiciously at me, scowling and shaking her head as she pushed past me, through the doors and out into the corridor.

I felt awful. I'd been delighted when I'd seen it was my Gran who'd burst her balloon. I thought it might mean that my Gran had remembered who she was again. But she'd been stood right in front of me. And hadn't recognised me. And now she was just wandering away up the corridor, with the nurse following and saying, 'Vera Madeira! I just don't know what's got into you today, Vera.'

I stood there in the corridor, with Twinky and Norman, watching her go.

And Norman said, 'Fuckin' hell, Fly! I'm fuckin' never gonna get old.'

I just nodded. And I felt awful, for my Gran. And for my friends. Because I'd wanted them to meet my Gran, my proper Gran. Not this person who'd changed so much that she didn't even recognise me any more.

We started walking back up the corridor, towards the exit signs. And that's when it began to dawn on me; when I was thinking about how much my Gran had changed in such a short time. That's when I realised; that it wasn't only my Gran who had changed! And that the reason she hadn't recognised me might not have anything to do with what was happening to her mind.

'Come on!' I shouted at Norman and Twink as I ran back down the corridor. And as I got round the corner, I saw my Gran and the nurse, just about to go into a room.

'Gran!' I shouted. 'Gran!' She turned and she looked and as I ran up to her, I said, 'Gran! It is! It's me.' I was smiling at her. 'It's Raymond!' I said.

She frowned at first. But then I saw it in her eyes, the sudden spark of light and the recognition. And then her face just crumpled up like a rag and she started crying. But as she did, she stretched out her arms and hugged me to her as she said, 'Son ... son ... Raymond ... what's happened to you, son? What's become of you?'

'Gran! Gran!' I said. 'It's all right! Nothing's happened to me, Gran! I've just got thin again, that's all. That's why you didn't recognise me; because I've lost all the weight, Gran. Look.'

I stood back and let my Gran look at me.

'See!' I told her. 'It is me! I'm just slim again, that's all, like I used to be.'

My Gran stared and stared. And then the nurse, who'd been stood there looking a bit suspicious, said, '*Do* you know him, Vera? Do you know this young man?'

My Gran slowly turned her head and fixed the nurse with her glare. 'Don't be so stupid!' my Gran said. 'Know him? Of course I know him!'

The nurse shook her head and gave my Gran a huffy look. Then she turned to me and said, 'Well, she's all yours then. And you're welcome to her and all. I don't know,' the nurse said as she started walking off, 'I don't know what's got into you today, Vera. You're just not yourself at all.'

But she was wrong, that nurse. Because my Gran was herself! She was completely and perfectly herself. She just stared at the disappearing nurse and said, 'Go on, bugger off. Go and rattle your bloody balloons and leave me to see my gorgeous grandson.'

I said, 'I've brought y' some biscuits, Gran.'

'Oh!' my Gran said as I handed them to her. 'Garibaldis! You couldn't have brought me anything better, son; I've been longing for a biscuit with a bit of character to it. The biscuits they give us in here,' she said, 'they're just these puffed-up little things with hardly a bite or a bit of backbone to them!'

And I knew for definite then that my Gran was my Gran again. I just stood there smiling at her. Then I remembered Norman and Twinky, who were stood there further down the corridor.

'And Gran,' I said, 'I've brought my friends to see y'.'

My Gran looked down the corridor to where Twinky and Norman were stood. 'Now then,' she said as she squinted at them, 'who's this?'

'It's Twinky and Norman, Gran,' I told her. 'It was Twinky and Norman who helped me to get all slim again.'

My Gran stared at them both for a second. Then screwing up her eyes, she said to Twinky, 'I know you, don't I?'

Twinky nodded and my Gran said, 'Of course I do! Aren't you that little homosexual lad who took such a good part as the Virgin Mary?'

Twinky just nodded at my Gran. And then his big bright smile lit up the whole of his face as he said, 'Yes. And aren't you that wicked old witch from Failsworth who used to frighten me shitless, trying to get me to dance in Sainsbury's?'

My Gran smiled back at Twinky. 'You wouldn't do it though, would y'?' she said. 'You wouldn't dance no more, not after that Nativity.'

'He dances now though, Gran,' I said.

My Gran looked at Twinky. 'Go on then,' she urged him, 'go on, give us a pirouette.'

And Twinky obliged, my Gran clapping her hands and watching him with her eyes all sparkling as he came pirouetting all the way up the corridor and fell at my Gran's feet in a splendid if somewhat ostentatious curtsy.

My Gran bent down and helped Twinky to his feet. And he just stood there, staring at my Gran. And I could tell, from the way he stood there smiling, that he was enchanted by her. But my Gran was looking down the corridor again, where Norman was still stood, looking nervous and ill at ease.

'And what's wrong with you?' my Gran said. 'You look like you've been sucking lemons, lad; what's the matter with you?'

Norman just shrugged and said, 'I don't . . . it's just . . . I fu . . . I just . . . I don't like it,' he said.

'Norman's a bit frightened, Gran,' I explained, 'because he doesn't like it in here. He's a bit frightened of all the old people.'

'I don't blame him!' my Gran said. 'I'm frightened of them myself. But I'll tell y' what,' she said, 'they're not half as frightening as the nurses!' My Gran grasped my arm then and she was gripping it dead tight. And she suddenly looked all pathetic, my Gran. 'They keep trying to make me have fun!' she said. 'They keep trying to give us fun! And it's all right on my forgetful days, it doesn't seem to matter then. But then I have days like today and they keep on doing it to me, Raymond, trying to make me have fun.'

I stroked my Gran's arm. 'Well, it's all right now, Gran,' I said, 'because we're here now and we won't try and make you have any fun at all, will we, Twink?'

Twinky shook his head and looked very gravely at my Gran until she looked relieved and reassured and said, 'You're good lads, all of you, good lads.'

Then she looked at Norman again as she said, 'And I certainly don't think he's in much danger of suddenly breaking into fits of frivolity, is he?'

She called out to Norman then and said, 'Come on! Come on, Norman! Come on into my room and we'll all have some Garibaldis.'

Norman started slowly moving up the corridor towards us then. And my Gran waited. And when Norman got to us, my Gran reached out and took hold of his arm. I could see that it was difficult for Norman and he didn't even like an old person touching him. But he didn't try and move his arm away. And as my Gran held onto him, she turned to me and Twinky and said, 'You shouldn't laugh at Norman, y' know; just because he doesn't like to be around old persons, you shouldn't laugh at him.'

'We don't, Gran,' I said. 'We'd never laugh at Norman.'

'Well, you shouldn't,' my Gran said, 'because he's right to be frightened, Norman is. And do you know why?' she asked me and Twink. 'Do you know why it makes him scared to be in a place like this?'

Me and Twinky just shook our heads.

'Because Norman can feel it,' my Gran said, 'feel it all around him.'

'Feel what, Gran?' I said. 'What can Norman feel?'

'Death!' my Gran said. 'Death!'

Me and Twinky just stood there, staring at my Gran. But my Gran nodded and said, 'Oh it's everywhere! In a place like this, it's in the walls, it's in the air, it's everywhere. And that's why Norman's so frightened and uncomfortable. Isn't that right, Norman?'

Norman stared down at my Gran. And then slowly started nodding his head. And my Gran said, 'Of course it is. And who can blame y',' she said. 'A young lad like you, brimful of life. You've got every right in the world to be afeared, Norman. Who wants to be with the almost-done and the soon-to-be-departed when you're young and teeming with life like you young lads? And when you're your age,' my Gran said, 'death's nowt but a bloody bastard, is he?'

Norman was just staring into my Gran's face. He even smiled a bit, at hearing my Gran swearing. And I knew that my Gran had captivated him then because when she let go of his arm as she headed for her room, Norman quickly took hold of her hand and put it back on his arm again. And it was almost like Norman was escorting my Gran as they walked into the room, with me and Twinky following and my Gran saying, 'But when y' get to my age, Norman, there's nowt much to be afeared of from death. Unless,' she said, 'unless I've got it wrong and there really is a heaven up there. Now that *would* be something to be afraid of,' my Gran said as she sat down in her chair and Norman kneeled down at the side of her.

'Christ almighty!' my Gran said. 'Heaven! It's bad enough here with balloons and cheerful chirpy nurses, silly sodding songs and bloody biscuits with fancy coloured wafers and nowt to get your teeth into. So God knows', my Gran said, 'what sort of a hell you'd be in if you ended up in heaven.'

Me and Twinky just sat there on the bed and nodded at my Gran.

But Norman was sat at my Gran's feet, staring up at her with a sort of awed admiration now. And that's when he said, 'I think you're fuckin' right, Gran. Because when you think about it, it could be a right fuckin' shithole, heaven, couldn't it?'

My Gran just stared at Norman. I looked at Twink. But he was just sat there with his eyes closed, slowly shaking his head in despair at Norman and his language. Then I looked at my Gran again. And that's when I saw her smile, as she reached out and stroked Norman on the hair of his head as she said, 'Well, Norman, yes, I suppose you could put it like that!'

It was brilliant that day; the last day I ever properly saw my Gran. I knew that Twinky and Norman loved my Gran, just like I loved her. Twinky asked my Gran if he could do her hair for her. And my Gran said he could, just as long as he showed proper constraint and didn't go overdoing it with backcombing and kiss-curls and making her look like what she wasn't. Twinky said he wouldn't dream of backcombing my Gran's hair because it was lovely and thick and natural just like Katharine Hepburn's. And my Gran was pleased with that because she always said Katie Hepburn was the only film star she'd ever admired because she was suitably sombre and looked like she had some intelligence.

So we all sat around eating Garibaldis as Twinky gave my Gran an intelligent-looking hairdo and my Gran told us all sorts of things about the world and living in it. And one of the things she told us about, before we left, was Giuseppe Garibaldi.

Twinky said, 'I never realised that, Gran.'

And Norman said, 'I just thought it was the name of a fuckin' biscuit, Gran.'

So my Gran told us about Giuseppe Garibaldi and how he had to cross the Straits of Messina before Italy could become united. But all that Garibaldi had was a leaking ship, a few ragged volunteers, hardly any weapons and nowt but a couple of salami sandwiches between the lot of them.

'And that's why', my Gran said, 'nobody ever thought he'd ever do it. Nobody believed he'd ever amount to much. But you see, lads, what nobody ever saw, not until it was too late, was that Giuseppe Garibaldi and his volunteers, inside of them they had something that more than made up for the lack of salami or the want of proper weapons; they had unity, they had purpose; and they had love for each other.'

My Gran nodded at us. She said, 'And you lads, always try and remember that. Remember that you've got love for each other. And if you can keep hold of that, boys, if you can go on looking after each other and looking out for each other, you'll always find a way to cross the Straits of Messina.'

And that night, before we left her, we all told my Gran that we would always stick together, and always look out for each other. And I know that when we told her that, Twinky and Norman and me, we were each telling my Gran what we believed to be true. We never doubted, that night, never doubted for a single second that when we had to do it, we'd all be crossing the Straits of Messina together.

I was really happy that night. I couldn't believe what a lucky person I was, having a Gran like my Gran and friends like Twinky and Norman. But I should have known! I should have known how dangerous it is to be that happy.

It was Chantelle Smith who gave me the letter. It was just before the last lesson on Tuesday afternoon. It had been a crap day because I hadn't seen Twinky or Norman. They hadn't shown up for school and I'd just gone through the day trying to tell myself there was nothing to worry about and it was probably nothing more than Twinky had come down with a cold or Norman had overslept and missed the bus. If one of them ever had to miss school, the other one always stayed off as well. So I'd been telling myself it was probably just that. But when we were changing lessons, I was walking along the top corridor when

Chantelle Smith came past. She just flung this envelope at me and said, 'Here! The little queer said I've got to give you this! I'll bet it's a Valentine,' she said, 'and it's not even fuckin' Valentine's till next week!'

Chantelle ran off. And I just stood there, looking down at the envelope. And I knew, even before I opened it, I knew!

Dear Raymond, dearest Fly,
We have gone. We had to do it, Fly. We wanted to take you with us. But it would not be right, Fly, because we would be getting into big trouble if we took you with us when you are still so young. We thought we could wait, till you were old enough. We love you, Fly. And that is why me and Norman thought we could wait till you were sixteen and old enough to leave school. That is how we planned it, so that we could wait for you. But in the end we just could not wait. It is Norman's dad, Fly. Last night, Norman turned up at ours. His dad had battered him up again. I had to take Norman to the hospital and they said he had got broken ribs. But he has got more than that, Ray, because he has got a broken heart with what that bastard has done to him. And I know that Norman cannot take it any more. I know that if his dad tries to touch him again, Norman will go for him. And if Norman does do that, it could be the end of him because he will probably kill his dad or hurt him so much that he will get into all the sort of trouble that he has managed to keep out of for so long now.

So that is why me and Norman are going, Fly. If anybody asks you about it, just say that you don't know where we have gone and it is probably somewhere very far away where we can never be found.

When we get sorted and we have got somewhere to stay, I will write again. I know that this will hurt you, Fly, and I wish with all my heart that I did not have to write it. But I do, Fly. And I am just sorry that you are not coming with us.

Norman sends his love and says to tell you that he is sorry too. And he also says that we *will* be together again one day. I know that he is right. I know that there will be a day when we will *all* cross the Straights of Merseener together.
Love,
Twinky and Norman

PS I am very sorry about my writing. I know it is ugly. But it is something I never properly learned to do.

I was just stood there staring at it, the tears at the back of my eyes making Twinky's lovely, stilted writing look like words floating on water as I looked at them and tried to understand.

But I couldn't understand anything. Because this was all wrong! It wasn't meant to be like this. All the plans we'd made; about how we would always stay together, all go to London, together; all be in the Wonderful World of the West End, together. And now they'd gone without me. Twinky and Norman had left me behind.

I didn't know I was crying, not till I became aware of the voices, and people around me whispering, saying, 'He's crying! Fly's fucking crying!'

They were asking me what's up and what was wrong. But I just turned around, walked off along the corridor and went running back down the stairs with everyone shouting and asking me where I was going. But I just kept running, down the stairs, out of the school and across the field, running and running as fast as I could, tears swimming in front of my eyes and this pain inside of me, all mixed up with a sense of panic and dread and the feeling that everything was just falling apart. They'd left me! Twinky and Norman had left me behind! I kept running, running hard and fast like Norman had taught me to do; running, running across the field and over the ditch and into the woods where I'd ran with Twinky and Norman;

running and crying and shouting out their names as I ran, running hard and fast, like Norman had showed me, running beyond the pain, through the barrier so that it wouldn't hurt any more. Only this time, no matter how hard I ran, I couldn't stop the hurting.

I leaned up against the tree and read the letter again, trying to understand, trying to tell myself that they had to do it, that Norman couldn't go on like that. And I *did* understand that part of it. I didn't want my battered friend to keep on getting hurt and getting into trouble; but still, they'd gone. My friends . . . had gone!

I stood for ages and ages beneath the tree where me and Norman, and sometimes Twinky, used to sit and have a rest at the halfway point when we'd been running; where Norman used to measure my pulse rate and my heart recovery rate. And he always used to say, 'Fuckin' brilliant, Fly. Fuckin' A1 at Lloyd's!'

And Norman never even had the first idea of where that saying came from.

He said, 'I just know it means that you are one fit fucker, Fly!'

And so I'd told him, told Norman about Lloyd's of London and the big brass bell that only ever gets rung when there's been a disaster at sea.

And Norman had said, 'Fuckin' hell, we'll go there, Fly. When we all run away to London together. We'll all go to Lloyd's and look at that fuckin' bell! And when we do, when we get to London, we'll all be fuckin' "A1 at Lloyd's"!'

Only that was never going to happen now. And it didn't matter any more, that I was 'A1 at Lloyd's', that I was slim again like I used to be. They'd gone.

The wind was starting to howl now as I stood there beneath the beech tree. And I began to feel how cold it was, with the ground frozen as solid as stone and the mean February wind biting at the bare twig ends of branches, making them tremble against the darkening sky. Once, the speckled sun had shone through those same branches and made a kind of heaven. But there was no sun any more.

I didn't want to go home. I didn't want my Mam asking me what was wrong. My Mam wouldn't understand, just like she'd never been able to understand, about Norman and Twinky. Like she'd never really understood anything, not since *he* had been around, not since the Invasion of the Lert! I didn't want to go home. I wanted to go to London. And be with my friends. But I was too young to go to London. I didn't even have any money to get to a place like London. And even if I could get there, I didn't know where I'd find them, Norman and Twinky. I had to go home.

By the time I got back to the school it was all closed up and the minibus had gone. It was starting to get dark and I had to walk it all the way back to Wythenshawe. But I didn't care. And I didn't care about the cold or the wind that was slicing through me. I didn't care about anything any more. I thought there was nothing worth caring about, not now that my friends had gone off without me. It didn't even matter that my Mam wouldn't understand. Nothing mattered; that's what I thought.

Until I was back in Wythenshawe, coming round the corner of the block next to ours and walking over towards the car park.

I wasn't even surprised! I was just stunned; stunned like I'd stood on a cable carrying ten thousand volts of electricity; as I saw it, the Lert's car. And inside it, silhouetted against the light spilling out from the downstairs maisonette, the two dark shapes inside the car. I didn't want to believe it. I wanted to turn away and run. But my legs were like posts that had been hammered into the ground and my feet were like leaden lumps, so that all I could do was stand there in the dark, watching and trying to believe it wasn't really them, that it must be somebody else; somebody else leaning across towards the passenger seat; somebody else whose arms were outstretched and enfolding him;

342

somebody else he was hugging; two other people, not them! Not my Mam! Not my Mam and the Lert, sat inside a car, kissing each other! But then the car door opened, I saw my Mam get out of the car; and I knew, I had to believe it then. I saw her, smiling as she waved and said tarar. And I saw that same smile start to freeze on her face as she glanced across the roof of that car and saw me stood there, watching her from the shadow of the maisonettes.

It was like my voice wouldn't work properly, the words coming out all thin and quiet as I stared back at her and said, 'What are you doin'?'

She lifted up her hand. 'Now hold on,' she said, 'hold on!'

'What are you doin'?' I asked again, the words stronger now, all the horror rushing up from my belly. 'What are you doin'?'

But the other door was opening. And he was getting out of the car, smiling! Saying, 'Hello, Raymond,' saying, 'I'm just dropping your mum off.'

But I ignored him and I screamed! Screamed at my Mam and said, 'What are you doing?'

And then! Then they looked at each other. He walked round to the other side of the car. He took my Mam by the hand. And I could hear my Mam saying, 'No, Ted! Not now, not now!'

But he said, 'No, Shelagh. That's not fair. Raymond deserves an explanation.'

Then he turned back to me, smiling at me again. And I knew! Before the words came out of his mouth, I knew what they'd be! Knew that they'd be lethal words, bullet words, poison-tipped, killing words, words that he aimed straight at me as he walked around the car and I was already raising my hands, trying to get to my ears and cover them as he fired off the first round of the volley, the smile still on his lips as he said, 'Raymond. Your Mum and I have got some news.'

I clamped my hands hard to my ears, trying to shut

it out, to protect myself and save myself. But still I could hear it, the muffled shots of words.

'You see,' he said, 'I've asked your mum, I've asked Shelagh, if she'll do me the great honour of becoming my—'

I started shouting, my hands still clamped to my ears and my own words filling up my head and keeping his words out; repeating it, all the time saying out loud, 'Earmuffs, earmuffs, earmuffs,' over and over and over, all the time so that I wouldn't hear him, 'Earmuffs, earmuffs, earmuffs, earmuffs, earmuffs, don't listen, don't listen, don't listen, he's trying to kill me, don't listen, earmuffs, earmuffs, earmuffs, keep me safe, don't kill me, don't listen, don't listen, earmuffs, earmuffs, earmuffs . . .'

I could see my Mam lowering her head and shaking it. I could see him coming towards me, coming towards me with his mouth moving, his lips moving as he carried on talking, never stopping talking; keeping on talking, always talking, talking, trying to get me, trying to hurt me, trying to aim the words into my ears, trying to kill me.

'Earmuffs, earmuffs, get the sheriff, earmuffs, earmuffs, he's trying to kill me, keep them out, the words, the words, earmuffs, earmuffs, keep them out, keep them out, he's trying to kill me, trying to kill me, trying to kill me . . .'

I could see my Mam as she opened her mouth, yelling, screaming at me, but doing it all in silence because I couldn't hear anything outside my own head as I kept up the words that kept out the words that the Lert was trying to kill me with. 'Mam, Mam, Mam, don't let him kill me, don't Mam, don't Mam, don't Mam, please, he killed her! He did, his wife, he did, he did. It wasn't the mussels, it wasn't the mussels, Mam. He killed her, he did, he did did did. And he'll kill you like he's trying to kill me, like he tried to kill the Shoeshine Boy. Earmuffs, earmuffs, earmuffs, Mam, don't let him kill you, put your earmuffs on . . .'

But my Mam was taking no notice. My Mam was just leaning up against the car and now he was coming towards me, his arms outstretched as he moved forward, his lips still moving as he came towards me, still talking, talking, talking as he came towards me. And I knew, I knew, I knew, if he got to me, he'd get me, get me with the words, get under my hands and into my ears and into my brain with the words, the words, the words, the words that were made to kill me. I was backing away, backing away from him, backing away from the look in his eye, the shock in his eyes, the startled shock; because he knew, because he knew he'd been found out. The Lert, the Lert, the Lert was coming after me, trying to catch me, trying to get me. But I was running, running, running away, over the car park, between the blocks and into the dark; away, away; away from the Lert; running, running, leaving him behind, running, scrambling to get out of range, where they couldn't reach me; the words that he wanted to fire into me! The dumdum bullet words that I knew would shatter on impact, sending bits of shrapnel and shards of steel spiralling through me; and leaving me dead!

Morrissey, I know! I know it does seem as if I was mad. I even think I probably *was* mad, that night. But not mad like they said I was mad. The real insanity, Morrissey, the obscene, crippling insanity was what he had tried to tell me! My Mam! And that Lert! My mother, getting married, to *him*! That was the true madness. That was the lunacy; the schizoid, psychotic, moon-touched, deranged daftness that defied all sense. That was the real madness, Morrissey. The madness that made me run and run and run.

But if I'd been truly mad that night, if I'd been mad like they said I was mad, I would have tried to run all the way to London. I didn't try to run to London though! I ran to where I thought I would find some sanity, Morrissey; ran to the one person, the only person in all of the world who would somehow make it all right.

The nurse asked me if I was OK. She said I looked frozen to my bones and asked me why I wasn't wearing a coat on such a cold and bitter night. But I told the nurse I wasn't cold at all. I told her I'd come to see my Gran. Only when she asked me what my Gran's name was, she suddenly looked a bit anxious and asked me to wait a minute. Then she disappeared into the office and another nurse came out. She told me that my Gran wasn't very well. She explained that my Gran had had a little setback. And they were waiting for the doctor. I think that was when I started crying. The nurses thought I was just crying for my Gran. And said that perhaps if I didn't stay for too long I could go in and see her then.

When the nurse showed me into the room, my Gran was just slumped there in a chair. I could see her eyes watching me. But nothing else seemed to be working. Her mouth was just hanging open and drooping at one side.

'Look, Vera!' the nurse said, her voice all bright and cheerful. 'Look who's here; it's your grandson.'

But my Gran didn't flicker. And the nurse, still talking to my Gran as if she was a deaf daft woman, said, 'He can't stop long, Vera, because we're waiting for the doctor. We think you might have had a little mini stroke, Vera.'

The nurse bent down in front of my Gran then and said, 'Ah. Poor Vera Madeira.' She reached out then to try and take hold of my Gran's hand. But as she did, this red thing rolled out of my Gran's lap. The nurse took no notice of it. But I said, 'What is it? What's that?'

The nurse looked. And picked it up.

'Oh, Vera, look,' she said. 'It's your red nose,Vera!'

Then turning to me, the nurse said, 'Ah, and she was having such fun as well. We've all been practisin' wearing our noses and getting ready for Red Nose Day. Everybody's been so looking forward to it. We came up with this marvellous idea, where all the guests are going

346

to be the comedian of their choice for the whole of Red Nose Day. We're having custard pies and funny hats, tickle-sticks, and party-poppers. We had our first practice this afternoon. Didn't we, Vera? And it was hysterical, it was. Everywhere you looked there were Arthur Askeys, Frankie Howerds and Tommy Coopers, Hylda Bakers and Beryl Reids. And Charlie Chaplins? We've got some brilliant Charlie Chaplins.' She turned to my Gran, 'Haven't we, Vera?' she almost shouted. 'Haven't we seen some fantastic Charlie Chaplins today?'

But my Gran just stared as the nurse nodded and said, 'Mind you, your Gran was very good an' all. I'm not so sure that everybody understood exactly which comedian she was being; because I think your Gran must have lived abroad at some time, didn't she?'

I just frowned at the nurse and shook my head.

'Oh,' she said, 'well, it was definitely a foreign-sounding name. When we asked your Gran which comedian she was, she came up with this name, I thought it was German. And I suppose they must have comedians, even the Germans, mustn't they?'

I didn't have the first clue what she was talking about. And then I heard it, heard my Gran making this noise.

'What was that, Vera?' the nurse said.

And my Gran took a big struggling breath and said it again, '. . . Wit . . . Wit . . . Wit.'

She had spit dribbling out the side of her mouth. And the nurse thought that that was what my Gran was trying to say, 'spit'.

'Well, we'll soon clean that up,' the nurse said, reaching for a tissue. But as she went to wipe her mouth, my Gran pushed the nurse's arm away and, her eyes fixed on me, she said, 'Witt . . . Witt . . . Witt . . . gen . . . stein.'

'That was it!' the nurse suddenly shouted. 'That's the comedian your Gran was being. Vitgen, that's it, Vitgen someone. I told you it sounded German. And you were very good, Vera.' The nurse said, 'You got some good laughs today, didn't you?'

Then the nurse stood back and looked at my Gran. 'Ah,' she said, 'she was having such fun.'

The nurse nodded at my Gran. Then she said, 'Shall we put it back on again, Vera? All right, come on,' she said, lifting up the piece of red plastic and attaching it to my Gran's nose.

And that's how I last saw my Gran. Another nurse arrived and said the doctor was here, so I'd have to leave. And for ages after that, whenever I thought about my Gran, I saw her like that, her speech all gone, a red plastic nose stuck to her face; her body looking like all the bones had been pulled out of it; as she sat there, slumped in a chair; stricken dumb by fun, Wittgenstein, the Red-Nosed Philosopher!

I don't know why I went there. I didn't live there any more. Twinky and Norman weren't there any more. And my Gran would never be coming back there, not now. I don't know why I went. But there was nowhere else to go really, nowhere at all. I was just walking around, that's all; walking around Failsworth, where I used to live. I didn't know he was out looking for me, Wilson. I was just walking, that's all, looking at all the old places, at my old school in Binfield Road, where I'd first known Norman and Twinky; the recreation park where I used to play football and superheroes and camp out with my friends in the summer; the house where we used to live, all different now since the council had fixed it up, a different-coloured door, a different-coloured gate. Then I went to my Gran's house, expecting it to be dark and locked up but still looking like I'd always remembered it. Only it wasn't locked up and it wasn't dark. All the lights were on and it looked like the people inside were having some kind of a party. There was a new glass porch around the front door. And a brand new satellite dish up there on the roof. I wondered if my Mam knew! That he must have sold it, my Uncle Bastard! Sold my Gran's house, without telling anyone.

But it didn't matter, not any more. My Gran was never coming back, not now. My Uncle Bastard, his Sickening Spouse and the Brainless Brats could do what they liked. It didn't matter. None of it mattered any more.

But, Morrissey, I wasn't doing what they said I was doing. I know I ended up walking down the cut, past the bread shop, through the gate and down past the allotments. But that wasn't the reason, Morrissey, what they said. It was the ice! The ice! That's why I couldn't get back; because of the ice! I could see the frost on the ground; and up in the clear sky, the big bright yellow moon, lighting up everywhere into a sort of daylight, stretching my shadow out behind me as I came out of the lane and over the bridge and down past the backs of the bungalow houses. And of course I knew where I was going! I knew exactly where I was going. But the reason I was going there, Morrissey, the reason had nothing to do with madness and Lerts or earmuffs and mussels and Psycho The Rapists or witches in sandwiches, felonious uncles, fictitious friends and their American fathers; or anything else that was on the computer.

The only reason, Morrissey, the only reason I ended up back there, standing there on the bank, there, in that place at the side of the canal, the only reason, was that my heart felt like it was all broken. And I *know* it couldn't be fixed, just by me standing there at the side of a frozen canal at a place where I'd once disappeared! I *know* that! I knew that when I was stood there; knew it wouldn't make anything better or bring my friends back, make my Gran into my proper Gran again or stop my Mam from taking a hideous husband. I *knew* my going back to that place wouldn't do anything like that. But I just went there! That's all. Just went there! Because I didn't have *anywhere else to go*! That's why! That's why I went there. And the only thing I was doing was thinking. Just standing there thinking. And wondering. Wondering what had ever happened. To me. And to the little girl. Wondering about her. And what had ever become of her. And I'd never blamed her, Morrissey. I'd never blamed that little girl. Because what had happened to her had been terrible, much more terrible than anything that had happened to me. But if she hadn't said, if she hadn't said it was the Beast of a Boy, I knew I wouldn't be back standing where I was at that canal, my teeth chattering and the sharp thin wind cutting through my shirt as I thought and wondered, and stared at the moon's reflection on the glassy surface of the frozen water.

And I would have gone back home, Morrissey, in the end. I would have turned around and just gone home. Because I knew there were no answers for me, not there at that canal. I think I knew, even then, that there aren't no answers anywhere. Like my Gran always said, 'It's the questions, son, they're what matter; the questions; the answers are barely worth bothering with.'

In the end, I'd had enough of walking round Failsworth; had enough of standing, frozen, by the canal. And I'd remembered the other thing my Gran always said, that thing about self-pity and how it never ever peeled a single potato.

And that's why I never would have done it, Morrissey, not what they said. I was even turning to go, turning around and away from the water. And it was the shock. The sudden shock; the noise of it suddenly cutting through the calm quiet air. It just startled me, the big shape of him rushing towards me and the shout, almost a scream exploding in the quiet frosty air as he yelled, 'RAYMOND!'

I felt my foot as it juddered and slipped and missed; the frost on the coping stone wiping my foot from under me and sending me sprawling, backwards. I was already half turned and toppling, reaching out and grasping nothing but thin air as I saw who it was who'd

shouted and startled me, him, the Lert, running down
from the bridge towards the towpath, shouting,
screaming at me, 'No, no! Raymond, DON'T DO IT!'

But I wasn't, Morrissey; I wasn't doing it. I wasn't
doing anything. It was just happening to me, that's all.
And I couldn't stop it. Because I was in mid air and
falling, my forehead smacking against the solid stone
lip of the bank before I crashed down onto the ice
where I lay and felt the warm blood from my head as it
trickled down the cold skin of my face. And just for the
smallest moment of a second, I thought it would all be
all right and that I'd just get up and clamber back up
the bank. I even reached out my arm and started to try
and push myself up. Only that's when I heard it, the
scream of the ice; like something squealing in terrible
agony as it shattered beneath me, slowly at first and
then suddenly cracking open, setting free the icy
fingers of the water that reached out and grabbed me,
numbing me as they seized me and pulled me down
under the ice, into the water. I tried to come back up,
Morrissey. Even with the pain that was in my head and
the paralysing cold of the water, I tried to come back
up. But it was the ice, you see, the ice; it had closed
back over me and it wouldn't open again, not from
underneath. I kept pushing at it, kept trying to find the
place where I'd slipped through. But the pain in my
head, Morrissey. And the numbness, Morrissey; pushing up at the ice, it was like trying to push the whole
of the world; it wouldn't move. And the more I tried to
push it, the more my arms just lost their strength. Till
in the end it didn't seem like it was worth pushing any
more. It felt sort of nice when I just gave up, gave in.
Even the pain in my head started to disappear. And all
the paralysing cold of the water seemed like it wasn't
even cold any more; seemed almost like it was a warm
blanket wrapped all around me.

And that's when I saw him, the Nice Boy. He was
just there, swimming in front of me, swimming
towards me, his face smiling as he approached me, as

351

he lifted up his arm and waved to greet me; as he stretched out his hand towards me. And with the last shred of strength that was in me, I reached out, took hold of his hand. And started to softly sink, down and down, gently down; and into the darkest depths of the water.

Yours sincerely,
Raymond Marks

Dear Morrissey,

I know I shouldn't be here, I shouldn't be anywhere near here. I never ever meant to come to Plinxton. I'd never even heard of it before tonight. But I had to come, Morrissey; even though it's meant I'm miles out of my way by now, miles and miles and miles. But I had to come to Plinxton. Because something's happened, Morrissey. And that's why I had to come here!

I always thought Country and Western people were to be pitied. And avoided! I thought they were like morris dancers and stamp collectors, people who polish steam engines and those who wax lyrical on the beauty of real ale; harmless but hideous!

I even felt a bit guilty about getting into the van; especially when I was still three places down in the hitchhikers' stacking system, with the salvation-seeker and the body-metal girl with the shaved head still ahead of me. But the van had driven straight past them and stopped specially for me. I was still sitting there on the grass when it pulled over and I heard this voice saying, ' 'ey up, partner. Jump in!'

353

So I did. Somebody pushed open the back doors and I jumped in the van as quick as I could, with the salvation-seeker and the tongue-studded girl shouting at me and saying I was a bastard for jumping the queue!

But it wasn't them who were being offered the lift, it was me.

The Dewsbury Desperadoes had seen me sat there and spotting my guitar, they'd assumed that like them I was a Country and Western artiste, headed for the Country Music Convention that's being held at Plinxton Allied Butchers' and Architects' Club. And good Country cousins that they are, the Dewsbury Desperadoes had stopped and picked me up. But it was only when I was sat there parked on a flight case with the van pulling away that they got a good look at me. And when they did, when they saw my Morrissey tee shirt, I think they were all a bit disappointed. They were too polite to ask me to get out again though. So I just sat there, trying to be as comfortable as I could with the Dewsbury Desperadoes all staring at me.

When they did finally speak, it was Cindy-Charlene, the Desperadoes' country chanteuse, who nodded at the picture on my tee shirt and said, 'Who's that then?'

I said, 'It's Edith Sitwell.'

Cindy-Charlene just nodded, somewhat cautiously. And the Desperado called Deak, who seemed to have a particularly peptic disposition, scowled and said, 'Who?'

I said, 'Edith Sitwell.' But Deak just looked at me rather blankly; and concluding that he must be the drummer with the group, I said, 'Edwardian poet, performance artist and English eccentric.'

'And right ugly fucker and all!' Deak said. 'Look at the gob on her!'

I didn't say nowt but I thought, I'll bet Dolly Parton and Emmy Lou Harris are not looking too shit hot when they get to be nearly ninety!

354

They just ignored me after that though. And Sowerby Slim, the big bass player and obviously the boss of the Desperadoes, told them all it was time for their vocal warm-up. Deak the drummer muttered something about what was the point but Cindy-Charlene turned on him then and told him that as well as being a shagawful drummer he was a right bilious bastard.

'And the *point*,' she told him, 'the point is that we've got to rehearse. And we've got to do this gig. Whether you like it or not, we're doing it; for the sake of the Cowboy; for his memory.'

I didn't know who she was talking about. But Sowerby Slim started singing then, the others joined in and I just had to sit there and suffer it all as these musically retarded unfortunates polluted the air with a compendium of wrist-slashing Country classics such as 'I've Never Been To Bed With An Ugly Woman But I've Sure Woken Up With A Few'.

It was all so depressing and melancholic that I even started to feel quite at home actually. But then, in the middle of something excruciatingly appalling called 'The Dog Don't Wag His Tail Since You've Been Gone', Desperado Deak just banged his fist against the side of the van and in a somewhat tortured tone, he wailed, 'It's wrong! We shouldn't be doing it. I don't care what any fucker says, we shouldn't be doin' it. It's wrong playing in that place, that place where it all happened, it's not right.'

Cindy-Charlene began to remonstrate with him again. But Sowerby Slim appealed for calm and said, 'Deak, it's hard, it's hard for all of us, mate. But be strong, Deak, try and be strong. Tell y'self you're doing it for the Cowboy. For the memory of the Cowboy.'

Deak just nodded and snuffled a bit then. And Cindy-Charlene handed him a paper hankie but he declined it manfully and just wiped away his snuffles with the back of his hand. Mercifully, though, they didn't do no more rehearsing after that. And instead they all just sat there looking depressed and deflated.

And I don't even know why I asked because I've never had the slightest interest in Country music or the sort of people who feel compelled to inflict it on a world that's already seen enough suffering. But I heard myself saying, 'What happened to him then? The Cowboy person?'

They all turned and looked at me like they'd forgotten I was there. And I thought I might have upset them by being nosey or talking out of turn. But it was the opposite of that and they were like persons who've been bereaved and want to rekindle and relive the memory of the departed, by telling a willing listener all about their long-gone loved one.

Cindy-Charlene asked me what my name was and when I told her it was Raymond, she said, 'Well, Raymond, if you could have seen him! If you could have met him yourself and seen that Cowboy. The Kexborough Cowboy. What a man!'

I just nodded. Because I wasn't paying that much attention really. If they'd been telling me about you, Morrissey, or The Smiths then it would have been different. But I couldn't muster much enthusiasm for hearing about some obscure Country singer with a somewhat unfortunate name.

'We didn't even know who he was,' Cindy-Charlene said. 'We didn't know him as the Cowboy, not then. He just turned up, y' see. He just appeared, arrived un-announced one day, from out of the west.'

I looked at Cindy-Charlene and nodded. 'America?' I said.

'No, Bolton,' she said. 'Bolton or Burnley or some-where like that, somewhere in Lancashire, the other side of the moors, judging from the way he spoke. We'd certainly never seen him before, not on the Country circuit. We didn't know him. He was just the stranger. The Stranger who turned up at that audition.'

'We were just packing up, y' see,' Sowerby Slim said. 'Three days we'd been auditioning, trying to find a replacement guitarist. But we were getting nowhere fast. We'd seen just about everyone. But no matter who played with us, there just didn't seem to be that . . . spark. Anyroad, end of that final day of auditions we were right down in the dumps, none of us saying nowt, just starting to pack up the gear and wondering if we'd ever find a guitarist to suit.'

'And that's when we heard it,' Cindy-Charlene said, 'coming from somewhere back down in the dimness of the hall; we heard this cough. And then this voice, all sort of hesitant and a bit shy like, saying, "Erm . . . I'm sorry to erm . . . I'm very sorry to bother you but I did hear how you might be lookin' for a guitarist." And then he appeared, this Stranger; just sort of materialised out of the gloom and stood there at the foot of the stage, guitar in hand.'

'I was for not bothering, me,' Deak said. 'I'd already dismantled my hi-hat and my foot pedal. But that's when Slim nudged me and nodded in the direction of the Stranger. And I noticed it then; the guitar he was carryin'.'

Morrissey, I've got to tell you! By this time I was wishing I'd kept my big mouth shut and never asked about the sodding Kexborough Cowboy. All I'd wanted to know was what had happened to him. But the Dewsbury Desperadoes were telling it like it was something out of Marcel bleeding Proust! I didn't think I could stand much more. I even thought about asking them if they could stop the van and drop me off. But then, Morrissey, with Sowerby Slim having taken over the narrative, that's when it started to happen to me, the 'something' that happened in the Dewsbury Desperadoes' van. Because that's when I suddenly started to realise what it was he was saying, Sowerby Slim, as he recounted that moment in the audition hall and began to describe the guitar that the Stranger had been clutching hold of!

'A pre-war, bevel-fronted, small-bodied acoustic Guild,' Sowerby Slim said. And then, with some reverence, added, 'Authentic mottled fish-shell scratch board. Original ivory tuning pegs.'

Sowerby Slim saw me then, saw me staring at him with my mouth half open and my eyes wide and wondering.

'Are you all right, young man?' he asked.

I just nodded. And then I said, '*All* of them? All *six* original ivory tuning pegs?'

Sowerby Slim leaned forward then and patted me on the knee as he said, 'Now then, young man, that's what I like to hear, a person who pays attention to detail when he's talking about serious matters such as musical instruments.' Slim lifted up his finger then and said, 'Now, it's funny you should mention those tuning pegs, young man. But as a matter of fact, no, they weren't all there. There was one peg missing. Just one, mind. And I remember it because whoever had replaced it, that missing peg, they'd done a real cack-handed job on it. I'd never have done it, not to an instrument of that pedigree. But whoever had replaced that peg, they'd used a bog standard, cheap silver thing. And, oh . . . it was a crime, it was! A crime to repair an instrument of that quality using nothing but . . .'

Slim just carried on talking then, going on about the slipshoddiness of some instrument repairers. But I was no longer listening, Morrissey. I didn't want to hear any more about the guitar. I wanted to know about the Stranger who'd been carrying it.

'What happened?' I asked them. 'What happened at the audition?'

The Desperadoes all glanced at each other and all smiled, even Deak the drummer. And Sowerby Slim said, 'Young man, there are auditions and there are *auditions*! And I think I can say with some confidence that I'll never again have the experience I had that day, the day the Cowboy auditioned.'

'Was he good?' I asked. 'Did he play good?'

'Good?' Cindy-Charlene said. 'Good? He got up on

the stage with us and we said, "Right then, friend, what would you like to play?" Well, he just sort of shrugged, a bit shy. And then, quietly spoken, very quiet, he said, "I was wonderin' if you know 'Country Boy'?"'

Cindy-Charlene just paused and stared at me then, nodding her head all knowingly as if I should understand the significance of such a title.

'Well, we knew,' Cindy-Charlene said, 'we knew we were in for something then all right. Nobody tackles a tune like "Country Boy" without knowing his way around a guitar.'

'That's right,' Slim concurred. 'I've seen many a picker, many a good picker come to grief over "Country Boy". I've even seen Albert Lee himself lose his fingering on some of the licks in that treacherously taxing tune.'

Slim just sat there nodding at his memories. But I wasn't interested in Albert bleeding Lee, whoever he was.

'But what about the Cowboy?' I said. 'What was the Cowboy's fingering like?'

'*His* fingering?' Sowerby Slim said. 'His fingering . . . it had to be seen to be believed.'

'*His* fingering?' Cindy-Charlene echoed. 'We counted him in, four beats on the snare from Deak; and the Cowboy, he's straight in there, right into that first solo, foot beating perfect time, going off like a metronome, his head thrown back and his eyes closed like he's so into the number that he's possessed. And fingers! I've never seen fingers that could dance up and down a fretboard the way that that Cowboy's fingers danced.'

All the Desperadoes just fell silent then, with smiles on their faces as they seemed to savour the memory of that special moment. And I was smiling too, smiling a big smile that seemed to have come up from somewhere deep in the very soul of me.

And I said to the Desperadoes, 'It must have just

been so brilliant, that. Just so brilliant seeing him, the Cowboy, playing like that.'

They looked at me, the Desperadoes. And I looked back at them with the big warm smile still on my face. But Cindy-Charlene was slowly shaking her head and looking somewhat crestfallen now.

'But he *wasn't!*' she said. 'That's the whole point! He wasn't *playin'* anything. All he was doing was just skittering his fingers anywhere and everywhere. And there wasn't one single note he played that bore the slightest resemblance to "Country Boy"; or to anything that could be reasonably described as music!'

Sowerby Slim shook his big bearded head and sorrowfully declared, 'It was awful. Truly awful.'

'And right embarrassing,' Cindy-Charlene said. 'Because we didn't know what to do. We didn't want to give offence. So we just had to keep playing along and carrying on as if it was a normal audition. And every time we got to one of his solos, the Stranger, he'd shriek with delight, leap up in the air or drop down on one knee, giving it loads and thrusting out the neck of the guitar as if he was Hendrix, Clapton, Django Reinhardt and Chet Atkins all rolled into one.'

'And the worst of it was,' Deak said, 'when we got to the end of that number he just stood there, smiling at us all and asking us if he'd got the job.'

'We just stood there saying nowt,' Cindy-Charlene explained. 'Because y' could tell, even then y' could tell as how he was ... oh, such a mild-mannered, innocent sort of chap. I was trying to think of something a bit diplomatic like, wondering if perhaps we could find a way to let him down gently. In the end though, it was Deak who just threw his sticks up into the air and said, "Got the job? Got the fuckin' job! We're lookin' for a guitarist, mate, not a ten-thumbed bastard who wouldn't know a crotchet from a fuckin' hatchet."'

Cindy-Charlene shook her head at the memory of that appalling moment. 'I felt awful for him,' she said.

'I felt right dreadful when Deak told him that. It might have been the truth but it's not easy, is it, it's not easy for a person to be told he's no good.'

'The weird thing though', Sowerby Slim piped up, 'is that he didn't even seem to mind.'

Cindy-Charlene nodded and said, 'That's right. He didn't take the slightest bit of offence. He thanked us all, shook us all by the hand, even Deak; and he said he was very very grateful and it had been a particular honour for him to audition with us. Then he just walked off the stage, clutching his guitar, and headed off towards the exit.'

Cindy-Charlene shook her head, somewhat ruefully. 'And that might have been it,' she said. 'In fact that *would* have been it if the caretaker hadn't already locked up the front of house. He thought we were all done, y' see, so he could lock up and leave us lot to go out the back. So when the Stranger got out into the foyer, he found the doors locked. And not being the sort of man to cause a fuss, he just perched himself on a beer crate, quite content to sit there waiting till someone came along and unlocked the doors.'

'But we didn't know about that,' Slim said. 'We didn't know he was out there in the foyer. We were just sat there in that empty hall, depressed by three days of fruitless auditions and especially by having had our hopes suddenly raised and then dashed by the ten-thumbed Stranger with the bevel-topped Guild.'

'And when we first heard it,' Cindy-Charlene said, 'at first we thought it was somebody playin' a record.'

'Aye, but what a record!' Deak said.

'What d' y' mean?' I asked.

'Well, we were sitting there,' Cindy-Charlene said, 'and we heard it drifting through.'

'This . . . sound,' Slim said, 'a sound that . . . just wrapped itself around your heart. A sound that made y' want to weep an' . . . wail with joy at the same time.'

I looked at Sowerby Slim. 'What do y' mean?' I said. 'What sort of sound?'

'Singing.' Sowerby Slim nodded, 'Melody. A voice . . . singing. But singing like you'd never heard singing before in your life.'

'It was a voice,' Cindy-Charlene said, 'a voice like a perfect sweet-and-sour sauce; sweet and tangy at the same time; full and soft and curving like a woman but hard and muscly like a man; brittle, yet supple; gentle and jagged at the same time. It was a voice that sounded like it had been marinated in the kitchens of heaven. And every note carried through to that empty hall as if it was being borne on the wings of angels.'

'And we all just sat there,' Deak said, 'sat there thinking we must be listening to some rare and priceless record. Until it started to dawn on each and every one of us and we began to look at each other as we realised it couldn't be a record. Or else we'd have heard some instruments as well. Then it stopped, this magical melody, just stopped mid-phrase and we heard George, the caretaker, shouting something in the foyer. Then we heard the rattle of keys. And that's when we started moving, all of us, running down that empty hall and out into the foyer. Only to find it empty except for George who'd just let the Stranger out and was locking up again.'

'For a second,' Cindy-Charlene said, 'we stood there staring at George himself and wondering if it was somehow him who'd made that incredible sound.'

'I was even starting to think we might just have imagined it,' Slim said, 'but that's when Cindy-Charlene pointed out through the glass doors and said, "Look".'

'And there he was,' Cindy-Charlene said, 'the Stranger, strolling off across the car park.'

'I couldn't believe it,' Deak said. 'I couldn't see how it was possible. After the vomit he'd spewed from that guitar. I couldn't believe it could be one and the same creature.'

'But I knew,' Cindy-Charlene said, 'I knew! I couldn't get those doors unlocked fast enough. He was almost out of sight by then, the Stranger. We ran like hell across that car park. And when we got to the gates we thought we'd lost him. But then, halfway up the high street, we saw him outside Hendleys Music Mart, stood there staring through the window. When we caught up with him he was just about to go into the shop. He looked all puzzled and perplexed when he saw us. But I just said to him, "Sing!" '

'He was all reluctant,' Sowerby Slim said. 'He just stood there blushing and a bit embarrassed and asking us why we wanted him to sing.'

'In the end,' Cindy-Charlene said, 'I just started singing myself. People at the bus stop were stood there looking at us like we were all soft. And there was me, singing away in the street, trying to get the Stranger to join in. But he just watched and smiled and kept saying it was lovely. And I started to think I might as well pack in. Started to think perhaps we'd got it wrong and it wasn't his voice we'd heard at all.'

'But then,' Deak said, 'just as we were about to give it up as a bad job, quietly, really quietly at first, the Stranger opened his mouth and softly started singing along with Cindy-Charlene.'

'And oh,' Slim said, 'what a harmony! What a glorious sound he made; singing perfect thirds to Cindy-Charlene's top line. And then swapping with her and him taking the top line, Cindy-Charlene the harmony and the pair of them making a sound that could soothe the inconsolable soul. It was like that street was suddenly dripping in honey. Those folks at the bus stop, they couldn't believe their ears; they were stood there in raptures; there must have been three buses came along but nobody made the slightest effort to get on one. And the last bus, the driver just kept it there at the stop with the doors open and him and all his passengers listening to such sweet beauty in the ordinary street.'

'And the applause,' Deak declared, 'the shouts and the whistles when the song was done.'

'But *he* just stood there frowning, didn't he,' Cindy-Charlene said, 'the Stranger? Like he couldn't understand what it was that everybody was applauding.'

'But we didn't hesitate,' Slim said. 'We hadn't even been looking for a male vocalist. But right there in the street, we asked him if he'd like to join the Dewsbury Desperadoes.'

'Well, if you'd seen the look on his face when he heard that,' Cindy-Charlene said. 'He just looked from one to the other of us as if he couldn't believe his ears. And all his face lit up then. He closed his eyes for a second like he'd just been given the most precious thing in all the world. When he opened them again, he said, "Do y' mean it? Do y' really mean it?"'

'We told him of course we bloody meant it,' Deak said. 'And we could see that he finally realised we were making him a serious offer.'

'Aye,' Slim said, 'and that's when *we* realised an' all. Because that's when he lifted up that bevel-topped Guild guitar of his. And lifting it to his lips, he kissed it and said, "At last, old girl; at last we've done it! We're on our way!"'

Sowerby Slim nodded at me. 'That's right,' Slim said, 'he thought we were asking him to join as a guitarist!'

Sowerby Slim shook his head and Deak did the same, saying, 'It's beyond me. It was always beyond me; when it came to singing, he could move me to the very depths of my heart and soul. But when it came to playing guitar, the only thing that moved in me were my bowels!'

'We tried telling him,' Cindy-Charlene said. 'We all went back over to the club and tried to make him see it was a crime, not allowing a voice like that to sing. But he just stood there frowning all the time and saying, "Well, I don't know . . . I just don't know really."'

'"You're a singer," we told him, "a singer, not a guitarist."'

'But it was like he couldn't get it into his head and he

said, "Y' mean . . . y' mean, I can sing with y' . . . but I'd have to give up the guitar?" And the way he looked at his guitar when he said that, it almost broke my heart.'

'But that's what gave me the idea,' Slim said, 'when I saw him looking at that Guild like it was his favourite whippet that was about to be put down. I didn't know how he'd take it but I said, "Look, how's about a compromise? How about . . . you come and sing with us . . . and you keep your guitar . . . But . . . but y' don't . . . actually . . . plug it in!" Well, he frowned at first, a big deep frown. I thought I'd blown it. I thought it was all up with the feathers then. But he said, "On stage? I can have the guitar on stage with me?" We all nodded. "But I won't be plugged in?" We all nodded again, but cautious this time. We just stood and watched him; and it seemed like an eternity as he stood there, debating with himself, wrestling to try an' come to a decision. And when he finally looked at us, all he said was, "Well, I think perhaps a chap gets to the point where he has to be a bit realistic, doesn't he?"

'We didn't dare say a word. We just stood there staring at him, crossing our fingers. Then he nodded and it was almost like he was talking to himself as he said, "I've never wanted to be a singer. Always thought I'd be an instrumentalist. Always saw myself singing with my fingers, really. Never thought about singing with my voice." He looked at us then and he said, "But I can have the guitar with me, up on the stage?"

'We all nodded again, furiously.

'And that's when he said, "Well, perhaps . . . perhaps it's for the best. As I said, sometimes a chap has to be realistic, doesn't he?" He smiled at us all then. And he said, "All right then. I'd be very pleased to accept your offer, to become a Dewsbury Desperado."'

Sowerby Slim sighed then. Deak and Cindy-Charlene sighed as well. And suddenly the atmosphere in the van went back to being somewhat melancholic.

'What's up?' I asked. 'I thought you all wanted him to join.'

Cindy-Charlene sighed again and said, 'We did.'

'So why've you all gone so sad and depressed again?' I asked them.

Cindy-Charlene turned her head and stared out the window. And Sowerby Slim told me, 'Don't mind Cindy-Charlene, young man. It's painful for her. It's painful for all of us.'

'Why?' I said. 'Why is it painful? It shouldn't be painful,' I said, 'because I think it's brilliant that you made the Cowboy sing. What was the point,' I said, 'what was the point in him wasting his time for ever, pretending he could be a guitarist when he never could? And all the time,' I said, 'all the time, he had an instrument that he *could* play, one instrument that he could play brilliantly . . .'

I tailed off then because I could hear my voice beginning to crack and I could feel tears starting to form at the back of my eyes. So I just blinked and said nowt. But Sowerby Slim said, 'Hey up. Now hold on. There's no need for you to be getting upset, young man.'

I nodded and I said, 'I'm sorry, I just . . . it . . . I'm . . .' But I couldn't say nowt because all sorts of things were tumbling through my head. And I didn't know if I should tell them or not. But then Cindy-Charlene turned round again and looked at me. And she said, 'The reason we all find it a bit painful, Raymond, is because we all feel guilty!'

'But why?' I asked again. 'Why should you be guilty when all you did was make the Cowboy see what he always should have seen? Made him see that he was a good singer! Wasn't he happy?' I said. 'Wasn't he happy being a singer?'

Sowerby Slim nodded and said, 'Oh, he was happy all right. As long as he could keep his guitar with him he'd sing all night. We had some wonderful years, we did; some wonderful years with the Cowboy.'

I looked at Cindy-Charlene and I said, 'So why should anybody feel guilty?'

And that's when Cindy-Charlene said, 'Because . . . because if we hadn't brought him into the Desperadoes, he never would have met *her*, would he, never would have taken up with her.'

'Who?' I asked.

Cindy-Charlene's petite pretty face suddenly transformed itself into a mask of repulsion and loathing as she said, 'The Slut! *Her*. That spread-legged slut from Silkstone Common!'

Deak the drummer shook his head and said, 'He didn't stand a chance. Not with her. The Cowboy, y' see, he was as gentle a man as y' could ever wish to meet. Throughout the whole of the Country circuit the Cowboy was renowned for the mildness of his manners. That man, he had the touch of a butterfly and the heart of a dove.'

'And that's why,' Cindy-Charlene said, frowning darkly, 'that's why she was able to walk all over him. She led him like a lamb to the slaughter, the brazen bitch!'

And all the Desperadoes told me then about the woman called Patsy, who the Cowboy met and married. The Country music groupie who couldn't keep her hands off nowt.

'Even on their wedding day,' Cindy-Charlene said, 'at the wedding breakfast she was at it. The ink not yet dry on the marriage certificate and she's leg-spreading already. She said she was going into the function-room kitchen just to have a look in the oven and see how the sausage rolls were doing. But the sausage rolls ended up being burnt black, didn't they! Because instead of checking sausage rolls like she should have been doing, she'd been at it in the walk-in pantry, her and that mean-lipped mandolin player from the back of Halifax. But what did he do, the Cowboy, when he was walking past that kitchen and he smelt the sausage rolls burning? And looking for some oven gloves to lift out the hot trays of burning sausage rolls, he opened the door to the walk-in pantry and saw that slut of a bride and that mandolin player tangled together, panting and whimpering and lost in lust – what did the Cowboy do? Did he walk out on that slut? Did he take that mandolin player by the scruff and stuff his miserable mandolin down his lusting throat?'

I stared at Cindy-Charlene. 'Well?' I said. 'Did he?'

But Cindy-Charlene just shook her head. 'No!' she said. 'The only thing that the Cowboy did was to send out for fresh sausage rolls.'

'That's how he was,' Sowerby Slim said to me, his eyes filled with tears and admiration. 'That was the Cowboy, you see.'

And that set them all to reminiscing then about how, through many years of marriage, the constantly cuckolded Cowboy could always turn the other cheek.

Cindy-Charlene shrugged and said, 'I'll never understand it. Not till the day I die, I'll never understand it. But the sad fact is that, slut that she was, he still loved her.'

Deak and Slim both nodded and added their own solemn testimony to the deep depth of hopeless love that the Cowboy harboured for the undeserving Silkstone Slut.

'He put up with it all, y' see,' Sowerby Slim explained. 'The Cowboy's heart was a heart that was bigger than the heart of a humpety-backed whale. And he bore the burden of all that indignity and held all the humiliation there in his big big heart. He loved her! And to the Cowboy that was all that mattered. It's like he was with that guitar of his. It didn't matter that he couldn't play it, couldn't plug it in. As long as he could just have it there with him, that's all that mattered. And it was the same with *her*; as long as she remained his, that was all he asked.'

Cindy-Charlene shook her head in palpable disgust and said, 'He turned a blind eye and a deaf ear to all her goings-on. He gave her enough leash to twirl two times around the world but still it wasn't enough for her! What did she do in the end?'

And apparently what she did do, the wife of the Kexborough Cowboy, was to tell him she was going to a Tupperware party in Todmorden. When she returned home three days later wearing a kiss-me-quick hat from Blackpool and a satiated smirk on her lips the Cowboy just smiled at her fondly and said, 'Well, Patsy, did you get lots of nice new Tupperware then?'

And Patsy told him then, told the Cowboy that she hadn't been in Todmorden at all and that there'd never been no Tupperware party. The tungsten-hearted temptress recounted in delighted detail how she'd been in Blackpool for three days with the ponytailed pedal-steel guitarist from the Hebden Bridge Hoboes. And pausing only long enough to tell the Cowboy that if it hadn't been for their dog she would have left him years ago, Patsy packed her case, put her arms around Duke, the mongrel, kissed it and was gone.

In his hour of need, the Country music fraternity rallied round the forsaken Cowboy and bitter as the deed that had been done to him, everybody sought to reassure the singer, telling him as how his pretty Patsy had always been a voraciously insatiable slut and that therefore he should look on the bright side and see her departure as the blessing it truly was. And in response to such expressions of comfort and concern the Cowboy always nodded and smiled and murmured his thanks for such sympathies.

'And we all thought he was getting over it, you see,' Cindy-Charlene explained. 'As the weeks turned into months the Cowboy gradually talked less and less about her.'

'It was like he just accepted it in the end, wasn't it?' Sowerby Slim said. 'He never talked about her no more and we all thought he'd come to terms with it. We never would have accepted that booking at the Allied Butchers' and Architects' if we'd known that beneath his stoic demeanour his heart was still rent asunder.'

'We never should have accepted it anyway!' Deak exclaimed. 'We should have cancelled it the second we found out who we were sharing the bill with. If we'd done that then the Cowboy would still be with us today.'

'Deak,' Cindy-Charlene said, 'he wanted to do it! The Cowboy said he could handle it. Time and time again he said it didn't matter that we were sharing the bill with the Hebden Bridge Hoboes, he said he had no grudge against them, not even their pedal man. He said he could handle it. We had no alternative, we had to play that gig!'

And the Dewsbury Desperadoes did play that gig. And, apparently, everybody agreed that that night the Kexborough Cowboy sang with such matchless and tender beauty that it was almost as if he was harbouring a premonition that the Plinxton Allied Butchers' and Architects' gig was to be his swansong.

'It would have broke your heart to hear him that night,' Cindy-Charlene recounted, her eyes all glistening as she recalled that particularly poignant performance. 'By the time we were going on for our opening spot, the Hoboes hadn't arrived and I was beginning to think that with a bit of luck and with them only doing the one spot after us we might avoid coming face to face with them.'

Cindy-Charlene stared out the window for a moment. And then added, 'But some things are just not meant to be. We were halfway through our set, the Cowboy had just gone into the first chorus of "Silver Dagger" when I looked down into the audience, and there at the back, just coming through the function-room doors and making their way along to the bar at the back of the hall was him, the ponytailed Pedal Man, and her, the Teflon-hearted trollop, with a skirt slit right up the side, displaying a flash of flesh and a dark blue suspender belt, testifying as ever to her disregard of decency; not to mention the risk of cystitis!

We all looked at each other on stage, wondering if he'd seen them, the Cowboy. And in actuality there was no way he could have avoided seeing them; they were stood there propping up the bar, the pair of them laughing and indulging in all sorts of lascivious banter. But the Kexborough Cowboy, true professional that he'd become, he stood there on that stage in the Allied Butchers' and Architects' and he sang more beautiful that night than he'd ever sang before. He mesmerised that audience, the Cowboy, mesmerised them all. Apart from her, that slingbacked hoor, and him, that pedal player, behaving for all the world as if they were out to taunt and torment that Cowboy; the pair of them up against the bar, in public, their hands full of each other's flesh, chewing the mouths off each other, swapping tongues and saliva and bits of honey-roasted peanut.'

Cindy-Charlene shuddered at her own flesh-creeping recollections and Sowerby Slim picked up the narrative then, telling me, 'And even though we knew him to be as mild-mannered a man as Jesus of Nazareth, the public provocation as he had suffered was such that we considered it discretionary if a proper distance was maintained between ourselves and the Hebden Bridge Hoboes. When we came off stage after that first set we thought the wisest course of action was to keep the Cowboy away from the dressing-room area where the Hoboes and their pedal player would shortly be arriving to prepare for their own performance. So in an effort to distract him I said, "Come on, Cowboy, why don't me an' you go and admire the exhibits in the Trophy Room." '

And the Kexborough Cowboy, who was apparently in something of a trance-like and pliable state, allowed himself to be meekly led away from the dressing-room area and into the quiet harbour of the Trophy Room where his loyal bass guitarist kept him distracted by pointing out various artifacts and trophies and memorabilia which sat there a-glistening and a-gleaming in their display cases. Keeping half an ear cocked for the opening bars which would testify that the Hoboes and their pedal man were safely on the stage, Sowerby Slim promenaded the Cowboy from one display case to another, all the while providing what pertinent comment he could muster on the quills of architects whose artistic endeavours still stood proudly in Plinxton and thereabouts, long after their begetters had gone; and the gleaming cleavers and keen-edged chop knives which in the nimble fingers of bull-necked butchers had carved and cut out countless hearts, slicing flesh from bone with the kind of flourish and finesse that is so often found wanting in what passes for butchery these days. And just as Slim was running out of things to say about the Great Gold Fillet Knife which the butchers of Plinxton had won from the butchers of Burnley for the third and final time in the bitterly fought pork-filleting competition of 1963, Sowerby Slim heard the opening bars of 'Orange Blossom Special' and knew then that the Hebden Bridge Hoboes were safely on the stage. Leading the way to the big oak doors of the Trophy Room, Sowerby Slim told the Cowboy, 'We can go back to the dressing room now, Cowboy.'

But when he got to the doors of the Trophy Room, the Kexborough Cowboy said, 'I don't want to go to the dressing room thank you very much, Slim. I've the intention of going out front to the bar and having myself a pot of beer.'

And that's when Sowerby Slim stood in front of the Cowboy, frowned and cocked his head and said, 'Come on, Cowboy; you know who's out there. Come on, don't cause yourself no more pain than is necessary.'

But with his customary good grace the Cowboy just thanked the big bass player for his concern and told him, 'Slim, you can't break a heart that's already in pieces.'

And pondering both the wisdom of this and the possibility that it could be quite a good title for a new

Country song, Sowerby Slim just stepped aside and the Kexborough Cowboy headed out to the bar and asked for a pint of ale. And while it was being pulled he turned and looked along the bar and saw his own wife leaning there, her back against the bar rail, a stilettoed foot tapping out time and her nail-varnished fingers wrapped around a long thin glass containing a cocktail called Do-It-Till-Dawn.

Taking a sip of his beer, the Cowboy dallied with his pint for a moment, and eyes fixed on the creamy whirl of froth he said, 'I miss you, Patsy. Me and the dog, we both miss you.'

And that's when the leg-spreading lady turned her head for a moment and just looked at him as she chewed on her chewy. And when the Cowboy raised his eyes from his pint pot and looked at her, the tungsten-hearted tart just opened up her mouth and laughed and laughed before turning her attentions back towards the stage where her new and thrilling lover, who sported the proudest ponytail in the whole of the British Country circuit, was playing the opening bars to 'One More Tequila Sheila And We'll Make The Border Tonight'.

The Cowboy edged along the bar a bit towards his wife and told her, 'My heart's in two pieces, Patsy. And there's not a glue on this earth that could bind it back together. My heart's in lumps, Patsy. But so is the dog's. Me and Duke, we're both broken-hearted without you, Patsy.'

But the pitiless Patsy ignored his words and kept her lustful gaze on the stage and the pedal-guitar player who was pedalling and playing and starting to stare back at the goings-on at the bar.

'I know that you'd never come back for me,' the Cowboy insisted to his wanton wife. 'But, Patsy, what about the dog? The dog never done you no harm, Patsy. Wouldn't you come back for the sake of the dog?'

On stage the pedal player glared and stared. And

fluffed the opening notes to his instrumental break.

'Not for me, Patsy,' the Cowboy was telling his wife, 'just for the dog. Y' see, the dog won't eat a thing since you've been gone and it's all I can do to look at him these days. And if you don't come back, Patsy, I'm going to have to take our Duke to a veterinary surgeon and have him put down in a humane manner.'

And that's when Patsy turned her head slowly, her nostrils beginning to flare and her gaudy red lips pressed tight together in disgust as she slammed down her neo-exotic cocktail on the bar and declared, 'You heartless bastard!'

And that's when the pedal player put down his plectrum and stood up, leaving all the other Hoboes grinding to a clumsy shuddering halt in the middle of 'One More Tequila Sheila And We'll Make The Border Tonight'.

A sudden and eerie silence descended upon the Allied Butchers' and Architects' Club, a silence observed by everyone in that hall, apart from the Cowboy, whose pleading words to his wife echoed all through the function room as he told her, 'Patsy, the fate of our Duke is in your hands.'

But the Cowboy's appeal for such canine consideration only served to harden the pitiless Patsy's tungsten heart. Reaching for her drink, she told him, 'Fuck it then! Have the dog put down if y' like. What do I need with a dog these days? I don't need a dog to stroke no more.' And inclining her head to the stage and to the ponytailed Pedal Man who was stood there staring and glaring she said, 'Look, just look at the ponytail on that!' And turning back to the Cowboy, triumph on her lips and insolence in her eyes, she told him, 'Up there's a head of hair that gives me all the stroking I'll ever need.'

'Please,' the Cowboy said then, 'please, Patsy, please,' as he reached out his hand to touch her arm.

And that's when a deep growling voice from the stage said, 'Hey! Cowboy!'

And the Cowboy turned and saw, on the stage, the pedal-steel guitar player pointing at him.

'What d' y' think you're up to?' the pedal player demanded.

The Cowboy looked up at the stage and said, 'I'm not up to nowt that need concern you, Pedal Man.'

The Pedal Man stared and narrowed his eyes then and said, 'But, Cowboy, it does concern me.'

'Well, it needn't do,' the Cowboy said. 'If a chap wants to have a word with his wife about their dog then I think he's got the right to.'

Everybody turned and looked at the Pedal Man then. And the Hoboes' bass player shrugged and said well that was reasonable enough, wasn't it, a feller talking to his wife about their dog? And assuming the matter to have been settled, he counted in four bars and tried to lead the other Hoboes back into 'One More Tequila Sheila'. But the Pedal Man just kept standing and 'One More Tequila Sheila' bit the dust again.

The Pedal Man pointed his finger then. 'Cowboy!' he said. 'You listen to me; Patsy's not your woman no more. Pretty Patsy's my woman now!'

And the Pedal Man glanced at Pretty Patsy, the leg-spreading slut who was loving every minute of it and whose cleavage was heaving with pride for the pugnacious Pedal Man.

'And I don't want you talking to her,' the Pedal Man told the Cowboy. 'I don't want you talking to her about nothing, not dogs, not nowt, understand?'

All eyes were on the Cowboy again then, waiting to see what the Cowboy would do. But the Cowboy did nowt except look. And the Pedal Man pointed his finger and said, 'Now you move away from Pretty Patsy, go on, move.'

There were some in the crowd as shouted out then and told the Cowboy that he should stand his ground and others who said as how he should take that pedal-steel guitarist outside and give him a good thrashing. There were even some as shouted and said he was a shitawful pedal-steel player anyway and the only reason he was in the band was on account of his ponytail. And everyone agreed that he was right out of order and therefore deserved a thrashing from the Cowboy.

But those who offered such advice were unaware of the mildness of the Cowboy's manners and the Gandhian goodness of his heart. And instead of taking such advice the Cowboy merely nodded at the Pedal Man and said, 'Yes, I do understand. Patsy's your woman now.'

There were those in the crowd then who started yelling at the Cowboy, telling him he couldn't just ignore it and shrieking, 'Don't be a bollocks, get up there, Cowboy, and give that ponytailed prat what he deserves.'

But disregarding the vehemence and passion of such exhortations, the Kexborough Cowboy just put his pint pot down on the bar, turned and walked slowly out of the hall and the frustrated and disgruntled cries of the audience were drowned out as the Hebden Bridge Hoboes went back to telling Sheila that after one more tequila they'd all make the border tonight. And Pretty Patsy, almost limp with lust, ran her tongue in a slow circular motion over her bottom lip as she stared at the stage and wantonly contemplated her ponytailed hero.

The Cowboy just walked. He didn't know where he was going and he didn't care. He just walked and walked until eventually he came to a church. And though not a man of any particularly devout religiosity, the Kexborough Cowboy, in need of solace, found himself pulling back the latch on the churchyard gate and sitting himself down to rest on a bench beneath a gnarled and twisted yew tree of some considerable antiquity. And it happened that the Cowboy's eyes were drawn to a floodlit display board that had been erected in that churchyard and on whose bright yellow hardboard surface, in dark red lettering, were written the words, *The meek shall inherit the earth*. And intended though it was to bring comfort to those who would never have nowt and to bolster and make bearable the grief of the perpetually put down and trampled upon, this bald beatitude had exactly the opposite effect upon the Cowboy, who reflected upon the meekness and mildness of his own demeanour and concluded that far from gaining him the earth, such consistent gentility had gained him nowt but a cold lonely house in Kexborough, a fretting dog and a broken heart. And rising from that bench, the Cowboy's formerly gentle hands seized the stanchion that held aloft the hardboard lie and in an anger born of years of restraint and humiliation he ripped that post clean out of the hard earth and battered and buckled the hardboard beatitude until its words could be read no more. And knowing now, knowing in his pounding and excited heart that it was not the meek who inherited nowt, that it was all the bad bastards who inherited the earth and who always would, the bad bastards, the dubious, the barbarous, the brutish and the biggest, the hardest and the toughest and the determinedly unscrupulous, they were the ones who inherited everything. And walking once more, only this time striding purposefully back towards the Allied Butchers' and Architects', the Cowboy laughed out loud, laughed and laughed at his own craziness, at how he'd been such a dove for his Patsy, such a meek and mild-mannered man, believing that such consistent consideration and gentility would be rewarded with her love. All along he'd been a dove and she'd upped and left him for a prick of a ponytailed Pedal Man with dubious left-hand technique. And the Kexborough Cowboy, laughing hysterically as he marched past the houses and cottages, had already concluded that to win back the heart of the woman he loved, the dove must fly and the brute must out!

'We were out looking for him,' Cindy-Charlene explained. 'The Hoboes only had another few numbers and then it was our second spot. We were up and down

Plinxton in the van looking everywhere for the Cowboy but he was nowhere to be found. We just had to go back to the club, find the Concert Secretary and tell him we wouldn't be able to go on for our second spot. But by the time we got back, the Concert Secretary had other things on his mind because the Concert Secretary and such other committee members as were in attendance that night were all running round the foyer like blue-arsed flies, some of them almost weeping, others running and looking out the doors and saying weren't the police here yet, and others huffing and a-puffing and declaring to whoever would listen that this was what you had to expect when two-thirds of the youth of Plinxton regularly smoked ecstasy, LSD and crack cocaine. And the cause of such consternation to the committee members was there, in the Trophy Room, where a glass display case had been shattered asunder; and from which had been stolen the Great Gold Fillet Knife.'

'And my blood ran cold,' Sowerby Slim declared. 'As I stared down at that shattered display case I suddenly knew, knew why we hadn't been able to find the Cowboy in the streets of Plinxton.'

Sowerby Slim paused then, his eyes wide as if seeing it all again before him, 'Because when we'd been looking for him, the Kexborough Cowboy was already back in the club, was already plunging his fist through that glass display case and seizing hold of the Great Gold Fillet Knife, a blade with as keen an edge as ever came out of the great steel mills of Sheffield.'

'I saw the blood draining out of your face, I did,' Cindy-Charlene recalled. 'It put the fear into me, seeing you like that. And when you didn't answer me when I asked you what was wrong, when you suddenly started running towards the function-room doors, I just knew then, I knew it was something grave and awful as was about to happen.'

'I knew he'd snapped, y' see,' Sowerby Slim explained. 'Because for all the mildness of his manners and the goodness in his heart, a man is just like a guitar string. It can be the finest string ever wound; but stretch it too far, and it snaps! And that's why I went rushing into that function room.'

'But we thought it was her, didn't we?' Deak said. 'We thought it was *her* that he'd go for. That's why we all rushed out to the bar.'

'I didn't rush!' Cindy-Charlene declared. 'She'd brought it on herself, leg-spreading slut that she was. And if she could taunt like she taunted the Cowboy, pushing him beyond breaking point, then she had no-one to blame but herself.'

'But it wasn't her I was worried about,' Slim said, 'it was the Cowboy. Because I knew that if he did anything to her in a moment of madness, he'd regret it for the rest of his life. That's why I rushed out there. Because that's where I expected him to appear.'

'But when we got to the bar,' Deak said, 'there was no sight of the Cowboy anywhere. *She* was still stood there, eyes glued on the stage and that Pedal Man of hers who was in the middle of a solo, whipping up the crowd, the way he did by twirling his head and sending that bloody ponytail spinning as he picked out all them flashy slides on the steel guitar.'

'And she's stood there,' Cindy-Charlene said, 'cleavage still heaving, lips wet, groin slowly grinding in time to the music. And not the faintest idea that she'd caused a mild-mannered man to lose his mind; caused him to shatter glass and seize hold of a lethal Fillet Knife.'

'She saw me watching her,' Slim said. 'She even asked me what I was gawping at. Then she just curled her lip and sneered at me, before turning her eyes back to the stage again. But little did the brazen hussy know that shortly she might have cause to be thanking me, when the Cowboy appeared. Because I knew, I knew if I could get to him before he got to her, I could talk to him. I could talk to the Cowboy and make him see sense. I knew he wouldn't hurt me. An' if I could persuade him to hand over that Great Gold Fillet Knife before the bobbies turned up, then there wouldn't be much harm done that couldn't be mended.'

Deak shook his head and sighed and said, 'But we got it wrong, didn't we? We were in the wrong spot. Backstage, that's where we should have been.'

Slim nodded and said, 'I knew. I was stood there, my back to the stage, watching *her*, watching her face. And when I saw her eyes suddenly open up like saucers, when I saw her mouth gaping open as she stopped chewing, I knew then. I turned and followed her gaze. And there, on the stage, coming through the backcloth, behind the unsuspecting Hebden Bridge Hoboes, was the sight that I dreaded; the sight of the Cowboy, a murderous madness in his eyes and the Great Gold Fillet Knife in his hand. Some of the crowd, they started cheering, thinking it was part of the Hoboes' act. And that Pedal Man, when he heard those cheers he thought they were for him and inspired to even flashier flourishes on his slide guitar, he played up to the crowd, smirking at his own supposed brilliance and circling his head faster and faster till his ponytail was almost a blur, rotating round his head like a propeller.'

'And most of that crowd,' Deak said, 'they just sat there cheering.'

'They didn't know,' Slim declared. 'They didn't know. But we knew. And *she* knew.'

'She started to scream,' Cindy-Charlene explained. 'As the Cowboy made his move, the slut began to scream.'

'But it was too late,' Slim said, 'it was too late for all of us. I was running, pushing my way through and trying to get to the stage. But then I heard the yell! A yell like I've never heard before and never want to hear again. The Hoboes stopped playing, all of them turned around and to a man they just froze, rigid, unable to do nowt but just stare, terrified, at the awful apparition of a mad-eyed cowboy stood there at the back of the stage with a razor-sharp Fillet Knife in his hand. And everybody knew then, everybody in that hall. There was nowt but silent staring people. Even the bobbies, who'd just arrived, were stood there like statues, not one of them daring to move as they peered at the stage where the Cowboy, the Hoboes and the Pedal Man were stood, transfixed, as if time itself had suddenly stopped. And then! Then the Pedal Man tried to run! But the Cowboy was too fast for him. As the Pedal Man panicked and ran for the wings, the Cowboy leaped, shot out a hand and the Pedal Man's head snapped back as he was seized by his legendary length of hair. Screaming, pleading with the Cowboy, he dropped to the floor and the Cowboy dragged him, legs kicking, into the centre of the stage. Then everywhere in that hall there was uproar, people screaming, the slut herself screaming the loudest of all, committee members yelling at one another and the bobbies rushing forward to try and get to the stage, before they were stopped in their tracks as the Cowboy lifted up the knife and silenced everybody in that hall; everybody except the terrified Pedal Man who lay on that stage, whimpering and helpless, the Cowboy's iron fist holding him fast by the hair of his head, the Fillet Knife poised and ready to plunge.

'And that's when the Cowboy looked out across the hall; looked all around, scanning the sea of faces until he saw her, his Pretty Patsy. That's when he said, "Well then, Patsy, here's a rum do!" Then, watery-eyed, wistful and choking back the tears, he said, "You never loved me, did y', Patsy. You never even loved our Duke! And that dog, that dog worshipped you; like I worshipped you. But we was wasting our time, wasn't we, Patsy. Me and Duke, we was wasting our time being good to you. Because you never ever loved anything that was good for y', Patsy. A bit of badness, that's all you ever loved, didn't y'?" He paused then, the Cowboy, paused, his gaze fixed upon the pleading eyes and the anguished face of his trembling wife. "Well, I can give you badness!" he said as he slowly raised the Fillet Knife. "I can give y' all the badness you need, Patsy! It's easy," he said as every eye in the room followed the glinting gold of the knife as it rose in his hand like a guillotine being slowly hoisted, as it stopped and hung there suspended above the neck of the Pedal Man.

' "You want badness?" the Cowboy said. "Well, all right, Patsy, I'll give you badness. How's this for badness?"

'And then, the Great Gold Fillet Knife flashed as it plunged down towards the neck of its prey. And with one razor-sharp slice, the Pedal Man's ponytail was scalped from the Pedal Man's head!

'For one second, just for a beat, it was like people couldn't quite take in what had happened. Then from somewhere in the crowd a voice was heard to say, "Fuckin' hell! He'll not be known as the Cowboy after this. He'll be the fuckin' Apache now!"

'And that was the cue for a sort of pandemonium. The Cowboy was waving the length of the severed ponytail above his head with a sense of wild triumph as he screamed down at Patsy, demanding to know if she loved him now, now that she'd seen the badness he was capable of. But the Cowboy never got an answer because the rest of the Hebden Bridge Hoboes piled on top of him then and brought him down and that pedal-steel player started kicking lumps out of him, all the while fingering the stump of a tuft at the back of his head and screaming at the Cowboy, telling him he'd fucking kill him for the maiming of his follicles. The bobbies were doing their best to get through to the stage but were constantly being sidetracked by the various disputes, fracas and fisticuffs that had broken out amongst the crowd. The Concert Secretary and committee members who were in attendance were running round the hall appealing for calm. And in the middle of all this me and Deak managed to get up onto the stage and start dragging some of them Hoboes off the Cowboy who, despite his former mildness of manner and dove-like demeanour was managing to give a reasonably good account of himself. And with me and Deak weighing in on the Cowboy's behalf it soon became something of a stalemate, with us and the Hebden Bridge Hoboes just stood on either side of the stage, facing up to each other. But that's when she appeared on the stage, the suspender-belted slut in all her cleavage-heaving glory. And the Cowboy, God love him, that tender-hearted Cowboy, thought she was coming for him, thought that he'd won her back with his badness. "Y' see, Patsy," he said, "I've got all the badness you need. And him," he said, nodding at the Pedal Man, "look at him now! Now y' can see him for what he is, Patsy; nowt but a soft little pony, who hasn't even got a tail any more." She stared at the Cowboy for a second, flicking her tongue across her cherry-red lips. The Pedal Man called out to her from the other side of the stage, saying, "Patsy . . . come on, Pats . . . let's get out of here." But she ignored the Pedal Man. And eyes still fixed on the Cowboy she started stilettoing her way across the stage towards him, her hips rolling and her bosom thrust before her. She walked straight up to the Cowboy, her breasts pressed tightly up against him and her head thrust back as she stared up into his face. And the Cowboy gazed back down at her, gazed with the joy of a man whose shattered heart was about to be put back together again. That was when he started to embrace her, as he told her, "Patsy . . . Patsy. Our Duke's tail's gonna do some wagging tonight, when he sees that you've come home."

'But that's when she slipped from his grip, her lip curled up in disgust and her eyes flashing as she told him, "You think I'd ever get back with you? Just because you've docked a bit of his hair, you think my stallion's been turned into a little pony? Well fuck you, Cowboy. Fuck you! Y' think you've claimed his tail? Well, I've got news for you! He might be a bit sheared right now. But that stallion of mine . . . he'll soon grow another tail. I'm gonna see to that. Because y' know what it is, don't y', Cowboy, y' know what it is that brings on a stallion's tail? It's the riding! The riding he gets. And oh . . . am I gonna ride that stallion of mine; and in no time at all, he'll be sporting a length of tail with a thickness and a fullness that the likes of you couldn't even begin to dream of.''

'She turned away then, strode back across the stage. And that's when I looked at the Cowboy and saw the light fading from his eyes. I knew then he was a broken man.

'A couple of young bobbies were up on the stage, approaching with some degree of caution, for the Cowboy still had the Fillet Knife in his hand. But they had nowt to be afeared of from the Cowboy. Such fight as had been in him had gone for ever now. I just took hold of the Great Gold Fillet Knife, gently slipped it from his limp fingers and handed it to the bobbies as they took the Cowboy by his arms and started leading him away and out through the function-room doors of the Allied Butchers' and Architects'.'

Sowerby Slim, Cindy-Charlene and Deak the drummer all fell silent then, each of them lost in their own thoughts. And maybe they were too tired out with the telling, to tell the rest of their tale. Or maybe they were just reluctant and didn't want to bring back the memory of what had happened to the Cowboy after that. So I helped them out. I said to the Desperadoes, 'He lost his voice after that, didn't he?'

They looked at me with puzzled faces, all of them staring at me like they'd forgotten I was there. Until Cindy-Charlene, frowning, said, 'How do you know? How do you know that?'

I shrugged. 'I don't know,' I told her. 'I just guessed.'

Cindy-Charlene began to nod. And that's when I knew, Morrissey, knew beyond all doubt.

'How?' I asked. 'How did he come to lose his voice?'

The Dewsbury Desperadoes looked at each other.

And then they started to tell me what happened that night, after the Cowboy had been arrested; and how, before they drove him off to the police station, one of the policemen came back into the club, saying that the Cowboy was asking for his guitar.

'And we never thought,' Cindy-Charlene said. 'We were only too glad that the bobbies were letting him take it. Because we knew it might provide some small comfort, having his beloved guitar with him.'

'We didn't realise,' Slim said. 'Even though I'd seen him broken that night, I never knew just how deeply mortal were the wounds that had been inflicted upon his heart. We just handed over his guitar and the bobbies took him off.'

'By rights,' Cindy-Charlene said, 'they never should have let him have the guitar in the cell with him. But with the Cowboy back to his usual placid and mild-mannered demeanour and with the desk sergeant who booked him in being a bit partial to the occasional Country song, it was decided it wouldn't do no harm and might even help the passing of the night's long hours, if the Cowboy was allowed to croon a tune or two. So they let him have his guitar in the cell with him.'

'He didn't try and play it though,' said Slim. 'Apparently the Cowboy just sat there, huddled in the corner of his cell, arms wrapped around the instrument as if that guitar was his Pretty Patsy and him cradling her in his loving arms and crooning softly through the lonely hours, every sad song he knew.

'The desk sergeant said it was the quietest Saturday night in the cells that he'd ever known. He said the Cowboy's melancholic crooning seemed to be a balm for the soul of every other inmate that night; the drunks, ruffians, roustabouts and Saturday-night fighters in all the other cells causing none of their usual disturbance, each and every one soothed in their breasts and made meek like lambs by the sorrowful lyrics and tearful melodies floating into the air and out through the bars of cell number twenty-nine.'

'And nobody checked on him, did they?' Cindy-Charlene said. 'As long as they could hear him singing and crooning, they reckoned he must be all right. But what they didn't know was that after an hour or two, instead of the Cowboy just sitting there crooning as he cradled his guitar, the Cowboy was slowly unwinding the strings; all the while still singing, still letting everybody believe that he was doing nowt but crooning away the night.'

'Only he was making his preparations,' Deak said. 'All the while, he was preparing; removing the E string and the A string and the D string. And looping them together.'

'But he never stopped singing,' Slim said. 'Never once stopped singing as he twined those silver-plated strings together, as he made a loop at one end.'

'And attached the other end . . .' Deak said. 'All the while, still softly crooning . . . as he attached the other end to the light fitting . . . as he reached for the chair and placed it carefully below the light . . . as he climbed up onto that chair . . . slipped that noose around his neck, still singing . . . still singing . . . In every other cell, they could hear the Cowboy singing. Until!'

Deak shook his head, tears in his eyes, unable to go on, leaving it to Slim who said, 'The singing suddenly stopped!'

Slim frowned deeply. Cindy-Charlene was just staring down at her high-heeled boots, and Deak was starting to cry now.

'They began calling out,' Slim said, 'the other prisoners, addressing the Cowboy himself at first, calling, "Come on, mate, keep on singing, singer, don't stop now, mate." And then, when their words had no effect, they started banging on the bars of their cells, shouting to the sergeant, telling him to go and have a word with the singer and ask him to croon up his sad songs again. The sergeant told them to shut the fuck up, called them rabble and scum and not fit for this earth. But knowing how the Cowboy's sad-hearted singing had kept all the rabble quiet in their cells, the sergeant relented, said he'd go down to cell twenty-nine and try and persuade him to sing a bit more.'

'And that's how they found him,' Cindy-Charlene said. 'That desk sergeant found him hanging there by the strings of his own guitar.'

Cindy-Charlene shuddered at the memory.

'The sergeant managed to save him,' she said, 'cut him down in time.'

Sowerby Slim lowered his big bearded head and shook it sadly. 'But they couldn't save his voice. The strings had severed his vocal cords.'

Deak nodded, wiping at his tears with the back of his hand.

And I sat there, on a flight case; with my mind all confused and jumbled up, not knowing what to think or say or do. Because what can you do? What can you say or think, when you've just been told all kinds of things that you never knew; things about your own father! And not only that; because you know now that you met him! Day in and day out in Swintonfield, sat with him on summer afternoons, drinking sugary tea with not much milk, listening to the wind in the branches of the big chestnut tree. And never ever, not once did you even begin to guess that that same gardener man, the one who had lost his voice, the man who'd made you a present of his guitar, was the man who was your father.

That's what I was thinking about, Morrissey, when I heard Deak saying, 'Here we are then.' I looked up and saw we were passing the sign that said we were coming into Plinxton.

'Where did you say you were headed?' Slim asked me. When I said, 'Grimsby,' they all looked surprised.

Deak said, 'Fuckin' hell, you should have got out miles back at the M180.'

I just shrugged. 'It doesn't matter,' I said.

Deak stared at me like I was a bit soft.

We were pulling into a car park. And when we all got out, I found myself staring at it, the Allied Butchers' and Architects' Club. All sorts of people with stetson hats and beer bellies were queuing up to get in. Some of them even wore spurs and lurid tee shirts saying things like *I'm doing fine. I'm walking the line: now that I'm into Country.*

'Are y' comin' in with us?' Cindy-Charlene asked. 'Y' could catch our gig if you like.'

But before I could even shake my head, Deak said, 'For God's sake, Charlene! Come on!'

'What?' she asked.

But Deak turned to me and he said, 'Look, no offence, son, but dressed like that, at a place like this, well, it's not really on, lad.'

Cindy-Charlene started to argue with him but I just nodded and said, 'It's all right. I've got to get off now anyway.'

I didn't have the heart to tell Deak he needn't worry and that I'd rather catch dysentery than catch their gig. So I just thanked Cindy-Charlene and said I had to be on my way. I could tell Deak was relieved. Slim shook me by the hand and wished me all the best for getting to Grimsby. Then he told Deak they'd better start getting the gear unloaded. And in their own way, they'd been really nice to me, the Desperadoes. That's why I knew that I couldn't just go off without telling them. We were stood around the back of the van. Deak and Slim were getting busy sliding out the amps and the flight cases. And I said, 'Before I get off, I just want you all to know something.'

'Yeah, what's that then?' Deak said in an un-interested fashion as he picked up one end of a flight case and Slim grabbed the other.

'Well, I just wanted to tell y',' I said, 'the reason I

knew that the Kexborough Cowboy had lost his voice was because he was my Dad. He was my father.'

They looked at me. I just nodded at them all. And they looked at one another like they were a bit embarrassed. Then Deak and Slim started off towards the doors of the club, carrying the flight case. And that's when I heard Deak laughing as he said, 'I fuckin' told y', Slim. I said we should never have picked him up in the first place. Y' could tell, from fifty yards away; a kid like that, y' could tell straight off he was Care in the Community!'

They both disappeared inside the club then. I just nodded at Cindy-Charlene who was staring at me with a concerned expression on her face. But I just smiled and told her tarar and started walking away across the car park. I'd almost got to the gates when I heard her running up behind me. And when I turned around she was looking even more worried and concerned. And she said, 'Now look! Are you sure you'll be all right? It'll be getting dark soon, y' know.'

I shrugged. 'I'll be fine,' I said.

But she wasn't convinced. She frowned and she said, 'Are y' sure you know where you're going?'

'Yeah,' I said, 'Grimsby!'

'Well, how will you get there?' she said. 'Have y' got any money?'

'It's all right!' I said. 'I don't need any money. I'll be fine.'

'Here,' she said, and she was opening up her handbag and taking some money out.

'Look,' I said, 'you don't need to do that, I've . . .'

But she wouldn't listen and she said, 'Come on, here, take this.'

'It's all right,' I told her, 'I'm not really feeble-minded, y' know. Y' don't have to worry.'

But I could see that she was worried; worried about someone who was soft in the head and leaving him in a place he'd never been before. I just took the money and thanked her. Then I told her, 'It is true, y' know. He *was* my Dad.'

But she just nodded and winked as she said, 'Yeah. Sure . . . sure.'

But it was just like people used to say that sort of thing when I was in Swintonfield; so I knew she didn't believe me.

'You just make sure you look after yourself now, won't y'?'

I nodded and she started making her way back towards the club. And that's when I realised, when I remembered what I was carrying. And I called out to her then, 'Charlene . . . Cindy-Charlene, wait.'

As I began walking over to her I started opening the zipper on my guitar bag. 'Look,' I said.

Cindy-Charlene frowned. 'What?' she asked.

I pulled back the cover on the bag revealing the neck of the guitar and the head with the missing ivory tuning peg. Cindy-Charlene stared, her eyes widening as an involuntary hand was lifted to her mouth and in barely a whisper she said, 'Oh my God.' She looked up at me then. 'Oh my God!' she said again. And I saw that her eyes had filled up with tears. And then, her voice beginning to choke, she said, 'I loved him!'

I nodded.

'I know!' I said, 'I know that. And I just wish that he'd loved you instead of . . . y' know.'

Cindy-Charlene's face creased up with the tears. But then she pulled herself back together as she said, 'Come on! Come back with me, into the club. Show them, Deak and Slim, show them the guit—'

But I shook my head and zipped up the guitar case. 'No. It's all right,' I said. 'I just wanted you to know. But I've got to be going now.'

She grabbed me by the arm. 'Where is he?' she said. 'What's he up to? What's he doing these days, is he all right?'

I just shrugged. I said, 'I don't really know.' I said, 'It's years since I last saw him. And then, when I did, I didn't even know he was my Dad.'

Cindy-Charlene frowned.

And I shrugged and said, 'But he wasn't the Kexborough Cowboy any more.'

Cindy-Charlene was crying. Then, behind her, Deak started calling from the stage door, telling her it was time for her to do her soundcheck. Cindy-Charlene nodded. Then she stepped towards me and hugged me to her. As she stood back, she took my head in her hands and stared at me. 'He was a star,' she said, 'your dad. He was a real star.'

She stood there blinking back the tears, until Deak called out again and told her to get a move on. And Cindy-Charlene, who'd loved my father, turned and went high-heeling it back to the stage door of the Allied Butchers' and Architects' Club. The last I ever saw of her, she was stood silhouetted in the light that spilled out from the stage door, her hand raised as she blew me a kiss.

And on behalf of my Dad, I blew one back for Cindy-Charlene.

Yours sincerely,
Raymond Marks

The Big Bite Services,
A1(M),
Nr Doncaster

Dear Morrissey,

It's nice sitting here, overlooking the motorway; looking out and seeing nothing but the headlights and the tail lights coming and going in the dark. It's really quiet in here. I suppose that's because it's so late. And all those people down there in their cars or their lorries, I suppose they're all wanting to get home.

It's all right in here though. The lights are all dimmed and it's quiet; like being in a hospital at night, where the only sounds you can hear are far-off sounds and you can't quite make out what they are.

I got a taxi. With the money Cindy-Charlene gave me I got a taxi back to the motorway. And I know I should have just started hitch-hiking again. I came in here though, for something to eat.

And I'm sorry, Morrissey; I really am sorry. But suddenly it didn't seem to matter that much. If there'd been something decently vegetarian on the menu then I would have had it. But when I came in here I just felt a bit low, I suppose; like I wanted something to warm me up and fill me up, so I wouldn't feel so empty.

I am sorry, Morrissey. I know I could just keep quiet about it and then you wouldn't even know. But I couldn't do that. I just couldn't write to you, Morrissey, if I was holding anything back and not telling you the whole of the truth.

And the truth is that I did it!

I ordered chicken casserole. And I ate it!

I'm not trying to make excuses, Morrissey, but I did check with the lady on the counter and she said that they only ever used free-range chickens that had been fed properly on corn and stuff. So at least, Morrissey, at least the chicken in the casserole was a chicken that had had a relatively reasonable lifestyle and most likely lived quite a happy life.

I know you're probably deeply offended and appalled, Morrissey. Normally I would have been appalled myself, at the thought that I could so easily break my vegetarian vows. But after what had happened, after finding out about my Dad, it somehow seemed all a bit pointless really, worrying about what I ate.

I never knew, Morrissey, that my Dad had tried to kill himself.

That's what they said *I*'d been doing, the night they pulled me out from beneath the ice. The night they put me into Swintonfield.

They said I'd become a danger to myself. They said I needed protecting from myself. That's why my Mam signed the consent forms. But what else was she supposed to do? My Mam thought she was helping and protecting me. And that's why I don't blame my Mam; I don't blame her at all because everybody told her that Swintonfield was the best place for me.

And nowadays my Mam says me being ill had nothing to do with my Dad. She says that if I *was* mad, back then, it was only because I got driven mad by everything that happened. And my Mam says that if she blames anyone, she blames herself. But I don't blame her. Paulette Patterson's dad, my Uncle

Bastard Jason and Wilson the Lert, that's who I blame.

The night they took me there, the night I'd got trapped under the ice, they said the unit in Swintonfield was the safest place for me. I couldn't stop the jabbering; jabbering, stop jabbering, couldn't stop jabbering at all, jabbering jabbering.

Even when I was pulled out from under the ice, concussed and half unconscious, that's what it was like, Morrissey. I kept saying things over and over again.

And Wilson told my Mam that this latest attempt on my own life was something he'd been expecting for some time. He said he'd seen all the signs. And afterwards, he said my Mam shouldn't even hesitate to sign the consent papers because that was the only way I could truly be protected from myself.

Everybody said he was a hero, Mr Wilson; breaking through the ice, risking his own life to rescue me from the frozen water. My Mam knew she had very great cause to be grateful to Mr Wilson. Everybody said he was a hero. And nobody ever said *anything* about what a stupid bastard he was; and if he hadn't just leaped out of bleeding nowhere and startled the shit out of me then I never would have needed rescuing in the first place. Nobody said nothing about that. They just said he was a hero.

And Corkerdale, the consultant, said Mr Wilson had shown remarkable foresight in knowing exactly where I'd be that night. Mr Wilson was very modest about that though; he explained to the consultant that for a man who'd been able to observe my behaviour over quite a period of time, for a man who'd made himself familiar with my unfortunate history, it hadn't taken much to work out where I might end up that night. And Mr Wilson just thanked the lord he'd been able to get there in the nick of time. But the consultant insisted and said that as well as thanking the lord, there was a great debt of thanks owing to Mr Wilson himself.

They got on very well, Mr Wilson and the

consultant. Dr Corkerdale said it was always a great help in cases such as this, having the benefit of an understanding and articulate third party, one who could provide vital insights and information regarding the patient. And Mr Wilson said perhaps the doctor would like to see the file that he'd kept as part of his Open University studies; not that he wanted to step on the toes of the professionals, as it were.

But the doctor said on the contrary, and how sometimes it's the informed layperson who can provide the sort of clues and insights that can elude even the best professional. They got on very well together, Wilson and Corkerdale. They both agreed that my Mam was doing the best thing, in signing the consent forms.

The male nurse said I'd been as quiet as a mouse for the last couple of days. He said I'd quietened down considerably now they were trying me on this new medication. All the jabbering, jibbering jabbering, running off at the mouth, it had all stopped, he said.

And that's why he thought it would probably be all right now, me seeing the visitor. Brendan said he thought it might even be nice for me, to see my rescuer, that brave man who'd put his own life at risk in order to save mine.

'Raymond,' I heard Nurse Brendan's voice, somewhere far off in the distance, 'Raymond, come on, look. You've a visitor. Come on now.'

I didn't want to be bothered though. I just wanted to lie there with my eyes shut, with everything far off in the distance.

But Brendan was gently shaking me by the shoulder, saying, 'Come on, Raymond. Look. Look who's here.'

And I thought he might leave me alone, if I just opened my eyes and took a quick look at whoever it was. So I concentrated, concentrated really hard so that I could drag open my eyes and look. And that's when I saw *him* stood there at the foot of the bed.

That's when I started screaming and shouting and Nurse Brendan started trying to calm me down, saying it must be the concussion. But it wasn't the concussion and I couldn't calm down because there was a Lert at the foot of my bed, a Lert who'd come to get me and I told the nurse, told the nurse, get him out, get him out get him out. I was struggling in the bed, trying to get away, trying to move, trying to escape, to escape. But Nurse Brendan wouldn't let me and had hold of me, holding me down on the bed and shouting for someone to come and help. And I was screaming, screaming and crying about how the Lert had kidnapped my Mam and how the Lert had made me fall, made me go crashing through the ice. And how the Lerts were taking over the world! Taking over my world. I was screaming and thrashing about on the bed, with Brendan still trying to hold me down. And then suddenly there was blood everywhere and Brendan was cupping his nose with his hand and all this blood seeping through his fingers as other nurses appeared and more hands grabbed hold of me and pinned me down on the bed as I screamed and screamed and told them, told them, kept telling them and telling them it was the Lert, it was the Lert; the Lert who'd made me get trapped beneath the ice, the Lert who'd kidnapped my Mam; and now there he was, at the foot of the bed, come to kidnap me.

I tried to tell them. I tried. But they didn't listen. And the more I shouted, the more I screamed, the more they pinned me down. Then somebody was telling somebody to stand back. And somebody was saying, give me his arm, give me his arm. Then somebody was sticking a needle in. I was still shouting, still screaming, at first. But then everything started to feel far off in the distance again.

And it was nice like that, with everything far off in the distance and my eyes just starting to close. It was nice. And he wasn't there any more, the Lert at the foot of the bed.

And for ages after that, I hardly ever knew if I was awake or dreaming. Sometimes it seemed like there were other people at the foot of the bed, people like my Mam, looking like she was trying very hard not to cry as she explained that I'd become a danger to myself. But I didn't want to know about any of that. I just wanted to know how she'd managed to escape from the Lerts. When she came to hold my hand, when she kissed me, I asked her how she'd managed it. But she only looked at me with a puzzled look on her face. And from the far-off place inside my head, I managed to find the words and tell her, 'A1 at Lloyd's, Mam. A1 at Lloyd's now you've escaped from Lertland.'

And then she did start crying. And tried to tell me that I'd be all right and I would get better and once they'd found out the right medication and got me stabilised, I wouldn't be like this any more and I'd be able to go home.

Then she said, 'Ted says you'll be fine, once they've sorted out your medication and got you stabilised.'

That's when I snatched my hand away from hers; when I knew that this person *wasn't* my Mam; when I knew she was just another Lert, a Lert who'd smuggled herself onto the ward by disguising herself as my Mam. It wasn't safe! It wasn't safe in there. The Lerts were coming! The Lerts were taking over and coming from everywhere and I couldn't just lie there in my bed, waiting for them, waiting for them to come and get me. She was shouting, shouting at me and still pretending she was my Mam, shouting, 'Raymond, where are you going? Get back into bed!'

But she wasn't fooling me. I wasn't getting back into any bed. I wasn't staying there where a Lert could just walk in at any time and get me. If the nurses couldn't keep the Lerts away then I wasn't staying there. They were just watching me, the nurses, as I got to the door and went to pull it open. And the baldy one, the baldy one with the earring was laughing as he said, 'Raymond! Where the hell do you think you're going?'

'Out!' I said, pulling at the door. 'Out, where the Lerts can't get me. I'm not stopping here! It's the Lerts, there's Lerts in here, Lerts everywhere, I'm going I'm going, getting out!'

I couldn't open the door though! The door wouldn't open. And the nurse with the shaved head was laughing and waving keys at me, saying, 'Raymond! Look!'

The doors were locked, they were locked, locked doors. And now the Lert disguised as my Mam was heading for me and I was trapped, trapped against the doors. I started running, dodging past the Lert woman, running for the doors at the opposite end of the ward. And there were people laughing, people laughing everywhere as I ran for the doors, ran for the doors, ran for the doors! But they were locked! They were locked. And I was screaming then, screaming and telling them to open the doors and let me out. But they didn't let me out. They wouldn't let me out and I just slid down and ended up curled into a ball at the foot of the door, whimpering and telling them to make all the Lerts go away. Nurse Brendan picked me up; he just picked me up off the floor. And carried me back to the bed.

And he sat with me then. He told me it was all right, told me to try and calm down. But I couldn't calm down because she was still there, the Lert woman, there by the doors and looking back at me as she stood there, crying and still pretending she was my Mam. But I knew! I knew who she really was. And I didn't start to calm down till she finally gave up and the other nurse unlocked the door to let her out. I just watched her, keeping my eye on her, making sure she really was going and not just tricking the nurses again. She turned and waved to me, still trying to pretend and trick everybody into thinking she was my Mam. But I didn't wave back to her. I just watched, watched her closely as she disappeared through the doors. And it was only then, when the nurse locked the door after her, when I knew I was safe again, it was only then that I started to calm down.

Then Nurse Brendan asked me why I'd been so afraid of my own mother. So I explained to him. I said, 'That wasn't my mother.'

He raised an eyebrow as he looked at me. 'Is that right?' he said.

I nodded. And I explained to him that it was one of the Lerts who'd disguised herself up as my Mam. I nodded. 'And you shouldn't let any of them in here,' I said. 'They're dangerous, the Lerts.'

Brendan looked surprised.

'Is that so?' he said. 'Is that so? And there was me thinking what a nice woman she was, your mother.'

I shook my head. 'No,' I said, 'because that's what they're like, the Lerts; they always seem nice! But that's how they get in, you see; that's how they get in everywhere, because they do seem nice and so everybody thinks they're harmless. But they're very very dangerous, the Lerts. See, that's why I'm in here,' I said, 'because of the Lerts; the chief of the Lerts; it was him who made me fall through the ice. Everybody thinks he was being nice, because he pulled me back up from under the ice. But he wasn't being nice, because it was him who'd made me fall through the ice in the first place.'

Brendan was nodding as he stared at me. 'Oh, right,' he said, 'I get it now. So it was these, what do you call them, Raymond, these . . . Lerts, is it? These Lerts who chased you down to the water and made you fall in?'

I nodded. 'They're trying to kill me,' I said, 'the Lerts.'

Brendan stared at me and then nodded his head and patted my arm as he said, 'Ah Jesus, Raymond. Don't you be worrying now. A few Lerts? We'll soon have them on the run.'

I shook my head. 'It isn't that easy though,' I told him. 'You can't just get rid of the Lerts like that. It's not that simple.'

He looked surprised. 'Raymond, come on,' he said, 'a few Lerts? In here, Raymond, we've seen off far worse things than a few feckin' Lerts. See your man over the way,' Brendan nodded over at the bed opposite me, 'Tony, there; when he first came in here, I'm telling you, Raymond, he was demented. Pursued day and night he was; and not just by a few feckin' Lerts. The fish it was, with Tony, the piranhas, y' know, coming from everywhere; he couldn't bathe, couldn't go the lavvy, couldn't even take a drink of water for the fear of the piranhas. But look at him now.'

I looked. At the boy opposite me. He was sat there in the chair at the side of his bed; sat there, staring out.

Nurse Brendan called across to him, 'Tony, how are y'?'

And Tony slowly turned his head, like he was trying to locate where the voice had come from.

'Tony!' Brendan said again. And the boy focused then, focused on the nurse.

'Y' OK, Tony?' Brendan asked. And Tony smiled then, as he slowly nodded his head.

'I was just telling Raymond here,' the nurse said, 'about the fish, the piranhas.'

Tony nodded again. Then Brendan said, 'Where are they, Tony? Where are all the piranhas now?'

Tony smiled then. And in a voice that sounded thick and slow he said, 'Gone!' He nodded his head, still smiling as he said it again, 'Got fucked off. Fucked off now, the fish.'

'See!' Brendan declared with a note of triumph as he turned back to me. 'We've had them all in here, Raymond, the CIA, the MI5, aliens, assassins, Napoleon Bonaparte, all of them queuin' up to get in here and disturb the patients. But we find a way, Raymond; we find a way to keep them all at bay. And if we can stop the piranhas coming up the lavvy, Raymond, we can soon be doin' away with a few Lerts.'

Brendan was wrong about that though. Because even when they weren't there at the foot of my bed, the Lerts kept coming into my head, thousands and thousands of them, all with the same face and the same voice as Wilson. And it was like I was looking at all those Lerts from somewhere up above as more and more and more of them arrived in this big wide field. And in the middle of it was a white tent, a marquee, and all the Lerts were queuing up to get into this tent. And even though it looked as though it wouldn't fit more than fifty or sixty people, there were thousands and thousands of Lerts pouring through the entrance and going into it. I didn't want to follow them; I didn't want to go inside that marquee. I was trying to resist it, trying to hold back and keep myself out of that tent. But then I was looking down and the tent had no roof to it and I could see all the thousands and thousands of Lerts. And I knew then what they were there for. I knew it was the wedding! And there, at the front, I could see her, my Mam with her arm linked in his. And she was turning and smiling and looking up at him. And he was lifting a veil from off my Mam's face and the thousands and thousands of Lerts were starting to clap as he lifted off his top hat and turned his big, red, bulbous lips towards my Mam! And I knew I had to get there, before it was too late. Knew that I had to get out of that bed and get to that field and rescue my Mam. I knew I could do it, I knew I could get there, knew I could run fast enough and hard enough, through the pain barrier, running like liquid like liquid like liquid. Easy easy easy, running like Norman, like Norman taught me, running with the head and the breath and the muscles and even doing a pirouette, pirouette like Twinky, running, pirouetting, gliding, gliding, to rescue my Mam, rescue my Mam. Take this, take this, take this Raymond. It's only a tablet. That's all right, that's all right, take it as I'm running, pirouetting, gliding, take it take take the tablet, doesn't matter take it, take it take it . . . . take it . . . . take it . . . . takeit . . . . ta . . . . ke . . . . . tay . . . . kit . . . tay . . . . . . kit . . . . . kit ache . . . . . . tayk

401

..... hit ..... hit ...... hake .... tayk ...... slow
...... slow ...... slow ..... down ...... slowed
...... down ...... tay ..... kitslow ...... tay ....
kits ...... slow ..... down .... sloooooo ......
doooooown .... timefor ...... timefour .....
fortimefouryour ..... medi .... kay ..... medi
...... kay ..... shun .... medi ... kay ... shun.
   All gone.

That's what it was like, Morrissey, once they'd got me
stabilised and on the right medication. After the first
few weeks, the Lerts stopped coming for me. Once
they'd got me properly stabilised and on the right
medication everything slowed right down in my head
and stayed like that. And there were no more Lerts
after that; or, if there were, they just didn't seem to
matter any more; they didn't bother me. My Mam was
just my Mam again after that and Mr Wilson was just
Mr Wilson. They came in together to visit me; and it
didn't bother me, apart from the fact that I wanted to
stay in the recreation room and carry on watching
Lucky Ladders or *Going for Gold*. Or anything.
Brendan said I had to come back to the ward though
and be with my visitors. My Mam hugged me, like she
always hugged me. But I wanted to go back and sit
there in front of the telly. Only they wouldn't let me.
So I just had to sit there by my bed, while my Mam
gave me whatever present she'd brought me; and Mr
Wilson patted me on the knee and said how much
better I was doing. And I just nodded my head, or
stared at them. Or looked at the floor. And wished I
could go back to the telly room. Mr Wilson said I was
doing very well, very well indeed, he said. My Mam
said why didn't I open my presents. Mr Wilson said it
was amazing, the change in me and how much better
I was doing. And my Mam said did I want her to help
me unwrap my present. Mr Wilson said he'd had a
long talk with the consultant, who'd told him he was
very pleased with me. My Mam held up the book she'd

just unwrapped for me and said she thought I'd like it. Mr Wilson said I was making excellent progress. And if I carried on like this, I'd soon be able to go out for a couple of hours one afternoon. And he'd take us somewhere nice, me and my Mam, somewhere nice in his car. My Mam said it was supposed to be a very good book indeed, the autobiography of Bob Geldof. And then she read out, from the back of the book jacket, some of the things the newspapers had said about it. Mr Wilson told my Mam it must be a real tonic for her, seeing how well I was responding to treatment. My Mam didn't answer him though.

Because now my Mam had her head bent down, like she was trying to read the Bob Geldof book. But what she was really doing was crying. And it should have upset me, really, seeing my Mam sitting there trying to hide the fact that she was crying. It didn't upset me though. It didn't upset me at all. I knew it should have done; I knew I should have been feeling sad in my heart and worried because my Mam was silently crying. But I wasn't sad; I wasn't anything. It was as if a place inside of me had been closed down and shuttered up, the place that normally registered things like upset and sadness and worry.

Mr Wilson said it was miraculous these days though, what they could do with the right treatment. With every single day that passed, he said, they were learning more and more about my sort of condition. Then he said the same thing again in about ten slightly different ways. But it didn't matter though because it was just like the game shows on the telly that keep on doing the same thing over and over and over again; that's why I liked watching them, because they just stayed the same. He didn't notice though, Mr Wilson, when he kept telling me about the miracles of modern medicine, he didn't notice that my Mam was crying as she sat there, bent over the Bob Geldof book.

It was only when she was wiping her eyes with the hankie that he said, 'Are you all right, Shelagh?'

And my Mam said she'd just got something in her eye, that was all. And he frowned a disapproving frown as he said it was probably mascara. My Mam nodded. And he looked a bit huffy and brassed off then as he said he couldn't understand it, why my Mam used such stuff as that, painting her eyes like a common person when her eyes looked perfectly all right in their natural and unadorned state.

My Mam didn't even look at him. She just nodded as she tried to smile at me while Wilson switched his attention from make-up to footwear and said my Mam's high heels were far too high and quite un-necessary. He said it was now widely acknowledged that shoes such as my Mam's could lead to a person suffering from severe lower back problems in later life. My Mam just nodded again and kept staring at me. Then he said my Mam's bad habits in footwear were the result of unfortunate patterns established in her youth. But when they were married, he said, he'd be able to convert his membership of the Ramblers' Association into a joint membership and once my Mam got out there in the bracing air, rambling and roaming the rugged moors, she'd soon start to appreci-ate the indispensable value of sturdy footwear.

He carried on for ages. But my Mam wasn't even listening to him. Because my Mam was just looking at me all the time. And then, right in the middle of him lerting on about how a waterproof cagoule was an absolutely indispensable accessory for anyone ventur-ing out onto the moors, even in July, my Mam just clutched my hand, and squeezing it, told me, 'You will be all right, you know, son. You will, I know you will because—'

But he interrupted her, sounding a bit peeved as he said of course I'd be all right and anybody could see I was making marvellous progress.

I didn't want to listen to him! I wanted to listen to my Mam and what my Mam had to say to me. But it was like he wouldn't let my Mam do any kind of talking. Whenever my Mam tried to say *anything* he kept interrupting and saying things for her, as if he knew better than my Mam what it was she wanted to say. And in the end my Mam just gave up, left all the talking to him and just sat there like she was a bit of a spare part. And somewhere far off in my mind, behind the cotton-wool fog of all the medication, I understood that my Mam was a woman who'd been taken hostage. But I couldn't rescue her though, I knew that. I didn't have the energy to rescue anyone or anything. All I could do was sit there, not even listening as Wilson talked and talked until it was time to go; and my Mam kissed me and hugged me, hugged me and hugged me, till Wilson said, 'Come on now, Shelagh, come on; you don't want to smother the boy.'

My Mam kept hold of me though, just for a few seconds longer. And she whispered in my ear, saying, 'Son, I'm sorry, I'm so, so sorry.'

It sounded like my Mam was about to start crying again. And when she let go of me, when she stood back and looked at me, I could see that she was struggling to hold back the tears.

I was glad; glad that I was on the right medication, glad that I was stabilised and somewhere far off inside my own head. Because it meant it didn't upset me, watching my Mam fighting back the tears, watching her as she kept turning her head and waving back to me as Wilson led her down the ward. Then they were both gone. And I was glad because that meant I could go back to the telly room. *Going for Gold* had finished. But *The Sullivans* was on. So I watched that. I liked it; sitting there in the recreation room, watching the game shows and the quiz shows, all the talk shows and cookery shows, puppet shows and soap shows; all the shows where nothing ever ever happened. And everybody laughed or applauded wildly at all-the-nothing that kept on happening.

And then she was suddenly stood there, on her own,

my Mam. And I didn't know if it was the same day or another day. I don't even know if she was really there at all; or if it was me, just dreaming in front of the telly.

She said, 'Tell me! Tell me where they live in Failsworth and I'll go and see them. When *he*'s not around, I'll bring them in to see y'.'

I looked at her. I didn't know what she was talking about. But she bent down then, clasping hold of my hands, her eyes staring fiercely into mine as she said, 'I'll bring them, your friends! Just tell me where they live.'

And then I realised it was Twinky and Norman she was talking about. I shook my head though and my Mam's face started to crumple up as she said, 'Raymond, come on! Just tell me where they live. I thought you'd *want* to see them.'

That's when I frowned at my Mam. Because I didn't, not any more. I didn't want my friends to see me, not now; now that I was fat again. I wasn't properly fat again, not fat on the outside. But inside of me, that's where I was fat; where I was fat and all slugged and slow and daft, where my brain wouldn't work any more and I didn't want to think about anything. So I told my Mam, 'They've gone. My friends have gone.'

'What do y' mean?' she said, frowning as she crouched there in front of me. 'What do y' mean, Raymond?'

I just shrugged and I sighed and said, 'They don't even live in Failsworth any more, Twinky and Norman. They went to London.'

I tried to watch the telly then. But my Mam was still clutching hold of my hands and she shook them as she said, 'All right! So just tell me where in London, I'll get in touch with them there. It doesn't matter.'

But I shook my head. And I don't even know if I just dreamed it anyway. Because the next time I looked up, my Mam wasn't even there. And I don't even think it was the same day. Because it was the afternoon now and *Emmerdale* was on.

And instead of my Mam being stood there, it was *him* stood there, standing right between me and the telly so that I had to move my chair to see it properly.

He pulled over another chair and sat down beside me then. I thought maybe he wanted to watch *Emmerdale* with me. But he started talking. Straight away he started talking. He said, 'Raymond, I'm afraid your mum's not going to be able to come in and see you tonight. She did want to, Raymond. But in the circumstances, I managed to persuade her that erm . . . well, it might be better if I came and saw you this afternoon instead.'

He was looking at me. But I was still watching *Emmerdale*. Then I felt it, his hand on my arm. I looked at him then.

And his voice became all grave and suitably solemn as he said, 'It's your Gran, Raymond.'

I looked at him. I said, 'What's my Gran?'

He sort of sighed a bit and frowned as he said, 'Your Gran, she's gone.'

'Gone where?' I said.

He looked down at the carpet. '*Gone*, Raymond,' he said. 'She's gone.'

I felt it coming up from somewhere deep inside me. And then I felt it breaking out all over my face; this big smile. When he looked up at me again he had this severe frown on his face.

'Raymond,' he said, 'did you hear what I just said? Your Gran . . . has *gone*. Do you understand what I'm saying, Raymond?'

I nodded. And then turned back and stared at the telly again. Only I wasn't seeing *Emmerdale* any more. All I could see was this picture of my Gran legging it down the drive of Stalybridge Sanctuary for Seasoned Citizens, legging it like mad with everyone chasing her, clowns and comedians and hearty folk singers, all the chirpy nurses, with balloons in their hands and red noses on their faces as they legged it down the drive, trying to catch my Gran. But they didn't stand a chance, because my Gran was too swift for them and went hurtling down the drive and into the road just as the bus appeared; the big black bus with the sombre tyres, swerving in and slowing slightly as the extremely elegant frock-coated conductor with the long white hair leaned down from the platform, his arm outstretched as my Gran leaped and seized it and was pulled up onto the big black bus. And the two of them stood there together on the platform as the bus picked up speed and roared off up the road, leaving behind for ever the cheery chirpy nurses with their bright red noses, the hearty folk singers and all the peddlers of fun.

Then the big black bus was approaching me, passing the place where I was stood. And it slowed for a second, just for a second. And they were there, waving to me from the platform, my Gran waving and smiling at me; with Thomas Hardy, the Master of Misery, by her side.

'Did you hear me, Raymond?' he said. 'I'm afraid your Gran has passed away.'

I nodded then. 'I know,' I said, 'she'll be very glad about that.'

He just looked at me. Then he sighed as he got up. He stood there looking at me. He was blocking the telly again though and I had to move my chair again. He sighed and shook his head. And he said, 'Your mum *was* hoping you'd be fit enough to attend the funeral.'

It seemed all wrong really; somewhere at the back of my head, it just seemed wrong, everybody dressed up like that and having a funeral for my Gran. It was a good job she was dead! That's what I said to them, in the back of the big black limousine; I said, 'It's a good job my Gran's dead, isn't it?'

They all glanced at each other; apart from Mark and Sonia, who were still sat there staring at me like they'd been staring at me ever since I'd got into the car.

Mr Wilson patted me on the arm and said, 'It's all right, Raymond.' Then he smiled at my Uncle Jason and my Aunty Paula who were sitting facing us.

And he said, 'Don't mind Raymond. It's bound to be somewhat strange for him today. You have to remember he's not used to being out in a normal environment.'

My Uncle Jason glared at me and my Aunty Paula shot me a nervous glance. Then she said, 'It's very good of you, Mr Wilson . . . Ted. It's very good of you. It's not everyone who'd do this. Because it's a big responsibility, isn't it, when they're like that.'

She nodded at me, without looking at me. And Mr Wilson said, 'Well, it's not such a huge responsibility, Paula. Raymond and me, we understand each other and we get along just fine; don't we, Raymond?'

I nodded.

And he smiled at my Aunty Paula as he told her, 'Normally, you see, the hospital would have insisted upon one of the nurses being in attendance. But Raymond's consultant didn't consider that necessary, on the strict condition that he would remain in my care for the day.'

'Well yes,' my Aunty Paula said, 'because they'd trust you, wouldn't they, Mr Wilson. You see, a man like you, they know, the authorities, don't they, they know that you understand all this stuff, don't you, with the mind and that?'

Mr Wilson smiled again.

I leaned forward and looked across at my Mam who was sat there on the other side of him. She looked so sad and sorrowful, but still lovely though; my Mam, all dressed in black. She didn't look back at me though. She was just staring somewhere far off out of the window. And I knew she must be thinking about my Gran, who'd been her Mam; and now my Mam didn't have a mam any more. And I didn't have a gran.

I just leaned back in my seat again.

And I said, 'It's a good job she's dead, isn't it?'

But my Uncle Jason blew a big huffy sigh and said, 'For Christ's sake, can't somebody bloody shut him up!?'

'Raymond!' I heard my Mam quietly tell me.

So I just sighed and sat there saying nowt, watching Moronic Mark as he leaned into his dad and tried to whisper.

We all heard it though, everybody heard him saying, 'Our Raymond's mad, isn't he, Dad, he's mad.'

My Aunty Paula tried to tell him to be quiet and just look out the window at the scenery.

But Wilson felt compelled to get involved and told him, 'We try not to use words like that, Mark, words like "mad". Your cousin is poorly, Mark, certainly. But being poorly in the mind, Mark, that deserves just as much sympathy, as much understanding, as somebody who is physically poorly.'

Moronic Mark just gawped at Wilson and shrunk back into his dad as he tried to work out whether he was being bollocked or just patronised to death. My Aunty Paula laughed her nervous laugh and came to his rescue, saying, 'Oh that's what he *meant*, Mr Wilson; didn't you, Mark? You meant Raymond was poorly, didn't you?'

But by now Moronic Mark didn't know what he meant, so he just carried on gawping as another awkward silence ensued.

And I said, 'So it's a good job, isn't it, because if my Gran wasn't dead, she wouldn't be coming to this funeral, would she?'

'For Christ's sake!' my Uncle Jason declared. 'I don't know if I can put up with much more of this, y' know!'

My Mam said, 'Raymond!' again. So I tried to remember to be quiet.

Sickening Sonia was looking at me. And I just smiled at her. But she moved up closer to her mam and whimpered, 'He's looking at me, Mummy. He keeps looking at me.'

I just kept smiling at her though. Somewhere at the back of my head I could remember that she sickened me and I couldn't stick her. But she didn't seem to bother me now. Like nothing seemed to bother me any more, even the funeral for my Gran. I knew they shouldn't be doing it, giving my Gran a Christian burial. I knew I should be shouting at them all really and telling them it was a blasphemy, having a church service when my Gran had always hated the church and said it was nowt but a font of false hope and fantasy for the faint-hearted. And my Gran never wanted a funeral neither because my Gran always said she just wanted to be put in a biodegradable box and buried beneath a majestically melancholic oak tree.

And that's why I was glad she *had* gone; because I knew she wouldn't know anything about it, this funeral they were giving her; so it didn't matter, none of it mattered. That's why I just did what I was told, did what they said I should do, went where they said I should go.

And the only thing I said about it all, as we sat there in the back of the funeral car, was, 'Well, I'm glad for my Gran and it doesn't really matter what kind of a box she's in, does it, because she's off with the Master of Misery now and so she's probably ecstatically unhappy.'

Only that's when my Uncle Jason erupted, saying he'd had enough, when he waved his finger at me and told my Mam that if she couldn't shut me up then he was stopping the funeral car and I'd have to walk the rest of the way to the church.

My Mam quietly told him I wasn't walking anywhere.

So my Uncle Bastard Jason started kicking off at my Mam then, saying he shouldn't be expected to put up with all this when he was in such grief and mourning for the loss of his beloved mother.

And I don't know what it was that made me remember; I don't know if it was my Uncle Bastard Jason shouting at my Mam or whether it was the way he was pretending to be sad about my Gran when all his life he'd never done nowt but scrounge and cheat and take from her. Like he took her satellite dish! And that's what made me remember, made me remember about that freezing cold night when I'd been back in Failsworth and I'd gone to my Gran's house. Only it hadn't been my Gran's house, not any more. Because there was a new porch and people partying inside. And stuck there in my Gran's garden had been a *For Sale* sign; with the word *SOLD* pasted right across it.

'So anyway', I said, 'it *is* a good job she's dead because—'

'Right! That's it!' my Uncle Jason snapped. 'I'm stopping this car, I bloody am! I'm too distressed for this. I'm stopping this car and he can get out and walk.'

But I just carried on and said, 'Because if she wasn't dead, my Gran'd be a homeless person. Because she wouldn't have anywhere to live any more, would she?'

I stared at them, my Uncle Jason and my Aunty Paula, who were both sat there now, each one of them staring back at me like two kids who'd been caught in the Kwiky with their pockets full of Mars bars.

'Not now,' I said, 'not now that my Gran's house was sold while she was in Stalybridge Sanctuary for Seasoned Citizens!'

They were staring at me, staring like a pair of rabbits caught in the headlights. But Mr Wilson intervened then and said, 'Come on now, Raymond, just try and be quiet for a while.' Then he beamed a smile at my Uncle and my Aunty and told them it would soon be time for my next medication.

'You can always tell,' he explained, 'just from Raymond's behaviour you can always tell when he's due for his next dose; he starts slipping into repetitive speech patterns again, and generally making less and less sense.'

My Aunty Paula quickly nodded her head and said, 'I suppose that's what we've got to remember, isn't it,

Ted? It's a sickness after all, isn't it? I suppose he doesn't even know what he's saying himself half the time, does he?'

I could see them then, my Uncle and my Aunty, relaxing like they'd just wriggled off the hook again. And they might just have swam away and all. Wilson was explaining to them about my condition, telling them that one of the problems is that sufferers often experience paranoid delusions and make all kinds of accusations. And the thieving pair of them thought they'd got away with it then.

Only that's when my Mam bent forward in her seat and stared at me, her brow all creased up in puzzlement.

And ignoring Wilson and the others, she asked me, 'What did you just say?'

'Shelagh,' Wilson interrupted my Mam, 'don't get upset, he doesn't really know what he's—'

But my Mam ignored him and she said, 'Say that again, Raymond, about your Gran's house.'

Everybody was looking at me then. And it was like I was on *Blockbusters* with Unbearable Bob and everybody looking at me and waiting to see if I could answer the question.

But that's when I started to get a bit panicky; and began to wonder if it was just like the Lerts all over again, not real, just something in my head, and perhaps my Gran's house hadn't been sold at all; because maybe it was like Mr Wilson said and it was nearly time for my medication, so that's why I was starting to hate him again, my Uncle Bastard Jason.

That's why, instead of saying anything more to my Mam, I just shrugged instead. And my Bastard Uncle shook his head, like he was being all sympathetic and considerate as he sighed and said, 'It must be hard though, mustn't it, when y' can't tell the difference between what's real and what's just tricks in the mind.'

He shook his head some more.

And Mr Wilson said I'd be fine as soon as I'd had my

413

medication. Then he was explaining, telling my Uncle Jason how the drugs acted as an inhibitor and kept everything suppressed within my brain so that I remained levelled out and calm. He nodded, my Uncle Jason, nodded like he was interested. But I could tell, I could tell that even my Uncle Bastard Jason was being bored to bits by Mr Wilson.

That's when it first started coming back into my mind again, for the first time in ages, about Wilson being a Lert. And I sat there thinking that with a bit of luck, Wilson might just be able to bore my Uncle Jason to *death*.

But before there was even a chance of that happening we were at the church and all of us getting out of the car. And as I stood there on the pavement, that's when my Mam, looking as sad as a woman of constant sorrow, stepped forward, quickly linked her arm through mine, and said, 'Come on, son; let's you and me walk into church together.'

And I was made up with that, because I wanted to be with my Mam.

But he said, Mr Wilson said, 'Shelagh! Shelagh, he's got to have his medication.'

My Mam looked even sadder then. And she frowned and said, 'It'll only be an hour or so. It can wait just an hour, can't it?'

He looked at my Mam, Mr Wilson, looked at her as if she was a very very stupid child sort of person.

So my Mam nodded then. And slipped her arm from mine. And she walked into the church on her own as Mr Wilson led me into the vestry and ran some water from the tap so that I could take my tablets.

He said it was very important, Mr Wilson said; it was extremely important that I took my medication at exactly the right time every day; because it was all about maintaining the balance, he said; it's the imbalance, the chemical imbalance within the brain, he said, that's what causes everything to go out of kilter.

'And on a day that's as naturally stressful as this,

414

Raymond,' he said, 'we don't want you having to cope with more than is absolutely necessary, do we?'

I shook my head and he handed me the cup of water as he went fiddling in his pockets to find my tablets.

I liked taking my tablets, anyway. I didn't feel things when I took my tablets. And I didn't want to start feeling things, and imagining things; and having strange funny things start happening to me again.

So I don't even know why I did it really!

But I think it might have been something to do with my Mam; and seeing her having to walk into the church all on her own, without me.

He put the tablets carefully into my hand. Then he stood there watching me as he said, 'Go on then, Raymond. You take those, then we can go inside and join the others.'

And I was just lifting up my hand, about to swallow my tablets, when he walked in, the new young vicar, and said, 'Hello there. Is everything all right in here?'

He turned around quick, Mr Wilson, saying, 'Hello, vicar. Yes, absolutely fine. Raymond here just needed a drop of water for his tablets. How are you?' he said, walking over to shake the vicar's hand.

The two of them stood there then, with Mr Wilson asking the vicar how he was finding his new parish and was he settling in in Failsworth.

That's when I realised that they both had their backs to me. And that's when I saw he'd left the tap running in the sink. And as he stood there talking with the vicar, I just flicked them really; just flicked the tablets into the sink and stood there watching them as they dissolved away and disappeared down the plughole. I was staring at the sink, wondering why I'd done it.

But then he was turning round again so I took a gulp of water out of the cup as if I was washing down my medication.

He said, 'All right, Raymond? All done?'

I just nodded. And he reached out, took the cup out of my hand and swilled it under the tap.

'Come on then, Raymond,' he said. 'This way.' And he took hold of my arm and started leading me out of the vestry and into the church.

And that's when I began to get worried. Because the chemicals in my brain would all start to go out of balance now, without my medication. I started to feel really panicky and wonder why I'd done such a stupid thing. I didn't know what was going to happen to me.

But then we were in the church and he was leading me down to the front and into one of the pews. But it wasn't the same pew as the one where my Mam was sat; me and Mr Wilson were sat behind her where a few of my Gran's friends from the Positive Pensioners were sat.

My Mam turned round and pointed to the spare place next to her. But Mr Wilson leaned across and whispered, 'He'll be better here with me, Shelagh, at the end of the pew. Then if I need to take him out we won't be disturbing anybody.'

My Mam stared for a second. And then slowly nodded as she turned back to face the front. I wanted to be there. I wanted to be with my Mam, alongside her. I said to Mr Wilson, 'It's all right,' I said, 'I won't need to go out. I want to go an' sit there. I want to sit by my Mam.'

I was getting up. But he got hold of my arm and he was holding onto it dead tight.

'No, no, no, no, no,' he said. He was smiling at me. 'Come on now, Raymond,' he said, 'you sit down.' He was pulling me then. 'You just sit down here with me and everything will be all right.'

That's when I noticed it, branded across his forehead, the word *Lert*. That's when I knew I should have taken my medication. Because the Lerts were coming back again. Things were starting to happen to me again. I was starting to feel really panicky. So I thought I'd better just do what he said and sit back down.

And it was all right then because he was Mr Wilson

again. He smiled at me. And said, 'That's it; that's a good lad.'

So I just sat there, hoping everything was going to be all right. Hoping I wouldn't become unbalanced again. The organ music was playing quietly in the background and I tried to concentrate on that.

But things kept happening! Because in front of me, I saw my Aunty Paula putting her arm around my Mam, comforting her, as if she was my Mam's friend. And I knew she was no friend of my Mam's! Just like she'd never been a friend of my Gran's! That must have been what got me riled up. I couldn't help it; it just came out of my mouth without me meaning it to.

'You flogged it!' I suddenly heard myself saying, 'You and my Bastard Uncle, you flogged my Gran's house!'

They were staring at me, further down the pew, some of the Positive Pensioners turned and were staring at me. Mr Wilson was smiling and nodding at them all while out of the side of his mouth he was telling me, 'Come on now, Raymond, you're not back on the ward now! This is a church. You can't just blurt things out the way you do back on the ward.'

I told him I was sorry.

But then I saw my Mam was still turned around and looking at me.

And my Appalling Aunty Paula was telling her, 'Come on, Shelagh, take no notice. You've got enough to put up with today, haven't you, love. Now take no notice and you let Ted deal with it; he knows what he's doing.'

Then she put her arm around my Mam as though she meant to comfort her. And I was trying to be quiet. I was trying to just sit there and be good but it just came out: 'They did, Mam!' I said. 'They dumped her in Stalybridge and then sold my Gran's house before she'd even died.'

'Stop it!' Mr Wilson said, hissing at me and glaring. 'Come on, just calm down, Raymond!'

And then he grabbed a hymn book and said, 'Look, look here . . . now this is the hymn we'll be singing in a few minutes. Look! You just look at this, come on!'

But I was looking at my Mam instead. She was crying. And I knew that I must have upset her. I knew then that I should have taken my medication; because I was upsetting my Mam. And I knew it must be because she could see the paranoia coming back.

So I said, 'I'm sorry, Mam. I didn't mean it, Mam, I didn't mean it, didn't mean it.'

But my Mam wasn't even looking at me by then. And she wouldn't be comforted because when my Aunty Paula tried, my Mam shrugged her arm away and my Aunty Paula looked all surprised and offended.

I just stared at the hymn book. And then the organ music started to swell and I got to my feet along with everybody else. I wished I hadn't been so stupid though, washing my tablets away. I could see my Aunty Paula stood in front of me, with my cretinous cousins; all of them sobbing now that the coffin was coming in, hanky-dabbing and crying and pretending that they cared when none of them had ever done nowt for my Gran. I could feel myself hating them! Hating all of them.

But I knew I mustn't say anything because it was just all the paranoia coming back. I should have taken it, my medication. Only it was too late now. So I tried. I tried really hard to just concentrate and stop the feelings, and make my mind go somewhere in the far-off distance. I looked up at the big stained-glass window and tried to just concentrate on the picture.

Only that was when I started seeing things!

At first it looked just like an ordinary stained-glass picture, with the sun shining on it from the outside sending down shards of light and making the dust in the air of the church become all sparkly. And in the picture itself, it was where Jesus of Nazareth was still a young teenager and he'd gone missing and his mam and his dad had been out of their minds with worry about their Jesus and where he'd got to. But now they'd found him again and he'd just been in the temple all along. And you could see they were dead happy and relieved, Mary and Joseph the Carpenter, because they'd found their son and he was safe and everything was all right.

So I just kept staring at that glass picture and trying to forget about everything else as my Uncle thieving Jason and the other pall-bearers walked past me, down the aisle with the coffin. I didn't look. I didn't want to see my Uncle Bastard Jason. And I didn't want to see the coffin either, because it wasn't biodegradable cardboard like my Gran had wanted so that she could soon be mingling with the worms.

I just kept my eyes fixed on the coloured glass picture, of Jesus with his mam and dad.

And that's when it happened!

Because the faces in the picture suddenly stopped belonging to Jesus and Mary and Joseph the Carpenter; it was Norman's face looking down at me now, from the head of the Carpenter. And the Virgin's face had become Twinky's; Twinky's face with the lovely big smile he sometimes smiled for me. And the face of the teenage Jesus was the face of the Nice Boy, looking back at me; the face of the nice boy that I used to be.

It frightened me, frightened me at first, seeing those three faces. But it was lovely as well, in a way, seeing them up there in the glass, all back together again, the Failsworth Three.

I knew it must be all the chemicals in my brain starting to go ballistic because they weren't getting the medication they needed. I blinked, I blinked really hard as everybody started singing the hymn and Mr Wilson was singing it dead loud at the side of me. But they were still up there, still staring back down at me, the faces of the Failsworth Three. So I just closed my eyes then. And kept them shut dead tight until the hymn had finished. And when I opened them, I didn't look up at the stained-glass window again. I looked at the vicar instead, listening to him as he said he hadn't had the pleasure of knowing my Gran personally, but nevertheless had spent the past few days building up a picture of her, a very vivid picture made up of the memories and recollections of those who knew and loved her; and especially, he said, those gallant nurses in Stalybridge who'd devoted so much time and care into making my Gran's last months on earth such a rich and joyous time.

'And listening to ... the recollections of those nurses,' the vicar said, 'hearing their ... stories ... and ... their ... impressions ... I feel ... that ... through ... their combined ... memories ... I was afforded a privileged glimpse of the ... *real* ... Vera Bradwell.'

He smiled then, the vicar.

'Or, as she was more ... affectionately known ... amongst her dear friends in Stalybridge ... Vera ... *Madeira*.'

He chuckled! And then I heard Wilson chuckling beside me. I wanted my tablets! I wanted to be far off in the distance!

'In remembering Vera Bradwell today,' he said, 'let us try ... and keep ... that image, that wonderful image in mind, of that ... happy-go-lucky ... lady, Vera ... *Madeira*.'

I couldn't bear it! I couldn't bear it! He was a Lert! The vicar was a Lert! I started chanting in my head so I wouldn't hear it no more, chanting chanting, chanting in my head, talking and talking and talking to myself saying nothing, saying something saying anything, talking, keeping it out, keeping it out, keeping it out. I was stupid, I was stupid, I was, not taking my pills not taking them, washing them down the plughole, shouldn't have done it should have taken it, my medication medikayshun medication. I tried to concentrate, concentrate, keep my mind, keep it still keep it calm, keep it still. Then I saw it, the coffin, the coffin, the coffin in the chancel. It was all right, it was all right. Staring at it, staring at it; calmed me down, calmed me, knowing, my Gran, my dead Gran, my Gran was gone, she wasn't here, it was all right, all right; because she wasn't here to hear it, it didn't matter what they said; didn't matter, not now, not any longer, it didn't matter.

It was all right. It was just a drone now, the vicar's voice. Just a drone, somewhere far off. And I was all right, just staring, my eyes fixed on the coffin; the lerting drone of the vicar just something in the background.

I stared at the shiny coffin, and the shards of light spilling down from the stained-glass window and into the chancel, making stripes of sunlight across the coffin lid. It was all right. It was all ri—

And that's when I saw it!

On top of the coffin. Just in front of the flowers. Just sitting there on top of the coffin. A packet.

A packet of Garibaldi biscuits!

I felt my heart leaping up with delight.

But then I remembered, I hadn't taken my tablets. So the Garibaldi biscuits, they probably weren't even there and I was just seeing things again. I knew then it must be the chemicals kicking off in my brain. Because people didn't do that, people put flowers on top of coffins, not packets of Garibaldi biscuits. I could see them though. All the way through the funeral service, I could see them sitting there on top of the coffin. And even when the coffin was being carried out, when they were carrying it past me, I could see the packet perched there on top of the coffin lid.

Then when we went out and everybody started mingling around the grave and it was sitting there, the coffin, waiting to be put into the ground, I could still see the packet of biscuits. And even though I knew it was probably just the imbalance of the chemicals in my brain, I stepped forward to have a closer look. But as I did, he grabbed my arm, Wilson. And he said, 'You just stay here, Raymond. Just stay here alongside me and you'll be all right.'

It was like he was my bleeding jailer! And the only reason I did stay there was because I knew I couldn't trust myself, not while I was seeing things. And I didn't want to start blurting things out again and risk upsetting my Mam. She was upset enough already, I could see that. She was stood on the other side of the grave, but stood right back like she couldn't bear to look at it. She was just stood there, all on her own and staring, just staring. I saw my Uncle and my Aunty trying to get my Mam to come and stand by them. But my Mam shook her head and wouldn't even look at them; and you could tell that my Mam just wanted to be on her own. I thought she mustn't want anyone near her, anyone at all. It was like she was all locked up inside herself, with nothing but her sadness. I could barely look at my Mam, for all the sadness that was upon her. And that's why I looked away; looked beyond her, far off towards the wall, at the back of the church.

And that was when I saw them!

It was like I was seeing them in a dream, the way they moved, slowly like they were gliding across the grass, moving in and out through the tombstones, like they were floating just above the earth, these two figures who looked exactly like Twinky and Norman.

I snapped my eyes shut! Screwed them up as tight as I could, to make it go away, the awful painful picture of my two best friends gliding towards me as if they were really there. I missed them. I missed them so much, my friends. But when I was on the medication, when everything stayed in the far-off distance, it was all right, I didn't think about them very much and when I did it was as if Twinky and Norman and Sunny Pines were all just a far-off memory.

But now, now that the medication had worn off, now that I was hallucinating and seeing pictures of them in my mind, it just made me want to cry, for the loss of the friends whom I had loved.

And that's why I was stood there at the side of my Gran's grave with my eyes screwed up tightly shut and bits of tears leaking out from the corners of them. And when I opened my eyes again, it was only because of him, Wilson, because I suddenly heard him as he said, 'What the . . . What the hell's . . .'

When I looked, he was quickly moving forward towards the coffin that was sat there at the other side of the grave. And I watched him as he bent down and snatched up the packet of biscuits off the top of the coffin!

I just stared at him as he strode across to the bin by the corner of the church, the packet of biscuits in his hand.

They were real!

They weren't just in my mind, the Garibaldis, they were real. He was pulling open the litter-bin lid and flinging the offending biscuits inside. And across from me I could hear my Aunty Paula saying wasn't it disgusting and how could anybody do something like that, leaving a packet of biscuits on top of a deceased person's final resting place.

But I wasn't listening to my appalled and appalling Aunty.

Because the biscuits were real! And if the Garibaldis were real—

I looked up again! And they were there! It really was them, it really, really *was* Twinky and Norman.

And if I had any remaining doubts, they were completely swept away when I heard her again, my Appalling Aunty, saying, 'What are *they* doing here?'

And then my Aunty was nudging my Uncle Jason and pointing at Twinky and Norman as the pair of them approached the grave, both of them sombre and sad, Norman's face all streaked with tears and both looking like they were going to start crying again as they came and stood by me and Norman put his big bear arms around me as he hugged me, his voice all choked up as he said, 'Fuckin' hell, Fly, I always thought we'd see her again.'

Then Twinky took hold of my hand and squeezed it dead tight as he said, 'Are you all right, Fly? You going to be all right?'

And I was crying as I nodded, crying as this big big smile swelled up from inside of me and broke out all across my face as I told Twinky, 'A1 at Lloyd's, Twinky, A1 at Lloyd's.'

Then Twinky, Norman and me, we all just hugged hold of each other and then stood there, clinging together as we turned to face my Gran's coffin, the Failsworth Three of us standing there silently staring at it, paying some sort of respect. Until through his tears, his voice cracked and breaking, Norman said, 'Fuckin' hell, where's Gran's biscuits gone?'

And that's when Wilson arrived back at the grave and said to Norman and Twinky, 'Was that *you*? Did you put those biscuits there?'

Norman nodded. And Wilson looked disgusted. 'I suppose it's a joke, isn't it?' he said. 'Is that what it is, your idea of a joke?'

Norman frowned. 'No!' he said. 'It's not a joke! They were Garibaldis. We wanted her to have some biscuits when she got to the other side.'

'Her favourite biscuits,' Twinky said.

Wilson stared at them. And that's when *he* piped up, my Uncle Jason, calling across from the other side of the grave and saying, 'Come on! Let's be havin' y'. Come on, sling your bloody hooks. It's a private funeral, this is.'

That's when I felt it all start bubbling up inside of me, bubbling bubbling.

Twinky and Norman looked at each other like they didn't know what to do.

Then my Aunty Paula joined in and said, 'Go on! You've no business here, go on, the pair of y'.'

Norman looked all upset. 'We got the coach,' he said, 'we got the coach from London.'

'Yes, well, you can just go back there, can't y'?' my Uncle Jason said.

Then Wilson joined in and he said, 'Now come on, you can see that this is a very upsetting time for the family as it is.'

I could feel it, the bubbling bubbling; it was like all this bubbling happiness at my friends being there, but all of it mixed up with this fizzy bubbling sort of hysteria inside of me as well. But it didn't matter! Everything was going to be all right now, everything was going to be happy and lovely because my friends had come back for me, my friends were with me again!

Norman shrugged and said to Wilson, 'We only came to say tarar. We just wanted to say tarar to Gran.'

'Gran!' my outraged Aunty Paula almost screamed. 'Gran! Who gave *you* the right to call her Gran? You didn't even know her! Now go on! On your way.'

That's when I shouted, shouted out and told my Aunty Pigging Paula, 'They're not! They're not going anywhere! Thief, thief house-robber, felon cheat cow!'

And holding onto both of my friends, I said to them, 'Don't move, move don't don't don't. Take no notice, you don't don't don't have to go nowhere . . . don't don't don't.'

My Uncle Jason was shouting at me then, yelling and pointing and blaming my Mam, saying I never should have been allowed to come to the funeral when anybody could see what a spastic-brained bastard I was.

I ignored him, hugging and holding onto my friends and telling them, 'It's all right, it's OK, take no . . . don't worry, it's only him, the thief robber felon; take no notice.'

But that was when I saw that Wilson was really frowning at me. And then he stepped forward, saying, 'Now come on, Raymond, these boys are causing a great deal of upset.'

'They're not going!' I said, holding on tightly to Twinky and Norman and pulling them closer to me.

425

'They're not going anywhere! They're my friends and they've come back!'

I stood defiantly glaring at him then, seeing all the Lertiness oozing out of him now, the peeved, pissed-off look in his eye and the thin set line of his lips as he glared back at me. And then the shrug as he changed tack, looked up and called across to my Mam, saying, 'Shelagh, I'm afraid I'm going to have to take Raymond back to the hospital.'

I saw my Mam, her bowed head slowly rising like she was slowly coming out of some kind of trance. And when she looked at me, it was like she was a bit puzzled, as if she was seeing me for the first time.

'He's spoiling it, Shelagh!' my Aunty Paula suddenly declared. 'Spoiling it for everybody.'

'I think it's just proved too much for him,' Wilson said. 'Better for everybody if we get him safely back.' He reached out, grabbing me by the arm and trying to pull me away from my friends as he said, 'Come on! Come on, Raymond, let's get you back to the ward.'

That's when I heard it, my Mam's voice, firm and clear as she said, 'No! No no no!'

And then she was stood there beside me, pulling Wilson's arm away and telling him, 'Leave him alone, just leave our Raymond alone.'

Wilson gawped at her. 'Shelagh, now look,' he said, 'take my advice and let me deal with this.'

But my Mam was shaking her head. And I could see it now, all the fire and the steeliness in her eyes, the stubborn steeliness that I used to see in the eyes of my Gran. And for a second, it was almost like my Mam had suddenly turned into my Gran! Everybody was looking at her.

'You just leave my son alone,' she told Wilson. '*And* his friends, you just leave these lads alone.'

He glared at my Mam. And then, half raising a finger, he said, 'Now look, Shelagh, I understand that this has been a very stressful time for you and my advice would be . . .'

426

'I said, *leave them*!' my Mam insisted. 'I *asked* these lads to come here today. I wrote to London and I invited them here. So you leave them alone, all right? And you leave me alone!'

There was a pause as Wilson stood there, frowning at my Mam. And in the background I heard my Uncle Jason start kicking off about how he wasn't having his mother buried in the presence of a pair of poofs!

'Shelagh, what are you saying?' Wilson asked my Mam.

But my Mam ignored him. And that's when she reached out and took my hand in hers. And on her other side she reached out and took Norman's hand. Until my Mam, me, Norman and Twinky were all stood there, hand in hand at the side of the grave. And I think I loved my Mam then more than I'd ever loved her in all my life; when she held the hands of me and my friends.

And turned her back on the Lert.

And I didn't even realise I was saying it out loud, I thought I was just saying it in my head, in my joyous joyous head as I said, 'My Mam's free, she's free, she's free, she's free of the Lerts at last. Escaped, got out got out got out. Mam Mam Mam, my Mam's free, Mam's free.'

Lerts don't give up that easily though.

Because that's when Wilson went across and started speaking to my Uncle Bastard Jason. And then they were coming across towards us, Wilson, my Uncle and one of his mates who'd been helping to carry the coffin.

And Wilson said to my Mam, 'I'm sorry, Shelagh, but it's my opinion that your present grief is affecting your judgement. I've got to insist, Shelagh; you might be his mother, but Raymond's welfare has been entrusted to me for today. And that means that as long as I am acting *in loco parentis* I have to insist that, for his own good, Raymond comes back to the hospital now, with me.'

I felt my Mam's grip tightening around my hand as she defiantly glared at Wilson.

And I was saying, 'Good good good good Mam I'm not I'm not going, not! I'm with my friends, my friends I love my friends friends I'm with love . . .'

That's when my Uncle Bastard said, 'Sod this!' as him and his mate pushed past Wilson and moved towards me. And I knew they were going to grab me then and pull me away from my Mam and make me go back with the Lert, locked in the car with the Lert and carried back to Swintonfield and locked in the unit with my friends all gone and disappeared, Twinky and Norman gone and then the Lert would capture my Mam again and I wouldn't have anything or anybody, just the far-offness in my head.

And that's why I let go of my Mam's hand; that was why I leaped across the open grave and started running. Before my Uncle Bastard could get his hands on me. Before Wilson could stop me. I knew, I knew now, the real reason Twinky and Norman were here. They'd come for me at last, they'd come to collect me and take me back to London with them. We had to get to London! We had to run fast, fast; they were telling me to stop, Norman and Twinky, were telling me to stop as they ran after me. But I shouted back as I sped across the grass, dodging the tombstones and calling to my friends, 'Come on, Twinky, Norman Norman Norman, come on, they'll never catch us, catch us now they never will cos we're too fast, the Failsworth Three fleet-footed faster than fury, come on!'

I scrambled across the church wall and dropped down onto the road, legging it along the pavement, Twinky and Norman trying to catch up with me and shouting, telling me to stop, to wait.

But I couldn't understand what they were on about because we had to hurry up, all of us, we had to get to the coach the coach the coach! It might be going be going without us, for London leaving, leaving without us if we didn't hurry, hurry hurry up Twinky hurry up

Norman. We'd get the bus, we'd have to get the bus, the bus to towntown there and there we'd get the coach, the coach the coach to London. Running running running down the road, Twinky, Norman behind me, running running behind me trying to catch up but they couldn't couldn't even Norman and he'd been my train train trainer, couldn't catch me I was so so fast so fast and got to the bus stop got to the stop stop without them and stood, waiting for them to catch up, laughing laughing laughing, doubled up hyena laughing and pointing at Twinky and Norman as they came running up towards the bus shelter, me doubled up and laughing, pointing and shouting and laughing, telling them they weren't fit weren't fit and the people in the bus shelter looking at me, looking at me, moving away from me, moving away, giving me more room room room.

'Going to London,' I told them all. 'Me and my friends my friends, look these are my friends, here they are Twinky and Norman, my friends.'

The people at the bus stop trying to look away, trying to look anywhere and me laughing laughing as my friends caught caught up and came running up to the bus stop, the two of them stood there looking at me as they gasped to get their breath back and I laughed and told the people in the bus queue, 'We're the Failsworth Three but when we get to London London we'll probably be the something else three something else three something else Piccadilly pick a lily pick a rose pick a pocket or two, Piccadilly lily lilylilylilylilylilylily.'

I was laughing, smiling at them all the persons persons in the queue, laughing laughing laughing.

And then they had hold of my hands, Twinky and Norman, gently holding me and leading me out of the bus shelter and away from the people till we were standing by the wall. And I just kept laughing and laughing, laughing every time I looked at my lovely friends and felt all the lovely bubbly niceness washing up and over me, making me laugh laugh laugh.

Only, my friends weren't laughing. Twinky and Norman weren't laughing at all. Norman looked really upset. And Twinky was just staring at me. Then Norman was crying and shaking his head as he said, 'Fuckin' hell, Fly! What have they done to y'?'

I tried to tell him, tried to tell Norman that nobody had done anything to me. 'A1, Norman,' I said, 'A1 at Lloyd's.' And I laughed again so Norman would know that I was all right.

But Twinky and Norman just looked at each other. And it was stupid because it was like they didn't get it didn't get it didn't understand and I said I said, 'We're going, we're going, we're going and we're all going together this time aren't we, all crossing the Straits of Messina together.'

That's when I saw the bus and I ran back towards the shelter, telling my friends, 'Come on come on, this is it this is it, this goes to the coach station, come on, the coach might leave might leave for London, the coach might leave without us.'

They followed me, Twinky and Norman, followed me into the bus shelter. And I was telling them, telling all the people in front of us how we were on our way now, me and my friends on our way to London. We got to the front of the bus shelter, all the people in front of me had got on. And then I was just about to step onto the platform. But that was when I felt this pair of arms wrap themselves around me and suddenly I couldn't move. Then the driver was looking down and saying, 'Come on! Are you lads getting on or what?'

And that's when I saw Twinky, at the side of me, slowly shaking his head. And I felt myself being lifted off my feet and carried back into the bus shelter as the bus doors hissed shut and the bus began to pull away and I couldn't stop couldn't stop couldn't stop the jibberjabberjibberjabberjibbering telling my friendsmyfriends we'd miss the coach now missthecoachmissthecoach! And I knew IknewIknewI knewknew the way Twinky was looking at me, the way

Norman was holding onto me and saying he was sorry and Twinky was saying he was sorry and I knewIknewIknewIknew. I was crying Iwascrying Iwascrying, because Iknewknewknew IknewIknew. I wasn't going.

Twinky said, 'Fly, you know that we love you, Fly. But we've got to take you home. Not to London, Fly. We've got to take you home to your Mam.'

And Norman had tears running down his cheeks as he said, 'You've got to fuckin' trust us, Fly. Me an' Twink, we'd fuckin' love you to come to London with us. But Fly, you can't fuckin' go anywhere, not like this. You should hear y'self, Fly, because honest, you're as fuckin' mad as a demented fucker.'

And I knew that. I knew I *was* a demented fucker. I knew that I couldn't go anywhere.

Twinky held my hand then. And he said, 'Do you think you could do it, Fly? Do you think you could trust Norman and me?'

I nodded my head at Twinky. And through my tears, I told him, 'You knowyou know you know I'd trust you. I'd trusttrust trust you and Norman more than I'd evereverevereverever trust any any anyone.'

That's when Norman began to release his grip on me.

And Twinky said, 'Come on then, sweetheart, let's get you home to your Mam.'

You see, the thing is, Morrissey, that my Mam didn't have any choice. She said, she said she'd do everything she could to make sure I got out of there at the earliest opportunity. But for now I had to go back, she said. She hugged me. And told me again like she'd told me a hundred times already how sorry she was and what a stupid, *stupid* person she'd been to have ever got involved with Wilson in the first place. My Mam said she doubted that I'd ever have ended up in Swintonfield if it hadn't been for Wilson and his interfering. But even so, she said, she blamed herself; blamed herself because she'd been desperate,

431

desperate about me, desperate about not being married and maybe having to live the rest of her life on her own. And because she'd been desperate, she'd become daft as well as desperate, allowing herself to be taken in and taken over by a know-all interfering menace who seemed to feed and thrive on the misfortunes of others.

My Mam even apologised to Twinky and Norman. She said she was ashamed of herself, the way she'd let Wilson turn her against them when she hadn't even known them and all the time they'd been such nice lads and such good friends to me.

That's what made me cry again, hearing my Mam say that and knowing now that my Mam liked my friends, that's what made me start crying; right in the middle of laughing, start crying again.

And my Mam explained how she *had* to take me back to Swintonfield. She said, 'Look, Raymond, even your friends, your friends can see that you're not well, can't you, boys?'

Twinky and Norman nodded. But my Mam didn't even need to explain. She didn't need to say she was sorry, because I knew I wasn't well; one minute I'd be crying, the next I'd be jibberjabbering, laughing my head off at things that weren't even funny. I was crying about my Gran and then laughing and laughing and telling my Mam, telling Twinky and Norman about the big black bus and the Master of Misery who'd come to collect my Gran but he wouldn't be taking her to heaven because it would just be hell for my Gran in heaven and like Norman had said, when you think about it, it could be a right shithole in heaven.

They took me in a taxi, Norman, Twinky and my Mam, the three of them being really nice to me, all of them sitting with me and holding my hand. And I never knew, not till a long long time afterwards, that they'd been holding me down, holding me safe and keeping me from harm as I jibber-jabbered, cried and laughed and jibber-jabbered all the way back to

432

Swintonfield, coming up with brilliant ideas like why didn't we all run back to Swintonfield instead! That's why I kept trying to open the door and get out of the moving taxi, believing it wouldn't do me the least bit of harm to open the door and walk out of a taxi at forty-five miles an hour.

Morrissey, it's occurred to me for some time now, what you might be thinking from reading these letters; and how you might very well be tempted to conclude that perhaps I really am an unfortunate mad person. I wouldn't even blame you if you did think that, Morrissey; because there were all sorts of people, people who knew me, and they all thought I was mad, thought there was something wrong with me and I'd never be right again. But it wasn't like that, Morrissey.

That's why I just want to reassure you; because I know that a person in your position gets all kinds of unwelcome attention and correspondence from people who have somewhat lost the plot. Just from talking to other fans, I know there are plenty of people who start to confuse reality and end up believing they have some kind of affinity with you personally. But Morrissey, I'm not such a person.

I know I wasn't well. But when I did go through that period where I'd lost touch with reality, it was just because of everything that had happened. And my Mam says that even if I was a bit mad, back then, it was only because I got *driven* mad.

It was just a phase, you see, Morrissey, just something I was going through at the time. And after I finally got out of Swintonfield I never ever had any sort of attacks. They said they thought it had been brought on because of all the stress and the pressure and anxiety about things. And keeping me on the drugs, they said that would provide my mind with the rest it needed.

I told them I didn't feel under any pressure or stress or anxiety. After the funeral, when my Mam and

Twinky and Norman took me back, I told them I wasn't a bit depressed. Even when I was crying I was happy. And as my Mam and my friends led me through the doors and up to the reception, I was buzzing like a bee, charged up and loaded, all cylinders firing, elated, ideas pouring into my head and out of my mouth about all the things we were going to do and no-one could stop us and anything that we ever ever wanted to do we could do it, without a doubt or hesitation, without fear of any kind of consequence. As my Mam spoke to the nurse on reception and told her I was back, I was telling Twinky and Norman how they could both come and stay with me on the unit and then we'd all be living there together and my Mam could come and visit us and bring us nice things to eat and we could have picnics on the ward. Twinky said that sounded divine. And Norman nodded.

But there were tears in everyone's eyes as they looked at each other.

Then Brendan was there, and the shaved-head nurse and some others. They had hold of me by the arms and were talking to me like I was a child person. And then they were leading me towards the lifts. But nobody was coming with me. Twinky and Norman and my Mam weren't there any more. I tried to turn round to see them, but the nurses kept marching me towards the lifts. And I *had* to struggle because they wouldn't stop, they wouldn't let me turn round and see my Mam and see my friends. I wasn't trying to hurt anyone or hit anyone or anything like that. I was just trying to get them to LET GO OF ME so that I could turn round and look. And when I started shouting out, I didn't mean to frighten anybody or startle the old lady who was coming out of the lift. I was just trying to MAKE THEM LET GO OF ME. Because all I wanted to do was turn round and see my friends and see my Mam. But they WOULDN'T LET ME. Brendan and the nurses WOULDN'T LET GO OF ME. And that's the only reason I made my legs go limp beneath me, dropping to the floor, wailing for my friends and my Mam as I twisted and struggled and cried and shouted until they LIFTED ME UP off my feet, carrying me into the lift and holding me there; where I finally managed to twist myself round before the lift doors closed; and I saw them, Twinky, Norman and my Mam, still stood by the reception desk, my Mam with a hand raised to her mouth, Norman turned away, his head bent down. And Twinky, looking at me, his hand half raised in a wave, before the doors of the lift closed over; and it seemed like everyone was gone for ever.

I'm not denying that I was ill, Morrissey. I know I was. And I'd never try and deny that. The day after the funeral, when my Mam came to see me, she said she was so shocked at how ill I looked she tried to take me back home again. All the jabbering and the jibbering and gabbling had stopped. But it was like everything else had stopped as well. My Mam said it was like my brain had stopped. She said it was like seeing a lump of jelly lying there.

She told them she was taking me home. She even started trying to get me out of the bed and get me dressed. Brendan had to stop my Mam and explain to her that it was just because of the drugs they'd had to give me, because I'd been so manic. My Mam was crying though, trying to get me dressed and out of there. They had to send for the consultant. And Dr Corkerdale explained to my Mam that the reason I looked like a wrung-out dishcloth was just the natural result of both the depression and the therapy. He told my Mam it was quite normal. It was much much better, he said, that I was calm now and resting, instead of gabbling and babbling manic, because that was when I was at most danger from myself, when I was hyper manic and self-inflated and full of grandiose schemes.

'Because it's at times such as those,' he told my Mam, 'that the patient can form the illusion that he is indestructible. And I don't think we want that now, do

435

we, mummy? I don't think you'd want him leaping off bridges or buildings or in front of trains. Or, indeed, into canals again, now would you?'

And then, when my Mam shook her head, calmer now and frightened for me, the smiling consultant told her I'd probably be a lot brighter when she next came in. He said that as soon as he was confident the manic phase was over he'd reduce the lithium; and then I'd soon be back to something like my old self.

Only I never was, Morrissey, not while I was in Swintonfield; I never did get back to being my old self.

I tried to tell them at first, about it all being a mistake, and I'd never ever made any suicide attempts. But Dr Corkerdale just used to smile at me and then ruffle me by the hair of my head as he told his students, 'You see, this is fairly typical of bipolarisation. This young chap's already recorded at least two suicidal episodes but continues to remain in denial, largely, I'd suggest, because of the tendency in some b.p.1s towards schizoaffective disorder. In his current, controlled state he denies or simply fails to recognise episodes associated with his previous manic phases.'

The students nodded and made notes while the consultant smiled and played with one of his cuff links.

I kept on trying, for a while; trying to tell them that I hadn't ever tried to commit suicide; to tell them that the person they kept on talking about wasn't the person I was.

But when I attempted to do that, Corkerdale just ruffled my hair again and told his students that consistent with schizoaffective disorder was the tendency for the patient to present with multi-persona symptoms.

Then he said I was a good chap again.

I tried to tell him, to make him understand. But already he was off, moving down the ward, his students following.

And I think that was when I first started seeing things again! When I was watching Corkerdale and his

436

students following behind him, all in a line, disappearing down the ward in their white coats and stethoscopes. Until the line of bodies suddenly became this one long bloated creature that wobbled through the ward like a fat caterpillar, its bleached bloated body pushing and heaving its way out through the doors.

I started seeing all kinds of things after that; like turnips growing out of the wall, and the man who looked like his head was on upside down. His clothes were too small for him. And he wanted to hurt me. He'd just appear at the window, after dark, waving to me, calling and trying to get me to go with him. That's why I kept telling the night nurses to make sure the curtains were properly shut, properly, properly shut, not half shut, not-shut, not with slits and open slats and gaping gaps and bits in the middle where the cloth didn't meet; shut, shut, shut, properly shut curtains so the man with the upside-down head couldn't come through.

They didn't understand though, the night nurses. Sometimes they got fed up and said things like, 'For Christ's sake, Raymond, will you shut up about the fucking curtains! They're shut, they're shut, they're already shut! Look.'

They weren't though!

And I'd have to lie there all night, knowing he was watching me, the Man with the Upside-Down Head.

I think that's why I was so tired all the time. That's why I didn't want to get up out of bed, because I never got any sleep at night, with the sound of the turnips growing out of the walls, and the man staring at me through the gaps in the curtains.

I know now, Morrissey, I know it was all just things in my head, things that weren't there. Sometimes they were nice things. Like sometimes I'd look up and see my Gran and she'd be carrying Jaffa cakes, a bottle of dandelion and burdock and a bag of filled finger rolls. And I'd know that she'd come to collect me and take me out for the day, like she did when I was little and we used to go and have a picnic at one of the Greater Manchester graveyards.

I liked it when it was like that, when it was nice things I was seeing, when it was people like my Gran; or my friends.

I'd look up and see them, Twinky and Norman sitting there at the foot of my bed, smiling at me and telling me about how they'd been to have tea with Petula Clark.

And once they even told me that they'd come back to Failsworth for the weekend to visit Twinky's mum who'd been traumatised and upset on account of her spaniel dog had been knocked over by a dial-a-pizza van. Norman said when they got back it was all over Failsworth!

I thought he meant Twinky's mam's spaniel dog. But Twinky said the dog was all right and only had a broken foot.

It wasn't the dog that was all over Failsworth; it was the news! The news about Paulette Patterson's father and how he'd been arrested; how everybody was saying it had been going on for years; before Paulette it had been her older sisters. And how the eldest sister, who was married now, had finally decided to speak out.

That's what Twinky and Norman told me. Or that's what I *thought* Twinky and Norman had told me. That's why it made me glad at first, because they'd finally know now; that I'd never done it, never done anything to the little girl. And perhaps now me and my Mam could go back and live in Failsworth again. That's what I was telling them, Twinky and Norman. But when I looked up, I wasn't talking to anyone. There was no Twinky and Norman. And that left me feeling a bit sad, knowing that it must be just like the turnips, just something inside my own head.

So that then, when it was my Mam sat at the side of the bed, sat there telling me about the little girl, telling

438

me the same thing that Twinky and Norman had told me, I just ignored it and stared at the window, waiting till she disappeared again; taking no notice as she said she'd already been on to the housing to see about getting us moved from Wythenshawe and back to Failsworth where we belonged. I just kept staring out of the window; wondering if the night nurse would remember tonight, to make sure the curtains were properly closed.

I don't know exactly how long I was on the unit at Swintonfield, I just know it was winter when I went in there. And by the time I got out again it was past the middle of summer.

And what I used to think, Morrissey, was that the time I spent in Swintonfield was just this slice of my life that had been wasted. Like it was all just a void.

He said, Dr Corkerdale, he told my Mam that what he wanted was for my mind to be kept at a minimum level of activity and function. Just like one of the modern television sets, he enthusiastically explained to my Mam, one of those where you can select *sleep* mode, so that the set is almost but not quite fully switched off!

And that was what he wanted my mind to be, *almost* switched off. Because it was his theory that if allowed proper rest, the mind could best heal itself. And the drugs, he explained, they were merely a means of relieving the mind of pressure and stress and anxiety; so the mind could be given the opportunity to restore and reset itself.

That's why I thought it was all just wasted time; when I was a turned-down telly, a stopped clock. When I was nothing. When my life was put on hold. When it was just empty time, in which nothing happened.

But I didn't know. Not then. There wasn't any way I could have known.

They started saying that I had to take some exercise. But I didn't want to take any exercise. I didn't even care that I'd started getting fat again. I just wanted to stay in bed.

In the end they got my Mam to persuade me. She said now that the weather was getting warmer it would be nice, just taking a gentle stroll around the grounds. That's the only reason I started going, because it was with my Mam.

That's who I was with, the first time he saw me. And he must have seen my Mam as well. He wouldn't have recognised me unless I'd been with my Mam. She didn't see him though. He ducked back, behind the chestnut tree. But as we were walking past, I saw him hiding behind the trunk of the tree, still watching us. I didn't know; I didn't know if he was real or not. Sometimes I thought he was the man who lived in the chestnut tree. He was always there, peeping out from behind the tree when me and my Mam went past. And sometimes I thought he must be real. That's why I tugged on my Mam's sleeve and began pointing. But I knew then it probably *was* just me seeing things because when my Mam looked up, he wasn't there. He was never there when my Mam looked up, the man who lived in the chestnut tree; the man with the warm soft eyes who always peeped out, but hid behind the trunk whenever me and my Mam went by.

When it was one of the nurses though and not my Mam who was taking me for a walk, he always used to come right out from behind the tree. He always waved and smiled at me then and stood there watching as I went past. But I could never wave or smile back, not then, not when my eyelids were still as heavy as sandbags and my brain a ball of wool; and my legs always felt like I was wading through water, deep dirty water, wading through water, deep dark and wide.

It was only when I was starting to get a bit better, when Dr Corkerdale had began reducing my medication, it was only then that I found out that he was real; that he was the man who did the gardens and tended the grounds at Swintonfield.

There was this day when he came right up to me; the day when he started walking alongside me and the nurse. He pointed at me, then made signs with his fingers. The nurse smiled and nodded and, like he'd asked her a question, she answered him, ' "Raymond". That's right, Raymond; our latest addition, young Raymond Marks.'

He nodded. And smiled at first, but then it was like he was choking back the smile and trying to stop himself from crying. Then he opened his mouth, like he was trying to talk. But the sounds that came out were all broken and strangled and sounded like someone who was gasping for air. His eyes were all warm but his voice made me frightened and I stopped and I clasped at the hand of the nurse. But she said, 'It's all right, Raymond, there's nothing to be afraid of. He's just saying hello, being nice. Aren't you, John?' He stood and he nodded as the nurse reassured me and explained that the gardener didn't mean any harm. And it was just that he'd lost his means of talking, she said; on account of how his vocal cords had been badly injured.

'But if you'd been here as long as I have, Raymond,' said the nurse as we started walking again, 'you'd get to understand his signs and his croaking, the sounds that he makes and what they all mean. Wouldn't he, John?' said the nurse, and he nodded. And the three of us started walking again.

Later on, Morrissey, when I'd been on reduced medication for weeks without ending up manic again and jibber-jabbering or trying to throw myself out of the window or anything like that, that's when they started letting me walk the grounds on my own if I wanted to. And that's when I started going to see him every day, John the Gardener. I liked him. We'd sit there outside his hut behind the big chestnut tree, drinking sugary tea with not much milk. And the nurse had been right because even though he had no voice any more, I soon learned to understand his croaking and his gurgling and his signs with his hands. That's how we used to talk. And he'd ask me things about myself like why I was in Swintonfield and I'd explain to John the Gardener and tell him the bits I could remember; about Twinky and Norman running away to London and about the Lert and my Mam nearly getting married; about my Gran and how she got struck dumb and died. And I told him about the Wrong Boy. Not everything, not about flycatching or anything like that, but just about how I'd turned into the Wrong Boy. And how I'd become my mother's wound.

John the Gardener used to look at me with all the sadness in his eyes when I told him things like that. But sometimes it seemed to make him really angry because he'd frown as he stared at me and shake his head and make this growling sound that I didn't properly understand. Because I never knew!

I never knew that he was my Dad.

And that he was growling and angry because of what had happened to his son.

Why didn't he tell me, Morrissey? Grown-up people aren't supposed to be stupid. Why didn't he tell me? Did he think I wouldn't like him? Because he couldn't talk? Because he was a gardener? And all those years before, he'd never even come back with the turf and laid a simple lawn; for me and for my Mam. I don't know why he didn't tell me, Morrissey, but he never did. Unless, when he gave me his guitar, he *was* telling me, in some sort of a way. He just went off into his hut one day. And when he came back he was carrying this old-fashioned, beaten-up guitar. He held it out towards me. But I frowned and told him I couldn't play the guitar. He didn't seem to understand though. He kept nodding his head and offering me the instrument. I just took hold of it in the end. And he stood there, watching me, nodding his head and encouraging me to try and play it. I couldn't do it though. Not properly. I just messed around with it really. And all I could pick out of it was just a bit of a one-string tune that I'd remembered from when I'd learned the recorder at school. It was supposed to be 'The Ink Is Black The Page Is White' but it was all clumsy and faltering, out of time and barely recognisable as any sort of tune.

John the Gardener seemed to be made up though. He was clapping his hands and jumping up and down with delight, his face all excited as he kept shouting out saying, 'Yargaarrra! Yaaaaaar. Yargaarra,' which in the language of John the Gardener meant, 'You've got it. Yes. You've got it.'

I couldn't understand how anybody could get so excited about such a rudimentary picking out of a plodding, boring tune like 'The Ink Is Black'. Anybody could have played it. But to hear John the Gardener, you would have thought I'd just played an entire guitar concerto. That's how dads are though, aren't they? With their own kids. If my Dad had never gone away he would have probably watched me doing Lego when I was little and then gone bragging to the neighbours that I was the next Isambard Kingdom Brunel. He might have watched me playing football with my friends on the recreation ground, then gone home to tell my Mam that I was the next Georgie Best. He might have done all sorts of things; if he'd never gone away.

Just like I might never have ended up in Swintonfield.

Morrissey, I'm sorry about the chicken. I know I only ate it because I was hungry and feeling sorry for myself. But I feel ashamed now, Morrissey. Because I used it as an excuse, what I'd found out about my Dad and how it had made me feel, I just used it as an excuse to behave badly. I don't even like chicken!

And I know now it's pointless, sitting here feeling sorry for myself. And feeling sorry for my father.

It made me sad. But it made me angry as well. Everything he'd ever wanted, my Dad, he'd had it there all the time; there, in his voice; the musical instrument he'd always wanted to play and it was there, all the bleeding time, in his voice, in his vocal cords. And he'd ruined it, wrecked it. The only instrument he'd ever been able to play; his only means of letting out all the melody that was in his heart; and he'd thrown it away, thrown it all away on nothing more than his hopeless love for a slutty woman from Silkstone Common who'd turned him into a fool.

And what I've been thinking, Morrissey, as I've been sitting here, is that it's just pointless sentimentality, wallowing in the what-might-have-been. Because the fact is that my Dad was never my dad, not really. I never even knew him. The Dewsbury Desperadoes knew him better than I ever did. And if I ever had a real Dad, it was my Gran; she was a dad to me. Because it was my Gran who taught me about important things, things that mattered. Like she told me about spuds and self-pity. That's why I know I can't sit here much longer, mourning the life and the memory of the Dad I'd never had.

I'd grown up without him. And nothing could ever alter that. My Gran always said it was the wanting of what he never could have that drove my Dad's mind in the wrong direction.

'Many's the life, Raymond,' she said, 'many's the life that was nowt but a catalogue of frustration and despair with the wanting of what can never be had. Look at me!' my Gran said. 'Don't you think I would have liked to have been Simone de Beauvoir or Daphne du Maurier? I would. I would have liked it very much indeed, all those tea parties on the lawn with clever people and flunkies to cut the crusts off my bread. I certainly would have liked it, Raymond. But it was never meant to be, son; I wasn't Daphne du Maurier. And I never would be. So I just had to get on with being the best Vera Bradwell that I could possibly be.'

And my Gran was right; I knew that. I knew that my Dad had spent all his life wanting what could never be. So he'd never really lived the life he'd been given.

And I know that what I have to do now, Morrissey,

is to get on; get out there on the motorway again; carry on trying to get to Grimsby.

And trying to be the best Raymond Marks that I can possibly be.

Yours sincerely,
Raymond Marks

17 June 1991
A Shelter,
The Esplanade,
Cleethorpes,
Lincs
(Mon. morning)

Dear Morrissey,

Sometimes I wonder what would have happened if I'd turned out like the rest of them; if I'd ended up just being a normal sort of person, like all them others, the Darren Duckworths and the Geoffrey Weatherbys, the Kevin Cowleys and the Albert Goldbergs and all of them.

I see some of them when I'm in town, mostly the ones who haven't got jobs. Sometimes they shout things out, especially if there's a few of them hanging round the benches or outside the off-licence. They just shout stupid stuff, like, 'Hey, Marks! Are y' looking for Spencer?'

They think it's dead hysterical, that. Sometimes they shout out things like, 'Psycho' or 'Spazzie' or 'Mong'. And if they're particularly energised, they'll shout something like, 'Look out! It's Raymond the Retard!'

I just ignore them. And most of the time they just

ignore me. It's like we come from different planets.

Some of them went away to university, like Geoffrey Weatherby did. And some of them got jobs, working in places like banks and building societies. And I see them, sometimes, when I'm walking down the boulevard or through the Precinct. We don't even look at each other. They get nervous when they see me; because they think I might try and talk to them. And then they'd be really embarrassed because they'd have to pretend they didn't know who I was or, even worse, have to stand there in their unisex hairdos, distressed denims and mock moccasin Hush Puppy shoes, praying that nobody would come past and see them, with me!

And they don't know, not one of them, that the person who would be really embarrassed would be me! Because I wouldn't want to be seen dead talking to nauseatingly normal persons like them.

That's why I didn't care! I didn't care one bit about them just walking past me. I was always really glad that they walked straight past! Even Geoffrey Weatherby. And the day he did stop, that day I was walking through the Arcade and I saw him, coming towards me with his girlfriend, the two of them all entwined with each other and laughing, I wish he'd just carried on walking, ignored me, pretended he never knew me.

But he suddenly crossed over and came walking up to me, leaving his girlfriend stood outside WH Smith's.

He nodded. Then he asked me was I all right. I just shrugged. I didn't even know why he'd stopped. He'd never spoken to me since all those years ago when he'd ridden past me on his bike and called me Fatso.

'With being away at uni,' he said, 'I'm not that in touch with what's going on around here these days. But I . . . heard . . . I heard you had a bit of a hard time.'

I could see his girlfriend stood outside Smith's and looking in the window. She was really pretty. She

447

looked like somebody he must have met at university.

'The thing is,' he said. And then he cleared his throat and looked somewhat sheepish. 'I just wanted to . . . I mean . . .' He turned round, checking that his girlfriend was still out of earshot. Then he lowered his voice and he said, 'You know that . . . erm . . . years ago! You know when we were at . . . remember all that stuff . . . at the canal . . . with Albert Goldberg and those others?'

I looked at him then, properly, for the first time. And I was suddenly glad! Even though it was after all this time and it was too late to make a difference now, I was still glad that Geoffrey Weatherby was trying to own up and sort of say he was sorry about things. Once upon a time he'd been my all-time best friend. And I'd never wanted him to be the bastard he'd become; the one who'd ripped up our secret document and never ever talked to me again. And that's why I was glad.

'Well the thing is,' he said, 'when we were kids, I always meant to say . . . you know . . . I always wanted to tell you, really . . . that I thought they were all bastards, all those others, Goldberg, Duckworth and Kev Cowley . . . I thought they were real shits the way they all left you to it and let you take all the blame.'

He nodded. And even reached out as if to touch my arm, before stopping and drawing back his hand, saying, 'I just wanted you to know that. I thought they treated you really badly, those guys.'

I just stared at him!

And tried not to vomit at the putrid whiff and the sickly sweet stench of his patronising cant. Suddenly I knew why the smiles of the homeless people and beggars cannot conceal the hate in their eyes as you hand them your money.

I watched him as he went back to join his girlfriend and the two of them moved off through the Arcade. She turned round and glanced back over her shoulder, looking at me as she laughed at something he was telling her.

And I didn't care! I didn't care about any of them. Because I had something that none of them could ever have. That's why I could just ignore them.

I carried on to the music shop, to buy a new set of strings.

They didn't matter. I could even sort of feel sorry for them. I'd have hated to be like them, like any of them, with their cars and their careers and their Saturday night clubbing it; their crap CDs and student railcards, I hated all that. That's why I didn't care and never wanted anything that they had.

Apart from a girlfriend!

She looked really nice, Geoffrey Weatherby's girlfriend.

But even that didn't matter.

Because I had something that was nearly as good as having a girlfriend. I had something that none of them others would ever have; I had you, Morrissey. And that's why I loved it so much, being in my bedroom in Failsworth, waking up in the morning and seeing you there on the walls. I'd lie there in bed, before the getting-up time, looking at every single one of the posters and pictures and record sleeves of you and The Smiths, all of them making me feel warm and lovely and reminding me how much I was a part of something. That's why I loved it.

And now?

Now I'm here, Morrissey, like a displaced person, huddled in a wooden shelter, looking out across the sea. *Here!*

I'm HERE, Morrissey! Two miles down the road from Grimsby.

And a million miles from home.

He always said, my Uncle, he said, 'Well, it's not as if you do fuck all else, is it, except sit around in that bedroom of yours, playing your records or your stupid fucking guitar. So it's not as if you're giving anything up, is it? You never go out. You never do fuckin' nowt, so what have you got to lose? It's not as if you're living any sort of bloody worthwhile life here in Failsworth, is it?'

And I never even bothered trying to tell him, Morrissey; because how could he ever understand, that unfortunate uncle of mine; how could he have comprehended that I was never ever ever just doing 'fuck all'.

I was being a Morrissey fan!

Twenty-four hours a day, every day of the week, that's what I was doing! I was listening and reading and thinking and dreaming. And writing. All day long, in my lyric book. Writing my words and my songs and my ideas and thoughts about you, Morrissey, and The Smiths. And other things too, things about my Gran. And even some things about myself.

I was never an 'idle tosser'. I was busy, all the time; busy being myself. Because that's what you'd allowed me to become, Morrissey, myself. And I loved it. Knowing I was all right. Knowing it was perfectly, absolutely, one million per cent positively all right, to not be normal. That it was even better than that! That it was the *best* thing of all, the brilliance of not being normal.

And that's what I'd seen, Morrissey, when I'd looked up at the telly screen and seen you for the first time; seen all that sublime not normalness of you.

There, on the telly in our front room. And I didn't even know who you were. I hadn't ever really listened that much, to pop music. I'd never heard of The Smiths. But I sat spellbound on our settee in a jumbled state of ecstatic serenity as you sang 'Half A Person', 'Cemetery Gates', 'The Boy With The Thorn In His Side'; and in the wave of recognition that swept over me, I suddenly knew that *I* am known! I understood that *I* am understood.

It's just that nobody else seemed to understand!

My Mam was always saying she was fed up seeing me sat around the house and doing nothing and wasting the most precious time of my life.

She said, 'It's like you've never really done *anything* since you came out of hospital, Raymond. And I always thought, I thought that once we were living back here in Failsworth again you'd start to come out of your shell and buck your ideas up.'

That's what my Mam was always saying. She always thought that.

As soon as we'd moved back to Failsworth, after they'd prosecuted the little girl's father and locked him up and nobody could blame me any more, my Mam thought we could just go back to the beginning and start all over again. I think she wanted me to go back to becoming the boy I'd been meant to be. Only I couldn't. Because time had moved on. And I'd become a different boy instead.

I tried to tell her though, about how she didn't need to worry about me. Because I was perfectly happy.

And I was, Morrissey, after that day when I'd discovered you, I was always happy after that. Even when I found out that I'd left it really really late and The Smiths had already broken up, I was still happy, because I'd found you. I don't mean I was frivolous happy; not jumpy-up-and-down stupid happy, frivolity-fuelled fun-filled happy, not that. It was *real* happiness, Morrissey; a calm and quiet happiness deep down inside of me. It was like being a kid and having the loveliness of catalogued comics all over again.

I wasn't being a 'bone idle bastard'!

I was being a Morrissey fan. And being myself. That's why I went and found it, Morrissey, stuffed under the stairs where it had been for months and months, neglected, forgotten. I'd even thought about dumping it or giving it away because whenever I'd caught sight of it, all it had ever done was remind me of my time in Swintonfield. And so it had stayed there in the cupboard under the stairs: the guitar, along with my *Star Wars* stuff, my cobwebbed comic collection and all the other things I'd grown out of; all that stuff which seemed to belong to a person I could barely remember.

Now though, now that I'd found you, Morrissey, now that I'd started learning from you, even beginning to try and make up songs of my own, finding that guitar in the cupboard beneath the stairs, pulling it out from under all the junk and the don't-know-what-to-do-with bits and pieces, it was like digging up a priceless piece of long-lost treasure.

And I hadn't even wanted it!

I'd told him, John the Gardener; I'd gone to find him and tell him I wouldn't be able to play for him on the guitar any more; or drink the lovely sugary tea with not much milk; or sit there on summer afternoons, listening to the warm wind in the branches of the big chestnut tree. I'd told him I was being discharged. And if I'd known, Morrissey, if I'd known who he really was then I might have understood the look on his face when I told him that. I thought he was ill at first. I thought something had snapped inside of him and he was having a heart attack or something. Because just for a moment, his face creased up with pain. And he whimpered out this sound that I'd never heard him make before, so I couldn't even translate it. And even though I didn't know why, I could see what sort of a monumental effort it was for him to summon up a smile and ruffle up the hair of my head as he made the choking growling sounds that I did understand; and I knew that he was telling me, 'Good! Good, I'm glad you're getting out of here. And going home, where you belong.'

The next morning, the day I was leaving, I woke up on the ward and it was there, by the side of my bed, the guitar. And I didn't even want it!

But I knew I had to take it.

And when my Mam came to collect me and asked where I'd got it from, I told her it was from the gardener. And I said we'd have to go and see him

452

before I went home; go and see him and thank him. And say tarar.

But, of course, when we got there, he was nowhere to be seen. The hut was empty; like it always was, whenever I was with my Mam.

I wonder what he would have been like, Morrissey, if he'd heard me play it properly? I don't mean brilliantly, Morrissey, because I'd never be able to play the guitar brilliantly, not like the genius Johnny Marr. But I learned enough, Morrissey. After I'd rescued it from under the stairs and polished it up and got new strings, I practised and practised every day, my fingers aching and stinging in agony from making the shapes and pressing the strings; until gradually my fingers became supple enough, the tips grew smooth and hardened up and I could press the strings and play the chords without feeling any pain.

Then day after day, from listening and listening over and over again, I worked out the chords to 'Handsome Devil', 'Back To The Old House', 'Ask' and 'Panic' and 'Cemetery Gates'; and 'Please Please Let Me Get What I Want This Time'.

And it was like I *had*, Morrissey; like I had got exactly what I wanted; because I'd found a way of being me.

And that's why they didn't matter, the Darren Duckworths and the Kev Cowleys. That's why I could carry on without caring about the Geoffrey Weatherbys. And the girlfriends that I didn't have. It didn't matter. Because I had a way of living.

Until!

Last night, Morrissey, when he picked me up in the silver Mercedes, I couldn't believe it was possible. It should have been the lift of a lifetime, really. I'd never ever met a *real* American person before. And I'd certainly never ever met a middle-aged person who knew almost every lyric from every track on *The Smiths' Singles* cassette. He said it was his son, back in

New York, that's who'd first introduced him to your music. And that's why he'd stopped for me, he said, because normally he would have thought twice about picking up a hitch-hiker at that time of night. But then he'd seen my tee shirt and recognised Edith Sitwell. I hadn't even been hitching. I'd just been sitting there by the petrol station.

And then I'd heard this voice saying, 'Hey, kid! You need a ride?'

I looked up and saw him standing there by his car.

'Where you headed?' he asked.

When I told him Grimsby, he said, 'Come on, you're in luck.'

He said the place he was staying was a few miles south of Grimsby and so he could easily drop me off.

I know, Morrissey! I know I should have been ecstatic at getting a lift like that. Especially when I was sat there in leather-seated, air-conditioned luxury, gliding down the motorway in that big silver Mercedes with the glorious sounds of *The Smiths' Singles* pouring out from every speaker. It should have been brilliant. But it wasn't. He was really nice, the American man. It wasn't like he was *pretending*, like a vicar or like those teachers who pretend to like music that's far too young for them and so they end up being the most excruciatingly embarrassing form of sub-human life that's ever been known. He wasn't like that at all, the American man. Because it was like he understood, like he *really* understood everything about you and your lyrics, Morrissey. He said that sometimes he could hear a line of yours and it would reduce him to tears, the way that you could capture the 'strange joy of heartache'. And sometimes, he said, the 'sheer audacity of a Morrissey line' would momentarily rob him of his breath.

That's why it should have been the most magical lift I've ever had, Morrissey. But it wasn't. Because with every track we were getting nearer and nearer to my destination. I think the American man must have known. Because he stopped talking to me, like he understood.

And it was like *you* understood, Morrissey. Because every line that you sang, it was like you were singing it for the very first time; and singing it just for me; like you knew that finally this was it, that there was no more getting out of it, no more putting it off. And this time I really was going to Grimsby! Going to work. Growing up!

I looked out of the window, saw the lights of Scunthorpe flickering in the distance, across the fields. With every mile, I felt it growing heavier, the weight of where I was going to; the weight of all I was leaving behind. The weight of what I was about to do.

I'm sorry, Morrissey!

I don't want you to think of it as a betrayal. See, what you've got to understand, Morrissey, is that in a place like a building site, you've got to do everything you can just to survive. You see, they wouldn't understand, Morrissey. You'll always be there in my heart, inside of me, Morrissey. It's just that . . . on the outside . . .

It doesn't mean I'm no longer a fan or that I don't respect and care for you as much as I've always done. All it does mean, Morrissey, is that I'm just trying to get by without being mocked and made miserable and being griefed-up all the time.

And that's the only reason I agreed, Morrissey. That's why I let my Mam get them for me, the black vests! She got them from the Army and Navy, along with the jacket, the builders' boots, the stonewashed jeans and the grey slacks and vee-neck jumpers for the nights and weekends, when I went out with my new friends!

My Mam said they really suited me, the black tank-top vests. She said I'd grow into them, once I started building up my muscles and filling out a bit. And with the jeans, she said, the jeans and the boots and the tank-top vests, I could almost be taken for a young Bruce Springsteen.

'And a person like that,' my Mam said, 'someone

like Bruce Springsteen, he'd never look out of place on a building site.'

Morrissey, I'm sorry!

That's the real reason I ate the chicken!

So I could try and start getting used to it. So that I won't seem different; so I won't be out of place any more.

Morrissey, it doesn't mean that I'll have forgotten you though. Even if I do end up looking ordinary and normal, even though I might have to listen to unforgivable things like U2 and learn how to tell jokes and talk all that shag-brained sort of stuff that only men can do, I won't ever forget you, Morrissey.

I know you'll think I'm letting you down; and letting myself down.

Last night, when I was in the silver Mercedes, I even felt like I was letting the American man down. There he was, thinking he was talking to a real Morrissey fan. And all the time I knew I'd soon be swapping my Edith Sitwell tee shirt for something else. All the time we're driving along with your sublime singing filling the air; and in the back there's my bag, with my brand new costume of ordinariness and normality. And it's like I'm betraying everything. That's why I just stared out of the window, staring at the blackness; then watching Immingham, as we passed it by, all lit up like a spaceship in the night. Then back to the blackness, punctuated only by the motorway signs, the one that said *Welcome to Grimsby – Food Capital of Europe*. And the other one saying *Grimsby City Centre 5 miles*.

I stared at the outskirts, the shuttered-up shops and retail outlets; the neon signs and the sodium lights, deserted bus stops, theme pubs, houses, petrol stations, the hoarding boards for flights and beer, bras and fish fingers, pickles and pensions, films and cars. I stared at the gates of the schools and the playgrounds, the office buildings, the depots and yards; the signs for the docks, the museums and ferries; and one sign by the side of the traffic lights that said *Fish Dock Number 9*.

456

And next to that, tied up with string, a yellow card with a black arrow pointing and underneath, the mud-spattered lettering that said *Cinema Complex 200 yds. All Contractors' Vehicles MUST report to Site Office.*

That's what I was looking at when the car started slowing down and I heard him ask, 'This place you're staying – what was the name of the street?'

I pulled the piece of paper out of my pocket again and told him, 'Slinger Street.'

'You have any idea where it is?' he asked.

I shook my head. 'I just know it's somewhere near the docks,' I said.

He nodded, looking out the window, as he brought the car to a halt. 'Well, I guess this is the dock area,' he said, 'but I don't have a clue where this Slinger Street could be.'

'It's all right,' I said, 'you don't have to take me any further. You can just drop me off here and I'll find it.'

He frowned, looking a bit dubious. 'You sure?' he said.

'Yeah,' I said, 'I'll ask somebody.'

I started getting out of the car. Then he got out and said, 'You know it's real late. How can you be sure there's gonna be people to let you in once you find this place?'

'It's all right,' I said, 'they know I'm coming. My Uncle arranged it.'

He started nodding. 'OK,' he said, 'but you look after yourself.'

Then as he was about to get back in the car he stopped and said, 'So, what's your name, kid?'

When I told him, he said, 'Well, it's good to have met you, Ray. By the way, I'm Ralph, Ralph Gallagher.'

That's when he reached out and shook me by the hand. And I thanked him for giving me such a brilliant lift. 'I didn't know', I said, 'that such a mature person as yourself could be a Morrissey fan.'

He sort of looked at me. Then he said, 'Is that your way of trying to say that I'm ancient, Raymond?'

I shook my head and started to apologise. But he just laughed and said, 'Hey! Hey, it's OK, I'm only teasing.'

I nodded.

And then he said, 'Well, good luck, Raymond.' He shook me by the hand again and went and got in his car.

And it was only as I was walking away that I heard him calling out, 'Hey, Ray.'

I stopped. And he was leaned over, with the passenger window wound down.

'I meant to ask,' he said, 'what's in the book?'

I didn't know what he was talking about at first. I just frowned.

And then he pointed at me. 'Ever since I picked you up you been clutching hold of it like your life depended on it.'

Realising he meant my lyric book I shrugged. 'It's just my book', I said, 'that I write in.'

It was his turn to frown then. 'Yeah?' he said, 'Like what? *What* do you write?'

'Lyrics,' I said, 'my lyrics. And things like that. Ideas and stuff. And letters, to Morrissey.'

He stared at me, nodding his head. 'Lyrics,' he said. 'You like that, huh? Writing lyrics?'

I nodded. He seemed to think about that for a second. And I wondered what for.

But then he just smiled and shook his head a bit, before winding up the window and driving off.

I stood there watching the car as it began to pull away. And I even started to wonder if it was just something I'd imagined, the nice American man with his silver car and his greying hair; and his genuine feeling for the songs and the lyrics I love. I thought perhaps I'd just dreamed it all up. But it was like one of those dreams where you don't want to wake up because you know that when you do, everything'll just be ordinary again and you'll have to get on with all the things you've got to get on with. That's why I didn't want him

458

to drive off and leave me standing by a sign that said *Fish Dock Number 9.*

Watching the silver car as it moved away, it was just like something my Mam had told me years ago, about how she was once stood in a hospital corridor and knew that she was safe and secure, because she was with Dr Janice.

And when Dr Janice was walking away, my Mam wanted to stop her and make her stay so that my Mam could go on feeling safe. But she knew, my Mam, that it was a stupid thing, wanting to stop a person, a doctor person you didn't even really know, just so that you could still have that person near you.

And that's what I felt like, Morrissey, watching the American man drive away. I didn't want him to leave me there, on that corner of a street by the docks in Grimsby. Because he made me feel safe. But just like my Mam, I knew it was a stupid thing, wanting a person to stay close to you, a person you didn't really know; just so that you could feel safe again.

That's why at first I thought I might be dreaming it up again, when I saw the brake lights suddenly light up, saw the car stopping. And saw him, the American man, step out of the car and begin waving me over.

I started running. But it felt like I was flying! Like I was being lifted up and borne away beyond the roads and houses and shops, beyond the city of Grimsby, up and away and soaring free from building sites, black vests and *Fish Dock Number 9.*

But then, as I was running up towards the car I heard him calling out, as he pointed. 'I just happened to glance up,' he said, 'and there it is. Look! It's here, look, Slinger Street.'

I slowed down. Started falling back to earth. I managed to smile and say, 'Thanks.'

And he said, 'So, you're all set now, yeah?'

I nodded.

And he waved a hand as he started to get back into

the car, telling me, 'Hey! Raymond, keep good! OK? You keep good!'

I nodded again. And watched the car until it disappeared. Then I turned into Slinger Street. And I thought about how brilliant they were at being American; American people. They're the only people who can do it. Because if anybody from England had ever said to me something like *Keep good!* I probably would have vomited! But American people can do it and get away with it; because American people aren't embarrassed about being American.

That's what I was thinking about as I wandered down the street and found the guest house.

And I should have known, Morrissey, even before I knocked on the door and rang the bell, I should have known. In the end I didn't even care, really.

She said, 'I'm not bothered when y' booked; I can't be letting you have a room if you can't pay your deposit.'

'But my money,' I said, 'I told you, it was stolen off me. I'm starting work tomorrow though and I'll be able to get a sub and pay you the deposit then.'

'Well, that's fine,' she said, 'you do that! But I can't be having you stopping here tonight, not without your deposit being paid!'

I carried on trying, but it was useless. I gave up. I walked back down the hall.

'I've got a business to run!' she said. 'I can't be holding rooms for people who turn up at this hour and then say they can't pay the deposit.'

She carried on but I just left her to it and walked out.

I was glad! It smelt of cats and yellow fish.

I wouldn't have wanted to stay there anyway.

I just started walking. I didn't mind staying outside, not when it was so warm.

And that's how I ended up here, in Cleethorpes. It's only down the road from Grimsby but it's like it's a seaside resort. I'm in this sort of wooden sun shelter on the esplanade. I think it's a place where the pensioners must come and sit in the daytime, to feed the seagulls and talk about their sciatica. The benches are a bit hard but I used my bag as a pillow and I managed to get a few hours' sleep. But then the sun came up really early and I couldn't get back to sleep after that.

It's dead old-fashioned here, Morrissey, with a pier and roundabouts and all kinds of arcades and cafés and candy-floss stalls. They're all shuttered up at this time of the morning though. And maybe that's why it's sort of nice here, Morrissey; before Cleethorpes wakes up, comes to its senses and gets on with doing its day job of being a screaming shrine to fun and frivolity.

Now though, it's serene and sort of saintly, in the holy silence of the empty streets and the deserted esplanade. And far, far out beyond the sands, Morrissey, I can see the shapes of ships and boats in the distance as they lumber up the Humber, getting smaller and fainter as they move to the mouth of the estuary, head out into the North Sea and finally disappear.

And that's what I was looking at, just staring blankly out across the sand, when I first noticed her.

She was a good way off, walking along the beach, silhouetted against the silver glare of the sun on the water.

Or maybe I didn't even see her at all! Perhaps I just conjured her up in my mind.

She looked real though, shoes in one hand as she moved across the sands, a sort of spring in her step as she moved towards the morning sun.

And I know it was just something in my mind and she couldn't have been there really. Because what would *she* be doing in a place like Cleethorpes, the Girl with the Chestnut Eyes?

I told myself it must be because I'd had hardly any sleep, Morrissey. And that's why I must be imagining things. That's what I said to myself. But I was a bit worried as well, Morrissey. Because since I'd

461

left Swintonfield it had never happened to me again. I didn't do it any more, see things that weren't there, like the Lerts or the turnips or the man behind the curtains, the one with the upside-down head.

And I know that this was different, because this was seeing somebody nice, seeing the Girl with the Chestnut Eyes.

It was still seeing somebody who wasn't there though, seeing something that wasn't real!

It wasn't even as though it could have been somebody else, some other girl on the beach who just looked like her. I know that because I walked across to the pier where the telescopes were. I put in a 50p piece. And there she was! In close-up, right in front of me, her eyes as dark and shining as I'd always remembered. She was twisting and twirling around on the sand, with her head thrown back and her arms stretched out. And if I needed any more proof of who it was I was watching, I only had to look at the tee shirt she had on; it was the really really rare one featuring the picture from the Australian version of the *Viva Hate* album when it was wrongly titled *Education In Reverse*!

That's why I knew, Morrissey, I knew it couldn't be anyone else but her.

But then my 50p ran out.

And when I looked down the beach again, it was empty.

That's why I was worried. I didn't want to start seeing things that weren't there again, even nice things, like the Girl with the Chestnut Eyes. And the man!

The American man with the silver car and the Smiths cassettes. Had I just imagined him and all? Conjured it all up in my mind?

I'm tired, Morrissey; tired and worn out. Maybe that's why I saw her, because I *wanted* to see her.

And what I *don't* want to do is do what I have to do; to go back down that road; back towards Fish Dock Number 9; into that place where they're expecting me;

where I'll work, and be normal and ordinary and a part of it all.

That's why I've got to go and get changed in a minute and put on the stupid vest, the stonewashed jeans and the builders' boots. And worst of all, Morrissey, I've got to comb out my quiff.

There's a public toilet, further down the esplanade. I'll be able to get changed in there.

I hope you can understand, Morrissey, that I haven't really got any choice. I've *got* to do it. I'm not doing it because I'm ashamed, Morrissey, or because I want to wipe out the past.

It's just that things'll be different, you see. I might even end up making friends with some of the other people who work there. And if I do that well I'll probably have to join in and do all kinds of boring and embarrassing things that you wouldn't want to hear about; like going out to clubs and sometimes going for a drink after work; and even watching football, I suppose, sometimes. I know that you wouldn't want to hear about any of that kind of stuff, Morrissey. That's why I wouldn't bother you by writing to you about it. And the thing is, Morrissey, from now on, I don't think I'll be writing very much of anything in my lyric book.

I suppose there must be thousands of people like me, Morrissey, who became so captivated by you and your lyrics that they all thought they could write as well. But what we all forgot, Morrissey, is that you're a genius; and the rest of us are just fairly ordinary really. And not very remarkable. I think that's probably why I left the guitar, Morrissey. I didn't do it on purpose, not like I was meaning to do it. I just forgot it really. He'd put it in the boot. And I never thought about it, not till he'd driven off and gone. It doesn't matter though. I won't be needing a guitar any more!

You see, the thing is . . . I lied to you, Morrissey, I didn't come to Grimsby just because my Uncle forced me into it. I could have resisted it. I could have pleaded with my Mam or pretended that I wasn't well again. But I didn't, Morrissey. So I suppose you've got to know; I suppose it's only fair to tell you, Morrissey, that I came here for a reason! I came here to Grimsby because I wanted . . . *to leave you behind*!

Morrissey, I'm sorry. I'm really really sorry!

But I can't help it, Morrissey.

I'd just got exhausted, worn out with the effort of being not normal, being criticised and disapproved of, taking the sneers and the jeers and the jibes; and the isolation, the loneliness.

Morrissey, I'm all right on my own. I don't even mind being on my own. But I never *wanted* to be on my own. That was just how it turned out. And I tried to make the best of it. You helped me with that, Morrissey. You made it seem all right, feeling lonely. And it was, in a way, it was all right being lonely and misunderstood, because I had my love of you and everything that went with that, all the records and posters and videos and all the mementoes and memorabilia. I had all of that.

But sometimes I'd find myself thinking about the future, Morrissey. And that's when I'd get frightened. Because it's all right being a bit lonely when you're only nineteen and you can wear all that loneliness like it's cool and defiant and a bit mysterious; like it's something you've chosen. But when you're not nineteen any more, Morrissey, when you've ended up older and you're still sitting there in your room, on your own, with a brilliant collection of Smiths and Morrissey memorabilia, what then? I've seen them, Morrissey, when I've been at conventions and all the fans have been gathered to wallow in all the wonderfulness of you and The Smiths, I've seen them, the *older* fans, the ones who were probably fans right back at the beginning, back in the early days when you and The Smiths first emerged, when *they* were only nineteen or twenty-somethings themselves. And then, back then, they must have seemed really 'it', Morrissey, those early fans with their fledgling quiffs, their shy smiles, their Meat Is Murder and Morrissey-mania. They must have looked lovely in all their cultivated loneliness, giddy not-normalness and exquisite indie-superiority. But ten years on, hanging around at concerts or conventions, their quiffs somewhat wilted and starting to recede, they just look sad; and faintly cheesy, all their enigmatic loneliness looking more like quiet desperation. And do you know what occurred to me, Morrissey, what occurred to me is that you must *despise* them – fans like that. Fans so devoted that they became trapped inside their devotion, imprisoned by their idolatry; those who clung onto worship because they were afraid to let go; in case they discovered that outside of you, Morrissey, and beyond the bedrooms of their own minds, they didn't exist. Which is why they're still there, at all of the concerts and all the conventions, with all the right books and rare records and pictures, all the right poses and strike-the-right-attitudes, all the right facts, dates and figures, discographies, bios and trivia and Morrissey-lore; those who dared adore you for just a little too long, Morrissey; those whose love is so needy that it blinds them to that look in your eyes, Morrissey; that look of pained *contempt*.

And that's why you have to understand, Morrissey, that I've not done all this just for myself; I'm doing it for you as well, Morrissey. Because I promised that I would never ever do that to you; never grow into the sort of fan whom you would have to despise.

So it's for both of us, Morrissey, me *and* you.

I'm just going to try and get on with things now. That's why I'm wearing them, the stupid jeans and the tee shirt and the brawny builders' boots. And even though I hate it really and I'm a bit frightened, I'm going to try my very very best to fit in at this job. Who knows, Morrissey, I might even learn to like it. And if I enjoy it and I make some friends, I might even meet a girlfriend. Then I'll probably be fairly happy and won't have much time to think about things like lyrics and you, Morrissey; and the times when I wore my hair in a quiff, so that all the world could see that I was a Morrissey fan.

Yours sincerely,
Raymond Marks

Dear M . . . . . .

I don't know . . . .

Dear Mor . . . I can't, I . . . .

What? . . . I don't . . . Morrissey? . . . What . . . have I done, what have I done?

Where am . . . I

It's . . . . . dark . . . I shouldn't . . . . .

De . . . Dear . . . . . Morri . . . . . I tried . . . forgive me, Mor . . . . . .

I don't . . . know . . . I was . . . . . . wrong . . . so wrong . . .

I shouldn't be . . . It's . . . Where? Dear . . . . .

I think . . . .

Where am I? . . . . . . Morrissey please . . . . come back . . . I didn't mean . . . where am I

I can't . . . . . . just don't . . . . . . can't . . .

Morrissey . . . are you still there?

Morrissey, MORRISSEY? Help me, Morrissey . . .

Please . . . . help me . . . . MORRISSEY

Dear Morrissey,

All the walls were white. And there were flowers! A
vase of flowers on the table next to the bed. There was
a window high up, a small window set in the thick
white wall, with a shaft of yellow sunlight leaking
through.

I didn't move, apart from my eyes scanning the
white room, seeing the grey cabinet at the end of
the bed – like the ones in the hospital – where you
keep your personal things, your slippers and your
dressing gown. I'd seen them, rooms like this. Side
rooms, off the main ward. Rooms where they put the
worst cases. Or when somebody from the ward had lost
it, and had had to be sedated and then kept in the side
room for a couple of days.

I didn't move. I didn't even try to move. Because I
knew it would hurt! Like it was hurting now, even
when I wasn't trying to move but still it hurt, itching
and stinging across my shoulders, my neck and down
my back. And my head! It was that dull pain: the
heavy, leaden pain, like the inside of my skull had
been stuffed to bursting with pounds and pounds of
cotton wool; the sort of pain that you feel in your head

when you're just coming round, after heavy medication. I didn't move. I just lay there, trying to remember; trying to think back . . . in bits . . . just in bits, here and there . . . beginning to remember . . . the wallet . . . *my* wallet . . . but before that . . . the sun, blazing . . . burning . . . the headache . . . my eyes . . . the splitting pain behind my eyes . . . and wondering how I was going to tell my Mam . . . how I could even get home . . . get back . . . to Failsworth . . . and my Uncle Bastard . . . blaming me, blaming me, telling me I couldn't do anything right . . .

But I tried! . . . I know I did my best . . . I gave up everything. Gave up you, Morrissey. And still it didn't work!

I know now!

I know . . . it could never have worked. But I tried.

That's why I wore the boots, the stupid jeans and the hideous Springsteen top. That's why I didn't try and argue or even get gobby and answer back; why I just shrugged and said nowt, that morning, at the site when I turned up for work and the Ganger said I looked like 'a right fuckin' wanker!'

He asked me what I was doing bringing my bags to work with me. I told him I hadn't been able to get into my digs because I had no money.

'And that's why I was wondering,' I said, 'if I could have a sub till the end of the week, just a few quid, enough to pay my deposit.'

He looked at me with one eyebrow raised. And then he said, 'Where d' y' think y' are, son, Social fuckin' Services?' And then he just turned round and said, 'Come on, shift y' arse an' follow me.'

He went striding off and I almost had to run to keep up with him.

He kept glaring at me and then he said, 'There's no favours here, y' know. I'm givin' y' a start and that's all. The rest's up to you. Y' pull your weight or you'll be fucked off, uncle or no uncle! D' you understand?'

I nodded. And then I saw where he was taking me,

leading me towards the place where the big lorries with the cement-mixer backs were pouring out the thick wet liquid. And I knew then, I knew he was putting me on the Readymix. Just from listening to my Uncle Jason, I knew it was a killer, shovelling the Readymix, because it looks like nothing but it's so heavy and you can't stop or take a breather because it goes off so fast and you have to keep working it while it's still wet. That's why he'd said, my Uncle Jason, said, 'So they'll probably start you on something a bit easier, making the tea and doing some wheelbarrow work till you've had the chance to build up a bit of muscle on those spindles of yours. Arms like sparrow legs, you wouldn't last half an hour on the Readymix.'

That's why I said it to him, Morrissey, the Ganger man; I didn't moan or whinge but I just said, 'Is there nothing else I could do at first? Because my Uncle said I haven't got the muscle for the Readymix yet and it might be better if I build my muscles up a bit first.'

He looked taken aback. But then he recovered and said, 'Hey! What the fuck d' y' think this is, *Fitness World*? It's a building site, not a fuckin' gym. Your uncle!' he said. 'Your uncle! Forget your fuckin' uncle. *I*'m the Ganger on this site. Your uncle might be up the arse of the QS but I'm the Ganger here, I'm the one who decides what's fuckin' what on this site! So take your pick,' he said, throwing the shovel at me. I went to catch it but I missed and it just clattered onto the ground.

'Either get stuck in with them and start shovelling,' he said, 'or y' can sling your fuckin' hook.'

I looked down the bank, where the Readymix was coiling out of a pipe like giant grey toothpaste while a gang of stripped-shirt, bare-backed builders shovelled together in some kind of unison, like silent rhythm boys, like a chain gang, the sweat pouring off them. It was still only just gone eight o'clock in the morning, but even then the sun was already bright and burning and you could tell it was going to be one of those days

470

when the tar on the roads bubbles up like cheese beneath the grill.

I saw the brown-backed labourers looking back at me, looking peeved and pissed off as they started muttering to each other. Then one of them, the youngest one who didn't look much older than me, shouted up to the Ganger, saying, 'Y' not thinkin' of putting him with us, are y'? We need another man, not a fuckin' streak of piss like that!'

I just looked back at him. And I could quite happily have slung my hook right there and then. I was frightened, Morrissey; frightened that I'd make a fool of myself, that I'd be too shagged out and feeble and laughed at, or worse. But I knew; if it was a new start then it had to be a brand spanking new start. They didn't know me, none of them knew me; I wasn't Raymond Marks, I wasn't anybody, just a new face, that's all. They didn't know who I was or what I was. So I didn't *have* to be Raymond Marks. It *was* a new start! And that's why I suddenly bent down and snatched up the shovel. And pushing past the Ganger man, I walked down the bank, staring all the while at the labourer who'd called me a streak of piss. And when I got near enough, I stopped and I said, 'What the fuck's your problem?'

He slowly straightened up. But I didn't flinch, Morrissey. And I could see him sizing me up, wondering whether he should go for me. But then one of the older ones told him, 'Hey, come on, keep fuckin' shovellin'. In heat like this it's setting faster than plaster of fuckin' Paris. Now come on.'

The young labourer stared at me for a second longer, before lifting his shovel and filling it again as he told me, 'My problem, mate, is that my bonus is on the line here. So if we're lumbered with someone who can't hack it, I'm not gonna be very fuckin' happy, am I?'

I'd never really prayed before, Morrissey, not really. But I did then! As I moved across, lifted my shovel and swung it into the sludgy mound of thick wet mix, I just prayed with all my heart that I'd have the strength to carry it off, to survive.

It looked easy, looked like there was no weight at all, the way they swung their shovels like they were shovelling air. But I knew, as I plunged my shovel into the mix and lifted, as I felt the strain at the top of my arms I knew, as I bent and straightened and shovelled the mix deep down in the trench before turning and bending and shovelling and lifting and throwing it off in the trench again, I knew; that if he'd never been right about anything else in all of his appalling life, my Uncle Bastard Jason had been right about shovelling Readymix. It wasn't that each shovelful was particularly heavy. It was the accumulation, like all those single shovelfuls taking their toll and stretching the muscles, slowly sapping the strength from within, while outside, up above, the sun blistered down, baking the napes of the necks and the backs of the shovellers shovelling the mix and filling the trenches.

Nobody spoke to me. Nobody said a word. And I was glad, because it was taking every ounce of energy I had just to make even a respectable attempt at keeping up with them. I knew I wasn't doing very well, Morrissey, not compared with them, the rest of the gang, with their big thick muscles and their tender tattoos. The worst thing was that I was sweating so much that it kept running into my eyes and stinging them so that I had to keep lifting up the front of my vest and wiping my eyes so that I could still see properly. I know I wasn't very good. But at least I was trying, trying my best. And at least no-one was slagging me off or taking the piss. And I concluded that they must have just decided to ignore me. Which is why I didn't really hear him at first, the older one. But then he knocked me on the arm and when I looked up he was holding out a piece of rag. Then he motioned to me to tie it around my head. I was just about to tell him it was bad enough wearing a Springsteen tee shirt without having a Willie Nelson headband as well.

But he nodded and said, 'Keep the sweat out y' eyes.'

And so I didn't say anything, Morrissey. I just nodded back and tried to tell him thanks; but he was already back shovelling, as I paused, tying on the head-rag, grateful for the kindness; and grateful for the breather, for just those tiny seconds where my back could stay straight for a moment and my arms feel free of the shovel. I took the opportunity to pull off my soaking vest as well. And as I did, I noticed that my fingers were shaking uncontrollably. I could barely hold them still enough to tie the headband around my head. And then, when I finally did get it tied and picked up the shovel again, I was almost sorry I'd stopped, because after just that one tiny break everything felt twice as heavy and harder and ten times more backbreaking than it had done before. Maybe that's why I winced as I bent and began to shovel again. That's when I caught his eye and saw that he was watching me, the younger lad. I half expected him to laugh, or kick off again about his bonus and how I was holding them back. But he said nothing; and I wasn't entirely sure, but he seemed to nod at me. I just kept on trying to keep up.

Until I heard someone saying, 'Swing.'

I looked up and it was the young labourer. He was talking to me. 'Don't stab at it,' he said. 'Let the shovel do the work. Swing with it.'

He showed me what he meant, his shovel swinging easily and slicing into the mix like a knife into butter, his body following through and the filled shovel lifting up, before he turned and sent the mix shooting down into the trench, the whole graceful thing like it was one seamless movement. I tried it, letting the shovel swing like he said and bending into it as I did. Then I heard one of the others saying, 'That's more like it. Don't try and fight the fuckin' stuff because it'll kill y'. Work *with* it.'

'That's it,' the younger one said, 'keep the rhythm. It's easier if y' keep in rhythm.'

I nodded. And tried to do what he said, tried to do it like they all did. I knew I still couldn't keep up with them, not really. But doing it like they said, going with the rhythm of it, *feeling* the rhythm of the way it was working, I knew I could keep going. Even though I'd end up more knackered than I'd ever been knackered in my whole life, I knew I could survive it. And I think they all knew as well, because they seemed to relax a bit. The work didn't slacken but as they shovelled they started talking and laughing amongst themselves. And I was glad; because even though they weren't talking to me, at least they were able to forget about me instead of being suspicious and pissed off, worried that I'd hold them back and make them lose out on their bonus. I didn't even expect them to talk to me. That's why it didn't register at first. Until I realised the one with the snake tattoo on each arm was asking me where I was from. I didn't think they would have heard of Failsworth, so I told them Manchester. And straight away then, they asked me what team I supported. I was about to tell them that I didn't support any team and I never ever watched football. But I didn't, and instead I said, 'Manchester United.'

They laughed and jeered, and one of them said, 'Man United? Shite United more like!' They all laughed again. And I knew I was supposed to go back at them and counter with something suitably disparaging about their team. But I didn't even know who their team were. So I said, 'Who do you all support?'

They said, Grimsby Town. And even I knew that in the hierarchy of English football, a lowly Grimsby Town supporter didn't even have the right to *mention* Manchester United, let alone insult them! But still I couldn't think of a sufficiently authentic-sounding insult to throw back at them. And I could see it was expected, that if I was to have any credibility as a football supporter I'd have to come up with something. And maybe that's why it suddenly popped into my head, the little piece of verse I'd written when I'd

474

been on that coach with all them Grimsby trades-people.

So that's what I said to them, the Grimsby Town-supporting Readymix shifters. Still shovelling, I told them, 'Grimsby! Oh Grimsby/One look's all it takes/To prove even God/Can make mistakes!'

They suddenly all looked somewhat stunned. They even stopped shovelling! And I realised I'd gone too far. But then, as I was trying to figure a way out of it with them all stood there staring at me, almost as one they suddenly started laughing. And the older one even said, 'Tell us that again.'

So I did. And as we all went back to work, I heard him repeating it to himself, ' "Grimsby! Oh Grimsby/One look's all it takes..." ' Then he was chuckling to himself as he said, 'Fuckin' right that an' all!'

The younger lad said, 'Where did you hear that then?'

I just shrugged and said, 'I forget. I think I just read it somewhere.'

He nodded and carried on with the shovelling as everything fell quiet again.

And, Morrissey, I wanted to tell them that I'd written it! That bit of verse that had tickled them. It was me who'd made that up and I hadn't read it in a book. I wanted to tell them – it was the first time that one of my own lyrics had ever been aired in public!

Then I realised that I couldn't tell them. Because they'd probably think I was lying or mark me down as being weird. And anyway I wasn't a lyric writer! Not any more. I was just the new lad on the end of a shovel. I'd given up lyric writing. I was doing all right, managing to hold my own, as part of a gang on a building site. I'd had enough of being weird. I just kept on shovelling and kept my mouth shut about matters such as lyric writing.

I worked like they'd told me, going with the rhythm, keeping time, shovelling, lifting, bending and lifting and shovelling, shovelling the thick wet mix ... shovelling faster than ever today, they said, because of the weather, the hot hot weather, the blazing sun, the stripped-off shirts and the baking heat that blasts and burns and turns the Readymix block-solid and useless in no time at all ... no time to stand and fuck about when the weather's like this, when the sun's full out and blazing down, baking the napes of the necks and the backs of the shovellers shovelling the mix and filling the trenches till your body's not you, it's just a machine; and your mind disappears, goes off some-where else, lost in a kind of empty trance.

And that's why, at first, I thought it was just some-thing inside my head, because most of the time, Morrissey, sometimes without me even being aware of it, there'll be one of your songs buzzing away inside my head. But then I heard the moans and groans and shouts of protest and realised that, anyway, it wasn't even your voice I was hearing. It was his, Morrissey, the young labourer lad's. As he was working he'd broken into song and now all his mates were shouting at him, telling him to give up and give over and if he wanted to sing he should sing something with a bit of life to it instead of 'that fuckin' morbid dirge'.

He ignored them though, and I saw the devilment in his eyes as he wound them up and sang even louder, sang, '*I was happy in the haze of a drunken hour/But heaven knows I'm miserable now ...*'

Seeing me watching, he smiled and winked as the older fellers kept up their barrage of protest. Then he suddenly stopped singing and called out to the rest of them, saying, 'Shut y' whinging! Y' all fuckin' ancient, youse, y' know nowt. That's a quality song, that is!' He turned and looked at me again. 'Isn't it?' he said.

But I just shrugged.

And he said, 'Don't y' rate him then? Morrissey?'

I just shrugged again. And I said, 'He's all right. I suppose.'

Morrissey, I'm sorry! I wanted to tell him!

476

But he just broke out singing again, '*I was happy in the haze of a drunken hour . . .*'

And then all his mates ganged up against him and all started singing at the top of their discordant voices, singing 'Radio GooGoo', that stupid Queen song, singing it louder and louder and louder until they'd drowned out the young labourer so that he just gave up and went back to shovelling in silence.

And I wanted to tell him, Morrissey, that he wasn't alone, that there was another fan on that building site.

Only I wasn't, Morrissey, not any longer. I'd renounced you!

It was all right for him, the young labourer, he could be a fan and still get by, because he'd already proved himself in the gnarled-knuckle world of the building site. But if I'd gone there with my quiff and my tee shirt and all of my Morrisseyness intact, I never would have had a chance. And as it was, I was managing. I was getting by. That's why I just kept on shovelling, saying nowt; and doing my best to ignore all my natural instincts, Morrissey; to ignore *you*!

I just wanted to belong, that's all. And I know now, I know it's pathetic. But when I was with them, working, I felt as if I was achieving something and even making some kind of progress. And I know, Morrissey, I know it's ridiculous because the only thing I was doing was helping fill up a trench with a load of concrete, while getting baked beneath the sun and so shagged out that by the time it got to dinnertime I could barely begin to lift my legs and drag myself across to the corrugated-iron hut that served as a sort of canteen. It was only a couple of hundred yards away but it could have been a hundred miles, the way my legs felt as if all the life had leaked out of them. And I don't think I would have made it at all if I hadn't overheard them, the old feller and the labourer with the snake tattoos.

They must have thought I'd already gone across to the canteen, but I was just sat there slumped on the ground at the back of the Readymix truck. They were around the other side, washing their hands under the stop tap, and I heard him, the snake-tattoo man, as he said to the older man, 'Lookin' at him this morning, I thought he'd be a waste of fuckin' space. But he's not doin' so bad.'

'Aye,' the old feller agreed, 'I wouldn't have put tuppence on him *holding* a shovel, let alone using one.'

I heard them both laughing. And then the snake-tattoo man said, 'Aye, if he sets his mind to it, he's got the makings of a good little grafter!'

Morrissey, I know it was stupid! I'm even embarrassed just telling you. But when I overheard them saying that, I felt this small rush of pride! I don't know what was wrong with me, but as I struggled to my feet and started following after them, dragging myself towards the canteen I felt . . . I felt a small sense of belonging; of being part of something!

And I might have carried on feeling like that, Morrissey, feeling as if I was getting somewhere; feeling that, if nothing else, I was at least holding down a job. But even when I was making my way over to the corrugated-iron hut, I was already starting to feel a bit light-headed and woozy. I was starting to shake, and tremble, like I'd got the 'knock', like all my energy had been burned up and the only way to bring it back was to get some food inside of me like they do in the Tour de France when they've pedalled over the Pyrenees and burned up all their energy so they have to stuff Mars bars into their mouths to stop them shaking. And that's what I thought it was with me, just a bit of light-headedness because I was so starving hungry that all my insides were trembling and screaming out for the want of some food. By the time I got inside the hut and joined the queue at the counter, I knew that I'd never even begin to get through the afternoon and a load more shovelling unless I could get some strength back. That's why I decided I was going to have the biggest dinner I'd ever had in my life, with loads of carbohydrates like the athletes have, with double helpings

478

and extra chips, loads of bread and the thickest, stickiest pudding they'd got.

Then I put my hand in my pocket and pulled out my money. And remembered that all I had left from what Cindy-Charlene had given me was 65p! 65p! And even just a portion of chips cost 35p!

I was just stood there looking at the chalked-up menu board, realising that all I could afford was chips, gravy and one thin slice of bread. Or perhaps chips and peas instead of the gravy. Or just chips with two slices of bread. And then I was thinking it might even be best to have just peas with five slices of bread – when I saw him! Further along, down towards the front of the queue! Him! The truck driver who'd robbed all my money. The Greasy-Gobbed Get who'd robbed my wallet. And there it was! Being held out in his fat hands, one hand holding it open and the other extracting a ten-pound note and passing it over to the girl at the till, *my wallet*!

And then I saw him turning away from the front of the queue, with a tray in his hands; and I even remembered then, remembered him saying that his job sometimes took him all the way over to the east coast; the bastard, the Incredible Bulk of a bacon-chewing bastard who'd taken my wallet from my bag, leaving me penniless and destitute and having to hitch and beg and borrow just to get myself to Grimsby. Leaving me without so much as my deposit for my digs or enough to buy myself a decent dinner!

And now here he was turning away from the front of the queue, with a tray in his fat hands; and on it a big plate piled high with chips, two eggs, big black pudding pieces, sliced tomatoes, beans and mushrooms along with half a loaf of thick buttered bread and next to that a steaming pudding bowl. And all of it paid for with money from my wallet!

I know, Morrissey, I know now, I should perhaps have proceeded with a bit more caution. But I was starving and weak with hunger; and there was him lifting all his overflowing dishes from the tray and laying them out on the table. I watched him as he sat down and started laughing and talking with the other men at the table, the men I'd been working with. I watched as he put down the wallet, *my* wallet, at the side of his dinnerplate. And I didn't even have to worry, Morrissey, because I could *prove* it was my wallet. I could! Because what he didn't know was that inside the wallet, on the back panel, in purple felt-tip pen I'd inscribed it, Morrissey; inscribed it with words of yours. It was the night before I'd left Failsworth. The night that I knew I was going to have to give you up, Morrissey – give you up and go to Grimsby and try and make a go of it. And inside that wallet I'd written the words, '*Will nature make a man of me yet?*'

And that's why I left the queue and started picking my way through the tables, looking at him all the time, watching him as he opened his big mouth and laughed at something one of the others said, laughed like I'd seen him laugh before, with his fat mouth full of food so that you could see all the chewed-up chips and black pudding mixed up with egg yolk and sauce and saliva. He didn't see me though. Didn't look up, didn't notice. Nobody seemed to notice me, even when I was stood there at the side of the table. They were all talking, the labourers, laughing and talking and telling jokes. I ignored them. And kept staring at the Greasy-Gobbed Get, waiting for him to realise, to look up and recognise me. But it was one of the labourers who noticed me first, the one with the snake tattoos. 'Y' all right?' he asked.

But I didn't answer him. I just kept looking at the wallet robber. And in the end it was the young labourer who nudged him, so that he finally looked up from his plate. And, at last, he was staring at me, staring into the face of the person he thought he'd never see again, the person whose wallet he'd robbed.

'Yes! That's right,' I said to him, 'it's me!'

He tried to pretend! Straight away, he tried to

pretend. Looking at me with a puzzled frown on his fat face and then turning to the others, indicating me with a nod of his head as he said, 'One of your lads?'

The labourers all shook their heads. Then the older one shrugged and said, 'He was just with us this morning.'

Then the Greasy-Gobbed Get turned back to me and said, 'I think you've made a mistake, son. You've got the wrong party!'

But I didn't flinch, Morrissey. I just kept staring and even smiling slightly as I shook my head and said, 'Oh no I haven't! I've got exactly the right party! The party from Birch Services, on the M62!'

He still tried to pretend, Morrissey. He frowned at me and said, 'What the fuck are y' talking about, son?'

I nodded. I pointed at him. And said, 'I'm talking about you! And what you stole from me yesterday.'

All the others were looking at him then, Morrissey. And I knew he must be getting hot under the collar then, because he said, 'What are y', a fuckin' druggie or what?'

But I just shook my head, smiling at him, smiling in triumph as I said, 'I can prove it! I can prove that you stole my wallet.'

And I know that must have rattled him because he suddenly became really narked then as he pointed at me with his fork and said, 'Now listen! Fuck off, y' little twat. I've never even fuckin' set eyes on y' before. Go on, fuck off!'

But I didn't, Morrissey. I didn't 'fuck off', because I knew! 'Right then,' I said, pointing at it, 'all right! If that's not my wallet, then how come I know what's inscribed inside the back panel?'

He picked up the wallet from the table and pointing it at me, he said, 'I'll fuckin' inscribe you in a minute!'

But that's where he made his big mistake, Morrissey, because as he was pointing at me with the wallet, that's when I snatched it out of his hand! And the look of surprise on his face, Morrissey, it was like he was so

481

stunned, he couldn't even move. And before he could recover, I handed the wallet to the young labourer and said, 'Go on, go on. I haven't looked inside it, have I? But if you open it and look inside the back panel – go on, look in there and I'll tell you what it says, the words, the words in there. I know what they are because I put them in there and if it wasn't my wallet then I wouldn't know, would I, would I?'

They were all looking at me, Morrissey. All of them, even the Greasy-Gobbed Get, sitting there and looking mutely back at me. And I knew why, I knew why, because it was all up, the game was up and they all knew. 'Go on,' I told the young labourer, 'open the wallet.'

He seemed a bit apprehensive. But then he looked at the Greasy-Gobbed Get who nodded. He'd given up! He knew I'd caught him red-handed and there was no point denying it any longer. The young labourer opened up the wallet and looked inside.

'The panel at the back,' I told him. 'Look in there.'

He did. And then I said, 'Can you see what's written there?'

He nodded.

'Right,' I said, and they were all staring at me, 'written inside the back of the wallet are the words, *"Will nature make a man of me yet?"* '

The young labourer looked at me. Then he looked back at the wallet. I could see the rest of the gang, wide-eyed and waiting, like they were in the betting shop waiting to hear the results. I could see the Greasy-Gobbed Get, his face a stony mask, as if he was trying to pretend that none of this was happening to him. I almost felt sorry for him. And then I heard him, the young labourer, as he announced, ' *"Made in Italy"* !'

They all burst out laughing, Morrissey! And one of the labourers reached across saying, 'Here, let's have a look.'

They were all still laughing as the other labourer said, 'Y' right, *"Made in Italy"*. It says nowt else here.'

Morrissey, I want you to understand that I *wasn't* thieving. I thought they were lying, covering up for the Greasy-Gobbed Get. And that's why I did it. Why I snatched the wallet as it was being passed from one pair of hands to the next. And if none of them had leaped up and started coming after me, I wouldn't have run anywhere with it. I was only trying to get far enough away so that I could look inside and see for myself before they took the wallet back off me and carried on pretending that your words weren't inscribed inside, when I knew they were. That's the only reason I went running, dodging between the tables and out of the canteen, so that I could prove that they were all lying. And that's why I was pulling out the money! Not because I was taking it or trying to steal it! I was pulling it out so that I could see inside the wallet properly! Because I must have inscribed the words much deeper down than I'd remembered. Or maybe it wasn't even inside the back panel. Maybe I'd just got mixed up and written the words inside the *front* panel. That's why I was pulling everything out and just letting it all fall to the ground, the pictures of the baby, the driving licence, receipts, credit cards, club membership, the packet of condoms, bits of scrap. I wasn't trying to steal anything, Morrissey. I was just looking for the words; the words that weren't there!

If I'd been trying to steal anything, Morrissey, I would still have been trying to get away, wouldn't I? But when they all came running up to me, I was just stood there, feeling really woozy and light-headed again. I didn't like being back out in the sun. It was glaring into my eyes and making the skin on my arms and shoulders feel all uncomfortable and prickly. That's why I was just stood there, Morrissey. In a sort of trance really, with all the money and all the bits and pieces from someone else's wallet all around me!

They said I was a 'fuckin' thievin' bastard'. They told me to pick everything up and put it back in the wallet. I told them I was sorry. They ignored me. When I'd put it all back and handed it to the man, they told him to check that everything was there. I watched him going through it all, counting his money. And it's funny, but outside in the sun he didn't even look that fat. He didn't have an earring either. Outside in the sun, it was hard to believe how I could ever have mistaken him for the Greasy-Gobbed Get. I said I was sorry again. But they all just kept looking at me, looking a bit shocked and wary. That's when I said to him, the young labourer, I said, 'I made a mistake. But I'm not a thief, I'm not, honest. Because really,' I said, 'I'm a Morrissey fan, just like you.'

I thought he'd understand. But his face twisted into a look of complete disgust as he said, 'What! I'm not a fuckin' Morrissey fan! Just because you heard me singing that miserable shite? I'm no fuckin' Morrissey fan! I just do it for a joke, to wind them up!' He pointed at me then and said, 'Don't fuckin' accuse me of liking that twisted bastard!'

Him and his mates just stood there and carried on staring at me then, as if I was even weirder than I'd seemed before. The man with the wallet announced that everything seemed to be in order and none of his money was missing. They started debating whether they should call in the police. But as they were doing that, the Ganger came running up, saying he'd heard what had been going on. When he saw me, he said, 'Well, I should have fuckin' well known, shouldn't I? It obviously runs in the family with you lot, doesn't it? Like your uncle! Like uncle, like fuckin' nephew!'

And that's when he pushed me, Morrissey, pushed me so hard that I fell over, sprawling on the ground. And then he was pulling me, dragging me back to my feet and propelling me along, pulling me by my vest and dragging me with it, dragging me all the way to the Portakabin, where he told me to get my gear and get the fuck out of it before he called the police and had me arrested. Then he aimed a kick at me and sent me running and stumbling out of the gates and up the narrow lane, all the while trying to keep to the side that was in shadow, to keep out of the sun. I hated the sun! It was making me feel sick, whenever I looked at the light or felt the heat of it directly on me. I didn't know where I was going, didn't have any idea; I was just stumbling along, reeling from side to side like the drunk men do. And then I had to sit down, leaning my back against the building-site boards and just sitting there, feeling frightened and panicky and wondering, wondering what was happening to me; trying to tell myself that it couldn't be happening again. Only it was, Morrissey. I knew it was! Because it was starting to be like it was before, when I was in Swintonfield and being paranoid, when I was seeing things, seeing people who weren't there, seeing the Greasy-Gobbed Get when there'd been no Greasy-Gobbed Get. And that same morning in Cleethorpes, when I'd sat and stared out across the sands, I'd been seeing things then, seeing the girl; when there was no way that she could possibly have been there, the Girl with the Chestnut Eyes.

And even the man, Morrissey, the night before, the American man who'd dropped me in Grimsby. He was probably just somebody inside my head. I should have known, should have known that it was starting then, when a middle-aged grey-haired man was singing along to Smiths' songs and said he had a son back in New York City. Maybe he meant Malcolm! Perhaps that's who he was, Malcolm's dad who used to be in the Beach Boys.

But there was no Malcolm, was there? There was never any Malcolm. There was never any American man who'd driven off with my guitar in the boot. I'd just lost it somewhere and couldn't remember where.

It was all happening again! That's why I knew I had to try and get home, before it was too late; before I no longer knew who I was any more. My head was aching though, aching so much that I couldn't bear to open my eyes. And I had no money, no way of getting home. But I had to!

I pushed myself up and tried to move along the lane, leaning on the chipboard wall, stumbling along to the end of the lane till I got to the road that leads down to the docks. I reached the traffic lights, the ones with the yellow sign for the building site. But I couldn't bear it, the traffic, the noise of the traffic, the smell of the fumes from the cars and the lorries and the heat, the heat, coming down from the sky, coming up from the ground, the heat. I had to sit down again, sit down anywhere, just there, on the pavement, anywhere, it didn't matter, leaning up against the traffic-light pole, my eyes closed against the light, head spinning, my ears ringing with the noise, the noise of the traffic and the wheels and the squeals and the thundering roar and then the voice, the American voice, shouting, calling, saying, 'Hey, Kid! . . . Raymond?'

'Go away!' I started shouting at the voice, covering my ears to cut it out, starting to jibber and jabber so that I couldn't hear it inside my head, the voice . . . the voice saying, 'Jesus Christ! What the fuck happened? Raymond? Kid, come on . . . it's OK, OK.'

'Go away,' I told the voice in my head, 'go away go away go away . . . leave me leave me go away . . .'

But it wouldn't. It was still there, still in my head, saying, 'Jesus, what happened to you? Can't you talk . . . can you hear? Can you hear me?'

That's when I felt the hands! Hands on my hands, gently tugging them away from my ears as the voice said, 'Can you open your eyes? Can you try? Please . . .'

And I thought that might make it go away, like it sometimes did in Swintonfield when somebody had hold of me, like the Man with the Upside-Down Head, but if I opened my eyes then they wouldn't be there any more.

Only this time it didn't work, because he was still

486

there, Malcolm's dad, kneeling in front of me, pretending to be real, pretending he knew things.

'I've been lookin' for you,' he said. 'I didn't know where the hell to find you. I opened up the boot and there was your guitar. I looked for you. What happened to you? What happened to your clothes? I almost drove straight by you.'

I started frowning. I blinked and looked at him again. He seemed worried and anxious. His eyes were full of concern as he said, 'Jesus, you really are in a bad way.'

Morrissey, that's when I began to wonder! When I even started to hope that he might be real.

That's why I nodded when he said, 'Look, do you think you could stand?'

I pushed myself up as best I could, with my back against the traffic light pole till I was standing, and shivering now, shivering in the burning hot heat of the day. He was looking at me really intently. And he said, 'Hey! You're gonna be OK, you know that? You're gonna be OK.'

That's when I felt the salty sting of a tear running down my cheek; when I didn't even care any more whether he was real or not, because it was just so nice having someone who was smiling at me, being nice to me, picking up my bag and helping me and asking me if I could manage the few steps around the corner, where the car was parked.

I began walking, following, wishing that the pain in my head wasn't so bad, that my skin didn't sting, that my legs didn't feel like they were made of jelly; wishing that the man really was as real as he seemed; as real as the silver Mercedes parked in the side street around the corner, the same silver Mercedes that I'd seen the night before.

That's when I thought it was all right! That it *was* real after all! Really, really real. That's why I tried to start hurrying towards the car, so that I could get out of the sun.

Only I never made it. Because that's when I passed out!

When I saw her, sitting there in the back seat of the car, the Girl with the Chestnut Eyes.

Yours sincerely,
Raymond Marks

22 June 1991
Swallowbrook,
Heaton Wold,
N. Lincolnshire

Dear Mam,

I know that this'll come as a surprise but, honest, you really shouldn't worry about me; because I'm all right, Mam.

I know that my Uncle Jason will have talked to you by now and so you're probably all upset. But Mam, don't even bother listening to him because it's all right; it is, Mam, everything's all right.

I know it's a different sort of *all right* from the all right you expected it to be. And I know how much you were counting on it, me getting a job and settling down and just becoming an ordinary normal person who wouldn't be such a worry to you any more. I understand that, Mam. That's why I went to Grimsby in the first place, because I thought you were right. I even thought my Uncle Jason was right! I thought that if I just made the effort then I really could turn into the sort of ordinary normal lad that I know you've always wanted me to be. And Mam, *I* even wanted it to be like that as well! That's why I tried. I tried really hard. Only I think I've come to realise now, Mam, that if you're

489

not naturally normal then it's pointless really, thinking that you can change and become somebody who fits in. I think it must be a bit like being homosexual and if that's what you are then that's what you are; and that's all there is to it.

I don't mean that *I'm* homosexual, Mam! I know you've always thought that I might be. But I'm not. I know I always loved Twinky and Norman and I always will love them. And I wouldn't ever have minded even if I had been homosexual. But the fact is, Mam, that I'm not. All I am is not normal. And being here, where nobody seems normal, it feels quite normal really, not being normal.

That's what Jo said, she said, 'Looking at us all here, I'm not surprised you mistook it for a mental institution.'

She's really nice, Mam, Jo. She's not my girlfriend. But she's my friend. And although she doesn't live there any more, Mam, she originally comes from Failsworth! I didn't really know her before I came here although I did talk to her once, at the bus stop by the bottle bank on the boulevard. And then when I was trying to get to Grimsby, I saw her in a motorway service station. Unfortunately there was a bit of unpleasantness in there and so we didn't get to talk that time. But Jo says if she'd known I was coming over to this side of the country she could have given me a lift. She's only seventeen but she's driving already and she's got her own car. She says, 'It's just a bit of a bin really!'

But you can tell she's dead proud of it. Sometimes she gets up really early and drives over to the coast, to go walking on the sand as the sun's still rising. She says she likes it, being out at that time of the morning, and that's when she does some of her best writing. She let me read some of her poems. I think they're quite good really. In fact I think they're quite brilliant, some of them. But I might be a bit biased though.

Mam, I know that you probably won't believe me, but I really am truly all right! And sometimes I feel *so* all right, I get frightened that it might not be real and I might wake up at any minute.

I *know* I'm not on a building site, Mam, and I know you've probably had to put up with all kinds from my Uncle Jason and my Aunty Paula, just like you've always had to put up with them picking and patronising and pitying you because you had a son who turned out to be like me. I'm sorry, Mam. I never meant to turn out like I did. And I know how much you wanted me to be a normal, ordinary, invisible boy who just did all the normal things and never got picked on. Remember that summer, Mam, the first summer that nobody would play with me and so I couldn't go footballing or camping or playing tick and hide-and-seek on the recreation ground any more? And you said it broke your heart to see me like that; you said you couldn't wait for the day when you'd be able to look up and see me once again running with all the others, headlong and careless on the recreation ground, unaware and easy with the beauty of belonging.

Well, I know it probably seems as though it's taken for ever, Mam; and I know that you sort of gave up hope and don't even bother looking up any longer. But Mam, if you could see me here now, if you could see me sat beneath the beams in this converted barn, where I'm writing this with Jo sat across the table from me, the two of us scribbling away, each absorbed in what we're doing but each of us giving a sort of strength to the other, if you could see it, Mam, I know that it would be just like looking up at the recreation ground and seeing me there again, where I belonged.

Mam, that's what it feels like here; like I'm no longer out of place. And I wish you could see it, Mam, the house and the barn and everything; because you know that old biscuit box of yours where you keep your private things and all your jewellery, the box with the painted countryside picture of the house in the distance and the fields all full of the abundance of nature, well, that's what it's like here, Mam. The house is all on its own in the middle of fields and you have to come down a long dusty track just to get to it. We go walking sometimes, across the fields and down to the river. The river's quite low at this time of year and with the heatwave it's even more shallow than usual. Jo goes further down though, by the poplar trees where there's a deep pool and she says the water's so cold there, she thinks it must be fed by an underground spring and that's why it stays so deep even with the rest of the river nearly dried up. I'm going to go swimming there myself, when I can. I've got to wait a bit though because of my back and my shoulders.

I've been a bit ill, Mam.

But don't worry, I'm all right now. And I don't mean ill like I used to be! It's just physical, Mam. See, when I was on the building site, working outside in the sun, I didn't even know it was one of the hottest days of the year. Tom says that if I'd worn a hat or even a handkerchief over my head then it wouldn't have been quite so bad. He says my skin would still have got burnt and I'd still be peeling like I am now; but I wouldn't have ended up so delirious with the sun-stroke. I didn't realise that Tom was a doctor. But in his ordinary life that's what he is. And that's why, when Ralph found me, down by the fish docks, he brought me straight back here, because he knew that Tom would know what to do. Tom said it's the ultraviolet rays that do it – when your head's exposed to the sun for too long, the ultraviolet goes straight through your skull and so it's a bit like having part of your brain microwaved. And that's what makes you go all doolally and delirious.

Mam, it's all right though! My brain's back to normal now. My skin's still sore and peeling but I don't mind that so much, apart from the fact that it stops me going swimming with Jo. My arms and my back, Mam, they just look hideous and that's why I keep my shirt on. I told Jo I couldn't go in the water yet because I was too sore. But really it's just because I don't want her to see it, all my skin peeling and flaking and looking horrible. It might make her feel sick! Like it always made me feel sick when my Uncle Jason came back from the Canary Islands or the West Indies or somewhere and him and my Aunty Paula and the gruesome twosome were always sunburned to bits, like barbecued brats, and my Uncle Jason's big nose was always peeling and flaking and bits of it would fall off into his tea and he'd just carry on drinking it!

That's why I don't want Jo to see me flaking all over the place. I know it's stupid really, me still trying to hide something like that when I know so much about what Jo's had to go through. It's just that I don't want to make her feel sick. And I suppose I don't want to risk it that she might go off me. I know that she's not my girlfriend and I'm not even trying to make her become my girlfriend. But she's really easy with me and relaxed and when we're in the lounge at night with all the others, sitting on one of the big settees, listening to Ralph or somebody who's reading out a story, Jo sometimes just holds my hand or leans her head against my arm like she's snuggling up to me. And it's lovely, Mam! Because even though she's not my girlfriend, I know how much she likes me. And it's brilliant, being liked so much by a girl like Jo.

And I know really it probably wouldn't make any difference at all, even if she did see my scabby skin. I just feel a bit embarrassed about it, that's all. And I know it's stupid because Jo saw me when I was demented and delirious and even that didn't put her off!

It was the sunstroke, Mam, it made me woozy in the head and stumbling like a drunk man. And then I passed out and apparently I was in a sort of fever and became confused and delirious. That's why I thought I was in a kind of mental institution! When I first got here I thought it was a hospital! The day when I woke up, when I finally came round, I saw them out of the window, all the strange people wandering about on

493

the lawns, some of them with their lips moving ten
to the dozen but without any words coming out; and
others talking to themselves, mumbling and jibber-
jabbering and suddenly shouting out and swearing at
the tops of their voices, just like the Tourette's sufferers
always did in Swintonfield; and others talking all posh
and fluty, saying the same thing over and over again
like some of the old ones in Swintonfield when they
were all deluded and thought they were the late King
George or Bertrand Russell. It was just like that, Mam,
just the same; like at Swintonfield, on the nice afternoons, when all the pathetic patients wandered the
lawns on the march of the broken-hearted.

And the girl, Mam, this girl that I thought I kept
imagining, like I used to keep imagining the Lerts and
the man behind the curtain, the Man with the Upside-
Down Head; remember that, Mam? Well that's one of
the reasons I thought I was back inside some kind
of unit again, because *she* was with them on the lawn,
this girl that I thought I kept imagining, the girl I'd seen
by the bottle bank, the one with the eyes like bright
brown chestnuts.

And as I stared out, watching them all mingling on
the lawn, trance-like, some of them, possessed-looking
and repeating things over and over again, repeatedly
making the same movements like obsessive com-
pulsives, I even saw the American man amongst them,
the one I'd dreamed up somewhere inside my head
where he had a big car, a silver Mercedes, and a stack
of cassettes of Morrissey and The Smiths. I watched
him through the window of the white room, as he
appeared on the lawn and walked into the middle of
all the other patients. And that's when I thought he
must be the doctor, the consultant, like Dr Corkerdale,
because he clapped his hands and as he did that, all
the patients on the lawn stopped whatever they
were doing, stopped moving, stopped talking and
shouting, stopped picking things up and putting them
down, stopped walking round and round in circles.

And I thought the American man must be a really brilliant doctor because it was like all the patients just suddenly stopped being patients! He was standing amongst them, talking to them, talking like he was excited, you could see he was excited. And they were all looking at him, the people, looking and listening, all their eyes on him, following him as he moved around the lawn. And then they were laughing, all of them laughing at once, laughing properly like ordinary people.

And that's when he saw me watching him through the window. I tried to dodge back behind the curtain but he was waving at me with a big delighted smile on his face as he called out to me, saying, 'Raymond! Hey! How are you?'

Then everybody, all the patients, turned and looked, all of them staring at me, some of them pointing, some starting to smile, others lifting up their hands and waving and all of them starting to talk to each other. He was walking forward though, across the lawn, towards the window, talking to me, asking me how I felt and telling me he was sorry; telling me he'd forgotten that my room backed onto the lawn – and that if he had remembered he would have arranged to hold the workshop in the barn and not out on the lawn.

You see, Mam, they weren't mental at all, the people on the lawn! What they all were, were writers, Mam; people who come here to try and learn how to write better. And all they'd been doing on the lawn was going over their lines and rehearsing a play that one of them had written. That's what it is, you see, Mam, it's like a school for writers here.

That's what Ralph is, the American man who brought me here, he's a writer.

Don't worry, Mam, I know what you must be thinking already!

But Mam, honest, this time it's not like Malcolm or Malcolm's dad or anything like that. Ralph really is a *real* person, Mam, and he comes from New York City not Baton Rouge. And if you're worried, Mam, and you don't believe me, you can go down to the library or even to Waterstone's or somewhere like that and if you look under 'G' for Gallagher you'll probably find some of Ralph's books or his plays because even though I'd never heard of him, he's quite famous really, Ralph Gallagher.

It was Ralph who said he'd lend me the money to get back home. It was the day I'd started to feel better.

We were outside, in the shade between the house and the barn, stood on the big brown flagstones, still warm with all the sun they'd soaked up. We were looking out over all the meadows, field after flat field stretching away, all the crops, the green and the yellows shot through with reds and purples, the furthest fields lost in the heat haze that made the distant poplar trees look like dangling worms wriggling on the horizon.

I told Ralph, thanks. I promised that I'd send him the money back as soon as I could.

He nodded. Then he said, 'And what will you do, kid?'

I asked him what he meant.

'When you get back home,' he said, 'what will you do then?'

I just shrugged, and sighed. 'I don't know,' I said, 'I suppose I'll have to try and see about getting a job.'

'Doing what?' Ralph asked.

I shrugged again. 'I don't really know,' I said. 'I don't even know if I'll be able to get a job.'

Ralph nodded and kept looking out over the fields. Then he sniffed and said, 'So why the fuck don't you do what you *should* be doing, Raymond?' He was looking at me with his eyebrows raised.

I frowned at him.

'Ray,' he said, 'I read your book! Your lyric book.'

I could only stare back at him, the frown on my face growing deeper as I tried to understand.

Ralph just watched me. And then he said, 'You want

me to say I'm sorry? You want me to apologise for snooping?'

But he wasn't apologising because he was shaking his head and he said, 'No way, kid! You'll get no apology from me. I'm sorry I had to do it. I don't make a habit of sticking my nose where it don't belong. Only you've got to understand, Ray, when we brought you back here you were in a bad way. We didn't know who you were, where you were from. Jo told us the little she knew – she'd seen you in town, bumped into you in the motorway services. But other than that, we knew nothing. And like I say, you were in no state to make us any wiser. You were raving!'

Ralph nodded at me. 'And that's why I took the liberty of taking a look through your things, to try and find who he was, this kid with the delirium and skin like a spit-roast chicken!'

Ralph just watched me then, sort of studying my face as I stared out over the fields.

'You upset?' he asked. 'Offended? Outraged, just pissed? What?'

I shrugged. I didn't know what I was. I just felt faintly embarrassed really, with my mind racing back through all the private things that Ralph must have read about.

Then I heard him saying, 'Come on. Let's walk.'

He moved off and I followed him towards the arch that led out of the garden and onto the path leading down to the fields. We were walking along by the dried-up marshes. I didn't know what he was going to say, whether he was going to have a go at me about something.

But what he did say was, 'Ray, I love your Gran! Christ, she's wonderful. When she gives that what's-his-name . . . Akela? . . . when she gives him that flea in his ear, Jesus, I wanted to pick her up and kiss her! Fun! Christ, the way she hates fun, I just adore her for that alone.'

I couldn't believe it! Ralph was talking about my

Gran as if he knew her! Talking about her as if she was still alive!

And then he said, 'Do you sustain her throughout?'

I frowned at him.

'Throughout the story,' he said, 'she keeps coming back?'

I nodded. 'Of course,' I said. 'She's my Gran! Of course she keeps coming back until—'

But Ralph suddenly shouted, 'NO!' his hands up as he said, 'Don't! Don't tell me, I don't wanna know, don't give it away! Let me find out for myself when I read the whole thing.'

Ralph nodded again. 'I stopped reading,' he said, 'I forced myself not to go on reading because I knew you'd written it as a personal thing, a private manuscript. That's why I only read it in part. But,' he said, 'I'd love to read it all, if you'd give me permission.'

We'd reached the wooden fence by the cattle grid. Ralph leaned against the fence, looking back towards the house as he said, 'Because although I only read your manuscript in part, Raymond, I read enough to tell me that here is a kid who *needs* to write.'

Ralph looked at me but I didn't know what to say.

Then he nodded back towards the house and sighed as he said, 'See back there, the house? Well, I don't want you to quote me, Ray, but most of the people on this course, nice people, sweet people, probably better people than you and me; but most of them, they only *want* to write.'

He shook his head like it was something that made him sad. Then he turned and looked at me.

'So can you imagine,' he said, 'what a joy it is for me to find that I've got someone here who *needs* to write!?'

I just shrugged. I didn't fully understand him.

But then he nodded and looking back at the house again he said, 'Two or three others on the course, I think they've got it. Jo's one of them. I think she's got real talent. She's got great insight and she can express it. But I'm worried that it's not really working for her, this course. Part of the problem is that there's nobody remotely near her own age. And I think she needs that. I think she needs to be communicating with someone who's culturally closer.'

Ralph turned and looked at me. 'That's one reason', he said, 'that I hope you're gonna stay around. I think it'd be really good for Jo if she had someone closer to her own age.'

I frowned. And looked at him. Then I said, 'What's the other reason?'

Ralph smiled. 'So that I can get to read the rest of the book,' he said. And then, as he pushed himself away from the fence and we started walking back to the house, he said, 'And so I can try and help you be who you should be.'

You see, Mam, that's why I'm not coming home, not yet. But I want you to know that you don't have to worry. I know what my Uncle Jason will say, that I'm just fartarsing about in the country with a bunch of would-be poets and play-actors, being bone idle and useless like I've always been useless. But Mam, I'm not useless, or bone idle; not here. That's why you don't have to worry and fret any more. I'm happy, Mam. So happy that I'm almost frightened to say it; too frightened to breathe sometimes, in case something as soft as a breath could blow it all away.

With all my love,
Raymond

Dear Morrissey,

I know that I said I wasn't going to write to you any
more. But when I said that, Morrissey, it was just
because of all the pressure and me trying to fit in and
everything stupid like that. I know that I owe you an
apology over all that because it must have seemed like
I was trying to turn my back on you. And in a way I
was trying to do that. But Morrissey, I was trying to do
it for the wrong reasons and in the wrong way. The fact
of the matter is, Morrissey, that wherever I go and
whatever I do and wherever I end up and no matter
what happens and how long I live, you will always be
a part of my life. I know that whenever I catch a snatch
of a song leaking out from beneath somebody's door or
blasting out from behind a bar, wherever I am and whoever I'm with, there'll always be that rush inside of me;
a small rush of love and an inward tear for all the times
we shared. And it doesn't even matter and it won't ever
matter that you don't even know that we shared anything at all. Because even though you don't know it,
Morrissey, you did, you shared it all with me.

And that's why I'm writing you this last letter, Morrissey – to say thank you.

And to tell you, Morrissey, about the incredible thing that happened; the thing that even Ralph doesn't know about – and Ralph's even read the lyric book!

You see, she wasn't just here in my imagination, the Girl with the Chestnut Eyes. She was *really* here, Morrissey, here on this writers' course. She's trying to be a poet, you see. That's why she came here, to try and learn how she could be a better writer. Jo says that more than anything else in the world, that's what she wants to be.

And that's why she said she might not even bother going back to school after the summer and finishing her 'A' levels.

I think Ralph got a bit upset when he heard that. He tried to persuade Jo that she should take her exams and then go on to university. Ralph said that being a poet wasn't an occupation and even though Jo's work was really impressive, the chances of her being able to support herself through her writing were extremely slim. But Jo just shrugged and said, 'Ralph, I know that. I've always known that. But why should I spend my time doing "A" levels and going to university when I don't feel the need to?'

Ralph argued and tried to tell her that scholarship and study were not necessarily the enemies of creativity.

But Jo said, 'I *do* study, Ralph. I study really really hard. I'm studying here; I'll always study.'

Ralph kept arguing though, trying to come up with arguments as to why Jo really should go back and do her 'A' levels.

But in the end Jo just interrupted him and said, 'All right then, Ralph, what about you? Did you do your "A" levels, or whatever they're called in America? Did you go to university? And don't say you did because I read it on the dust-jacket of your book where it said you didn't have a formal education.'

Ralph had to admit that Jo was right. And Jo started laughing then, telling him not to be a hypocrite.

But Ralph kept trying to wriggle out of it, saying, 'No . . . look, listen, for Christ sakes stop laughing . . . listen . . . I was . . . I was lucky, OK? Even though I didn't do it formally I really did get myself an education. People I met and worked with, I learned so much from them. But it could've gone the other way. I just happened to be lucky.'

Jo just looked at him. And then she nodded as this smile broke out across her face and she said, 'I know! That's what I'm going to be: lucky!'

Ralph gave up after that. He said to me that with the sort of will Jo had it probably wouldn't matter if she didn't do her 'A' levels.

But even so, he said to me, 'Maybe she'll pay more attention to you, Ray. Try and make her see some sense, huh? She should go back.'

I sort of nodded. Only I never ever did anything about it. Because I knew that Jo would make up her own mind and it was nothing to do with me really.

The first time I'd ever seen her, Morrissey, at the bus stop by the bottle bank on the boulevard, she'd been back in Failsworth to visit her mother. She'd had to come all the way from the Wirral, where she was living with her sister now. That's why I never saw her around Failsworth after that one time at the bus stop; because she didn't come back there very often.

But I didn't know that, not then. The only thing I knew was that she was a Morrissey fan; and that she was the girl whose eyes were the colour of chestnuts.

She's not that now though; she isn't the Girl with the Chestnut Eyes any more; she's just Jo.

All the people here think that we're an item. Ralph says that always happens when there's two young people on the course; all the old ones always like to believe that the two youngsters have fallen in love with each other. Ralph says that's why it happens so much in stories; because it's one of the things that we *need* to happen.

So me and Jo just let them all think what they want. I suppose, in a way, you can't blame them really; with the two of us being together so much of the time. Some of them like to tease us and make these jokes about us being salt and pepper pots or joined at the hip or if you want to find where Jo is look for Raymond – and vice versa.

As you can see, Morrissey, their jokes aren't very witty at all. But like Ralph said, they're very nice people really. And that's why me and Jo just smile. And let them think what they want to think. We just like being together. Like sometimes we even stay up all night together, working side by side in the barn or talking till we fall asleep on one of the big settees in the lounge. Ralph came down to breakfast one morning and found us both curled up there. He didn't wake us up though. He just put a blanket over us.

I said before, Morrissey, that Ralph didn't know. But I sometimes wonder if he put two and two together and just never let on. I don't know. You see, I never even twigged it myself.

When I saw her, that first afternoon after Ralph had told me I could stay, I wasn't shy or anything like that because Ralph had asked me to team up with her and so I told myself I was just doing what Ralph had asked me, doing him a favour.

Even though it was almost evening, I was keeping out of the sun, sitting beneath the beech tree, trying to write something in my lyric book. And when I looked up she was crossing the lawn, walking towards the arch that leads out of the garden and onto the track.

I don't think she'd seen me, not till I stood up. And I said, 'What was the accessory she had, St Joan, when the flames began to melt it?'

She looked up. She almost frowned, hesitating, unsure. But then she smiled and she said, 'A Walkman of course!'

I shrugged. 'Sorry,' I said, 'it was too easy.' Then smiling back at her, I said, 'You still into him?'

She nodded but with a so-so expression on her face as she said, 'Yeah. Sort of.'

We just stood there, both of us nodding. And then it was funny because she didn't ask me if I wanted to go for a walk with her and I didn't ask her if I could come along but we were suddenly just walking along together through the arch and down the track and I was asking her about what sort of writing she did and which writers she liked.

She said she was into all sorts of people but she particularly liked Kit Wright and Liz Lochhead and Carol Ann Duffy.

I just nodded. I'd never heard of them.

And then she said, 'But I'm trying not to read any of them at the moment because their voices are so strong.'

I frowned. 'What do you mean?' I asked.

She shrugged. We were walking past the dried-up marshes where I'd walked with Ralph the night before.

'I mean,' she said, 'well . . . what I think I mean is that I'm trying to . . . sort of . . . find my *own* voice at the moment. But I know it's not strong enough yet. So when I read the likes of Kit Wright or Duffy, I just seem to get drowned out by the strength and power of their voices . . . and I don't mean to but instead of speaking in a voice of my own, I end up speaking in a parody of theirs.'

She nodded. 'I'm sorry,' she said, 'I'm probably not making much sense.'

'No!' I said. 'You are. You're making perfect sense. I know *exactly* what you mean. Because I've been writing songs,' I said, 'and it's taken me ages and ages to realise it but every single one I ever wrote was just crap because every one of them was just second-hand Morrissey. In the end they were all just worthless.'

She looked doubtful. 'Not *all* of them,' she said, 'not every single song you've written.'

I nodded.

'Don't you think you might be in danger of being a bit too self-critical?' she said.

I shook my head. 'No,' I said, 'I even got a second opinion. I played some of my songs to Ralph last night, in the barn. He said they were some of the most pedestrian tunes and execrable lyrics that it had ever been his misfortune to endure!'

She was frowning. But then she suddenly laughed and said, 'He didn't! You're winding me up. Ralph doesn't give criticism in that sort of way. He doesn't even talk like that.'

'I know,' I said, 'he was quite polite really. But that's what he meant! And anyway, I didn't even need Ralph to tell me because I'd come to the same conclusion myself.'

We were crossing the cattle grid, carefully stepping on the iron bits to make sure our feet didn't slip through. She was wearing red sandals. They were brilliant. And I've never really given much thought to sandals before.

'So are you just going to pack it in?' she said. 'Aren't you going to write any more songs?'

I thought about it. Then I sighed and said, 'No, I don't think so. At least not for a while; not until I can try and do it without hearing Morrissey in my head all the time.'

She looked at me. And she said, 'Aren't you into him any more?'

I sighed and I frowned as I thought about it and told her the terrible sort of truth, told her, 'I don't know.'

But it was like she understood because she said, 'It's terrible, isn't it? When you're into someone as much as you were into Morrissey and then suddenly it's not there, not in the same sort of way; the feeling's gone and no matter how much you want it to come back, it won't.'

I nodded. We were walking up the side of the dried-up marshy field. It was lovely, having someone who understood. That's what I wanted to tell her. But I didn't get the chance, not then, because as we moved down the bank towards the river she said, 'I always thought you were the biggest Morrissey fan of them all. Everyone always says that. The last time I was at a Smiths night I heard someone saying that that kid from Failsworth, that Raymond Marks, he's probably the most dedicated Morrissey maniac there is.'

We were walking along the river bed itself, where it was so dried up that it was almost like walking along a track. I thought maybe I hadn't heard her right.

'How did they know my name?' I said.

She shrugged. 'I don't know,' she said, 'I probably told them.'

I just carried on walking. And hoping that the sun wasn't making me go funny again.

'But how did *you* know it?' I said.

She shrugged again. 'Because I do,' she said. 'Because I used to live in Failsworth. I've known it for ages. I've known your name for ages.'

She was staring at me, looking straight into my eyes almost as if – as if she was challenging me.

And then she said it, Morrissey, her voice controlled and firm as she said, 'You don't know who I am, do you?'

I frowned. And shrugged. 'Just . . . Jo,' I said. 'That's all I know . . . that you're called Jo.'

Her gaze never flinching, eyes locked on mine, she nodded as she said, 'Yeah. But I used to be someone else. I used to be Paulette Patterson.'

They say, don't they, Morrissey, people who've survived explosions or had to face a terrible shock, they say it's the small, often unrelated detail that they remember most; like the fact that her eyes weren't really chestnut coloured at all, not when you could see them properly. Perhaps it was the sunlight making them appear much lighter, more amber than I'd remembered; but certainly the image of dark chestnuts was quite wrong, especially now that I was looking at

506

eyes that were wide with a sort of fierce defiance; eyes that were moist and swimmy from the tears that were welling up and spilling out, slowly rolling down her face.

I shrugged. And I said to her, 'Well, that doesn't matter.'

Then I shrugged again and said, 'I used to be the Wrong Boy.'

THE END

A REVOLUTION OF THE SUN
Tim Pears

'A HUGELY AMBITIOUS AND ENJOYABLE NOVEL'
The Times

It begins at the stroke of midnight on the first day of 1997. As
the year turns, a group of disparate individuals from different
backgrounds, from all corners of the country, embark on
separate journeys which will converge over the course of
the next twelve months: amongst them, Rebecca – mother-
to-be, Sam – amnesiac, Roderick – conservative MP, Jack –
lorry driver, Martha – cat burglar, Ben – hemiplegic child,
Solo – his father.

At the end of that year, their lives will have irrevocably
changed, some for better, some for worse, but changed
nonetheless. They cannot know what will happen to them
but their shared destination has an inevitability that will
prove impossible to withstand . . .

'TIM PEARS SPECIALISES IN GRAND PANORAMAS OF
OUR NATIONAL LIFE: TEEMING CASTS AND MULTI-
TRACKED PLOTTING HEAVY WITH THE SCENT OF
ZEITGEIST. FOR THIS, AND QUITE A LOT MORE
BESIDES, HE DESERVES THE HIGHEST PRAISE'
The Guardian

'THE SCOPE OF THIS NOVEL IS FAR REACHING. THAT
IT SUCCEEDS IN COMBINING ALL THE ELEMENTS AND
THRUSTING THEM EVER FORWARDS WITH HUMOUR
AND AFFECTION IS TESTAMENT TO PEARS' BOLD
VISION AND LARGE TALENT'
Daily Mail

'IF YOU'RE LOOKING FOR THE PERFECT READ FOR
YOUR HOLIDAYS, THIS IS IT – THE BOOK OF THE
SUMMER. BUT IF YOU HAVEN'T GOT ANY TIME OFF,
BUY IT AND TAKE A BREAK IN ITS PAGES'
Time Out

0 552 99862 1

BLACK SWAN

IDIOGLOSSIA
Eleanor Bailey

'HIGHLY ORIGINAL AND BEAUTIFULLY WRITTEN . . . A
BRILLIANT IMAGINATION AND GENUINE PSYCHOLOGICAL
INSIGHTS'
Sunday Telegraph

For four generations of women from the same family, madness is a
potent legacy. It tempts, it persuades and it destroys. But it can also
bring a strange kind of freedom. . .

Aggressive, demanding, eccentric, Great Edie curses the psychological
weakness that runs through the family like a fault. No one would
suspect that her psychic powers were anything more than a business,
security for her old age.

Her daughter, Grace, has languished in a mental institution for long
spells of her adult life, after a tragedy years ago. Grace's only child,
Maggie, grew up, working with her father on a fading cruise liner. But
the golden age of ocean travel is over, and a relationship with the
mysterious comedian, Rudi, leaves her pregnant and alone.

Now Maggie's daughter, Sarah, is truly dispossessed and, through
gratuitous sex, seeks revenge on her loveless childhood. She rejects
the world of overused clichés and overpriced coffee but can see no
alternative – except to let go. . .

'RELENTLESSLY BUILDING BENEATH AN ENTERTAINING AND
WELL-WRITTEN STORY. THE READER IS MADE AWARE OF THE
RELATIONSHIPS WHICH BIND US, NOT ONLY TO OUR FAMILY
BUT ONE BEING TO ANOTHER'
Daily Mail

'[BAILEY'S] UNSENTIMENTAL BUT SYMPATHETIC LANGUAGE
PENETRATES THE PRIVATE WORLD OF THE EMOTIONS IN AN
IMPRESSIVE WAY'
Daily Mail

'A BRILLIANT ACCOMPLISHED DEBUT . . . SLICK AND CLEVER,
HEARTFELT AND DEEP . . . BAILEY'S OBSERVATIONS ARE
STARTLING AND FRESH . . . THE SORT OF READ WHICH HAUNTS
YOU FOR WEEKS AFTERWARDS'
Sunday Express

'BAILEY IS AN INTELLIGENT WRITER, ELOQUENT ABOUT MEMORY
AND WOMEN'S STORIES. HER GRIP ON POETIC LANGUAGE IS AN
ASSURED ONE . . . AN AMBITIOUS FIRST NOVEL'
Independent on Sunday

0 552 99860 5

BLACK SWAN

THE DANDELION CLOCK
Guy Burt

'AMBITIOUS AND SUBSTANTIAL . . . BRILLIANTLY
CONJURED'
Guardian

*I used to think that perhaps everything that was happening
to me – my whole life – was just a memory. As if one
moment I could be eleven, and playing in the sun, and the
next I might – wake up, somehow, and find I was old and
dying, and the day when I was eleven was just a bright,
clear memory . . .*

Alex is an artist, preparing for a major exhibition. An
impulsive trip back to the Italy of his childhood forces him
to explore the unresolved questions of his past where, in
those seemingly innocent days, he swam and played and
explored the wild countryside with Jamie and Anna. Alex
has to experience again his first friendship with Jamie, and
his first love for Anna: to put together the pieces of a story
which brought the three of them together more closely
than they could understand, with a bond which seemed
innocent but which resulted in tragedy.

'A MENACING, SEDUCTIVE VISION OF MISSPENT
YOUTH'
Independent on Sunday

0 552 99824 9

BLACK SWAN

EDDIE'S BASTARD
William Kowalski

'A REMARKABLE DEBUT'
Time Out

Billy was deposited as an infant on the doorstep of Thomas
Mann's home in a simple wicker basket with a plain two-word
message pinned to his shawl reading 'Eddie's Bastard'.
Eddie, Thomas's son, had been killed in Vietnam three months
earlier, and his father had given up on life, having lost his
only son. But now, suddenly, Thomas has a grandson and
an heir – if not to the once-vast Mann fortune (for Thomas
recklessly squandered that in a foolhardy enterprise involving
ostriches just after his heroic return from the Second World
War), then at least to the long legacy of the Mann family
stories, stretching back to the Civil War.

In this rich, deeply resonant literary début, William Kowalski
explores the power of family, the meaning of history, and
the bonds of individual united and divided by love. By
turns hilarious, thrilling and heart-breaking, *Eddie's
Bastard* is a novel that stays in the mind long after the
reading is over.

'CLEVER, EMOTIONAL STORYTELLING WITH LAUGHS,
TEARS, AND LOVE'
The Times

'A BOOK WRITTEN WITH SUCH ELEGANCE, MATURITY
AND HUMOUR IT IS DIFFICULT TO BELIEVE THAT THE
AUTHOR IS ONLY 28 YEARS OLD'
The Good Book Guide

'WICKEDLY FUNNY AND GENUINELY MOVING'
Attitude

0 552 99859 1

BLACK SWAN

A SELECTED LIST OF FINE WRITING
AVAILABLE FROM BLACK SWAN

99313 1	OF LOVE AND SHADOWS	*Isabel Allende*	£6.99
99915 6	THE NEW CITY	*Stephen Amidon*	£6.99
99946 6	THE ANATOMIST	*Federico Andahazi*	£6.99
99619 X	HUMAN CROQUET	*Kate Atkinson*	£6.99
99860 5	IDIOGLOSSIA	*Eleanor Bailey*	£6.99
99824 9	THE DANDELION CLOCK	*Guy Burt*	£6.99
99686 6	BEACH MUSIC	*Pat Conroy*	£7.99
99836 2	A HEART OF STONE	*Renate Dorrestein*	£6.99
14698 6	INCONCEIVABLE	*Ben Elton*	£6.99
99587 8	LIKE WATER FOR CHOCOLATE	*Laura Esquivel*	£6.99
99751 X	STARCROSSED	*A. A. Gill*	£6.99
99801 X	THE SHORT HISTORY OF A PRINCE	*Jane Hamilton*	£6.99
99893 1	CHOCOLAT	*Joanne Harris*	£6.99
99796 X	A WIDOW FOR ONE YEAR	*John Irving*	£7.99
99859 1	EDDIE'S BASTARD	*William Kowalski*	£6.99
99807 9	MONTENEGRO	*Starling Lawrence*	£6.99
99580 0	CAIRO TRILOGY I: PALACE WALK	*Naguib Mahfouz*	£7.99
99875 3	MAYBE THE MOON	*Armistead Maupin*	£6.99
99874 5	PAPER	*John McCabe*	£6.99
99762 5	THE LACK BROTHERS	*Malcolm McKay*	£6.99
99785 4	GOODNIGHT, NEBRASKA	*Tom McNeal*	£6.99
99862 1	A REVOLUTION OF THE SUN	*Tim Pears*	£6.99
99817 6	INK	*John Preston*	£6.99
99783 8	DAY OF ATONEMENT	*Jay Rayner*	£6.99
99952 0	LIFE ISN'T ALL HA HA HEE HEE	*Meera Syal*	£6.99
99819 2	WHISTLING FOR THE ELEPHANTS	*Sandi Toksvig*	£6.99
99780 3	KNOWLEDGE OF ANGELS	*Jill Paton Walsh*	£6.99